For Caelyn & Abigail
Because strong women have never
been needed more in this world.
Your magic lies within.

CHAPTER ONE

The Direction of Death

Only three things in the world never truly rest—memories of the past, hope for the future, and a Healer with the ache of death in her bones.

Healers don't sleep. Generally speaking, Healers never really got much in the way of rest, but at least I inherited an uncanny ability to function on little sleep. Long days and nights tending to my patients rarely bothered me. It was accepted as part of the job—a job no one in Barnham ever truly thought I could take on, at least not for many years.

But necessity is a funny thing. Folks will allow you to set a broken bone at fifteen when the next closest Healer is over half a day's journey away. And they'll let you help birth a baby, especially when you're the only one in the village who knows what to do with a child who insists on a foot-first introduction into this world. No one expected me to take on the role of Healer three years ago, least of all me, but I had, and I'd like to think my mother would be proud.

Last night had been no different. The wind and rain raged on, the thunder rattling the tiny glass bottles on my workbench as the walls of the cottage reverberated with the worsening weather. At the height of the storm, Elric Asbury showed up at my door, fist pounding upon the wood.

"Moreina," he yelled from the other side. "Please come. He can't breathe!"

Brendon.

Without hesitation, I was up and moving, my heart thumping, my mind already working through the remedies and dosages needed for Brendon's episode. I didn't stop to think about how much things had changed since I'd become Healer. A few short years ago, neither Elric nor anyone else in the village would have been pounding on my door for help. I was too young, they said. But, necessity. Necessity led them to me.

I might have made it home long before dawn except I was pulled from the Asbury home to help deliver Elsie Ysack's fourth baby, a plump little thing whose howling screams rivaled the intensity of the thunder above.

Now, as I made my way home in the dim, early morning light, Aeros whickered at me from the paddock, the mare's ears pricked forward, dark eyes full of hope grain was on its way. As if sensing my nearness, the three milgoats stumbled from the barn into the paddock, fighting one another for the coveted lead spot and bleating in chorus. Placing my bag at the doorstep, I made my way down the sodden path to feed the hungry mouths that waited. Mucking could wait until after I'd slept.

I left my boots beside the door and peeled off my wet clothing, drawing a hot bath to wash the night's grime from my clammy skin. The water soothed away the chill that settled deep in my bones from the storm. Gray clouds still rolled overhead, but they had finally depleted themselves of rain, and I was grateful.

I sank deeper into the tub, expecting to feel my muscles soften with the heat of the surrounding water, but my body stubbornly refused to relax. The night had ended, my charges cared for, and yet my nerves remained raw. It hadn't been the storm. It hadn't been Brendon's asthma. It hadn't been Elsie's labor or the little screamer who had been born.

Something *else* was coming. My bones tingled almost as they did when death was close, and yet death had not made an appearance last night. Shifting in the water uneasily, I wondered what unpleasant surprise today might yet hold. I washed and rose from the tub, then ran a comb through my hair before dressing for sleep and making for my cot. Even the best Healer had to sleep some, and there was little doubt in my mind I was hardly the best, not with only three years under my belt.

No amount of unease could stop me from pulling the covers up to my ears and allowing sheer exhaustion to pull me into a deep sleep, a sleep where I'd no longer feel the ominous tingling of my bones, the looming promise of death somewhere in the near future.

Some hours later, I awoke to a knock at my door. Was this the *something else*? I rubbed the remnants of sleep from my eyes and stood with a stretch, shivering at the damp chill that hung in the air.

Wrapping a worn knit shawl around my shoulders, I opened the door to meet the dark, attentive gaze of Quinn D'Arturio. I had not seen him in some time, yet it didn't surprise me the man at my door no longer matched the memory of the boy I once knew.

Quinn had grown.

"I'm sorry to disturb you, Reina," he said, hardly seeming sincerely apologetic as he bent in a half bow and a lock of nearly black hair fell across his brow. "My father requests your presence."

My ability to function on little sleep was no less appreciated now than it had been last night. I estimated I had slept maybe three hours. It felt like seven.

With a nod, I assured him, "Let him know I'll come right away." I needed time to dress and since it clearly wasn't an emergency, I figured I might appease my rumbling stomach with a quick snack before heading out once again.

"If it's all the same to you, I'll wait," he said.

"Ah—" I hesitated, now wondering at the reason for my summoning. "All right, I'll just be a minute." No snack for me.

Clasping his hands behind his back, Quinn turned from me as I closed the door. I dressed simply, fastening my apron over my skirts and wishing now I'd had a chance to wash it of the Larkspur stains it carried. I stole a peek at Quinn through the condensation on my window, observing him as he surveyed my farm for some imperceptible danger only he might know.

There was a time when I had known much about Quinn and many of my former schoolmates, but past the days of school and childhood games, I had hardly spoken more than a dozen words to him since his return to Barnham.

I backed away from the window and fastened my hair into another knot, tucking the stray strands behind my ears. I pulled on my boots once more, flinching at the wetness still inside. Bag in hand, I opened the door and stepped outside once again.

Though still cool, the afternoon had pleasantly warmed

despite the occasional gust of wind, and an earthy dampness permeated the air. I stepped onto the well-worn walk beyond the cottage door and inhaled the familiar sweet scent of the violet and red kissing blooms that greeted me. The few tiny petal chalices that hadn't been blown off their vine by the storm harbored droplets of rain, but the majority of the flowers lay flattened on the ground, a stark reminder summer was gone. As was tradition on any farmstead in Castilles, my mother planted kissing blooms at the door of our tiny cottage, and they grew in vine-like abundance along a supporting trellis to remind our home's occupants never to leave without a parting kiss to the loved ones left behind—a custom I currently never needed to concern myself with.

I fell into step quickly and wordlessly beside Quinn as we made our way to his father's home. Stealing a sideways glance at Quinn as we walked, I studied the seriousness on his face. I tried to remember if I'd ever seen him smile in the time since our childhood days. He might be attractive if he did. His hair was shorter than the current style and the bottom half of his face seemed perpetually shadowed with the hint of a beard men twice his age would covet. His hawk-like eyes were always in motion and I forever had the distinct impression there wasn't much they missed…including my current observations.

I turned my eyes forward as we entered the village proper. "Is the governor well, Quinn?" I asked, attempting a chat despite knowing where it would get me.

"Aye, he's fine."

"His knees?"

"Good," he responded, effectively ending our conversation.

As I'd expected. I fought the urge to roll my eyes.

Where did you disappear to for the last two years? Why won't you speak to me? Do you remember me at all? There were so many questions I wanted to ask him. Instead, I nodded and let my gaze roam the town as we walked.

The place was a flurry of activity as the townsfolk cleaned up from the storm, assessed damage, and hacked fallen tree limbs into firewood. Small streams of water trickled along the edges of the streets, meandering between the cobbles, swiftly finding their way to gutters, to creeks, then to rivers beyond.

For the most part, it seemed the village had been spared major damage, though a large pine had come down on the corner of the Preswicks' roof, leaving a gaping hole in its wake. Three neighbors were already in the process of helping Jim Preswick to clear the tree and patch the hole.

A small swell of pride for my town at the sight had me clearing my throat to keep tears of gratitude from welling in my eyes. Barnham may not have been the biggest town in Castilles or the richest, but her citizens were no less than first class. Here, our neighbors were family. There could be no better place on Liron to spend one's days. Of that, I was certain.

As we neared the governor's house, small crowds gathered in doorways, their curious eyes on me and Quinn as we passed. Intriguing whispers carried to my ears in snippets and I listened intently as we walked, hoping to piece together what was being said.

"It's only a matter of time before Bruenner takes the west. He won't stop until he has all of Castilles bent to his will."

"You think Arden's going to search for it—"

"—putting together a candidate group."

"—force the prophecy to be fulfilled."

Indeed? Now my curiosity was piqued. This would explain my unease, the discomfort in my bones. *Something else*, for sure. Was it possible they spoke of the Prophecy of the White Sorceress? The timing was right. General Bruenner of the King's Army had taken King Edgar's premature death as a personal invitation to maneuver his way onto the throne. At least, he had tried. Almost as quickly as he had taken the throne, a Resistance Army formed to fight him.

We had almost become accustomed to the daily fear pervading every aspect of our lives. Would today be the day the troops would flatten our town? Tomorrow? Death was growing closer. My bones ached of it, virtually screaming of its nearness some days. Now, more so than ever, the ache was a constant reminder Barnham wouldn't remain safe forever.

It was easy enough to push aside the reality, to ignore the pain, when I threw myself into my craft, but the times in between…well, it seemed all we did was worry more often than not these days. Was this why death's presence seemed so near today?

With the thought still in my head, we reached the governor's house. Stepping into the foyer, I nodded my thanks to Quinn as he held open the heavy oak door. Inside, I was hit instantly with a pang of nostalgia. I spent many hours, days, and perhaps even years following Quinn through these rooms as a child on spring days too filled with rain for outdoor adventures. Now the warmth of the house greeted me like an old friend.

The scent of rising dough wafted from the kitchen, a

mouthwatering odor that instantly brought to mind Quinn's mother. If I ventured into the kitchen at that very moment, Mathilde D'Arturio would overwhelm me in a bear-like embrace smelling of briarmint, sage, and half a dozen other unnamed spices, all while covertly pinching my arm to determine the precise amount of fat on my bones. She would then sit me on a wooden stool, growl at me for allowing myself to grow so thin, and force-feed me a variety of dishes specifically made to match my meatless tastes. I smiled at the thought. If ever there had been anyone who could make me feel as though I still had a mother, Mathilde was it.

"Ah, Moreina," said Governor Arden, meeting me at the open door. He reached for my hands, covering them in his large grasp, and squeezed them in a greeting. His round, welcoming face was a contrast to Quinn's, all angles and sharp features. "My thanks for your coming to entertain my ideas."

"I'm always glad for a visit, Governor, but I'm afraid I'm not sure what ideas you mean to share with me."

"Quinn didn't tell you why I asked you here?" he said to me as he turned to face Quinn, a father's consternation apparent on his face. I may not have had a father in my life, but even I knew that look.

"I'm afraid not," I said with my best disarming smile.

"Quinn!"

"But," I continued, "there really wasn't much time to discuss anything on our way here. I was interested in seeing how the village fared in the storm. I'm afraid I distracted Quinn with all my questions." I didn't look at Quinn to gauge his reaction to my lie.

The governor seemed to accept my excuse and ushered me to a seat by the hearth. "Of course, of course. Please sit," he said, gesturing to a plush rose-embroidered armchair. "Can I interest you in a cup of kai?"

I nodded. "Please."

The governor offered some to his son, who declined with a shake of his head. He then poured two mugs with the steaming brew, handed one to me, and sat beside me in a matching armchair. Quinn took a watchful stance near the window, leaning against the wall, his arms folded across his broad chest. He seemed unable to relax even within the comforting walls of his childhood home. *Why?*

"And you got through the storm all right, Moreina?" Governor Arden asked. "No damage to the farm?"

"I haven't had a chance to survey fully," I admitted, holding the mug of bittersweet kai close to my face, my cheeks growing damp as the steam settled dew-like on my skin. "But it doesn't look like I lost any trees and the creek only rose half to the edge of the flood plain," I added.

"Good, good."

"It could have been much worse."

"The animals fared well?" he asked in a typical Governor Arden fashion. Eventually, I was sure I would learn why I'd been asked to come. Governor Arden was a talker, and if I intended to find out why I'd been called to his home, I'd have to wade through the chitchat first.

"Oh yes, everyone was tucked away before nightfall. Penny stayed safe and dry in Aeros's stall with her," I answered. Penny was a three-legged milgoat I had taken in to foster when she was only days old. Aeros couldn't often be found without the little goat by her side.

"That's very good. Glad to hear it," the governor replied as he sipped his kai.

The pause in conversation allowed me to sip from my own mug, and I let the bitter warmth of the spicy liquid slide down my throat.

"If I may, Governor," I began, "can I ask what ideas you're eager to share with me?" No point letting the small talk go on forever. I still had stalls to muck, eggs to collect, and goats to milk.

"Of course!" he said with enthusiasm. He set his mug down on a table beside him and folded his hands together in his lap. This didn't seem to satisfy him, so he stood, clasped his hands across the wide expanse of his belly, and walked the length of the narrow room as he talked. "Are you familiar with the Prophecy of the White Sorceress?"

So it *was* about the prophecy. I nodded. "Somewhat, though I confess I've never put faith in it."

The governor turned dramatically to face me, eyes hurt, his mouth agape in exaggerated shock. "That prophecy was the last in a long line of prophecies given by the last great sorcerer of the millennium! Every other prediction given by Magnus Tarrowburn has come to pass, and pass exactly as he said it would. How could you possibly believe this, perhaps the most important prophecy of them all, would not unfold before our very eyes?"

I gave a small shrug. "I don't put stock in such tellings, Governor. Truth be told, I'm not sure I've ever heard the prophecy in its entirety."

"Well, my dear girl, let me provide you with a copy," he said, pulling a book from his shelves. He slid a loose piece of yellowed parchment from the middle and handed it to me to examine.

I accepted it and read:

> *The last sorceress for a thousand years,*
> *Shall find herself needed not.*
> *Hide the pendant, hide it well,*
> *For a time when others know not what.*

> *When Cadnum's light shines from the east*
> *Hanging low in the morning sky.*
> *While Stellon follows Andra in oblivion,*
> *To the sun's path through Cadnum high.*

> *'Tis time for the magic to reawaken,*
> *The White Sorceress to be found.*
> *The talisman will make its choice,*
> *When evil, chaos, and uncertainty abound.*

> *A figure slight with hair so light,*
> *A saving grace to rescue man.*
> *Without her, the talisman lost,*
> *Its power useless to do what it can.*

> *Two lives are woven into hers,*
> *Able suitors though they may be.*

One is true and one is not,
Her choice determines all to see.

Should she choose the suitor right,
All that is good shall come to light.
But should she choose the suitor wrong,
No hope for Castilles or Liron.

Desolation, death, and despair,
All sit heavy in the air.
For choosing a suitor is not all,
Her duties continue through the fall.

Too long since the kingdom has lost an heir,
But hope remains he will return.
She must choose to find him again,
Before the impostor claims his turn.

She alone can end the fight,
She alone has the might.
The talisman shall show the way,
Truth can guide to save the day.

A slow burn lit in my veins as I handed the parchment back to him. It was unsettling, this confirmation of death as I viewed the prophecy. Which was silly because a piece of paper couldn't foretell death. I glanced out the window, wondering...

I understood why so many people wished to put their faith in it. It was a simple solution to the war, to the fear, to Bruenner. A savior to follow, a woman who would make all of our troubles disappear by making decisions for us, by unleashing a magic that could save us. I feared it was too good to be true and said as much to the governor.

"Eh!" he said, dismissing my concern, and taking a seat once again. "That's only because the prophecy isn't specific about *how* she'll be able to defeat Bruenner. I'm sure it isn't as easy as we make it seem."

"It also doesn't specifically name Bruenner as the one to bring about the kingdom's demise, either," I pointed out, though saying Bruenner's name aloud sent wicked chills down my spine. Bruenner was what my mother once liked to call a Very Bad Man, and she hadn't lived to see the brand of Bad he'd unleashed in recent months. Reportedly, the last two towns he'd rampaged had been burned to the ground, with residents blockaded in their homes. I shuddered again. And this was a man who thought he should rule a kingdom.

Governor Arden replied, "But the timing is exactly right. Tarrowburn specifies the position of the two moons and sun in relation to Cadnum in our skies when the White Sorceress is revealed to us. That time is now."

"So, what exactly do you propose?"

"We force the prophecy," he said.

"Supposing the prophecy is true," I answered slowly, "can that be done?"

"I don't see why not!"

"But isn't a prophecy, by definition, something that should come forth on its own?"

"Finally, a voice of reason." Quinn's voice startled me. I had almost forgotten he was in the room. "That's what I've been telling my hard-headed father for the last month," he said.

"Quinn, the council has met," the governor said. "It was agreed this is the best course of action."

Quinn answered with a snort. In stark contrast to his father, Quinn rarely said more than what courtesy required of him. After our school days, he had gone away for some time. When he returned, he was different in a way I couldn't put my finger on. Darker, maybe? Most girls in the village had long given up on hopes of catching his eye since attempts at conversation never seemed to lead where they intended, or anywhere at all.

"What course of action?" I asked.

"We're putting together a candidate group. We want you to be a part of it."

I raised the mug to my lips to drink once more, but promptly put it back down, sip untaken. I cleared my throat.

"Pardon?"

CHAPTER TWO

What Faith Will Bring

"Oh no, no!" Governor Arden waved a hand at me. "We haven't identified you as one of the likely candidates, but we'd like you to go with them."

Oddly, only a mild sense of relief washed over me. "Go with them where?"

"Based on the Semworth scrolls, the council has been able to identify where we believe the last known sorceress placed the Faranzine Talisman for safekeeping. It was predicted another sorceress would not come into existence for a thousand years—that sorceress being the infamous White Sorceress. The talisman could hardly be expected to be handed down from generation to generation for that length of time. Somewhere along the way it was bound to be lost, stolen, or sold in greed, so Sibyl Mariah hid it in order to protect it."

"And you think you know where it is?" I concluded for him.

"Yes!" The governor's eyes lit like a child's. "We are living in exciting times," he said.

I had my doubts. "Dangerous times."

"Dangerous, yes, but excitement doesn't often come without some degree of danger." When I didn't answer right away, he continued, "We live in a most amazing time, Moreina. It's been two years since the king's death, two years that war and famine have plagued our kingdom. This is the moment for which so many have been waiting. And we now believe we hold the key to making our destiny a reality."

My gut shifted uneasily, and I had no response. I wasn't even sure how to feel about such things. Medicinal herbs, those I put faith in. My mother painstakingly taught me which plants would cure a headache and which would make one worse. She showed me how to mix a *Lobelia* tincture and dispense it in a dose that would be effective without being lethal. Townsfolk were often mystified by such remedies and frequently asked what magic they contained, but years of study and a genuine passion for learning were all that were required.

Esmé di Bianco never taught me about things like destiny or fate and—call me a skeptic—I wasn't sure I believed either could truly be determined by an exceptionally cryptic prophecy about a thousand-year-old talisman and a woman who had yet to be born. And yet...

And yet, my own unease was a better indicator of what my life would hold than any barometer predicting rain. There was *something*. I felt it. Perhaps this was it.

"And where do you believe the talisman is hidden?" I asked, allowing myself to momentarily suspend disbelief.

The governor reached for a scroll on the corner of a table piled high with ancient looking papers and books. "Here," he said, unrolling it across the table and placing a finger directly on the Plymann Cliffs.

I stood and moved to the table, letting my eyes roam over the map in front of me. His finger pointed to a spot on the coast about three days north from Barnham Sound. The land there was wild, craggy, and essentially uninhabitable. The jagged cliffs made it impossible to launch or receive boats of any kind, and the caves below were rumored to flood regularly with each spring tide. To make matters worse, the *Brutales* winds made travels there at certain times of the month exceptionally hazardous. Enormous stone circles I'd seen only from afar eerily adorned the clifftops for miles as though warning curious humans against venturing farther if they valued their lives at all.

"It *would* be a good place to hide a treasure," I conceded, unconsciously tapping a finger on the table.

"Not just any treasure," the governor was quick to respond.

I contemplated. "How are the candidates being chosen? Have they already been named?" I was interested to know how a prophecy could be forced when there was no way at all to know who was likely to fulfill it.

"Yes, the most likely candidates were chosen when the council convened last."

"From Barnham?" I asked doubtfully. It seemed improbable that the White Sorceress would come from our tiny corner of the kingdom when the kingdom was nearly as vast as the number of home remedies for the common cold.

"Oh, no, not just from Barnham. Airdsbarg and Newcastle, too. Ancient text indicates the sorceress will hail from a western coastal town close to where Sibyl Mariah herself originated. The Sibyl was born in Newcastle, but we have every reason to hope the White Sorceress *could* be one of Barnham's own."

I turned to face him, wishing I had any hint of his enthusiasm for this mission. "So, what makes you think I have any value to this group you wish to send?" I asked.

"Oh, there are many reasons you're an obvious choice as an escort," he assured me. I winced at the word *escort*. If ever I'd been cast in the part of the old maid, now was the time. "First, and most importantly, there's an indication that the life of the woman chosen to be the White Sorceress is in imminent danger."

"And how could I be of service with that? I've not exactly Quinn's strength with a sword, I assure you."

Governor Arden laughed. "No, no, nothing like that. This particular source claims the White Sorceress will fall perilously ill and her life will be in danger as a result."

"Governor, forgive me, but I don't understand how all of these texts tie together. How can you know what's real and what's not? How many are there?"

"Hundreds," he replied. "If you count the false ones, thousands, but I've spent years debunking those. I've got a good grasp of which ones indicate the right path and I'm confident we're on it."

I wasn't so sure.

"And how can you be positive *I* will be able to heal her if she does fall ill?"

He sighed. "I cannot. But if anyone in the kingdom is capable, it's you, Moreina."

"I'm flattered," I said. "But I'm hesitant."

"My father offers no flattery," Quinn said curtly from his corner by the window. "You're the best we've got, Reina. If you cannot heal her when she falls ill, no one in this kingdom can."

My mouth suddenly dry, I didn't reply. What he said was

true, but to hear someone else say it was satisfyingly vindicating, given the years I had to prove to the residents of Barnham my own skills were on par with my mother's.

Quinn spoke again, softly this time, "I have faith in you."

His words transported me to another time, a day three years ago when my mother, bags packed and horse saddled, took to the road that would lead her to Irzan, leaving her fifteen-year-old daughter in charge as surrogate Healer for a week. Neither of us could have guessed how quickly a week could turn into forever.

"But what if I do the wrong thing? What if I do harm instead of good? What if I can't treat my patients?" I asked.

My mother stood beside the saddle and dropped the reins she'd been holding to embrace me in a soft hug. She held me at arm's length, and looked me squarely in the eyes, all the warmth and confidence in the world flowing through her gaze.

"Oh, Little Me, you are stronger than you know. Yes, being Healer is a big job, but you are ready. And I'll be back in a week's time." She hadn't called me Little Me since I was ten.

I tilted my head to her, the panic in my bones almost surely visible in my eyes. "I'm afraid," I said.

She smoothed a stray piece of hair back from my forehead. "Fear is normal. To be afraid of the unknown is to be human. Reina, there will come a time in your life when you'll be called upon to do something greater than you could even imagine. And when that time comes, I hope you choose to push aside the fear of uncertainty and accept that calling. It is why we are here." She paused as she mounted her horse. "I have faith in you."

I have faith in you.

Her words echoed in my ears. My mother's words. Quinn's

words.

"And, you've firsthand knowledge of the area, have you not?" Governor Arden said, snapping me back to the present.

I nodded, clearing my head of my thoughts, "Yes, you know that. It's the only place to find a decent store of some of the wild herbs I use regularly. I make that trip several times a year."

"So you know the roads that lead there well. You've probably been there more than anyone else in the village."

I chewed the side of my mouth as I considered. I was running low on seleniac, though I had not planned a trip for several weeks yet, as I was careful to plan around the *Brutales* season. Staring at the stains on my apron again, I ran a finger along one of the indigo splotches. Had I known I was visiting solely to discuss a prophecy, I wouldn't have worn it.

Finally, I asked, "How long will the journey take? Three days there and three days home, I assume…"

"And however long it takes to find the talisman in between," he finished.

"Supposing there *is* a talisman to find, so it could be weeks."

"I'm confident it won't be."

I narrowed my eyes. "How can you be so sure?" I asked.

"It's all in the prophecy."

"That's still a long time to be gone. Who will take my place here while I'm away? Janna Hess is due any day with her baby, and Anna Delantro isn't far behind. You'll need someone here who can deliver a baby, and you really shouldn't be without a Healer, either. Mason Kring is having episodes semi-regularly. They've gotten better, but we're still working on what's causing them." I said, uncomfortable with leaving my charges behind.

"Already taken care of. Mathilde's sister will stay with us as long as necessary. We expect her to arrive tomorrow night. She's years of experience in both areas. For the time you're gone, she'll be happy to help," he said, essentially wrapping my decision neatly into a package I couldn't refuse. "This is something big, Moreina, but we can't do it without you."

There will come a time in your life when you'll be called upon to do something greater than you could even imagine. And when that time comes, I hope you choose to push aside the fear of uncertainty and accept that calling.

My mother's words again. How could I ignore them? Could she have known I'd be tasked with something so important to the war effort? Of course not. There hadn't been a war when she'd said them. Perhaps she'd just been plying me with whatever she thought would keep me strong in her absence.

It had worked. Gritting my teeth, I vowed I wouldn't disappoint her. I would do what was asked of me. I would do it for my mother, for my village, for myself—even if I didn't know or understand how an old piece of magic jewelry could save us from Bruenner.

The door flew back on its hinges as I opened my mouth to reply, and John Ysack stood in the doorway, wild-eyed, gripping his hat in his hands. "Reina! Artos said you would be here. Something's wrong with the baby."

Death. Oh, God, no!

Not the baby. Grabbing my bag, I fled without a look back to Quinn or Governor Arden.

Though it was John who had found me, it wasn't the Ysack baby who had needed my help. It was Arella Engle, a two-month old infant who could have been saved had they called me three days ago, but the Engles were one of the few families in Barnham who *didn't* believe an eighteen-year-old could know anything about healing. And it had cost them. As I crossed their threshold, my bones lit like fire and I knew she was already gone. Pausing a moment, I closed my eyes in pain, bracing myself for what I would tell the family.

What was I to do? Did they think I was able to raise the dead? I cursed as I stood before the lifeless infant body. It took everything I had not to shake with anger while standing in their presence as Martina Engle howled, holding the tiny body in her arms, repeating unintelligible words through her tears. There was little I could say.

When I left their home, I walked to the narrow creek at the edge of the village, sat down on a large, flat rock and sobbed until I had nothing left in me. I slammed my palm into the stone, the biting sting on my skin a welcome sensation. The baby had *died*. For no good reason. I wanted to scream at the Engles. I wanted to march myself back over there and throttle them. But it wouldn't do any good, and it wouldn't convince them to call me the next time one of them was ill.

It was dinnertime when I composed myself enough to make it back to the D'Arturio house. I entered without so much as a knock, swinging open the door in my fury over Arella. Governor Arden, Mathilde, and Quinn had finished eating supper at their dining room table and looked surprised to see me standing in their entranceway.

Before any of them could say a word in greeting, I barked, "When do we leave?"

I was done with death. If I couldn't prevent the death of an infant, the least I could do was keep the White Sorceress alive long enough to do her job.

"So you *will* do it!" The governor rose to greet me, grasping my hands in his. "I knew you wouldn't let us down. The candidates will be ready to leave the morning after tomorrow."

That didn't leave much time to get things in order, but it could be done. The door opened behind me at that moment, and a blond head ducked through the doorway as Mathilde cleared plates from the table.

"Niles!" The governor dropped my hands and headed to the door to greet his newest guest.

Once inside, the new stranger stood to his full height and I was instantly taken aback, the pain from my experience with the Engles momentarily wiped from my mind. He was tall and lithe, with thick golden locks tied firmly at the base of his scalp and bright blue eyes that danced with amusement as they met mine. Sinewy muscles rippled beneath his deep green tunic. He was everything many of the young and single women in town would enjoy fighting over and a flush crept up my neck despite myself.

"Forgive me," Governor Arden said, "Allow me to introduce you. Niles Ingram, this is Moreina di Bianco, the finest Healer in all the kingdom."

I nodded my head in greeting, mustering the only thing I thought to say, "Very nice to meet you, sir."

"And you, ma'am," Niles said in a smooth voice I was sure

was excellent for serenading. I flushed again, not knowing where the thought had come from and willing it to go away quickly. Niles took my hand, lightly brushing the back of it with warm lips as he bowed in greeting, his eyes never leaving mine. It took every ounce of my strength to keep my knees from buckling.

I jumped when the door closed with a bang, my nerves uncharacteristically on edge. Pulling my hand back as he dropped it, I swore I could still feel the burn of his lips upon it. I clasped my hands together and rubbed the back of my hand lightly with my fingertips.

"Raised in a barn, Niles?" Quinn asked, glaring at Niles. "Or do you leave the door open at home, too?"

Niles looked amused. "A pleasure to see you again, too, Quinn."

Quinn snorted. Obviously, they knew each other.

The governor frowned at Quinn but did nothing to come to the defense of either man. "Niles is a Kenswell soldier," he informed me, attempting to return to civil conversation. "He and a small troop were given leave for the sole purpose of accompanying you and the candidates on their mission."

Well then. It seemed I would be spending a bit time in Niles Ingram's company in the very near future. Silently, I steeled my resolve to ignore the persistent fluttering in my stomach. Best to get myself composed now.

"He and Quinn will guide the expedition, provided"— Governor Arden glared at his son— "they can keep from killing each other in the process."

"I should think you know me better than that, Father," Quinn said. "I'd do no such thing in the presence of a lady, and I believe we'll be in the presence of several."

Niles laughed confidently, and Governor Arden rolled his eyes in exasperation. "Quinn, why don't you take Moreina home, and we'll plan to meet tomorrow evening to finalize details?"

"My pleasure," Quinn said, opening the door for me once again.

Niles nodded his head. "Until we meet again," he said.

"Yes," I answered with a nod of my own, wondering why my voice seemed an octave higher than usual. Turning to the governor, I added, "Tomorrow then, Governor."

"Yes, yes, of course. And, I knew you'd agree to do it, Moreina. Just knowing you'll go has eased my mind considerably. Thank you, my dear."

I had no chance to respond as he turned toward Niles and ushered him into the sitting room to examine the map he had shown me earlier in the day. They were deep in conversation within seconds, though I didn't fail to notice Niles's eyes upon me as we exited. Had it grown warm? I was grateful for the chance to escape into the cool air outside.

I brushed past Quinn as he held the door.

"Wait here a moment," Quinn said as he ran back inside. He returned a minute later with a covered bowl smelling mouthwateringly like whatever meal they had just eaten. "My mother packed dinner for you."

I smiled. Mathilde may have packed it, but only after Quinn returned to ask her to. "Thank you," I said, accepting it.

Quinn stayed by my side as we began the walk to my cottage. Curiosity burned in my mind and got the better of me.

"How do you know Niles?" I asked.

I didn't expect him to answer, not really, but Quinn responded, "Oh, I've seen Niles in action, when I've headed to the border wars with messages." Quinn never discussed why he hadn't joined with the army. I strongly suspected it was a sore point with him.

"Clearly, you don't like him."

He actually laughed, a deep rumble in his chest that took me by surprise as I'd heard it so infrequently. "Observant, Reina. No, I don't like him. Not at all."

"You've never struck me as the petty type, so I have to wonder what he's done to earn such scorn," I said.

"I have my reasons. Like him or not, I'll hold my tongue."

I took my cue and let the subject drop. When we reached the cottage, I thanked Quinn for walking me home.

"Happy to," he answered.

"Oh," I said, cocking my head, unable to suppress the kind of thoughts that inevitably got me in trouble. "So that was happy?"

He rewarded me with a smirk of amusement. Why it pleased me, I couldn't say. An odd expression crossed his features, and I was taken off guard when he said, "You lied to my father earlier, telling him that you kept me too busy with questions."

My smile died. I fiddled with my apron strings, a habit I had managed to quit long ago. "I did."

"Why?" His dark eyes searched mine, and for a moment I was afraid he might know my very thoughts, though I hardly knew them myself.

"I don't know," I answered truthfully.

I was thankful he accepted my response. With pursed lips, he nodded. "I'll come for you tomorrow afternoon."

"There's no need," I assured him. "I'm sure you have more pressing things to do than walk me to your parents' home. Besides, I've walked that path hundreds of times. I'm sure I can find my way."

"Then I'll come to chop the sycamore that fell in your back pasture last night."

I blinked, confusion clouding my brain.

"Tomorrow," he said with that same confounded smirk. With that, he turned and was over the hill before I could find a response.

I made quick work of milking and mucking, and by the time I was done, I was covered in a light sheen of perspiration. I wiped my brow with the sleeve of my dress and leaned the pitchfork against the wall. Fingering the ax leaning on the wall beside it, I grabbed the handle.

My feet were moving for the back pasture before I fully realized I'd intended to head there. Sure enough, half of the large sycamore in the rear of the field was lying across the alfalfa, split from the night's storm. Inadvertently, I let a very unladylike word slip from my lips.

Whether I liked it or not, it was a bigger job than I'd be able to handle by myself. Nonetheless, I began chopping the outer branches and gathering them for kindling. At least the physical work kept me from thinking too long on Arella Engle and the black cloak of death that saturated nearly every part of my day. The sun dipped lower on the horizon and I was forced to return to the barn to feed the animals yelling for their meals once more.

"Ye've eaten more than I have today, you greedy goats. Bottomless pits, that's what you are," I grumbled as I doled out their rations.

Aeros whickered in response. I paused to scratch her dappled ears as she ate. The chickens gathered around her legs to peck at the oats she dropped between giant mouthfuls.

"Slow down, horse, or you'll colic. Can't have that on my head. I was up too late last night. I won't be up walking you all night tonight."

Aeros snorted.

"I see how it is. Have it your way then."

The day finally done, I headed for my cottage to wash, to eat, and—if luck was with me—to sleep a long and dreamless sleep. Tomorrow would be another long day. I would do fine provided the pregnant women in the village could avoid laboring tonight.

I glanced at the sky above. The clouds had cleared, and the stars began to dot the velvety darkness. No, I'd rest easy. There would be no babes born in the village tonight.

CHAPTER THREE

Northward Journey

The sun had been shining for three hours by the time I made my way back to the fallen sycamore. After feeding the animals for the morning, I carefully cataloged my medicinal stores, packing the items I thought I would be most likely to need on the journey. Saints willing, I wouldn't need any of them, however unlikely that might be.

Though familiar with mucking and shoveling, my muscles weren't accustomed to the monotonous chopping from the day before. They protested at the mere thought of swinging the ax again today. Still, the work needed to be done, and preferably before I left for the Plymann Cliffs. I stretched my arms, swung them in circles, and threw my shoulders back. Intent on getting to work, I grabbed the ax and made for the back pasture once more.

But I arrived at the sycamore to find it already in at least a dozen large pieces on the ground. Quinn, stripped to the waist, was crouched atop the largest piece. Saw in hand, dripping with perspiration, he stood when he saw me and hopped with ease to the ground, landing curiously silently for his size.

"Morning, Reina," he said with a nod as he approached

me. Up close, he was more muscular than I'd realized. Why I should have noticed, I couldn't say. I'd spent many summers in Quinn's company, but had not ever seen until now the various scars across his back and shoulders. When had those appeared? *And what caused them?*

"Quinn D'Arturio, you said you'd come by this afternoon," I scolded, my hands on my hips. It was, perhaps, not the politest greeting I'd ever given.

"I said I'd come to get you in the afternoon," he said. "Right after I'm done taking care of the tree."

I pursed my lips. "I—thank you."

He gestured to the ax in my hand. "You started without me yesterday."

"I could hardly let you have all the fun," I replied.

He surveyed the branch pile I'd made the evening before. "Well, if you're going to help today, you can start chopping the smaller branches into kindling," he said.

My eyebrows lifted of their own accord. Was he assigning me work on my own land? I opened my mouth to protest, then realized my foolishness. What else was I truly fit to do? I wouldn't be able to cut into the thickest part of the trunk with ease as Quinn had.

Closing my mouth, I spun on my heel, headed toward the pile, and began fiercely hacking away at the branches. A few minutes passed before the rasp of a saw on wood resumed behind me.

The rest of the morning passed quickly, and when I had a pile of kindling as high as Aeros's withers, I fetched the wheelbarrow to haul it to the cottage.

When I lifted my head to gauge how far Quinn had gotten with the rest of the tree, a pang of guilt swept over me. The afternoon brought with it the sun's warmth. His hair was soaked and rivulets of sweat dripped down his back, making him glisten as though drenched in morning dew.

How ungrateful I must have seemed! He had been working for hours and uttered not a single complaint, and I hadn't so much as offered him a glass of water let alone food, though he must have been famished.

The pile of wood shifted as I leaned the ax against it, and I ignored the pieces that fell as I turned to traverse the field back to the cottage. I washed my hands in the basin on the bedside table, then splashed the cool water onto my face. Pulling a tray from one of the lower cupboards, I piled it high with thick slices of bread, cheese, and sliced applikens which filled the small bowl with their succulent juices. Quinn would probably have preferred his bread with savory slabs of heavily seasoned meat from the butcher, but, as I'd never eaten meat, I had none to offer. I filled a carafe with water from the pump and added it to the tray.

He looked up as I returned with the food and drink. He placed the saw against the tree, wiping his hands on his breeches as he offered to take the tray from me.

"I'm sorry I didn't offer sooner," I said. "It wasn't very gracious of me, was it? Here you are, helping me take care of all of this"—I motioned to the mess of logs surrounding us— "and then I go and starve you!"

"It was never a requirement, but thank you," he said with a nod as he accepted a glass of water and drank it down in hardly more than three long gulps. I poured another from the carafe.

We sat in the shade of one of the sycamores that hadn't fallen during the storm and ate our meal in relative silence, which, with Quinn, I surely should have expected.

After I returned the tray to the cottage, I rolled the wheelbarrow back to the field and began collecting and stacking the pieces of wood Quinn had already cut and split. By the time I'd completed my fourth run between the tree and the cottage, he had finished splitting the last large piece of trunk.

"There's a lot of wood here," he said. "And it's getting late. Perhaps it'd be best if we stack it here and haul it back another day, when we've returned from the Cliffs."

I agreed, and, when we'd stacked all of the wood, Quinn headed to wash in the creek despite my offer to draw a bath in the cottage and give him the privacy to bathe.

"Fine," I muttered as I hiked back to the cottage for what felt like the hundredth time that day, "You're a crazy man, Quinn D'Arturio, preferring the ice-cold creek to a warm bath." At least I could be sure I'd have enough firewood to last the winter. I planned on speaking with Archibald Greavner in a few weeks about delivering a load of firewood. Since it was clearly no longer necessary, I scratched that item off my mental list of winter preparations.

I washed with the tepid water from the basin and changed into a clean gown for the meeting with the governor, smoothing the course, gray material flat with the palms of my hands and noting I'd need to reinforce one of the round wooden buttons soon if I didn't want to lose it. As far as preparations were concerned, I was mostly ready. I needed only to pack my saddlebags for the trip and arrange for one of the older Asbury boys to care for my animals while I was gone, neither of which would take more than a quarter hour's time.

Quinn arrived at my door, clean and smelling mildly like the wild sage and mint that grew near the stream. His shirt was on and belted at his waist once again, hiding both the muscles and the scars that had surprised me earlier today.

"Are you ready?" he asked.

"As I'll ever be, I suppose," I replied, glancing around the cottage, tallying in my head the items I still wished to pack.

There it was again, the sudden unease in my gut I couldn't explain. I closed the door behind me, and we walked the path to the governor's house to receive instructions for a mission I didn't really believe could result in success.

I had shared my doubts with the governor, fully admitting I didn't believe in all of this White Sorceress Prophecy nonsense, and yet why I felt as though we were on the cusp of something big—something bigger than I'd ever known—remained a mystery.

Too much time in the sun, Reina. Chopping wood all day has addled your brain.

The council put more than a *little* faith in the prophecy. The evidence was plain to see as I observed the *women* before me. They were young—younger than I would have liked—all ranging between the ages of fourteen and seventeen and every one of them was fair-haired and even fairer-skinned. I recognized four of the eight as Barnham's own, one of whom I'd watched my mother bring into the world fourteen years earlier. Emylia's had been one of the first births my mother had let me attend. Given that I was four and finding someone to watch me was harder than not most days, it was hardly the last birth I would witness as a young child.

Now the girl stood before me, possibly about to be named the first sorceress in a thousand years. She was young, but she was quiet and serious, and I thought she might make a decent candidate if she ever learned to speak her mind. But fourteen? Were the council members out of their minds?

"Ladies, welcome," Governor Arden began. "I'd like to begin by thanking you for agreeing to take part in this journey. I truly believe we will recover the Faranzine Talisman and that one of *you* is about to become the sorceress who will restore peace to all of Castilles. I've gathered you here this evening to outline our plan and to introduce you to your escorts on this journey."

Niles stepped forth. A few of the girls had already been eyeing him, and I stifled a smile at the predictable doe-eyes that followed. It seemed Niles just had that kind of effect. At least it wasn't just me.

"This is Captain Niles Ingram. He and his soldiers have been granted leave from the borders to act as protection and escorts for your journey. Seeing as the Resistance troops are already outnumbered in this war, that should tell you the level of determination and faith we have in this effort."

"Thank you, Governor Arden. It's an honor to be chosen for such an important mission," Niles said in a voice like honey.

He turned to address the candidates. "Please rest assured I have chosen my four best men for this endeavor. We will do everything in our power to ensure we find the talisman and find it safely. Should there be anything you need during the journey, please do not hesitate to talk to me or one of my men. Our duty is to you."

Someone gave a breathy sigh, and I bit my lip to keep from laughing.

"Thank you, Captain Ingram." Governor Arden viewed the women before him. "Now what can I tell you that will ease your minds as you begin the journey? I'm sure you've questions," he said.

There were hushed mutterings as the girls turned to each other, not exactly knowing where to start or what to ask.

Finally another Barnham native—Selena Mayst, if I was correct—raised her voice. "What happens once the talisman is found? Can we assume the White Sorceress should know exactly what steps she's to take to end the war? And how will she know?"

"Ah, a good question. We can't be certain, but I believe the talisman should tell her all she needs to know. There's much to indicate the White Sorceress's power lies in the Faranzine Talisman itself. So I must assume the talisman will likely communicate to her the path she must take."

Selena put a hand to her chin thoughtfully. "Do you have plans in place if this is not the case?"

The governor gave a startled cough at the unexpected question and cleared his throat as he recovered. I guess Governor Arden hadn't expected any of his chosen ones to show a lack of confidence in his mission.

"It's a legitimate concern," Quinn said, offering support.

"Yes, I'm aware. It's certainly a fear, and not one we've overlooked. However, as we can't know for certain what will happen with the talisman until we actually *find* the talisman, we cannot anticipate exactly what will need to occur next. This is not cause for alarm, though. I have several thoughts, none of which I'd like to express until the talisman has been located and the identity of the sorceress determined. We'll convene again later and work out the details for sure."

Selena nodded, but did not look convinced. I liked the girl. A year behind me in our schooling, she was physically stunning with long, gleaming, nearly white hair, high, elegant cheekbones, and a pink-tinged complexion that always made her seem as though she had freshly applied blush to her cheeks. She and I could not have been more opposite, and yet somehow she seemed unaware of the looks the boys had always given her. More importantly, she had a mind as engaging as her looks—a rare combination.

I didn't know Selena as well as I knew Emylia, but I suspected she might make a good sorceress and if I had to hope for someone to rescue us, I might as well hope for her. She asked sensible questions with more than a shred of concern and intelligence. Were she to be chosen by the talisman, she might actually weigh her potential courses of action before leaping to conclusions. That was a start at least.

Placing a hand to my temple, I shook my head. I'd somehow already gotten caught up in the excitement of the mission and our journey, and we hadn't yet set foot from Barnham. Like the rest of them, I was beginning to place my hopes in an ancient prophecy, in the idea of a talisman, and the promise of a savior for the kingdom. And I didn't believe in magic.

"Are you all right?" Quinn asked, standing beside me.

I lowered my hand from my face. "Fine," I replied. He continued to observe me as I kept my eyes glued to the governor and listened to the explanation he was now giving to another question that had been asked. Finally, Quinn turned his eyes forward again.

Why *didn't* I believe in magic? By all rights, my own *sight* was considered by some to be a type of magic, and yet, I didn't feel it to be so. My visions had never been anything but normal. To me, anyway. I'd had them as long as I could remember, and I suspected my mother must have had them as well. Although she never said as much, my mother always had an innate understanding of them and never discouraged me from talking about them as a child. Perhaps she was the only reason I accepted them so readily myself. If I believed in my own visions, I *should* also believe in the possibility of other types of magic. Yet, I struggled.

My body's ability to sense death wasn't exactly a harbinger for normal life either, though at least *that* hadn't started until I was nine. I couldn't imagine the terror it would have invoked in a four-year-old. A single death sets my body ablaze in pain, a small fire instantly igniting in the longest bones of my arms and legs in flames that travel through to the tips of my fingers and toes before dissipating. Multiple deaths could easily cripple me, though it's true I've only had one instance to go by.

Sixteen months ago, a horrible fire overtook one of Barnham's homes in the middle of the night. No one saw until it was too late. In bed, I awoke from a pain so fierce I thought I might die. I wanted to run to the village to offer my help, but there was no point. The young family had already left this world, and nothing I could have done would have made a difference. Saints help me should I ever see the front lines of war.

I let my eyes roam over the faces of the candidates. One of them *must* possess something that would make the talisman work, something like my own abilities. It couldn't be chance. It *couldn't* be magic.

What would the girl do when she finally learned of her newfound powers? How would she handle the realization her life would never again be the same? Some of the girls in the room were flush with excitement, aroused by the possibility they would soon possess an ancient magic. But all I could think about was how much I didn't envy the responsibilities our sorceress would soon bear. *Whoever she is, I hope she's up to the task.*

The sun had not yet breached the horizon when I woke on the morning of our journey. Rising from my chair by the hearth—where I slept more often than not—I stood at the window and studied the dark landscape as I rubbed the sleep from my eyes. A whispered echo of a dream teased at the corners of my mind, remaining just out of reach of my memory. I couldn't shake the feeling there was something of importance I should remember, something from long ago. But then, maybe that was my sleep-fogged brain playing tricks on me.

As I gazed into the quickly lightening darkness, an owl swooped down from a nearby branch. It pinned a field mouse to the ground not five feet from my window. Clasping sharp talons around the struggling creature, it took to the air once more. Scarlet tendrils of light pierced the sky as the owl bore the mouse away into the depths of the towering pines.

I cursed. Whatever it was I couldn't remember from the dream would continue to elude me. Now fully awake, my brain was churning with thoughts of the things I needed to do, how best to do them, and with worries about what was to come over the next several days and weeks.

I settled for rechecking my bags, making sure I'd packed all I would need. Had I enough ground tumeria? Frowning, I searched the bag. I was sure I had packed it, but could find it neither in my bag, nor on my shelves. I had made a batch only three days ago. Crossing the room to my bench top, I moved aside jars, mortars, and pestles of various sizes to no avail.

I closed my eyes with a sigh, took a deep breath and focused, attempting to home in on the little glass jar containing the fragrant earthy brown beans ground into a fine powder that would dissolve instantly upon the tongue—a powder that dispensed numbing qualities along with a shockingly bitter aftertaste. Almost immediately, there was a mental tug low and to my right, a pinching sensation in my temple, not pleasant, but neither so *un*pleasant that I wouldn't think to utilize my ability. It was a convenient part of my vision.

Turning toward my bed, I knelt, opened my eyes, and reached a hand beneath the cot. My fingers closed around the cold glass jar, and I didn't need to read the label to know I had found the tumeria. It must have fallen from my sack when I'd packed it the day before. I tucked it snugly into its spot in my bag and cinched the satchel tightly shut.

When I was sure I hadn't forgotten anything, I drew a hot bath. It'd be the last one I might get for some time. I scrubbed my skin with one of the few luxuries I afforded myself—a bar of lemon verbena scented soap I could only purchase on my trips to Newcastle. I tried to use it sparingly.

Inhaling the savory, citrusy scent deep into my lungs, I closed my eyes and slid deeper into the tub, mentally focusing on what would happen over the next several days. My breathing slowed as I emptied my head of my worries and allowed the steam of the hot water to relax my muscles as well as my mind. Throughout the years, I found I was more likely to receive a vision if I focused on what I wanted to happen, even if it wasn't always what I saw.

Slowly, a sensation of warmth that wasn't due to the bath water washed over me. As it always did, it began with a tingling in my fingertips and spread until I could almost taste the warmth, a subtle sweetness caressing my palate.

And then I could *see*.

Ocean brine assaulted my nostrils as the scene unfolded, so strongly I was forced to choke down a cough. Then the image of stone flashed before my eyes—slick, dark stone devoid of colored veins or defining features. Voices echoed, but not the words that were being said, try though I might to hear them. They were muffled—angry—and it sounded as though I were listening from far away. Still, we would be successful in our journey. We would find the talisman, and the White Sorceress would be chosen exactly as the governor hoped. A flash of a brilliant aqua-hued gemstone nearly screamed as much to me. And yet, given the optimistic outlook, I was confused as to why I viewed the entire vision from behind the haze of a deep gray veil.

Auras almost never came into play in my visions. To see one so negative set me instantly on edge. I tried to see past the haze to determine what it was that caused such negativity, but my concentration had already been broken, and the vision dissolved into a grainy blur before disappearing entirely.

I opened my eyes and examined the ceiling of the cottage, slowly tracing the lines in the plaster with my eyes as I thought. Something wouldn't go as planned. We would find the talisman, but at what cost, I couldn't yet say.

I washed before the water had time to cool, scrubbing my hands and inspecting my nails meticulously. I wrinkled my nose at them and sighed. The dirt around the edges was nearly impossible to dislodge, but it was a small enough price to pay for doing what I loved. It wasn't as though I had anyone to impress.

Droplets fell from my body onto the wide wooden floorboards as I pulled myself from the tub. I drained the water into the trough that would carry it to my garden. It would soon be time to leave. Wrapping myself in a coarse towel, I sat upon my workbench stool and dragged a comb through my snarled locks, scowling at a particularly stubborn knot.

In the quiet of my cottage, as I pulled the comb through the ends of my hair, I could almost hear my mother now. *When I said you should do great things, Reina, I meant merely that you should stitch wounds and mend broken bones. That you should save lives. Heal. I never expected you to take me so literally.*

Oh, but I had. I had always taken my mother literally. And I *would* save lives. Perhaps on a greater scale than she had intended since I now knew the talisman would be found after all.

My gaze instinctively roamed to the dark, damp locks that spilled over my left shoulder, then to the peculiar white streak that ran from the base of my left temple to the very ends of my hair. I already had more white in that thin streak at eighteen than most of the women in Barnham did by age forty, but at least I was easy to find in a crowd.

Returning the comb to the bench, I reached for a glass jar of aloe and dipped my fingers into the fragrant balm. I massaged the cool substance onto my face, taking care to apply it generously below my lower lids, and rubbing the extra into the backs of my hands. My skin was not nearly as fair as most. Others said I always looked as though I'd spent too much time outdoors—and maybe I had—but my belly and breasts hadn't seen the sun, and they were just as golden.

I dressed in breeches and a tunic, as I always did when traveling. Despite the odd looks I got from most people in my travels, my saddle was a traditional men's saddle as my mother had always used. A man's saddle made it easier to keep my seat when Aeros made her way up a ravine or jumped a creek bank. But then, ladies probably weren't supposed to do such things.

I never cared what others thought, but once past my sixteenth year—the *Year of Choosing* for the young men and women of Castilles—I cared even less, which ultimately freed me from all expectations of what a woman should or should not be. Oh, they tried. With my mother gone a year, there had been many a townsperson who insisted it was his duty to choose a prospective mate for me, but I vehemently opposed any and all propositions. Thanks to my wildly stubborn nature and Governor Arden's penchant for compassion, I had been left to choose the path I desired without being sold like a prize goat.

I never understood the *Choosing*, why parents found it so critical to select their children's betrothed at sixteen. What did they think would happen if they waited? Was it because that's when schooling ended? Did parents suddenly feel an urgent need to usher their children into the world of adulthood by marrying them off? Not that anyone was actually married at sixteen. Betrothals lasted two years during which time young men and women spent their time either learning a trade or preparing a home.

Regardless of the fact that I had escaped the *Choosing,* there *had* been suitors, none of whom caught my attention for more than a week or two at most. I was glad to be able to throw myself into my healing craft, even if it took the townsfolk I cared for over a year to fully accept me in my mother's stead. Still, I never regretted my decision.

I was ready to leave by the time Elric Asbury appeared at the cottage. "Morning, Elric." I greeted him as I swung open the door to usher him in.

"Morning, Moreina," he said with a nod of his shaggy, sandy-haired head. His freckled face was open and friendly as always, and he was considerably more relaxed than he had been when I'd seen him the other night. While his younger brothers might say otherwise, Elric's mild disposition and always-agreeable attitude made him a trustworthy farm-sitter. He continued, "I hope it's all right that I settled Jex in the stall next to Aeros. Of all of our ponies, I figured she's got the best disposition for keeping Penny company."

"Perfect," I answered. Attention to detail was why I asked Elric to watch the farm when I was away. "Thank you." Then I gave Elric basic instructions and brought my bags to the barn to ready Aeros for the trip.

When I had the mare saddled and ready to go, I placed my foot into the stirrup and swung a leg over her back, inhaling the heady smell of worn leather and saddle polish. Aeros danced beneath me, a signal either that she wasn't used to being ridden after her lengthy furlough or that she was ready for an adventure. Ears pricked, she seemed eager to go. *Adventure*, I decided. I was ready, too.

"Okay, girl, let's round up the candidates and get moving, shall we? It's going to be a long journey. The sooner we get there, the sooner we get home. And that means extra grain and a warm stall for you."

Aeros jerked her head forward, nearly yanking the reins from my hand.

"Easy," I said soothingly as I stroked her warm neck. "You know the way, love. You'll care for me, and I'll care for you." It was silly, but I repeated the words before each of our trips, and never rode without speaking them. I'd been whispering them to her since I was ten.

You'll care for me and I'll care for you.

CHAPTER FOUR

Sincerity and Human Nature

We'd been on the road for two hours and I viewed the group before me with subdued interest and increasing disappointment.

The candidate group chattered amongst themselves, their excitement of the unknown having not yet waned. I figured it probably would by this time tomorrow, after their rears were sore from hours of riding and they had slept a night upon the cold, hard ground.

At the moment, however, they were twittering about like the flock of ayrelings that nested in my pines each year, giggling and discussing who was most likely to be declared the first sorceress to walk Liron in over a thousand years.

Niles handpicked the small group of soldiers that accompanied them and while they maintained a degree of chivalry, I noted their roving eyes upon the candidates. Niles himself rode near the front, keeping his brindle bay side by side with Selena's horse.

It seemed Niles exhibited a certain charm with Selena. I sympathized with the rising blush in her cheeks when my own mind drifted back to how he'd greeted me a day or so earlier.

But despite my initial observation, Niles wasn't about to

favor Selena over anyone else. After a while, he dropped his mount back to ride beside the next candidate, producing more rosy cheeks and shy smiles. To his credit, he was actually a relatively decent diplomat. He repeated the process several times, drawing out conversation and laughter with little effort.

Finally, he reined in and pulled his horse next to mine, drawing flattened ears and loud, unhappy snorts from Aeros.

"Do you always ride that feisty mare?" Niles asked.

"Aeros is only feisty when she wants to be," I answered. "And for a reason. I suggest keeping your distance. It appears she's not fond of your stallion."

"Surely she'd warm up to Bastian eventually?"

I gave him a dubious glance. "You may take your chances, sir, but consider yourself warned. I won't be responsible if Aeros displays her displeasure and leaves a mark on his gleaming hide. I can keep my seat in a saddle even with a good kick or two."

Niles gave a nervous laugh and nudged his horse aside to give Aeros room. "I actually cannot tell if you're serious or not," he said.

"Entirely," I answered with conviction. Aeros was twelve, but still often acted like a yearling. I couldn't be sure when the horse might do something silly. I'd been advised again and again that I should trade her for a more reliable journey horse, but I developed a bond with the mare I couldn't bear to break. She was my friend, perhaps at times a guardian. At the very least, Aeros spent more time in my company than any living human.

"May I ask you a question, Moreina?" Niles said.

"Mmhmm," I answered, wondering what he could possibly want to know.

"Have you been on your own long?"

Since I'd expected something at least remotely related to our journey, his question took me by surprise. My living alone never struck me as odd, though it would have been considered strange in most villages and it had taken some time for most of Barnham's residents to accept. If anyone in Barnham still thought it was unusual, none had recently shared their thoughts with me.

"Three years," I answered.

He gave me a look then—the one I was used to getting from people with preconceived ideas as to how old one needed to be to take care of oneself. In other words, it was the look I got from almost everyone I'd ever met, the look that usually involved estimating my age and counting backwards. "You're young."

"I wasn't always alone at the cottage. After my mother passed, they tried to convince me to move into the village. Governor Arden even offered me a place with his family. I almost accepted, but in the end, I couldn't give up the farm. It's my home."

"You couldn't have been more than, what, fourteen?"

"Fifteen," I corrected quickly—a little too quickly. *That's great, Reina. Show how much it irks you.*

"Extraordinary."

Not thinking so myself, I shrugged my shoulders in response. Niles watched me as we talked, showing either genuine interest or a very good impression of it.

"Governor Arden speaks highly of you. He tells me as long as you've been Healer, there's never been an illness that couldn't be cured."

I gave a half-laugh despite myself, "Is that so? Governor Arden says a lot of things," I told him.

"Yes, but I've never met a Healer so young with your skill."

Where was he going with this line of questioning? Was there a purpose?

"My mother taught me well," I replied. "There was no one available to watch a young child when she was called away, so I was her shadow. I began studying the healing craft long before I was introduced to grammar and arithmetic."

Niles gave a noncommittal, "Hmm."

I continued, "Barnham has been fortunate enough to have escaped most of the major plagues that have troubled the other towns and villages throughout the last several years. If we've been spared, it's not been my doing."

"Or have the plagues come to Barnham, but you've stopped them in their tracks? Have you worked a charm to prevent the vapors from disturbing the village? Have you some power of which the governor is unaware?" Niles challenged, seemingly wanting to believe that I was a witch as well as Healer.

I met Niles's eyes evenly, their blue seeming to shift and change as the sunlight caught them as it filtered through the rusty-hued canopy above. "If Barnham has escaped the plague, it is because we are a small village far from most others with few things to be desired by outsiders. We boast only the finest seascape and no more," I said firmly. "I assure you, if Barnham has been spared, it's not been because of me."

His eyes assessed mine in an uncomfortable silence. "Very well," he conceded, though he didn't seem convinced.

I took the opportunity to change the subject. "So, what news of the border wars? Has there been anything encouraging?" I asked.

Niles gave an almost imperceptible grunt and a shrug of his shoulders. "It's not what you'd think."

"And what should one think about war?"

"That it should be glorious. That the righteous should prevail. That good and evil should be easy to tell apart."

"Ah."

His eyes seemed to focus upon something beyond the road only he could see as he continued, "Then you're there, on the battlefield, and men are dying beside you and you can't figure out why you weren't the one who was sliced open instead, why you aren't staring at your own insides strewn across the ground. The thought eats away at you as you sleep." He sniffed. "What sleep you can manage anyway. And then comes the fear. The constant inescapable fear it *will* be you in the next battle, that you'll look up from the ground at the man beside you, and he'll be standing over you with a look of horror upon his face. And you'll know his thoughts precisely. Death will come for him, too."

I was struck by the morose detail in which Niles described the war. Real war was never the glorified version retold for children's textbooks, but this war had obviously impacted him in a way he never could have dreamed. Before joining the army, he'd probably been a naïve young kid who thought war was a march over the hill and a reclaiming of land and throne.

I shook my head in sorrow. "I'm sorry you had to know such things. How long have you been a soldier?"

"Six years," he answered. "It seemed a good, solid career

before Bruenner threw the kingdom into chaos by murdering the king."

I made an uncertain sound. "You seem pretty sure it was him."

"Believe me, if you ever met him, you'd be pretty sure, too. He's probably convinced himself he's doing the right thing. Following his destiny or some nonsense."

"So you knew him?"

Niles shrugged again. "As well as anyone who served under him *could* actually know him. I defected to the Resistance before he formally declared his intent. I knew what was coming. I just didn't realize the extent of the horrors he would unleash. That's why this mission is so important. This war needs to end. The killing needs to stop," he said, his jaw clenching with each word. "It can't do that unless the White Sorceress comes forth."

I let my gaze roam over the girls who rode before me, contemplating which would be the chosen one from my vision. "And you think that the sorceress will be able to stop the war?"

"It's in the prophecy, is it not?"

Slowly I said, "Yes, but the prophecy doesn't say how she'll stop it."

"I'm sure the talisman will tell her. It must!"

I wished I shared Niles's conviction. "That seems too easy an answer."

"Why must it be? Perhaps the talisman has untold powers we could only dream of. Maybe it has the power to decimate all of Bruenner's troops in one fell swoop. Or perhaps it can strike at him directly. I've a good feeling if we can cut off the viper's head, the rest of the snake will be harmless. Take out Bruenner and his troops will scatter like the wind. I have to believe most of his army doesn't really want to be fighting at all. I knew some of those men. I can't see them doing the things I've heard, the things I've seen..."

"Then let us hope that the talisman contains powers we have yet to know," I replied.

But I couldn't shake the vision I'd had this morning. Something wouldn't go as planned. Saints help us; maybe the talisman wouldn't do anything at all.

By the following evening, exactly as expected, the girls were sullen. Complaints of sore rears, the need for rest stops, and grievances about the sudden chill in the air abounded. I had expected no less. These girls had been raised in the village and knew better how to fix hair and prepare meals than they did how to pack for a demanding journey. Half of them hadn't brought decent heavyweight cloaks, which made me wonder how any of them could hold the wisdom expected of the White Sorceress.

And yet, I had seen the party successful, so the talisman would make its choice. I mulled over the options as I observed Selena dole out rations of the stew the soldiers had prepared over the campfire. She was sensible, unafraid of getting her hands dirty, and was happy to lend assistance where needed. Plus, she'd had at least enough brains to pack a thick wool cloak. Since the beginning of the journey, she'd remained quiet, though I didn't fail to note one of Niles's men had been flirting with her since yesterday morning despite the fact that she was already betrothed.

But then, there was that bit in the prophecy about there being two suitors, so who could say one of them wasn't among Niles's men? Perhaps the suitors would come into play as we made our journey. It was something worth considering at least.

A twig snapping behind me pulled me from my thoughts, and I turned to see Quinn standing next to me. Quinn had spent the majority of the journey riding silently either at the very front or the very rear of the group—usually wherever Niles was not. Occasionally, he'd scouted ahead after conferring with me about a turn in the road or what direction we needed to travel next, but otherwise he'd kept to himself.

"Care to share a fire, Reina?" he asked, offering a hand to help me stand.

I *was* chilly. I'd been staying away from the cooking fire since the smell of meat held no appeal and the conversation had been less than stimulating to say the least. I settled instead for huddling in my cloak and nibbling the dried fruit and cheese I'd brought.

Agreeing, I grasped his hand, registering its warmth, and used it to pull myself up. "Thank you," I said, following him to the small fire he'd started.

"Would you like some kai? I've got some already brewed."

"Please." I held out the tin cup he handed me and he filled it. Wrapping my hands around the mug, I sipped, letting the sweet bitterness warm my throat down to the depths of my stomach. "Mmm, thank you."

"Your hands are like ice," he said. "If you were so cold, why didn't you sit by the fire?"

I wrinkled my nose. "Stew," I said.

"Ah, that's right. I forgot."

I nodded and sipped the kai again.

"Why *don't* you eat meat?" he asked. "Your mother did."

"Why?" I echoed. He nodded. "Because I don't need to in order to live. If I can avoid taking the life of another, that's what I'll do, even if that *other* is an animal."

Quinn made no comment.

I continued, "I've looked into Aeros's eyes and surely as I have a soul, so has she. And that means the same for every animal. Every single one."

"Mmph."

I raised an eyebrow. "You don't agree?"

"Frankly, I think you're out of your head."

I scowled at him. "Well, I didn't ask for your opinion."

He laughed, and the sound surprised me. "But," he continued, "I admire you for sticking to what you believe."

My expression softened. "So it was only a half-hearted insult then?"

His smile died, and he caught my eyes with his. "'Twas not an insult, Reina." The firelight cut the shadows from his face and, for an instant, there was something familiar in his gaze, but I couldn't put my finger on it.

Sudden laughter from the larger group caught our attention. Two or three of the girls had decided to put on mock plays to keep themselves entertained. At least it distracted them from their complaints.

"I cannot say that any of those girls would stick to their convictions the way you do yours," he commented as he watched.

"That's harsh," I said, coming to their defense though my

mind regretfully agreed with him.

"Harsh?" he asked. "I say it because it's true."

More giggles followed from the group. Guilty as it made me feel, Quinn was right in his assumptions.

"They're young," I reminded him.

"Yes," he agreed. "Young and brainless. Niles's men are highly entertained."

"There do seem to be plenty of fluttering eyelashes," I replied, ignoring his brainless comment. "But to be fair, Niles's men are catering to it. Look at them!"

Two of the soldiers, Jinso and Ramus if I wasn't mistaken, were now acting as well. Arms flailing and sporting ridiculous expressions, they looked as though they'd begun an exuberant game of charades. Laughter carried on the breeze.

Quinn's mouth pressed into a hard line. "These *girls* are no more likely to be the White Sorceress than I am to be a court jester."

"You think this is a waste of time?"

"I do."

I bit my lip and contemplated how much I wanted to tell Quinn. "A day or so ago, I would have agreed," I said.

"And you believe otherwise now?" he asked, almost incredulously, motioning at the group.

I toyed with the handle on the cup I was holding. It had loosened, probably over many years of wear, and it made a satisfying clink each time I shifted it. I stared into the fire a moment before answering, "I might."

Quinn said nothing, no doubt waiting for me to elaborate.

"I had a vision," I confessed. My sight wasn't something I spoke of often, but those close to me knew I had it. "It showed our success."

"Then you already know which of our candidates is the One?"

I shook my head. "No, unfortunately."

I hesitated but didn't confide in him my fears of what could go wrong. The talisman would be found, and it would identify our sorceress. I couldn't truly be sure of anything beyond that. There had been more than one occasion when I'd translated visions incorrectly in the past, so I tried to refrain from interpretation where possible.

"So why is it that you seem to want to say more?" Quinn asked, studying me with more attention than he should.

"Just thinking," I lied. "We know the mission will be successful, but we still haven't determined exactly where we'll need to start looking once we reach the Plymann Cliffs."

"I've been considering that myself," he said, reaching into his bag. "I've got a few ideas."

I sidled closer to him to view his hand-drawn map. He'd traced the outline of the cliffs from Governor Arden's original map but had added detail and scrawled notations into certain areas. He pointed to an area marked *Stonehaven*.

"Right here," he said, "is where the Old Ones used to make their sacrifices. There's an altar of sorts, surrounded by rock walls. It's survived thousands of years and seems a likely place for something of importance to be hidden."

Chills slid down my spine as I recalled the flashes of stone I had *seen* the morning of our departure. "It's a possibility," I said slowly.

"Are you familiar with it?" he asked.

"Only from afar," I told him truthfully. The place had always had an ominous atmosphere that deterred me from going there alone, but I dared not tell this to Quinn. "I've never had the need to inspect it for any reason."

He accepted my explanation and moved on. "The next viable option is here." He pointed to a hastily drawn sketch. "The old monastery. Do the priests still reside there?"

"No," I said. "By the looks of the place, it's been abandoned for some time."

"So you've been there."

"It's the best spot for collecting seleniac and harkspun nettle. The walls are intact, as are the buildings, though they aren't in the best of shape. It could take days to search the entire place if the talisman is there." It, too, had stone walls. I tried to remember if it looked as I'd pictured in my vision.

"Mmph, well, those are the places I deemed most likely. There's not much else out there. Seeing as you're familiar with the area, have you any other suggestions?"

The places Quinn had mentioned were the only two manmade structures for miles. "No. I think you've determined the two most likely places. The talisman will probably be someplace where a person would go without being openly visible or easily found. Either of those places fits, and there's nothing else upon the cliffs for miles in any direction. But all of this depends on whether or not your father is correct in assuming the cliffs are where the talisman is located at all."

He nodded and folded the map once again, placing it back in his bag. I swallowed the last of my kai, rinsed my cup, and thanked him once again.

"If it's all the same to you," I said, "I'm going to check on

Aeros, and turn in. We've got a lot of ground to cover tomorrow. If we can convince the girls and Niles's men to move quickly, we might even reach the cliffs with time to start searching for the talisman before the sun sets."

"My thoughts, too. Night, Reina."

I nodded and made my way to Aeros. She and the rest of the horses stood tightly together, heads down, dozing. Sensing me, she pushed from deep inside of the herd to greet me, snorting lightly as she nuzzled my shoulder and blew a sweet, warm breath smelling of grass and grain into my ear. I ran my fingers along her sturdy neck, feeling the strength of the taut muscle beneath.

I let my hands travel lightly down the mare's legs to feel around her hooves. She was still in good shape, no sign of heat or injury. I had checked her hooves and pried a few stones from them when I'd dismounted earlier. Now, I checked hocks and fetlocks to reassure myself that the horse could still handle the journey at the pace we'd travel tomorrow.

She picked up legs when I asked and stretched them for me without trouble. I patted her neck again and gave her ears an extra scratch just where she liked.

"You've done a fine job so far, girl. Another day there and a few more days home and you'll be back in the paddock, eating yourself silly again. I promise."

As if realizing she'd been dismissed, Aeros turned from me and forced her way back into the middle of the herd. There was mild annoyance from some of the horses who tried to push back, but ultimately, as she always did, Aeros had her way.

"She's a bit bossy, isn't she?"

I started. I hadn't heard Selena approach.

"She is," I answered. "No one will ever tell her what to do."

Selena smiled in the darkness. "Including you, I assume?"

"Definitely," I said with a laugh.

We fell into silence and I waited, wondering what had encouraged Selena to seek me out. She fiddled nervously with her hands.

Finally, she cleared her throat. "Moreina, I know I've never told you this—and please don't laugh—but I just…well, I want to say that I really admire you."

My ears flooded with warmth at the unexpected compliment, and I found myself at a loss for words, not that I was very good at them anyway.

"I've been meaning to ask you for a while, but do you think, when this is all over and the White Sorceress has been found… well, if it's not me and I get to go back to normal life in Barnham, do you think you might take me on as a student?"

I couldn't hide the surprise from my voice. "A student?"

Selena nodded. "I love how you know so many remedies for ailments. I want that. I want to heal. It's so purposeful, so meaningful. I mean, what you do…it makes a difference. I want to do that, too."

I hesitated a moment before speaking. "What about Edrian?"

"We're still to be married next year, but he's a good one, Moreina. He was actually the one who encouraged me to talk to you. He said he doesn't want an unhappy wife and I should find something that I'm passionate about and go after it with all my heart," she paused before continuing, "as long as I can still find time to put supper on the table."

I laughed. It sounded like something Edrian would say.

"I wouldn't have thought to ask you on my own otherwise."

I thought. "Are you sure, Selena? It's a lot of work."

"I know, but I don't mind hard work, and I like to study."

"There *would* be a lot to study. It takes a long time. I learned mostly by assisting my mother from the time I was little."

"I could do that," Selena said, hope hanging on her words. "I could be your assistant. I'm not hoping to be proficient in a week or anything, I promise. I've got perseverance."

"Then I think we have a deal," I told Selena, sticking out my hand. "When we return to Barnham, if you are *not* the White Sorceress, we'll begin your training."

Selena ignored my hand and gripped me in a tight embrace. "Thank you!" she nearly squealed.

I fought back a smile at the unexpected gesture as Selena regained her composure.

"I'm so excited. Oh, thank you, Moreina!"

"Reina, please."

"Yes, all right. Reina. Thank you!" Selena disappeared into the darkness. Given the way she had practically skipped back to the camp, she wasn't likely to get much sleep tonight. I smiled.

It was a surprise. I hadn't thought there was anyone in the village interested in learning the healing arts. To discover Selena was not only interested, but that she outright *admired* my work, well, it was heartwarming. Teaching! It was something I had never considered.

All we needed to do was wrap up the talisman mission, return to Barnham, and I'd have an eager student ready to learn. And maybe, dare I say it, a newfound friend?

CHAPTER FIVE

Unpleasant Surprises

Selena spent the morning riding beside me, unwilling to wait until we returned to Barnham to delve into the art of healing. There wasn't much I could introduce her to in detail as we rode, but I recited the Healer's Oath and she repeated it time and again until she had every word memorized perfectly. Her thirst for knowledge seemed insatiable as she asked which ailments I encountered most often, how long the average woman labored, and whether it was better to let the body fight a fever naturally or treat before the rising temperature became dangerous to the mind.

I answered her questions at length until I thought my voice might give out. We stopped for a quick lunch at noon.

"You know, Selena," I said as I bit into an appliken. "All of this might be for nothing if you end up finding the talisman."

She pushed a platinum lock of hair from her forehead, tucking it firmly behind her ear. Pale blue eyes, nearly gray, but bright with curiosity met mine. "It's not," she replied. "Knowledge is never for nothing."

Had she been a year older, I might have had a friend in my school years. As it was, when I hadn't been following my mother around, my nose had always been stuck in a book about whatever ailment intrigued me that month.

"Mount up!" Niles called from atop his horse.

Already standing, I slung my sack over my shoulder and offered a hand to Selena as she shoved the last bite of bread and jam into her mouth. Brushing crumbs from her skirt, she grabbed my hand and stood, then stretched her arms to the sky.

"I'll tell you what," she said softly as she leaned in. "I'll be glad to be home away from Bossybritches over there, nice as he is to look at."

I stifled a giggle in response as my eyes unexpectedly met Quinn's. He had already mounted, and I caught his reproving gaze as I laughed at Selena's comment. My ears burned. I shouldn't feel guilty. I had nothing to be ashamed of, but Quinn's comments about brainlessness from the other night echoed in my ears and I wondered if I, too, must seem brainless to him.

We reached the cliffs a few hours later. As always during a double-full spell, the winds rolled from the surface of the ocean unpredictably in invisible waves, punishing all those in its path and forcing me to swallow involuntarily. I had always avoided journeying alone to the cliffs during a double-full for fear of being blown from the bluff. It would not have been the first time the *Brutales* would claim a horse as well as rider without warning. The only hint of the deadly wind's appearance was the curiously overbearing scent of sweet palinata blooms. Seconds later a wall of wind tore across the land, sweeping at all in its path. As palinata grew nowhere near the cliffs, the phenomenon remained a mystery.

The less docile horses objected to the sudden wind, stomping and dancing with nerves, their withers quivering with an equine sense more attuned to nature's wrath than a human's could ever be. For safety's sake, the group dismounted.

Though Quinn had avoided Niles for the duration of the trip, he approached him now, map in hand. They conferred for a moment before Niles nodded, spoke to his men, then addressed the candidates.

"Ladies," he said smoothly. For a moment, even the wind died down as if deferring to him. "It appears we have reached a very exciting time in our journey."

"About time," mumbled one of the girls, eliciting nervous giggles in response.

"Yes, we've all been impatient to arrive," Niles agreed. "It appears, at this point in time, there's not one, but two possibilities as to where we believe the talisman might be hidden."

With wary eyes, the girls glanced back and forth between each other as though waiting for one of them to voice an opinion on the matter. They hadn't expected to be faced with options. Selena met my gaze, eyebrows raised in question.

"We can either explore both as a group or break into two smaller groups and explore each option separately." Before anyone could indicate a preference, he continued. "It's my suggestion that we break into two groups. We will locate the talisman sooner that way and fulfill the prophecy that much quicker."

A fierce gust of wind nearly knocked him from his feet, and it was agreed the sooner we could leave the cliffs, the better.

I wasn't surprised Niles chose to lead one team while Quinn led the other. The remaining soldiers also split between the two groups, and we agreed to meet in two days' time should the talisman not be found before then.

I followed Quinn and four of the candidates, including Selena, to Stonehaven, but I wasn't entirely sure I wanted to visit the place even *with* company. The uneasy feeling that overcame me each time I thought about the stones wasn't one that could be fully explained, but I likened it to having gulped a large swig or two of belstem draught—a tingling cold that swept through my veins.

We arrived at the ominously towering stones in less than an hour, triggering chills that shot down my spine as the stones came into view. Though the sun had been visible moments earlier, an oppressive fog swirled around dozens of the rocks that stood upright, tall and smooth. The rocks themselves stood like sentries, alert and erect, awaiting our group's arrival, and it seemed to me, not entirely in welcome.

A thousand years of sea spray and wind. We have no chance of finding anything here. If the talisman had been placed in a crevice that existed a thousand years before, it might well have fallen into the dirt and gotten buried years ago.

Nevertheless, we searched high and low. Girls stood on saddles upon horses' backs to search some of the upper niches within the stones as I inched beneath the altar on hands and knees. The image of the three-ton stone collapsing in upon me, pinning my body to the ground, played itself in my mind. With a shiver, I banished the unwanted thought.

I ran my hands along the base of the stone, against the ground, trying to feel where rock met grass and praying I wouldn't stick my hand into a snake's den. While I carried a number of treatments with me, I had nothing that could battle the venom of a hibernating sluth viper and had no desire to feel the effects of a bite now or ever.

When I finished examining one altar stone, I moved to the next. It occurred to me then as I ran my hands along the surface of each stone that they were not cool to the touch as they rightfully should have been. I extended my fingers wide, flattening a palm to the rock to feel the heat emanating from the stone beneath my skin. Despite being wet with spray and exposed to the elements, the stones were warm without question.

I stood and made my way to the outer wall stones, hesitantly touching with my fingertips before running a palm across one. It, too, radiated warmth. Utterly bewildered, I examined the stone. There wasn't anything spectacular about it. Like the others, it was dark basalt with veins of an unknown deep green mineral dispersed throughout, rock typical of the area as a whole.

"Have you found something?" asked one of Niles's men when he realized I was staring intently at the stone in front of me.

I shook my head. "No, nothing."

He nodded and began to make his way to another stone before I called to him. "Do these stones feel warm to you, Antony?"

He placed a hand to the one I had been touching and looked back at me as if contemplating whether he was the victim of a poorly constructed prank or I had lost my mind. "No," he said. "Cold as, uh, stone."

"Thank you," I said, dismissing him with a distracted nod as he left to help lift one of the candidates to climb upon another standing stone.

My eyes searched the group until I spotted Quinn on the

other side of the circle of stones. Hands on hips, he was gazing upwards at the highest of them. *No doubt he's figuring out how he might get atop it.*

"Quinn?" I said as I reached him. "Do the stones seem right to you?"

"Right how?" he asked as he glanced down at me.

I pressed my lips together, thinking how not to sound like a lunatic. "I don't know exactly."

"The entire place gives me gooseflesh, Reina. There's something strange about it."

He feels it, too!

"Place your hand on that rock," I demanded.

He raised a questioning eyebrow at me, but did as I requested, his broad hand covering nearly twice the area mine had.

"Is it warm?"

His eyes narrowed suspiciously. "No."

I slapped my hand to the surface of the nearest stone. Like the others, it radiated heat. Had I been a barn cat, I would have happily curled up to a stone and slept, warm and cozy.

Hopes dashed, I let my hand drop to my side. I'd thought if Quinn noticed the strange air about Stonehaven, he might also feel the warmth of its rocks.

Acutely aware of Quinn examining my face, I tried not to relay emotion, but I was forced to elaborate on my odd question as he asked, "It's not cold for you, is it?"

Slowly, I shook my head.

"What do you feel?"

"Warmth. It's not hot exactly, but it feels like the healing stones I recommend to Edna Herrington for her chronic aches."

Quinn nodded thoughtfully, rubbing his chin with a hand. "Has anyone else felt it?"

I shook my head again. "I asked Antony. I have to assume that if you and he both felt nothing, then no one else would either."

"Is this the kind of thing that happens often?" he asked. Lowering his voice, he added, "You know, like your sight?"

I contemplated as the girls continued to search high and low, leaving no crevice unchecked. "No," I answered. "Other than my sight, I've never experienced anything out of the ordinary." *Liar. You can sense death better than any killhound. It might as well be your middle name. Moreina Death di Bianco.*

"What about your healing?"

"What of it?" I asked. "'Tis hardly a gift. It's knowledge obtained and properly applied."

"To you, maybe, but you have to know you've a reputation in Barnham," Quinn said.

Sharply, I turned to him. "And what does that mean?" I asked, perhaps a bit more accusatory than I meant to. "Niles said something similar."

"Did he?"

"He did."

"I won't speak for Niles," Quinn said. "I just meant that the capacity of your mind for medicine far exceeds that of most anyone else. It's a gift, Reina."

His words took me by surprise.

"Aye, well, thanks," I stammered.

He nodded and resumed searching for the talisman. Taking my cue, I returned to the altar and got on my knees once more, though I was far from saying any prayers.

The talisman eluded us for two straight days, despite our persistent scouring, and the stones continued to radiate a heat only I felt, lending to my unease of the place. By the time Quinn called for us to meet with Niles's group, I was eager to leave. Aeros seemed to share my sentiments and I kept a tight rein on the mare as we moved from the area.

Mumblings that the other candidate group had found the talisman ceased when we rounded the last bend and saw a shared dismay upon their faces. They had not managed to find the talisman either.

Arguments broke out amongst the girls as the two groups discussed who had had the more difficult past two days, but the fights weren't limited to the women. The soldiers' patience had worn thin over the last several days and they began regaling each other with tales of which group had had the more difficult time catering to the candidates who had clearly lost all excitement for their cause.

Listening to the incoherent jumble of words that grew louder the harder I tried to block it, I couldn't help but feel there was something I had missed.

Silently, I dismounted, left Aeros with the other horses, and walked a distance along the cliff's edge. *Brutales* forgotten, I stopped walking only when I could no longer hear the arguing.

I gazed into the water, the violent sea churning in the canyons below. Clearing my head, I attempted to let the vision be *seen* again, but was frustrated when I couldn't muster the focus. I was missing something. Something significant. What was it?

I flopped down upon the damp grass, not caring it would soak my cloak more than it already was. I let my gaze wander over the misty horizon and across the rocky landscape.

To my right, a portion of the cliffs jutted out in the resemblance of a thumb, like a weary traveler attempting to hitch a ride into town. Endless tidal pressure applied over years carved the rocks into an array of arches and columns, and I stared into their form as I reviewed the vision in my mind.

I thought back to the images of stone I'd seen, trying to remember what the rock looked like, its texture and feel. The girls had been crowded together in the vision, as if there hadn't been much room. A confined space. The light I'd seen in the vision had been provided by torches. Wherever the talisman was hidden, it was sheltered and dark. Unless maybe we were meant to find it at night.

And then it hit me—not a slow revelation as a child's understanding of a challenging arithmetic problem—but rather in a rush so powerful my breath was nearly swept from my lungs all at once, leaving me wondering how it hadn't all occurred to me sooner.

I jumped from my place in the grass and nearly ran back to the others, still bickering where I left them. I had to fight to be heard.

"I know where the talisman lies," I said urgently amongst the voices.

Only those nearest to me quieted, so I repeated myself louder. The group stilled in silence.

"What?" Niles asked.

"I know where the talisman is," I said, pointing to the jutting peninsula behind me. "It's in the caves."

"How do you know?" Niles said. "How can you be sure?"

"Think about it," I told him, unwilling to reveal my *sight*. I could only imagine what he would think. *Witch.* "It makes sense. Those caves have been here almost as long as the land itself. No human in his right mind would want to spend time in them. You can enter at low tide, but at high tide, they're likely filled completely. Even if one is brave enough—or foolish enough—to enter at low tide, there's only a few hours to get in and get back out."

"Why would anyone hide anything there?" asked Jinso.

"If you want to be certain that it won't be found for a thousand years, it's the perfect place to put it," I said.

"But, in this remote land, anywhere would have been fine to hide it. So, why there?"

"Maybe a thousand years ago anywhere would have been fine to hide it, but Sibyl Mariah couldn't begin to imagine what the land would look like this far into the future. The council couldn't predict if the *Brutales* would die down or even be eliminated. Perhaps the land would be cleared. Perhaps people would build homes here. Remote, yes, but it's not an entirely hostile land. The monastery is proof people *can* live here. If Sibyl Mariah wanted to be sure the talisman wouldn't be disturbed for a thousand years, what better place to hide it than a place where no one wants to go?"

"She's right," Quinn said. I let out a breath I didn't know I'd been holding. It was good to have Quinn's support.

Niles narrowed his eyes. "So what now? We can't just run in and grab the talisman if that's the case. That's far too dangerous."

"We wait. We watch the tides to determine the best time to go in and how long we have before we need to get back out," Quinn told him. "I'll explore the mouth of the caves to find an entrance worth considering."

"I'll go with you," I said.

Quinn nodded his consent.

Niles sighed and rubbed a hand along his neck. "We set up camp here then. Only not…here." He turned to the soldiers with him. "Let's get the women out of this wind." Addressing Quinn, he said, "We'll head down to the base of the cliffs, near the tree line, camp there for the night. Join us when you're ready."

Quinn appeared not to know whether he should be amused or annoyed with Niles's instructions, but said nothing. He pulled a bag from his saddle and handed his horse's reins to one of Niles's men. I did the same and Antony took Aeros.

The group slowly retreated from the cliff's edge and blustering wind. When I turned back to Quinn, he was already ten paces ahead, heading for the bluff. I hurried to catch up, peering over the edge as I reached him, the dizzying view forcing me to step back.

"There," Quinn pointed to the cove closest to us. "We can probably make our way down over there."

I followed where Quinn pointed, but I wasn't so sure. There was somewhat of a path—if it could be called that—from the top of the cliff downward, but after a distance it broke off and looked to take a straight drop to the ocean below.

I mentioned this to Quinn. "I don't think we'll be able to get farther than that point," I said.

"Maybe," he looked pensive. "But, I'm willing to bet there's a switchback to the side. See how the rock beyond it looks to be slightly different?"

I squinted but saw nothing unusual. I shook my head.

"The color. It's a slightly different shade of gray. I think the rock turns there and continues around the bend. I don't know where we go after that, but given there's no visible alternative, that looks like our best chance."

With that, we trekked through the tall grasses to where the path started. It quickly became obvious the *path* was nothing more than a slick, mossy drainage ditch carved by years of rainwater making its way to the ocean. I wasn't keen on following it, but from the new vantage point, there really didn't appear to be any other way down. With nerves rubbed raw by the persistent phantom odor of palinata blooms every few minutes, I began my descent behind Quinn.

It was mid-afternoon by the time we reached the turning point. Indeed the path turned in the direction Quinn anticipated, but it led to a drop off of its own, forcing us to once again reassess our plan. The drop was close enough to the cove below, allowing me to peer over the edge without feeling the need to step back again and the tide had nearly reached its low, but even with wet sand to land on, it was too far of a drop to comfortably attempt.

I met Quinn's eyes. "What now?"

His gaze roamed across the rock next to us, and he ran a hand along its surface until he found a small fissure.

"I think it's big enough," he said swinging his pack from his back and opening it. He pulled a metal clip, a small hammer,

and a length of rope from it. A few minutes later, he had secured
the clip to the fissure in the rock and returned the hammer to
his pack. He ran the rope through the clip and gave both sides a
hefty tug.

"I don't suppose you've done this before, so listen carefully.
I'll go down first. When I reach the bottom, I want you to pull up
the end of the rope and tie it securely around you like this." He
fashioned a harness between my legs and around my midsection.
His body was warm, so warm, as he bent almost intimately
close, and I felt a similar heat rising in my own cheeks. "It's very
important that this knot"—he pulled at the knot— "is secure.
When you've got it, let me know, and I'll help lower you down
from below."

I nodded and swallowed, not sure I trusted myself to speak.
He undid the harness and tied one for himself in a quarter of
the time it had taken him to tie it on me. Grabbing both sides of
the rope, he made quick work of the drop. Once he was down,
I grabbed the end of the rope and tied it around myself as he'd
instructed. Though the sand was only thirty feet beneath me, it
felt nearly an eternity before Quinn had me completely lowered
to the ground.

"The tide seems to be about at its lowest now," he commented,
his voice echoing on the rock above as we explored the mouth
of the cave. "If we can figure out the highest it can be to safely
enter the cave, the group can enter as the tide goes out and get
the most time to search before it comes back in again."

"It's almost double-full moon," I reminded him as I
clambered over a large rock, recovering as my foot slipped on
slick algae. I wrinkled my nose as I shook the seaweed from my

boot. "High tide will be higher than normal."

"Well, all we can do is wait and see. If it's too high to go in, we won't risk it. We'll camp out until we're able to go in safely."

"Niles won't like that."

"Frankly, Niles can go throw a stone. If he wants it done quickly, he can go in himself. I'll not risk the safety of any of my charges so that he can get back to a comfortable bed."

I pressed my lips together. "Doesn't he have to return to the war effort? I'd think he wants this done so he could get back to his post, not so he can cozy back home again."

"As far as he's concerned, Niles's only duty is to take care of his own hide."

I narrowed my eyes. "You're awfully tough on him," I said, coming to Niles's defense. "He may not be the hero you think he somehow should be, but he's seen a lot in battle. And like any soldier, maybe he's been a little scarred by the things he's seen."

"Ah, so he's told you his weepy tale, too, I see."

We'd made it to the mouth of the cave, and Quinn paused to light a torch. I grabbed his arm, forcing him to face me.

"What do you mean by that?"

He clenched his jaw as he moved forward once more, and I followed behind. "Nothing. He told my father the same story, that's all."

"Quinn, I know you don't like him. I understand you've had some exchange with him in the past that wasn't favorable, but right now I think we all want the same thing—to find the talisman and get back to our lives, to leave the rest of the war effort to the White Sorceress, whoever she may be. Whatever this thing is you have against Niles, can you please put it aside?"

He turned to face me. Surprised, I nearly ran straight into his chest. "No," he said quietly, looking down at me. "I cannot."

"Why?" I asked, searching his dark eyes for some hint of what could possibly be so awful. "What has he done that is so horrible?"

"Enough."

"Wouldn't it make you feel better if you talked about it?"

"Nothing would ever change what was done."

"No, but it might help you."

He gave a bitter laugh. "Reina, I don't need help with much, and for the things I do, there are few people who are capable of providing it."

I grew silent. Obviously, nothing I could do would lessen Quinn's resentment of Niles. Of all the terrible things I envisioned, I somehow could not imagine Niles doing any of them. Anxiety gnawed at my gut, and I forced myself to calm the imaginary demons. I'd talk to Niles later. Maybe then I could put my mind at ease.

We traveled onward for the better part of an hour. I followed Quinn from one cave to the next, trying to remember where we turned, and counting steps until the next turn. Finally, we reached a cavernous room that dwarfed all the churches in Millasboro. Though I'd only ever been there once as a child, I remembered the dozens of towering cathedrals, intricately decorated in carved stone and colored glass. The height of this particular chamber put them all to shame. I wished we'd had more light to see where open space met ceiling.

"These caves go on forever," I said, breaking the silence. My voice echoed back at me eerily. "How will we ever find it?"

Quinn didn't answer right away as he examined the walls of the room. He placed a hand to the rock, then turned to me.

"Feel this rock."

I did, and my eyes widened in surprise. "It's warm! You feel it, too."

He nodded. "What does it mean?"

Mentally, I tried to calculate how far we had traveled underground. I couldn't be sure, but I would have put a hefty wager on my only guess. "We're beneath Stonehaven."

He held the torch higher as he moved around the room, testing the feel of each of the stone walls. I closed my eyes, attempting to slow both my thoughts and my racing pulse. "This room," I said. "It's familiar."

Quinn was at my side. "You've *seen* it."

I swallowed as I nodded. "Yes. It's here, somewhere. The talisman is here."

"Tomorrow," he said. "As it is, we've been here too long."

We backtracked through the caves, a thousand thoughts flying through my head at once. We had found it. We had found the Faranzine Talisman. Well, almost.

After we'd taken nearly a half-dozen turns I didn't remember through the caves, I asked, "Are you sure this is the right way?"

Quinn glanced briefly at his arm as he continued. "Yes."

We made it to the mouth of the cave in ankle-deep water, emerging into the cool air and fading daylight. I didn't relish the thought of spending a night on the ledge we had to get back to, yet neither did I enjoy the idea of the tide coming in while we remained in the cove.

By the time we returned to the rope, the water was mid-calf.

I glanced upwards at the rock and realized suddenly I wasn't entirely sure I could get back up to the ledge at all. I'd been so initially preoccupied with being lowered down I hadn't given thought to getting back up.

Quinn quickly eliminated the problem. "I'll go up first. When I lower the rope back down, tie the harness same as before. I'll hoist you up."

I nodded gratefully as he swiftly scaled the rock using the rope as support. Quinn reached the top so quickly that I was left blinking, open-mouthed, in the cove below. When had Quinn taken up cliff-climbing as a hobby?

Shaking my head, I tied the rope as I'd been taught. The water was past my knees and the cold had begun to numb my toes. With Quinn's help, I partly scaled the rock as he lifted me to the ledge. I looked down only once I'd safely reached the top. The water rolled into the mouth of the cave with a force greater than I would have imagined, sucking sand with it as each wave washed back out to sea.

I began to untie the rope harness from my waist, but Quinn stopped me. "Let's not take chances," he said. "The wind has picked up, it'll be dark soon, and we've got a steep climb." He affixed the other end of the rope to his own body, fashioning a similar harness, as we began our ascent.

I wanted to pretend the wind didn't bother me, but with each gust, my teeth chattered. We were near the top of the cliff when an unmistakably floral scent washed over us. Eyes wide, I turned to face Quinn, who had already anchored his grip on a nearby rock outcropping.

"Hold on!" he yelled.

CHAPTER SIX

Friendship and Risk

A roaring filled my ears as a force unlike any I had experienced slammed into us. If I thought the *Brutales* winds would unleash their fury in one direction alone, I was sorely mistaken.

I closed my eyes tightly against the quickly shifting wind as it gusted wildly first in one direction and then the next, making it impossible to anticipate when the shift would come and which direction was safe to lean. My heart raced beneath my ribcage, and I grew dizzy as my senses were overwhelmed.

I did my best to pin myself to the ground in front of me, but my footing slipped on the slick face of the cliff. I grasped at the woody twigs growing between the rocks in an attempt to keep myself from sliding, but the weeds pulled free from the ground, sending my arms flailing wildly to keep myself from falling backwards. It was only the rope tying me to Quinn that saved me from a plunge down the gully and into churning waves below.

The force was over in seconds, but it felt like a lifetime. The roar in my ears dulled, then became a whisper until the wind died as though it had swept my hearing along with it. The ocean crashed below, but the sound now seemed to come from miles away. Heart pounding, muscles aching, pressed against the rock, I let my forehead rest upon the ground. Ragged gasps marked my struggle to catch my breath and the blood pounded loudly in my ears.

"Reina," Quinn's voice was hoarse. "Can you keep going? We have to get off the cliff."

Dully, I nodded, used the tension on the rope to right myself, and began climbing once more. It was almost dark by the time we reached the clifftop. Thankful for the solid ground beneath my feet, I collapsed on the grass.

"You're bleeding," Quinn said, touching a spot above my eyebrow as he sat beside me.

"Am I?" My hand went to my forehead. I dabbed at the cut with a finger and pulled my hand back to assess the amount of blood lost. It was minimal. "I think I cracked my head on the side of a rock."

"We were lucky."

"Remind me never to gamble with you," I mumbled.

Ignoring me, Quinn said, "Let's get off the cliff before we set up camp. We'll never get a fire started with the wind here." Though it had died down after the *Brutales*, the occasional gust had once again begun to blow hard.

When we reached a suitable spot, Quinn brought a blazing fire to life, pushing back the dampness and dark until there was a circle of warmth my bones drank in. Grateful for the heat, I pulled the water skins from my pack, took a long drink from one, and offered the other to Quinn. Sitting on a log, I pulled off my boots and stockings and placed them by the fire to dry. I wasn't about to remove my pants in Quinn's presence, damp though they were, settling instead for stretching my legs out by the warmth of the flames.

"It wasn't what I expected," I said, staring thoughtfully into the flames. "The *Brutales*."

"And what was it you expected?"

"I'm not sure," I answered. "I suppose I thought it would be more like a tidal wave, all at once and coming from one direction. The change of direction made it impossible to fight against."

He nodded. "Disorienting."

Quinn gave the fire another poke with a stick, then sat on a stump, removed a scroll from his pack and began hashing out marks on it. He looked back and forth between his arm and the paper.

"What are you doing?" I asked, peering over the flames at him.

"Making a more permanent map."

I laughed when I realized he'd used his arm to track our progress in the cave. A network of black lines and smudges decorated his muscular forearm.

"What are those smudges? Are those the larger caves?"

"No, that's sweat," Quinn said with a half-crooked grin.

While he worked, I made a dinner of toasted bread and cheese for us and as I later licked the last of the crumbs from my fingers, I spoke the thoughts that had been playing themselves through my mind. "The tide came in quicker than I expected. Scarily so."

"It did."

"Do you think we can get everyone in, find the talisman, and then get them out again in that amount of time? That's fifteen of us, although I suppose someone would have to stay back with the horses unless you want to lose one or two to the wind. Still, that's a lot of people to lower down a single rope and then get back up again, preferably before we have another episode with the *Brutales and* before the tide comes in."

"Can't be done," Quinn said.

"That's what I'm worried about."

"We'll have to find another way down. We can examine the other side of the bluff tomorrow and see if we can find a better path. There's no way to get everyone in and out in the short amount of time we've got."

"We have at least one advantage," I said. "We have a vague idea of where the talisman is."

"That won't mean much if we drown before finding it. If we wait a few weeks, low tide will be even lower and that's time we could use to our advantage. Truth be told, I'm no keener than Niles on the thought of waiting."

"Nor am I."

We drifted into silence, the soothing sound of the fire popping and the surf crashing in the distance our only company.

I stared at the embers from the fire as my mind wandered into childhood memories. I camped with Quinn more than once before, though it was long ago. Did he remember it as fondly as I? Did he even recall it at all?

"Do you remember the summer we camped in the field behind the cottage every chance we could?" I asked.

"I remember it well."

"Remember that night you split your knee on the creek bed?"

"I thought it would never stop bleeding."

"I wanted to take you back to the house so my mother could tend to you, but you refused."

He shrugged. "You had it under control."

I laughed. "My heart nearly failed. There was so much blood! I ruined my apron and caught hell from my mother the next day."

"You never told me that."

"Of course not."

He touched his knee absently. "I still have the scar."

I cocked my head and pulled at the grass beneath my hand, watching the mesmerizing flames. "We used to be close."

"We're still close."

"Not like that. Why did that end?"

"We grew up, Reina. We've no time to camp in the fields anymore."

I gave an exaggerated sigh. "Not that. I mean our friendship."

He gave me a quizzical look. "You're still my friend."

"You're impossible."

He shrugged again. "You chose to study your mother's craft, and I prepared for my future in politics. There wasn't much to discuss, I suppose."

"How did you manage to escape the *Choosing*?" I asked, honestly wondering why it was he hadn't been married off in the last year.

He waited a moment before responding, and, when I thought he wouldn't answer at all, he spoke. "As an ambassador for our village, and as a future public servant, I thought it best if I didn't yet form any family ties, I suppose. Better able to focus on what needs to be done that way. Especially given the uncertainty of war in the kingdom."

"And your father was okay with that?"

Quinn chuckled. "He had plenty to say. He always does."

I couldn't hide a smile. That much was true.

"Actually, it was my mother who took more of an issue with it, but I managed to persuade both of them in the end."

There was still something bothering me. "Quinn, didn't you *want* to *choose* someone?" It was true I hadn't wanted to have my entire future planned out for me, but most sixteen-year-olds looked forward to the ritual that so clearly defined the moment of their impending adulthood.

Quinn appeared to study the constellations before answering. "What I wanted wasn't as important as what needed to be."

"Well, that's cryptic," I said. When he didn't elaborate, I finally asked the question that burned in my mind, "You didn't not *choose* a girl because you're like Curtis and Edward, right? Because *they* married last year while you were away."

Quinn nearly choked on laughter. "What?!"

Well, I guess that answered *that* question. "Well, I just mean…" I let my voice trail off. There was no recovering now. Inwardly, I cringed.

"Are you really asking me if I prefer men?"

"It wouldn't be a crime if you did!" I tried to defend my words.

Uncharacteristically, he roared with laughter. My face burned in response.

"No, Reina," he said as he recovered. "No, I like women just fine."

We lapsed into silence, which was probably for the best given my penchant for saying the wrong thing. Quinn sighed, pulled his sleeping roll from his pack, and reclined on it. I did the same.

"Sleep," Quinn said as he adjusted onto his side. "There'll be plenty of time in the morning for figuring out what comes next. We're going to need the rest."

My gaze drifted above to the dark velvety sky. Stellon was near peaking, ever persistent in his chase of Andra, who was close to setting. Both moons gleamed brightly, Andra's fading glow casting a slightly pink shade to the ground while Stellon's silvery hue threatened to outshine her as he did every evening.

As a child, I had been told the ancient myths of the two moons and even though I knew they weren't true, I was fond of the familiar tales nonetheless.

The stories told of Stellon, the warrior, who fell in love with the king's daughter, Andra. She, too, fell in love with Stellon, but the mighty king had other plans for his only daughter. Rather than see her married to a common warrior, he promised her to a powerful prince of a foreign land.

Ever true to Stellon, Andra refused to marry the prince, but when the king threatened to have Stellon killed, she relented to her father's wishes in order to save the life of her one true love.

Andra knew she couldn't tell Stellon about her betrothal for fear he would anger and challenge the prince in a duel. The prince was widely known for never having lost a duel, and though Andra loved Stellon dearly, she couldn't stand the thought that she might be responsible for bringing about his death.

To spare Stellon's life, she told him she no longer cared for him. He pleaded with her to see reason and begged her to tell him what was wrong, for even though his heart was breaking, he could believe only that the words she spoke were untrue.

Finally, she asked him if his love for her was pure. He replied his love shined brighter than any star ever could.

"Then if you truly love me," she said, "please say no more and be on your way for tomorrow I marry another."

Crushed, Stellon dropped to a knee and promised to respect her wishes, but, in that same moment, he vowed he would love her forever. He promised no matter where she ventured in her life, she should know he would be but a step behind. Should she ever need him, all that was required was to turn around and he would be waiting, arms open to her always.

And so, Stellon forever chased Andra in the sky, night after night, always shining bright with love, but never able to touch the one he adored so completely.

It was a silly story. Yet I still felt close to it, still felt the passion of the forbidden romance that could never be. As a young child, before I'd shown any real interest in healing, I often play-acted in the field behind the cottage, the same one Quinn and I later camped in. I pretended I was Andra and that Stellon had declared his love for me, claiming he would never leave me. I was faced with the task of making him believe I did not love him in order to save his life. Eventually, I became responsible for farm chores like milking goats and feeding chickens, until there was no longer time to play the way I once had.

Now, I let out a long sigh with the memories as I stared at the two moons above. It had been some time since I'd thought of my childhood. I replayed scenes in my head as I slowly drifted to sleep, the rhythmic sound of the ocean surf a lullaby quickly working magic on my fatigue.

CHAPTER SEVEN

Of Things Lost and Found

Quinn and I scouted for three days before we found a suitable path that would allow our party to safely travel to the cave. By the time we returned to camp to meet with the others, both moons were beginning to wane, and I was relieved we likely wouldn't encounter the *Brutales* winds again.

The group broke down camp, eager to begin the final leg of the journey. It was mid-morning by the time we made it back to the bluff. Jinso volunteered to stay with the horses while the rest of our group headed down the path that would take us to the beach.

The tide was already moving out, and when we reached the cove, the water had receded enough to reveal the sand and the opening to the caves. It was later than we had intended to start, but eager to complete our journey, no one was willing to turn back.

We paused at the entrance of the cave to light several torches, and I allowed the candidates to walk ahead of me as I trailed behind. Quinn consulted his map from time to time and we navigated the turns from one passageway to the next, progressing to the giant cavern as quickly as we could.

It took an hour to arrive in the room with the cathedral ceiling. I doubted the water would ever fill the space entirely, but I wasn't eager to tread icy water, waiting for the tide to lower. *Please let the candidates find the talisman quickly.*

The torches set the room aglow. Whether it was the number of people in the cavern or the fact that I could see more of it, the room was not as wide as I'd previously thought. We spanned it and began to search.

"Can you feel how the walls are warm?" Quinn asked one of the girls.

She placed a hand to the wall and looked puzzled. "No," she said. "Feels cool."

"And slimy!" added another voice.

Quinn's eyes met mine. *Why?* he seemed to question. I shook my head, unable to explain it any more than he. Why I was able to feel the warmth of the stones at the surface and we were both able to feel the warmth below remained a mystery.

Torches were waved slowly back and forth to illuminate every crack and crevice. A large fissure opened along the floor against one wall, and I was glad Quinn and I had not ventured that direction a few days earlier. It widened along the one edge and could easily swallow a man—or woman—whole. I shivered.

"Where is it?" one of the girls exclaimed in frustration. I thought I recognized Nadine's voice. "How do we even know it's here?"

I was reluctant to admit how I was certain and was relieved when Quinn intervened. "It's here."

"Well, then why haven't we found it? And how do you even know?" There was an unhappy murmur by many of the girls.

"I'm tired of being led on a wild goose chase. We were told when we accepted this candidacy you knew where the talisman was. I'm starting to think no one here knows anything at all," Nadine said.

I shook my head. I should have counted on Nadine being trouble. The girl had never done more than half an hour's work in her life. This expedition was more than she'd bargained for. I searched the cavern for Selena, who still seemed to be preoccupied with scouring the lower crevices.

"Perhaps you need to stop complaining so much and concentrate more on searching," one of the girls said as she thrust an arm deep into a rift in the stone wall. It was hard to tell from where I stood, but I thought it was Emylia.

Nadine's jaw dropped, but Emylia's comment had the desired effect. She returned to searching without another word.

I closed my eyes and focused on feeling some sort of pull from the talisman within my mind. I felt its presence but couldn't pinpoint where its signal originated. Was it because of the rocks? It seemed almost as if there was an echo of the location, as though the talisman spoke to me from many directions all at once. I tilted my head from side to side, trying to home in on its location. At once, I realized why the feeling seemed to come from everywhere.

"It's above us," I said.

All eyes fell upon me.

"Where?" Nadine asked. I was glad she hadn't asked how I knew instead.

I scanned as high as the torches would let me see. "I'm not sure exactly. I thought I saw something."

"Why would she put it so high?"

"Wouldn't want the ocean tides pulling it back out," Niles said easily. "It makes sense. This room is probably the only one high enough to escape being flooded entirely, even with a double-spring tide."

I nodded in agreement. Niles beckoned to the three soldiers for their torches, and they raised the flickering beacons as high as they could. The front wall of the cavern was nearly sheer, offering few places for hand or footholds, but a distinct niche was visible about two stories from the ground.

Niles noticed it, too, and he searched for a place to begin climbing. He pointed and directed two of his men to help him up. They handed their torches to Quinn and the remaining soldier and hoisted Niles up. Once he was at the point where he could grab hold of the wall, Niles quickly scaled it with agility that rivaled Quinn's, pausing only when he reached the niche.

"Well?" one of the girls asked as Niles peered into the darkness. The single word echoed throughout the cavern.

"Can't tell," he said, as he repositioned himself. Carefully, he reached into the dark space and felt around.

He stilled and the expression on his face revealed all we needed to know. Slowly, he pulled the talisman from its thousand-year hiding place. It dangled from the chain, a teardrop shape glittering in the torchlight, as he held it out for all to see. The color wasn't visible by our meager light, but *I* knew the exact aqua hue it possessed. The pendant sparked—a quick brilliant flash—with my thought.

At that moment, everything became a blur of motion. Niles's foot slipped. He scrabbled at the rock to regain his balance. The talisman glinted in the torchlight, falling toward us. Several of the girls shot forward to grab it as it clattered to the ground. It flew from hand to hand, was lost in the shuffle as they argued, then reappeared briefly in the air as it was grabbed by another hand.

It all happened within seconds, but for a moment it seemed time itself stopped. My eyes widened as someone screamed and the pendant flew through the air at my face. I raised a hand to protect myself, squeezing my eyes shut and turning my head away...and felt it land squarely in my palm, an electric current shooting through my arm with the contact. When I opened my eyes, the pendant swung gently from the cool chain wrapped between my fingers.

In the dead silence, no one dared move a muscle. Slowly, I relaxed my arm, lowering it to examine the teardrop shaped tourmaline in my hand, flexing my fingers to coax feeling back into them after being shocked. What *was* that? Was that why no one had been able to hold it? Though the initial shock had dissipated, it vibrated on my skin.

I looked up and still no one moved, as though they were afraid to breathe. "What now?" I asked.

Wide eyes continued to stare. The only sound was the flickering whoosh of the torches and the click of Niles's boots on stone as he jumped the last few feet to the floor.

"You're it," Selena whispered. "You're the White Sorceress."

"What?" I said incredulously.

There were nods all around as the girls confirmed they thought so, too. A murmuring of assent filled the room. It might have been the first time in days they'd agreed upon something.

"Don't be daft!" I cried. "It was thrown at my face. I did what anyone would do!"

Ramus came to my side then and lowered his torch to the ground. "Not only did it choose you," he said, "but had you not caught it, it would have been lost forever."

"Just like the prophecy says," someone uttered.

I looked to where he pointed the torch and stepped forward. I hadn't realized that I'd been standing directly in front of the large fissure. Had I not been standing there, the talisman might still be falling into its depths. Had I taken half a step backward to duck from the object hurtling toward my face, I, too, might still be falling into its depths. I gave an involuntary shudder.

I returned my gaze to the group and found all eyes trained on me. Niles wore a half-smirk on his face as though he might have somehow suspected such an outcome all along, which was absurd. And Quinn looked as though he'd seen a ghost—a pallor that surely must have matched my own.

"All right," I began, "let's clear this up quickly. I am no more the White Sorceress than I am a soldier." I held out the pendant, feeling the curious electric current tingle through my arm again. "So, maybe I should close my eyes and toss it into the air so one of the true candidates can be *chosen*."

There were brief mutterings and the entire group as a whole shuffled a few steps back. I looked on in disbelief, mouth agape.

Niles shook his head and stepped toward me, holding his hands out, and clasping mine and the talisman within them. It sparked angrily, and I gave a jump at the sensation.

"I'm afraid you're it, Moreina. No one could have predicted this strange turn of events, but the prophecy states that the talisman chooses its wearer. You *are* the White Sorceress."

"That's ridiculous," I nearly hissed.

Quinn spoke up. "We could stay here and debate this all day, but I'd like to suggest that we continue this discussion back on the cliffs. The talisman won't be much good to anyone if we all drown. The clock is ticking."

It was enough for the group to shuffle back the way we had come, but instead of trailing as I had before, I moved to the front and pushed my way next to Quinn, talisman still clenched in my fist. Grabbing his hand, I pushed the talisman into his palm. He jumped at the contact and almost dropped it.

"What the blazes! It *shocked* me."

"It seems to go away after a minute," I said. "Hold this until it is claimed by the rightful sorceress."

Letting go of the stone, he held it by the chain instead. Glancing at the pendant, then back at me, his eyes were dark and serious as he shook his head. "I can't," he said as he draped the chain around my neck. The stone fell heavy onto my chest, the unpleasant electric sensation settling into a low hum of current. "I'm sorry, Reina."

Of all the people in the world to be influenced by silly and coincidental happenings, Quinn D'Arturio should not have been one of them. I refused to move until the rest of the group passed me by in a hurry to exit the caves. They avoided meeting my eyes as they passed. A feeling of unease settled deep in my bones.

Selena grabbed my hand and squeezed gently as she passed, a mix of compassion and disappointment showing in her face. "We'll talk later," she murmured.

I was struck with a sudden understanding of what the gray

veil in my vision had meant. This was the unanticipated surprise, but I never could have guessed it was meant for me. The soldier who trailed the group stopped and nodded to me, waiting for me to begin walking again before following. I gritted my teeth as I walked.

The water lapped at our ankles long before we were near the mouth of the cave and a wave of anxiety rolled through my stomach, all thoughts of the humming talisman around my neck forgotten. Judging by the way the group hurried forward, I wasn't alone.

Despite the increase in pace, the water continued to rise. By the time it reached our shins, some of the girls began to express their concerns, their voices echoing off cavern walls. Quinn pushed forward at a brutal pace while the water rolled in forcefully and pulled back out again with each wave.

"It won't be long," he said from the dimly lit passage ahead. "But if the water comes above our knees before we've reached the cove, I want everyone to link hands. No one will be separated."

My heart pounded harder against my ribcage. We had anticipated the possibility of occupying the cave as the tide came in, but I hadn't thought about the force of the water as it rolled into the cavern, not really. We should have waited for lower tides. The struggle exhausted everyone, but fear drove us on.

Moments later, hands were linked. My relief was nearly palpable when we reached the mouth of the cave and followed Quinn through the now waist-deep water around the edge of the rocks until we could see the path leading back to the bluff. My muscles had begun to seize with the cold and the sight of the path renewed my ability to keep moving forward.

But relief was short-lived when someone shrieked, and Selena lost her footing, dropped the hands of the two girls she'd been holding, and was quickly sucked out with the undertow. *No!*

Without a moment's hesitation, Quinn leaped headfirst into the current in pursuit of the bobbing head and hands that were repeatedly dipping beneath the water farther and farther away. His strong strides were no match for the current. To my horror, Selena's head appeared only one last time before disappearing beneath the surface. I knew the second she passed, a searing pain igniting in my bones with her last breath. Death, making its presence known. Ignoring the pain, I swallowed, biting back the scream that wanted to rip through my throat, and gripped the hands of those next to me even tighter.

Numbly, I couldn't help but dwell on the thought of my newfound friend, her excitement at the prospect of apprenticing. Then I thought of Edrian and of Selena's mother, and how we'd broken our promise to return everyone home safely. My heart shattered into a thousand pieces within my chest and breathing took effort.

"Keep moving!" Niles shouted at us, but I couldn't tear my eyes from Quinn's form, bobbing in the water, still searching futilely for Selena. "Now!"

We shuffled forward again, sobs escaping from several lips, tears openly falling. Nadine stumbled in front of me and her grasp reflexively tightened on my own, then slipped. She gripped tighter in response. Beside her, Emylia fell forward and slipped from the line, swiftly drifting as Selena had.

Instinctively, I lunged into the ocean, gasping at the cold as my entire body was immersed. The talisman let off a sudden, shockingly cold jolt where it met my skin. With five quick strokes, I caught up to Emylia.

Eyes wide and panicked with fear, she reached for me as she slipped below the surface. With one hand, I grabbed her collar, but my kicks were not nearly strong enough to take us both back to the shore. I sputtered as seawater assaulted my mouth and nose.

A strong hand grasped my own collar as I struggled. I was so thankful for Niles's help that even the anger on his face didn't upset me. A second set of hands appeared to help—Antony, and he took the bulk of Emylia's weight from me. Emylia struggled to kick, but she ceased moving when he yelled something to her.

Freed of Emylia's weight, I kicked myself back to shore, the frigid water numbing my fingers and toes as I swam. Niles released his grip on me only when I had sufficient control and would not find myself back in the current's grasp.

We joined the rest of the group as they emerged onto the path. I had never been so relieved to have my feet on the ground in my life. My teeth chattered so violently I wondered if they might not fall right out of my mouth. Dropping to my knees, I returned my eyes to the murderous ocean. There was no sign of either Selena or Quinn.

"What were you thinking?" Niles yelled at me, his voice hoarse, as he dragged himself to the shore.

"What was *I* thinking?"

He gripped my shoulders, shaking me, spraying droplets from my hair into the air.

"You could have been lost. You could have been sucked away," he said, pointing a finger to the ocean. "That could have been *you*. You can't behave as recklessly as you'd like, Moreina. In case you haven't realized, this entire thing—*all of it*—was to find *you*. And in a matter of seconds, you nearly threw away every hope Castilles has by trying to get yourself killed."

"Get myself killed? I was trying to help Emylia! Perhaps you haven't noticed, but she's still alive."

"That's *my* job," he said. "From now on your only responsibility is to keep *yourself* alive so you can figure out how to save the rest of the kingdom later."

I wanted to yell at him. I wanted to scream. My heart thumped furiously in my chest, but words evaded me, and I could only stare.

"Moreina," he said, his voice only slightly softer, but his eyes a pleading blue. "If we lose you, we lose everything."

His words shook me to the core. *There's been a mistake*, I wanted to tell him. Instead, I turned, pulled myself from the ground, and searched the darkening ocean for Quinn. Strong and capable though he might be, I worried I would not see him again. Only the absence of pain in my bones kept me from losing my mind. He was alive at least. At Niles's insistence, I followed the path, numbly placing one foot in front of the next, trying hard not to let my mind wander where it would.

Cold, wet, bedraggled, we reached Jinso and the horses, and made our way for the camp. By the time we arrived, the sun had set. Fires were lit to ward off the chill from wet clothing and lowering temperatures.

Not wanting company, I gathered enough wood to light my

own fire a short distance away. I promptly removed my boots and stockings and placed them as close to the flames as I dared. My teeth were no longer chattering, but a chill settled deep in my muscles.

Moments later, Quinn appeared, joining me in silence as he stoked the fire. Surprised, I jumped to hug him, grateful he had returned from the ocean's grasp. A testament to his own emotional state, he let me throw my arms around him. His clothes hung damp on his frame and saltwater droplets fell from his hair and clothes into the fire with a sizzle as I released him and he sat. His jaw was set in a hard line, and, though I knew the answer before I opened my mouth, I asked anyway.

"Selena?" I asked, my voice small.

He shook his head and stared into the flames.

"*Fiermi*," I breathed, tears springing to my eyes. I *knew*. Why had I asked?

He shook his head again and said quietly, "It's my fault. We should have waited for the tides."

I put a hand on his shoulder, but he stiffened, unwilling to receive the consolation. We *should* have waited. I should have insisted upon it. Why hadn't I?

Quinn made no further attempt at conversation, which was to his benefit as I was hardly in the mood myself.

My mind wandered, struggling to make sense of the purpose of our journey, the senselessness of Selena's death. What was the point of all of this? I was clearly not the White Sorceress from the prophecy. Selena had died for nothing, for a false savior.

Swearing to make things right, I vowed to find the talisman's true owner. Somewhere, somehow, I would fix this and return the talisman to the real sorceress.

And yet, my thoughts still would not settle, even with my mind made up. The somber group talked and ate around the fire, and I wondered if they felt responsible for Selena's death the way I somehow did. Every now and again, one of them would glance my way and the conversation became hushed.

Convincing them I was not the White Sorceress would be difficult. Inwardly I cringed at the thought. I could say nothing to convince any of them. All I could do was wait.

"Do you want to talk?" Quinn questioned after some time.

I looked at him, calculating for a moment. Was it worth it? Would he—or anyone—listen to what I had to say?

"No," I said, swallowing the dozens of biting responses I truly wished to issue. Instead, I turned into my bedroll and pulled the covers to my ears.

Quinn laid his bedroll near mine as he settled next to me. *Let him*, I thought. I was bound to have all sorts of company now that I had been declared the White Sorceress. The weight on my mind was nearly as heavy as the weight around my neck and sleep was a long time in coming.

CHAPTER EIGHT

A Shocking Truth

If I thought the morning light would clear my head or anyone else's, I was sorely mistaken. If anything, everyone seemed more determined that I was, indeed, the White Sorceress who would stop Bruenner, end the war, and find the rightful heir. It gave them a purpose behind Selena's death, a reason for the loss. If I were the White Sorceress, her death had not been in vain.

The enormity of the situation was overwhelming. I had to remind myself to breathe. I rubbed my grainy eyes and sucked cold forest air into my lungs. Selena's face haunted my dreams all night. She died a thousand different ways and I couldn't save her once.

Only Aeros remained unchanged in her opinion of me on the return journey. Niles had taken up residency at my side, despite Aeros's dislike of his stallion. He declared himself to be the Sorceress's Personal Guard and though his intentions were entirely well meant, I was not pleased about being singled out further.

I examined the talisman as we rode, in part due to curiosity and in part to keep it from sparking uncomfortably on my chest. The teardrop shaped cabochon was nearly as long as my middle finger and two fingers wide. It was tourmaline, deep blue in its center, the color morphing to a brilliant green along the edges. An indistinguishable blackened metal setting held the stone. I let my fingers graze the raised scrollwork of the metal though years of grime hid its intricacy from the naked eye. I had never seen anything like it. I doubted anyone had.

I understood now why the talisman had been hidden so well. Such an artifact could not have been protected from burglars and thieves throughout the generations.

"Any thoughts on how you'll stop Bruenner?" Niles's voice cut into my thoughts.

I let the pendant fall to my breast with a zap and readjusted the reins in my hands. "No," I told him sternly, shifting to slide the talisman so it lay flat on my chest. "And I don't plan on formulating any such thoughts since I am *not* the White Sorceress."

Niles nearly laughed, but my warning look stopped him. "Moreina, trust me. I don't believe anyone thought you would be chosen. You weren't even a candidate. Yet you cannot deny you *have* been chosen, just as predicted."

"Yes, well, *they* also predicted the sorceress would be fair-haired, didn't they? Isn't that why every candidate here was chosen first and foremost?" I gestured at the seven subdued candidates before me, their various shades of blonde hair glistening in the mid-morning sun.

"I've been thinking about that."

"Have you?" I asked, unable to restrain myself.

Niles paused only a moment at my venom. "I have. You see, the prophecy never actually said 'fair-haired.'"

He had my attention now. "Go on."

"That was our interpretation."

"But I read the prophecy. It said, 'hair so light.'"

"The original prophecy no longer exists and even if it did, you wouldn't be able to read it because it's not in our tongue."

The thought never occurred to me before.

"Translation gets tricky. Many of the old words had more than one meaning. We can only give our best guess at translation in those instances. I believe the original prophecy said a woman of white, not a woman of light hair."

"Woman of white doesn't make sense."

"Exactly. And that's why the other translation was chosen, but they deciphered it wrong. It did mean woman of white."

I waited for him to continue.

"Your surname, Moreina. Di Bianco is nearly synonymous with the old language for 'of white.' The prophecy never actually referred to hair color at all."

I swallowed, taking in what he'd said. I hadn't considered translation errors in the prophecy when I'd read it. I'd assumed— perhaps naively—I read it as it had originally been written.

"That, alone, hardly qualifies me to be the White Sorceress, Niles."

"No, but the fact the talisman chose you *does*."

I wasn't going to be able to get past this with him, but I persisted anyway. "Yes, well, let's concentrate on getting home as quickly as possible. I'm sure Governor Arden will be able to make more sense of this and assign the talisman to its rightful owner."

Niles looked as though he wanted to argue with me. "I suppose if anyone could make sense of what's happened, it would be the governor. He's been studying the Faranzine Talisman for most of his life."

"Oh?" This was news to me. Maybe he could explain why the talisman was so temperamental.

"When the heir to the kingdom was taken, the governor developed an obsession with the prophecy. The prince's abduction was the first indication the prophecy was about to unfold."

"You're saying he's been studying it for nearly twenty years?"

"Maybe longer. I doubt there's anyone else alive who knows more about it."

"But why?" I asked.

He shrugged his shoulders. "Why do you study your remedies?"

"Because it's my calling, my art."

"I believe Governor Arden feels the same way about his studies of the talisman. When I first arrived at Barnham, he told me he'd always felt a pull toward it, that he thought he'd someday be pivotal in finding it."

"Well, if you make yourself the subject matter expert, it's rather difficult not to be involved, isn't it?"

Niles nodded.

"Why did you come to Barnham, anyway?" I asked, guiding Aeros to the edge of the muddy path where the ground was firmer.

Bastian plodded through the center of the mud, his hooves squishing into the muck. Niles didn't seem bothered. "Governor

Arden sent a message to General Ott, requesting available troops for this assignment," he answered.

"Why soldiers, though?"

"Who else would he send to accompany candidates in search of the Faranzine Talisman? The villages don't have many young men who aren't already involved in the war effort, and the White Sorceress is deserving of the utmost protection we can afford."

I glanced at Quinn, riding slightly behind us. He stared straight ahead, careful to wear a blank expression, but he'd been listening to us, and it was easy to guess the direction of his thoughts.

"The five of us might not be much," Niles continued, "but rest assured these are my best men, and we would lay down our lives for yours if need be."

I nearly choked. "I assure you that won't be necessary."

On the morning of our final day journeying home, I awoke with hope in my chest and plagued with slightly less anxiety. Even the talisman seemed content to hum at my chest in contrast to its painful sparking over the last few days. Today I would get confirmation from Governor Arden that I wasn't the woman they wanted me to be. The governor *had* to have additional books or scrolls that would help us determine the next course of action.

We mounted quickly that morning and were on our way soon after rising, but I knew something was wrong long before we reached Barnham. Aeros sensed it too. Her trot had an extra bounce, making for a doubly uncomfortable ride.

By the time we were only a few miles away, acrid smoke made its way to my nostrils and we urged our horses into a gallop for the remaining distance.

As we crested the last hill, I gasped at the sight below. Most of Barnham's stone buildings were still intact, but many of the thatched roofs had been burned away and continued to smolder. Small flames licked at outbuildings.

From where we stood, the town appeared to be deserted. Signaling to his men, Niles instructed everyone to stay put and urged his horse forward.

"Like hell I will," I muttered.

Quinn grabbed my arm, his grip strong. I hadn't realized he'd pulled his horse next to mine.

"What are you doing, Reina?"

"I'm going to see what's happened to my town," I told him, mustering as much conviction into my voice as I could. "I should think you'd want to do the same."

Quinn's guarded eyes revealed nothing, but his voice was thick with concern. "I'll go with you."

The soldiers only mildly objected as we left to follow Niles down the road, and we ignored their protests. Aeros snorted and tossed her head as the smell of smoke grew thicker. We caught up with Niles after a moment, and, while he shot us a look, he said nothing.

As we had suspected, the town was deserted. We led the horses through the village, the eerie silence overwhelming. There was no sign of anyone in any of the residences, the mill, or the blacksmith's shop. We dismounted and entered the tavern, but it, too, was empty.

We turned toward the governor's house, traveling the empty streets quickly, hearing only our horses' hooves on packed dirt roads and the crackling of the occasional flame. Even the birds seemed to have gone.

Like many others, the door to the governor's house stood wide open. Dropping Aeros's reins, I slid from the saddle and followed behind Quinn, expecting the worst, but hoping to find the same emptiness we'd found everywhere else. I let out a sigh of relief when no one answered our calls. The house was abandoned.

But unlike anywhere else we'd been, there was evidence the house had been ransacked. The study stood in disarray, books pulled from shelves, maps torn from the walls, and half-burned pages littered the floor.

"Whoever they were, they were looking for something," I said.

Quinn surveyed the damage, sharp eyes assessing everything in their path. Leaning down, he picked up the leather-bound book that once contained the copy of the White Sorceress Prophecy I had read for the first time only a few short weeks before. The charred pages were badly smudged. Disgusted, he threw it back down again.

"Let's hope they didn't find whatever it was they wanted," he muttered.

"And we still don't have a clue where everyone is," Niles said.

"The church?" I suggested. They weren't dead. This much I knew. I would have felt the death of so many like a fire in my bones. It would have screamed itself to me the instant we set foot on Barnham's soil.

Quinn nodded, and we made our way to the church. It hadn't been burned. In fact, it was the only building that looked as though it hadn't been touched. The white spire stood gleaming, a symbol of Barnham's faith in the Saints above and all that was pure.

Atop the spire's point, the emblem of our faith—a knotted, interlaced copper triangle held within the silvered circle of life. Each of the triangle's green-hued, weathered tips swirled sideways as though blown by a hard wind, giving the elegant design a sense of movement, which was in essence exactly what the symbol represented. The triangle's tips symbolized life, death, and chaos—all three set in motion within the circle meant to embody our own lives. The emblems were everywhere in Millasboro, but in Barnham we had only one church, one spire, one symbol to remind us of life's balance.

Now, we pulled open the doors to that church, and only the sound of a pigeon flying to the rafters greeted us. The pews were empty, not a soul in sight. I said a quick prayer of thanks to each of the eight Saints that at least we had not found any bodies. The darkness of the church was unnerving. Dim light shone through the windows into the empty chapel, dust motes dancing in the beams to a music only they could hear. The candles sat flameless, motionless, waiting to be put to use again.

"Have they been taken?" I asked as we returned outside.

Niles shook his head. "By whom? That wouldn't make sense. Taking an entire village would require a large army, but the devastation here is minimal. I doubt this was done by an army."

"*This* is minimal?" I let my eyes roam across the rows of smoking, roofless buildings.

There was a haunted look in Niles's eyes when he met mine. "It is."

"So where is everyone? And if this wasn't done by an army, then who *is* responsible?"

"I couldn't say where everyone might be, but I have my suspicions as to who did it," Niles answered. "Quinn, does Barnham have a sister town? Is there somewhere else the people would have gone for protection?"

"Airdsbarg is the closest town, but it's at least a half day's journey. I wouldn't say they're a sister town, though we're friendly enough with them," Quinn answered.

"Is there anywhere else you can think they would have gone?"

Quinn and I both thought for a moment before Quinn answered, "The orchard is a few miles down the road and it's got outbuildings. It's out of the way, but if they suspected something like this was coming, they might have headed that way."

Niles looked to me for confirmation and I nodded.

"Lead the way," he said.

Quinn took the lead and we rode in the direction of the orchard. We found the townsfolk huddled within the outbuildings meant to house crates of applikens and fluted pears. The full, stacked crates of fruit permeated the air with a sweet scent.

The townspeople looked cold and frightened, but unharmed, and they came to life when they saw us approach. Someone called for Governor Arden.

The crowed parted way for him, and I inhaled sharply when

I saw his face. While there'd been no evidence of anyone else being hurt, the governor's face was covered in bruises and one eye was nearly swollen shut. He hobbled forward.

Quinn threw himself off his horse and gave his father a fierce hug. "What's happened here? What did they do to you?"

Governor Arden had tears in his eyes as he embraced his son. "I'm fine, I'm fine," he murmured. "Everyone is okay. We had warning. I sent everyone away."

Niles and I dismounted and joined Quinn at his father's side. The governor stilled as soon as he saw the pendant around my neck. The eye not swollen shut fixed on it.

"You found it?" he whispered, gripping Quinn's arms.

"We did."

His gaze slid from the pendant to my eyes. "You?" he asked.

"Yes," said Niles at the same time I answered, "No."

The governor looked thoroughly confused. "Well, what does that mean?"

He led us to an isolated corner of the building and we sat on empty crates. I relayed all that had happened in the cave and afterwards, then waited for Governor Arden's input.

"Selena's mother will need to be informed, and Edrian. We'll have to send a messenger to his post. He's going to be devastated. Saints, of all the matches, they were such a solid pair," he said solemnly with a sigh. The mention of the eager student and almost-friend I would never have sent a pang through my chest.

"I'll do it," Quinn offered. "I was the one who couldn't reach her in time."

"No, no, my dear boy. I'll handle it. Such is my responsibility, and it was never your fault."

Quinn looked as though he wanted to disagree, but with a slight nod, he conceded to his father's will.

"So, all this time, the translation was incorrect," Governor Arden said, running a hand across the back of his neck as he echoed Niles's earlier comments. If I had hoped he would agree that we needed to allow the rest of the candidates a chance to claim the talisman, I hoped in vain.

"Governor, that can't be the case. It just…can't."

"And why not? It makes sense now."

"Woman of white," Niles said.

"Yes, yes. Woman of white."

"This is absurd," I said. "Next thing you'll be telling me it's because of the white in my hair!"

The governor looked thoughtful as he examined my hair. "I hadn't thought of that, but that fits, too, doesn't it?"

I rolled my eyes. "For the love of Saints, have you all gone mad? I am not the White Sorceress."

"From what you, yourself, have told me, Moreina, I fear you underestimate yourself."

My mind reeled, grasping at whatever I could think of to prove him wrong.

"What about the suitors?" I asked.

"What of them?"

"I'm well past the *Choosing*, Governor. I have no prospects of any kind. Clearly, I am not the woman the prophecy was written about!"

Governor Arden's gaze shifted to my left and my right, where Niles and Quinn were seated to either side of me. I narrowed my eyes at him, almost daring him to speak his thoughts.

"That may be so, my dear, but there's plenty of time for that to unfold. And not everyone pairs at the *Choosing,* as you well know."

My jaw dropped. "Governor, you don't understand what I'm saying. Even if I had suitors, there would be none I'd be interested in. I am an experienced Healer, not a young girl looking for marriage. And I don't have a thought in my head on how I would possibly stop a war. I am most definitely not a sorceress, white, blue, orange, or any other kind!"

Governor Arden smiled a slow, frustrating smile at me. I was ashamed at my desire to hurl a fist at him, particularly when he was already covered in bruises. "We will see what we shall see," he said cryptically. "May I...may I hold the talisman?"

I pulled it from my neck, happy to hand it over as it had begun sparking angrily at me again. I didn't like the thing. It's temperament was unpredictable and whereas one minute it seemed to be happily humming along, the next minute it was just as likely to issue a sharp shock to my system, jolting me alert with annoyance.

"Please," I answered, handing it to him.

"The Faranzine Talisman," he said as he held the chain. When he got to the pendant, an audible *zap* caused him to nearly drop it from his grasp. "What the—" He looked up in surprise. "Does it always do that? Is that normal?"

As though any of us would have known the answer to such a question. "I kind of hoped you'd be able to tell me," I said dryly.

Hesitantly, he tried again, running his fingers across the surface of the stone, his lips moving as though he were asking it some private question. In response, the talisman let off a series of small static sparks that left him cursing and fumbling with it. "It's remarkable. Truly remarkable," he said aloud.

I made a noncommittal sound.

"I've never seen such craftsmanship in all my years," he said. "It's stunning. Not to mention the size of this stone."

"Not to mention the pain," I reminded him.

"Does it do that when you wear it? The whole time, I mean?"

I took it as he handed it back to me and felt the subsequent jolt of lightning to my shoulder, leaving my fingers tingling again.

"Only when I hold it directly," I answered as I placed it around my neck again. Shaking my arm, I tried to return feeling to the numbness. "Once it's on, it seems to settle into a sort of low buzzing. Annoying, but not exactly painful."

"Well, that's wonderful!" he exclaimed with a slap to his knee. "Further proof you're the right choice."

I gritted my teeth. "Humor me and pretend I'm not. Isn't there anyone else who could possibly help?" I asked. "There's got to be someone who knows something more about what to do."

The governor looked pensive. "The high council meets next week in Gillesmere. If you leave soon, you might make it there in time, but I'm sure they'll tell you the same thing I've told you, Moreina."

"Then I'll waste no time. I'll leave right now."

Anything to involve a voice of reason.

The council members came from all stretches of the kingdom to meet four times a year. During the king's time, there had been hundreds of members and they served him loyally.

After the king died and General Bruenner helped himself to the kingdom, what remained of the council met in secret locations that varied from meeting to meeting. Only a chosen few knew the location. Gillesmere was hardly close or easy to reach given the mountainous terrain, but I scarcely cared at this point.

"Then I'll go with you," Niles declared. He turned to Governor Arden. "If it's all right by you, Governor, I'll dispatch a messenger to the border to inform General Ott of the formation of the White Sorceress's Personal Guard and let him know that my leave will be extended."

"Of course," Governor Arden said with a bow of his head. "And you, Quinn?"

Quinn nodded his head, slowly and with less excitement than Nile's had shown. "I'll go, too."

I furrowed my brow at the governor, feeling very much like a puppet whose strings had just been pulled. The puppet master was enjoying his game entirely too much. Despite his bruises, a twinkle of the governor's eye didn't escape my notice.

"Father, you still haven't told us what's happened here," Quinn said. I was thankful for the change in subject.

"Bandits. Filthy bandits, and a large group of them, too."

"No," Niles said. "Not bandits."

The governor gave Niles a bewildered glance. "What do you mean?"

"How did you know they were coming?" Niles asked.

"The goatherd boy, Darian, saw them the day before they reached the village, camping near the beach. He found them only when one of the goats went missing. He said they didn't look like 'good folk' so he listened to what they were saying.

When he heard them speak my name—and not in good context either—the poor lad came running back to the village as fast as his legs would carry him.

"He was out of breath by the time he reached us. Could hardly form a sentence, but once he told us they planned to raid that evening, I cleared the village. Too many of them to safely fight and most of our able men off on the war effort already."

"But what about you?" Quinn asked, placing a hand on his father's shoulder.

"Me? Oh, silly thing. I got everyone out of the village and followed behind."

"And they got a hold of you?" Niles asked.

The governor waved his arm, dismissing the thought. "No, no, nothing like that, I'm afraid. Would have been much more exciting. No, my horse misstepped as we galloped through the darkness. We went down, and I tumbled head first into a rock."

"I'm glad you're all right," Quinn said. "I've told you to stay off Juniper. Clumsy horse nearly killed me two summers ago." He turned to Niles. "Who do you think is responsible?"

"Bruenner," Niles said without hesitation.

"Isn't he preoccupied with the war? We're a bit far from the borders," I said.

"He's done this many times before," Niles explained. "He hires a group of brutes to do his preliminary dirty work for him. If they deem a village has enough value to take over or enough young men to recruit, he moves in. He figures if he takes over enough of the important villages, the smaller ones will eventually give way and declare him rightful king."

"That will never happen," Quinn said.

"But Barnham is neither big nor important," I said. "Why would he send his miscreants here? He has no reason."

Niles eyed the governor. "He does if he believes he might learn something. Maybe he was looking for information."

The governor remained silent.

"If they got the information they needed, you can bet Bruenner will be sending his forces to follow," Niles continued. My thoughts flew to the scattered books and papers in the governor's study. "You've got a few weeks, maybe a month, before he sends his troops."

"What?" I cried. "This is madness! So what can we do?"

Niles's eyes met mine. "You're the White Sorceress," he said. "My faith lies in you."

"Well—well," I stuttered stupidly. "I'm leaving for Gillesmere, so if you're coming with me, be ready to ride. I'll make the pace we've been traveling at seem leisurely. There'll be no candidates to slow me down this time," I huffed, still angry at the title he insisted bestowing upon me.

"The town is in minor disrepair," Quinn said as he turned to his father. "A few days and it could be fixed. What will you do?"

"Good to know. I was going to send someone to check on the village. We'll go back this afternoon, start rebuilding. I'll set up watches day and night and send a messenger to Airdsbarg. We'll keep an eye out, and, when they come, we'll be ready to relocate."

"The entire village?" Niles asked.

The governor eyed him. "What would you have us do? We don't have the numbers to fight. Shall I have the women and children bear arms?"

Niles gave only a nod in response. "Will Airdsbarg receive you?" he asked.

"It's a lot to ask, but I can't imagine they wouldn't. They'll be next whether we come or not, and if we're there, at least there will be more of us to fight. We'd stand a better chance. At least they have walls."

"Then I suggest we all get moving," Niles said.

The governor nodded his assent. "I'll speak with the people." He turned back to me. "You'll take your leave now?"

"Yes," I answered, angry at turning away from Barnham once again. "No point in waiting, is there?"

Quinn and Niles returned to the horses, but Governor Arden grabbed my sleeve as I turned to go. "You must decide, Reina," he said.

"Decide what?" I asked, throwing my hands in the air. "It seems like the world has already decided for me."

He took a breath. "That may be so, but it's up to you how this unfolds. There is a great mantle of responsibility on your shoulders now. How you choose to handle that responsibility is up to you. Only you can determine your fate."

The talisman sent an angry jolt to my core and I winced, looking anywhere but at Governor Arden. "Except that my own fate now determines everyone else's. That's not very fair, is it?"

He squeezed my shoulder. "No," he said. "It's not."

We escorted the townsfolk back to the village and signaled Niles's men to bring the former candidates into the town. I stopped at my cottage only to rest assured that it had not been burned to the ground and that my animals and medicinal stores were still safe. All was well. I stocked up on the herbs I thought I should bring for our travels and silently cursed myself for not having harvested seleniac while we'd been at the cliffs. Then again, my mind had been elsewhere.

My bathtub mocked me from the corner, and I stared at it longingly, wishing that anyone else wore the talisman, that anyone else was faced with the task of going to council, and that Bruenner's men had stayed where they belonged—far from my beloved Barnham.

But I knew better. Wishes never got anyone anywhere. Action did. Resigned to that fact, I closed the door to my cottage and mounted Aeros. Elric had reassured me he would return to care for my animals as soon as he'd seen his mother and siblings settled at home, and I was certain that my homestead would be cared for.

Aeros was excited to be home, and I felt a bit of a traitor as I led the mare away from the barn once again. I hadn't even bothered to unsaddle her during our brief stay. She was clearly annoyed with me, chomping at the bit and making a show of angrily blowing air through her nostrils as we rode away. Penny yelled for her friend from the paddock, and another twinge of guilt raced through my veins.

I met with Niles as we headed toward the town. He had stubbornly refused to leave my side, insisting a guard should remain with his charge. I informed him that if, indeed, I actually was the White Sorceress, then he was actually *my* charge and I ordered him to stay put at the top of the hill.

The look in his eyes made it clear he didn't like the orders, but at least he'd listened. I congratulated myself on a brief moment of cunning, especially since I would soon speak with the council to clear matters up regarding the talisman's poor choice.

Quinn and Niles's men joined us shortly after and we journeyed onto the road, once again leaving Barnham behind us. With all that had occurred, how long would it be before I would see my village again? I fought against a sense of foreboding that Barnham would never again be as I remembered it. I needed Breunner to stay far, far from my home.

Saying nothing to my companions, I urged Aeros into a canter, a speed I—and the mare—could easily maintain. I intended to make good on my promise to keep a brutal pace. Aeros could handle it, and, if the soldiers had a single complaint, they would wisely keep it to themselves.

CHAPTER NINE

The Speed of News

Traveling with a large group had been annoying, particularly traveling with the young girls who complained at every turn and could hardly be expected to keep a remotely decent pace, but if I thought traveling with a group of men would be any easier, I was mistaken.

I was used to moving at my own pace, stopping only when I needed, and caring only for myself and for Aeros. Having six other men with me, particularly two who continued to watch my every move like a couple of nuhawks, was unnerving.

They were concerned when I tried to increase our speed, and worried when I wasn't yet ready to stop and camp for the evening. The fact that they needed daylight to hunt for dinner meant they needed to stop hours before dark to set up camp. I was well aware of every minute of that precious loss of time, anxiety eating away at me as I nibbled my own dinner of raw callogh root, nuts, fruit, and bread.

Neither Niles nor Quinn attempted to speak to me on the first day of our new journey and for that, I was glad. By the second day, I almost ran out of anger at the burden laid upon me, and by the third I finally forgave both of them for agreeing I was the White Sorceress and insisting on coming to protect me from whatever real or imaginary dangers we would soon face. Even the talisman settled for a muted hum at my chest as opposed to the angry shocks I had nearly grown used to. Things seemed to be improving.

I still wished we could have traveled the extra two hours each night, but I began to at least enjoy the company. Gillesmere was a ways off and I was concerned we might not reach it in time. I could not afford to miss the council meeting.

"What were you like as a child?" Niles asked me, leaning forward in his saddle as he broke the quiet and pulled me from my thoughts. We had slowed to allow the horses a break in pace that afternoon. "Were you always so serious?"

"Of course not," I told him, my mind wandering back to my childhood imaginings of Stellon and Andra.

"Then when was it you became so focused, so intense?" He studied me, his bright eyes expectant.

"Everyone must grow up sometime," I replied.

"Interesting."

I glanced at him, waiting for clarification on what was so interesting about people growing up.

"Are you always so evasive, too?"

Deflecting conversation away from myself had always been my best defense against revealing too much about my life— more accurately, my very private life. *At least*, I thought, *the very private life I once had.* Unless I could get the council to agree with me, I suspected it would never be the same.

I sighed. "What would you like to know, Niles?" I asked. "Did I play once? Yes, I loved to play. Long ago, once upon a time, I danced in pastures and play-acted my favorite tales. I frolicked with other children and raced bareback across the fields on my pony."

"Ah," he said. "So you *were* happy once."

I bristled. "I'm happy now," I informed him brusquely. "Or at least I *was* before this entire White Sorceress nonsense."

"Forgive me," he said. "I intend no insult. I only meant you were a child once, free and unencumbered."

"We all were once," I said, returning my eyes to the road. "I wasn't born a serious old maid, I promise."

His eyes appraised me. "Serious perhaps, but you are anything but an old maid, Moreina di Bianco."

I shifted in my saddle uncomfortably, swallowing back the self-consciousness that rushed in torrents to the forefront of my mind.

Niles didn't seem to notice and he continued, "So, in my mind's eye, I imagine a young Moreina, running through the field, her hair streaming out behind her, a smile on her face. Tell me, what did you play-act?"

I was reluctant to continue the conversation but found myself answering anyway. "Oh, I was Andra," I answered, giving an uncomfortable smile.

Niles threw his head back and laughed—a hearty, honest sound.

"Why should that be so amusing?" I asked, heat already flooding my cheeks.

"I'm sorry," he said, stifling another laugh. "Even then, you were doing your best to ward off men, imaginary though they may have been."

I stared at him in shock. "I don't ward off men!"

"Is that so?"

"You've known me but a few weeks, Captain Ingram. You can hardly claim to know my history in courting, or in any other area of my life for that matter."

"I know enough," he said. His eyes moved over my face, traveled downward *far* lower than my face, and back up again. "And yet," he continued, "not nearly enough at all."

I swallowed, completely at a loss for words, and my face burned as he continued to judge my reaction.

Slightly ahead of us, Quinn spurred his mount forward again and we cantered onward, conversation lost, but unfortunately not forgotten. I *wished* I could erase it from my mind. I almost wished I could erase it from Niles's.

I didn't understand why Niles's comment should have bothered me so much, but late that evening, as snores from several soldiers carried through the air, I lay awake staring at the dying fire, pondering his words.

Did I ward off men? Had I done so all my life? *No!* There had never been a serious suitor. I couldn't think of any boy who had pursued me so thoroughly so as to make me fall for him so completely that I would have wanted to *choose*.

I knew such emotions existed, but I had never been struck by them. I couldn't possibly have married just to be taken care of and raise babes of my own. That wasn't in my heart. It wasn't *me*.

Leaves crackled behind me, and I turned to see Quinn lean forward to stoke the fire. I hadn't realized he was still awake. I faced him and propped myself up on an elbow.

"Quinn," I said quietly.

He turned to me, the firelight flickering on his features.

Hesitant, I paused, unsure how to begin. "May I ask you a question?"

He sat beside me with a nod and laid his arms across his bent knees.

I struggled, uncertain of how to phrase my thoughts. "Did you ever think I—I mean, have I ever—Saints, I don't know how to begin…never mind."

Quinn's eyes were full of questions, but he waited patiently for me to try to gather my thoughts into a coherent sentence.

Finally, he said softly, "Do I think you've spent your life warding off men?"

"Yes," I exhaled, exceedingly relieved he'd spared me from speaking the words. "So you heard our conversation."

He stared into the fire, and I studied his face, hopeful of some indication I hadn't been haughty and angry toward the boys of my village. What would I do if he said I *was* awful?

The edges of his mouth twitched as he thought, and I wondered for a moment if he was laughing. "No, Reina, I don't believe you've ever done anything of the kind."

I breathed a sigh of relief. "Then why should Niles say such a thing?" I thought aloud, absently twirling a strand of hair around my finger repeatedly. "I shouldn't care. I know I shouldn't."

Quinn turned to study me. "Men will do whatever they can to get a woman's attention. It's clear Niles wants yours."

I rolled my eyes. "Yes," I said. "Your father insinuated as much."

I couldn't put my finger on it, but something about Niles's impression of me bothered me. I cared deeply for others—sick, wounded, newborn, dying—and here was someone who assumed I had scorned all men because I wasn't bound by marriage and serving one.

"Reina," Quinn said, breaking the brief silence. "If there have been no men who've successfully courted you, then it's because they weren't deserving enough of your affections, not because you looked down upon them. Anyone who thinks otherwise is a fool."

I flushed. "Thank you, Quinn," I said softly, dropping my eyes. "So you heard *everything* earlier."

"There's not much else to listen to amidst the trees. I assure you if I could give you privacy, I would."

"I don't want privacy," I said. "Well, I do, but not *that* kind. I miss my cottage. I miss Barnham."

"Aye, me too. It's not ever going to be the same. You know that."

I took an uncertain breath. "Yes, I know." I met his gaze. "You don't *truly* believe I'm the White Sorceress, do you?"

He studied me for an uncomfortably long while before answering. "I believe you are who you are meant to be."

"You've not answered the question, Quinn."

"Aye," he said. "I have. What does it mean to be the White Sorceress, anyway? It's just another title, Reina. It doesn't mean you're anyone different from the woman you were a day ago or a month ago. You're a daughter, a Healer, a friend, and a hermit, among other things. What's one more title?"

"I am not a hermit!"

He smiled. "Some titles are more preferable than others, I see," he said as he cocked an eyebrow.

I frowned at him. "I am *not* a hermit," I maintained.

He chuckled. "'Tis not a bad thing to be self-sufficient. You take care of yourself and you're so capable at it that, when necessary, you take care of all those around you as well. But, generally speaking, it's always been evident you prefer your solitude even to the winter festivities."

Damn him. He was right. I'd rather read a good book or dry my herbs by the warmth of a fire than venture to the town hall for the winter feast. I had always felt that way, however much I tried to hide it. I wished he hadn't noticed.

"Is my discomfort in a crowd that evident?"

"I wouldn't say it's obvious."

"Well, it must be somewhat obvious if you've noticed."

"There's not much that escapes my notice, Reina."

I'd always known that about him. Quinn could be in a room with two dozen townsfolk for fifteen seconds and know all he needed to know. Afterwards, he could recite what color shoes they wore and who probably needed to trim their toenails beneath the boot leather. Then he would likely proceed to calculate which of them had been born under double-full moon. As for me? I was good only at telling which of them had come to see me for earaches or digestive distress in the last six months.

"Yes, well, I suppose maybe I am a bit of a misfit," I conceded. "And you've still managed to avoid my question."

"I didn't avoid it," he answered. "You didn't like my

response. If you're looking for a straight answer, I don't have one to give."

I pursed my lips. "Well, what's that supposed to mean?"

"It means I haven't yet made up my mind as to whether or not you're the White Sorceress. I'll continue to watch and wait for some indication that you are or are not, but until then I have no answer for you."

I almost breathed a sigh of relief. So, Quinn maintained some sense of sanity amidst the craziness that consumed everyone else.

"But," he said, "I suggest that perhaps you become comfortable with this new title you've been given. Unless there is strong evidence against it, it seems likely it's yours to keep." As if to reinforce his words, the talisman sparked angrily on my skin.

I looked up to the stars winking in the endless darkness above. "That's what scares me."

The morning broke cold and clear, my breath easily condensing in the air. We didn't have long before winter would set in fully. A month at best, I guessed. Barnham was damp and chilly most of the year, but, as the town was seated along the coastline, few winters brought crippling snow. Heading toward Gillesmere meant facing dropping temperatures sooner than I had anticipated, and I was not eager to cross the mountain pass in snow.

We mounted early and followed the road to where it split.

Turning north, we continued, and I discovered the new *road* was nothing more than what appeared to be a well-used deer path. Cathonia deer were lithe and agile, and their antlers, when ground, were considered good for muscle growth in underdeveloped children. They were essential for muscle tissue recovery in a serious muscular injury—though thankfully I had seen little of that throughout my years as Barnham's Healer. Rather unfortunately for me, forest rats also found Cathonia deer antlers to be a delicacy, which meant finding them for grinding was all that more difficult each year.

"How do the people of Gillesmere travel?" I asked after Aeros's hoof slipped on another loose rock in the path, jolting me forward in the saddle. "They can't possibly use this route."

"No," Niles confirmed, turning to look at me. I had decided it was for the best that his stallion travel in front of Aeros, concerned the mare might decide to show her dislike of Bastian with a well-placed rear hoof to the chest at any moment. "There's a wagon path to the east of here, but it's long and slow. Commerce in and out of the city must go that way, but if you need to get to Gillesmere quickly, this is the only way."

"How lucky for us," I managed between gritted teeth as I was jostled in the saddle again.

The afternoon brought little warmth as we climbed in altitude. Slowly, the trees thinned until we were left climbing treacherous mountain terrain seemingly devoid of all life. Why would anyone choose to live near such a place?

"Not far until we're over the mountain now," Niles said.

I opened my mouth to reply, but a gust of wind swept the words from my lips, forcing me to swallow instead. I pulled my cloak closer around my neck. *At least it's not snowing.*

"We should stop before the peak." Niles reined his horse to a halt beneath a covered rocky ledge that widened barely enough for riders and horses to take cover from the wind. He dismounted as Quinn pulled up the rear of the group.

"Why've we stopped?" Quinn asked, scanning the surrounding peaks.

"We need to eat," Niles said. "It's as good a place as any to take shelter while we do. There won't be anywhere to stop once we start down the other side of the pass."

Quinn seemed uneasy. "I don't like it," he said.

"Relax, D'Arturio. We're not in battle," one of Niles's men quipped.

Quinn narrowed his eyes at the man, reluctantly dismounted, and propped himself against the rock wall while he ate.

I pulled stale bread and a wedge of hard cheese from Aeros's pack, and we ate a cold lunch as quickly as possible. Niles stretched his legs, first massaging one calf above the boot, then rubbing the other. My own calves were cramped from either the cold or the riding, or perhaps both.

Niles was aware of my gaze, and my ears grew warm when he glanced upward and met my eyes with a slow smile. I turned away, watching the empty air beyond the mountain instead.

I wasn't completely ignorant of what he'd meant when he said he didn't know enough about me at all yesterday, and yet I still wondered if he meant what it was he seemed to imply. I was eighteen, several years past the age when most girls on Liron would be looking for a suitor, but even I appreciated the way Niles's shirt stretched across his shoulders, whenever he removed his cloak anyway. I wasn't interested in a relationship, but that didn't mean I was blind to a pretty body.

My gaze settled on him again. Niles was perhaps twenty-two if I'd judged correctly by the comments I'd overheard from his men, and yet he'd seen a lot in battle so in some ways he was older than his years. Perhaps that's why he didn't view me as the old maid I sometimes felt.

He slowly paced back and forth across the ledge, stretching each leg, then he moved down the trail and out of sight. I contemplated stretching my own legs with a walk, but was reluctant to head into the wind, especially on a narrow trail where one misstep could easily send me plummeting to the icy river in the ravine below. Riding Aeros along the path was nerve-wracking enough, but I trusted Aeros's hooves far more than my own clumsy feet.

I finished the last of my meal and brushed crumbs from my lap as Niles returned. We gathered ourselves and remounted.

Emerging from beneath the ledge, I followed on Aeros as Niles led the way once more. The wind was still punishing, and the sun, which had spent all morning behind thick cloud cover, finally began to show itself. Though the warmth was welcome, the blinding reflection on the snow-covered terrain forced me to squint uncomfortably.

We hadn't ridden but five minutes when there was a sudden *thwack* I couldn't discern. I flinched involuntarily as Aeros danced on the ledge, the horse's hooves sending gravel skittering into the empty air beside us.

My eyes flew to an arrow lodged in the snow and rock inches to my right and my heart leaped into my throat, my pulse racing.

I registered what was happening only as the shouts from Niles's men began and commands flew from Niles's lips.

But I didn't realize the commands were meant for me.

CHAPTER TEN

Would-be Assassins and Would-be Admirers

"Moreina, *now*!" he yelled. "You must follow me."

Thwack. Thwack. Then, a yell from one of Niles's men.

A horse screamed as it was hit in the shoulder with an arrow. Attempting to retreat from the pain, it backed up blindly, its rear hooves finding air before it could move forward again. Then horse and rider plummeted into the air below, limbs flailing, futilely attempting to grasp at nothingness. My breath left my body, and for a moment, there seemed to be a vice on my lungs, squeezing them, keeping them from drawing vital, life-giving air.

"Moreina!" Niles's voice broke me from the horror, and I forced a ragged breath. Blinding pain assaulted my bones, causing stars to dance behind my eyes, as the rider and horse hit frozen water below, meeting instant death.

Eyes wide, I nodded at Niles and urged Aeros to follow as quickly as the mare would go, and probably much quicker than was safe on the narrow pass. But, there was no *safe* now. We were under attack. By whom, I did not know and could not begin to guess.

I risked a glance over my shoulder and watched the rest of

Niles's men—and Quinn somewhere behind them—fumbling with arrows of their own. I prayed to the Saints. For all the strength I professed to have at times, I seemed to have none now.

Niles and I reached a turn in the pass, the shouts dying in the distance behind us. As I followed, the trail descended steeply. It was the descent Niles had spoken of earlier. He hadn't lied when he'd said there was nowhere to stop once the downward journey began.

Nearly a half hour passed as we rode in silence, our horses' labored breath the only sound to be heard. Too afraid to speak, questions flew through my mind. Where had the attack come from? Why were we targeted? Who would attempt to kill us? Had it been an actual attempt to kill us or merely a warning to scare us off? Most importantly, where were Quinn and the others, and why had they not yet caught up?

After another half hour, when the pass widened enough for me to pull Aeros beside Niles, I finally worked up the courage to speak. "What happened back there?" I asked, not liking the way my voice broke.

"Not yet," Niles shook his head as he whispered, motioning for me to continue following.

Reluctantly, I returned to my spot behind him and followed obediently, my mind unsettled, my stomach sick with worry over the rest of our party.

Quinn had been a few years on his own, traveling and caring for himself, and Niles's men were competent soldiers trained in battle, but my mind continued to believe the worst regardless. I couldn't help but replay the scene of horse and man falling from the cliff and into the wide expanse below.

When the snow was behind us, and we finally reached what could be called a forest once more, Niles led us to a secluded area, away from the path so as not to be in plain sight, but close enough to observe whoever might follow in our footsteps. Aeros let her head hang, visibly fatigued from our escape. I allowed the reins fall to her neck as she closed her eyes to doze.

Niles turned in his saddle to face me, concern on his face. "You're all right?" he asked.

I nodded. "Fine," I answered, stroking Aeros's withers absently. "Scared, but fine. What *happened*?"

His eyes grew dark. "I don't know, but I take the blame. It never should have happened. I thought we'd have more time before something like this."

"What do you mean? You *anticipated* this?"

"Moreina, the talisman has been found, the White Sorceress declared. You didn't think the news would travel?"

"I am not the White Sorceress!"

Niles's jaw clenched. "Whether you wish to believe it or not is another story." His eyes narrowed. "I knew there was something different about you from the start. All the stories pointed to this."

I furrowed my brows. "What stories?"

Hard azure eyes focused on mine. "When I implied you had special abilities the other day, it was hardly my own opinion alone I voiced."

Taken aback, I waited for him to continue.

"Governor Arden had spectacular stories to tell of your healing powers, miraculous recoveries the likes of which I've never heard before. It seems people have wondered about you for some time."

"So what? I have medicinal knowledge, and perhaps more than most. That does not make me a witch!" Irritated with me, Aeros's head jerked with my rising voice.

"Not a witch. A sorceress."

I clenched my hands in my lap. "So who attacked us? Who tried to kill me?"

Niles's keen eyes searched the forest behind me and he answered between his teeth. "I do not know, but believe me when I say this, Moreina. I will find out."

"Well, what do we do now?" I asked.

"We wait. We wait, and we hope it's our men who are next to travel that path," he said, checking his sword in its sheath, pulling it free, and sliding it back again. "Because if it's not, this could get very ugly, and I want you to get away from here as fast as you can. Follow this road, and travel as quickly as possible. The road widens a few miles from here and will lead directly to Gillesmere."

My heart pounded. "Alone?"

"Only if we're given no other choice. I will not leave you, Moreina, but"—he paused for a moment as if searching for words— "I will not let them have you."

My mouth grew dry as I realized what Niles was saying. He would die before he would let harm come to me. Here stood a man who would actually give his own life before he would allow me to be taken, hurt, or killed. I'd never known such loyalty. But then, I'd never known Niles.

I grew silent, hoping—praying—that we would see Quinn and the others soon. Against my will, my mind replayed the scene of horse and rider falling into the air once more. I blinked the image away and ignored the bile that threatened to rise in my throat. Moments ticked by. I willed the rest of the group to return to us as I rubbed my aching knees. There was death. More death. But I couldn't begin to guess whose. Our men? Theirs?

We heard the movement before we saw them. Finally, four horses and riders came into view and I let out a breath I hadn't realized I'd been holding.

"Thank the Saints," Niles said beneath his breath as he urged his horse forward. I followed suit.

I had never been happier to see such a travel weary crew, and I was relieved they seemed relatively unscathed. I tried hard not to think of the one man who was no longer with them.

My eyes fell on Quinn as he brought up the rear. "You're hurt," I said to him, noting the red staining his shirt and the blood still dripping from a cut to the right of his eye.

"A scratch," Quinn said with a wave. "I'm fine."

"Nonsense, you've blood everywhere. Let me tend to you," I insisted, dismounting.

"Later," he responded.

"But—"

"'Tis not my blood, Reina."

My lips parted in shock. I paused, one leg over the saddle. "Oh…"

"Later," he repeated, and I placed my leg over Aeros's back once again, my foot numbly finding the stirrup. Quinn looked to Niles, who was already deep in conversation with his men. "Ingram, we need to keep moving, get as far as we can before we lose the sun."

"Agreed," Niles said.

So they can agree on something.

After the difficult crossing, the horses were in no condition to push hard, but Niles agreed to stop only when the sun threatened to leave us in total darkness.

"No fire," he ordered. There was no dissent from the group. The recent fight was still vivid in all of our minds, and no one had any desire to reenact the scene from earlier despite the fact that it meant empty stomachs and cold sleep.

I cleared my throat. "I need light if I'm to tend to wounds," I said.

"No. I will not risk an attack in the dark. We light a fire and we might as well trumpet our location for all to see. No one here is hurt so badly that he shall not live."

"Perhaps not, but the wounds need to be cleaned at the very least. Infection can kill as easily as any arrow," I argued.

"No fire," he repeated.

I scowled at him. "Fine."

Retreating to Aeros's saddlebag, I pulled out my satchel and sat on a flat boulder as I sorted through the bag. The wounds would not go untreated. Not if I had a say.

Andra had risen, though she was but a sliver in night's sky, and Stellon had yet to breach the trees. Even as a crescent, Stellon might provide enough light by which I could see, but by Andra alone I couldn't read the labels on the jars and packets I had brought.

Rather than wait for Stellon to rise, I *felt* my way through my stores of herbs, tonics, and powders with my sight as well as my hands. I closed my eyes. Concentrating hard on *Andral essence,*

I let my hands roam within the bag, across the various jars until they stopped on one precisely the right shape and size. I had at least six jars that size in the bag, but I knew without having to look I held the right one.

I opened the lid and breathed in. Sure enough, the musty scent of ground glow beetle penetrated my nostrils. I grabbed an empty jar and tapped nearly a full spoon of the *Andral essence* into it.

"What exactly are you doing?" Quinn had approached silently, and I jumped at his voice.

"Have you feline roots, Quinn?" I asked.

"None that I know of, but then, it's always possible, never having known my birth mother," he answered. "I could be part cat."

I stopped, turned my face to his in the darkness with a curiosity he could not see. He sensed my unasked question.

"I was orphaned. The sweat plague."

"I'm sorry," I said. "I always thought…" I trailed off, unsure of what to say. I had known Quinn all my life and had never known that he had been orphaned.

"Nothing to be sorry about. I had a childhood anyone would covet." I sensed, rather than saw, his shrug. "And, Barnham will be mine someday, so there's that." I gave a small laugh as he continued, "So, I ask again. What *are* you doing?"

"Oh," I turned my attention back to my medicinal stores. "Well, Niles says I can't have a fire, and I still need to clean and tend to wounds—especially yours, so I'm about to create my own light," I said, reaching for the proxide.

There was, what I could only assume, a confused silence.

Perhaps he thought I'd gone mad.

I poured the proxide into the jar with the *essence* until it formed a liquid paste. Stopping the lid, I tilted the jar back and forth half a dozen times. Nothing. I added more proxide and repeated the process. Slowly, a dim light began to emanate from within the bottle.

Quinn leaned forward until the light from the jar illuminated his features with a blue glow. The awe on his face was evident.

"That's amazing," he breathed.

"And here I'd thought you'd seen it all, Quinn D'Arturio."

His eyes shot to mine, then back to the jar whose contents had begun to glow brightly enough to illuminate both his face and mine.

"I've seen much in my travels, Reina, but this is nothing I've ever encountered. 'Tis almost"—he paused— "magic."

"Cease that, you nit," I warned him sharply. "It's naught but glow beetles and proxide." I didn't want to hear the word *magic* in my presence.

"But how?"

I sighed. "I don't know the workings of it. My mother taught me the mixture when I was maybe seven or eight. It's useful for collecting nightherbs. Tie a small jar to your wrist and you have light wherever your hands go without having to worry about burning yourself with a torch."

"Amazing," he repeated.

"Enough," I said. "Sit please and lean forward so I can clean that." I pointed to the cut beside his eye. The blood had dried to his face, making it difficult for me to tell for certain where the damaged skin actually was.

He sat while I prepared a clean cloth with distilled water. I wiped gently, careful not to touch his eye. He winced but didn't pull away.

"Sorry," I said. "It's dried. I would have preferred to do this when it was still fresh."

"It's fine."

His warm breath caressed my hand and I found myself all too aware our faces were mere inches apart. I tried to ignore his gaze as he watched me, but it was difficult. My heart gave an off-beat thump.

I swallowed, conscious of his eyes studying my face. "Had this been an inch to the left, you'd have lost an eye," I observed.

"Mmph."

I dabbed the last of the blood away. "It's actually not very deep," I noted, tracing the graze lightly with my fingertips. "But it will leave a scar."

I placed the cloth down and picked up a fresh one, soaking it with proxide. "This might sting a bit. I'm sorry."

He nodded as I placed it beside his eye but gave no complaint.

A hushed murmur of conversation carried from where the others stood, but I couldn't make out what was being said. The night seemed otherwise quiet, far too cold for the song of either bugs or birds. I continued to hold the cloth to Quinn's face as my gaze dropped to the dark stains on his tunic.

Finally, I asked the questions that had been burning in my mind ever since I'd seen the blood on Quinn's tunic, "What happened? To what chaos did we leave you?"

He did not immediately respond. Instead, he reached a warm hand upwards, closed it gently over mine as he pulled it down, and cradled my palm in his.

"Do not ask to know the details of death, Reina," he said, his eyes dark with emotion.

I opened my mouth to reply but was unable to find a suitable response. Did he think me too weak to hear of death? Did he think I'd never seen it myself? It was true most of my experiences with death were due to illness and old age, but I had seen blood, I had seen pain, and I knew what waited in the end.

"Ah, settle, Reina," he said upon seeing the fight on my face. "'Twas not an insult against you."

I didn't hesitate this time. "What am I to think?"

He covered my hand with both of his, rubbing a calloused thumb lightly against my palm. "You've too much life within you to hear of death. I would sooner steal the song from the meadowlark than dampen your light with talk of darkness."

Wide-eyed, I found my lungs reluctant to fill with air. "What talk is this?" I managed in a whisper.

Quinn dropped my hand.

"Antony," he said loudly. "You've a wounded arm. Let Moreina tend to you."

My eyes shot upward. I hadn't heard Antony approach. He stood only a few feet from us, his eyes fixed on the illuminated jar before me.

Quinn stood, stepped back, and with a slow nod of his head, he turned and disappeared into the darkness, leaving my mind whirling with a thousand and one thoughts at once.

Heart still thumping, I pushed my thoughts aside, focusing instead on the task at hand, something I was normally very good at doing. But a nagging sensation persisted in the corners of my mind and I seemed helpless to push it away.

"What *is* that?" Antony asked, seating himself where Quinn had been only half a moment earlier. "How did you do that?"

"It's nothing special," I told him, shaking thoughts of the previous conversation from my mind and explaining again how my mother had taught me to make the glowing mixture.

"Glow beetles," he said with wonder. "Who'd have thought?"

I was only glad he hadn't insisted it was magic.

He folded his sleeve nearly to his shoulder, revealing a puncture through the skin and deep into the muscle. It had missed the major arteries.

"An arrow?" I asked as I prepared a clean cloth with proxide.

He looked sheepish. "Aye. The bugger had a good shot, too. Had Quinn not released his arrow first, I'd not be sitting here now."

"Oh?"

He looked down and swallowed. "I'm only sorry we lost Ramus. He was a good man. I'll miss him."

I dabbed at his arm. "I'm sorry," I said, once again fighting the mental image of horse and rider falling into space. I could think of nothing more to say.

"Too bad D'Arturio couldn't get to him. I've never seen anyone move the way he did, and I've seen a lot. Did you know he's a one-man army?"

"Er…"

"It's true. Why has he not joined in the war efforts on the border?"

I wasn't sure, and I told him as much.

"Well, he's bloody amazing. Took out their two archers on

the opposite peak with a few arrows of his own, and then fought off the rest of them on our side with sword more or less by himself."

Quinn?

"Is that so?"

"The rest of us tried to help, but on that ledge, there wasn't much we could do with him standing between us and them. No way to get past to aid him, but that didn't seem to hinder him any." He gave a low whistle through his teeth. "I'll say this, though. If he were scouting the border, we might find ourselves in a very different position."

I tried to act as though this news were not a shock. "And what position are we in?" I asked.

Antony thought for a moment as I finished bandaging the wound. I motioned for him to roll his sleeve back down.

"Well, it hasn't been good," he said as he flexed his fingers. "Bruenner has his sights set on the crown, and he doesn't care who he plows down to get it. So far, he's been taking village by village, town by town. Our borders are growing smaller every day. He's got the numbers, unfortunately."

"And, why exactly does he have the numbers?" I asked. Who would want such a man as their king?

"You really don't know?" he asked. I shook my head. "He was King Edgar's top commander, his right hand, so to speak. The King's Army would follow him anywhere. They know him, trust him, though only Saints know why. With the death of the prince those years ago, there was no rightful heir when the king passed. Bruenner thinks that gives him the right to claim the throne for his own."

"I thought the prince went missing."

"Missing, dead, it's all the same, isn't it? If he didn't come forth on his sixteenth birthday to claim his birthright, one must assume he's dead. And it doesn't take much to believe it was likely Bruenner who had him killed. How difficult is it, anyhow, to kill a child? Physically, I mean."

My heart ached for a long-lost child who never had a chance at life. All for a crown and a throne—a stupid metal ring and a simple wooden chair.

I finished smothering a mint leaf with a paste made from antler grindings, rolled it, and handed it to him. "Chew this well before you swallow," I ordered. "It will help the muscle heal quicker. You'll need one twice a day for the next week."

He eyed the leaf warily as he took it, but obeyed nonetheless, putting it in his mouth with a grimace and chewing as instructed. He thanked me and returned to the rest of the party.

No one else had been injured beyond a scrape or two, which I quickly cleaned up and bandaged.

When I was finished, Niles sauntered to where I sat, eyeing me as he approached. "Do you always get your way?" he asked.

I glanced up at him as I wiped down some of the bottles and placed them back into the satchel. Drying my hands, I stuffed the last of the dirty cloths into a spare compartment in the bag, making a mental note to thoroughly wash them in the morning, and closed it tightly.

"Yes," I answered. This was not the truth, but I was still annoyed with him.

To my surprise, he chuckled. "I bet you do." He touched the glowing bottle, which, by that time, had begun to dim. "How does it work?"

"Magic."

He raised his eyebrows at me, and I huffed in response. Instead of elaborating, I uncorked the bottle and flung its contents onto the ground. The glowing blue remnants faded, then died.

"There," I said. "No more light."

"I didn't come here to scold you about the light," he said softly.

Stellon had risen now, and Niles's face was dimly illuminated. "Then what did you come here for?"

"To thank you." My confusion must have been evident. I had done nothing for Niles. "For taking care of my men."

"Oh," I paused. "Well, you're welcome. It's what I do."

"We'll ride early tomorrow. We should reach Gillesmere by late afternoon. We should all rest if we're going to make it there on time."

I agreed and followed him to where the others had set up camp. My bedroll had already been laid out. I climbed in, throwing my cloak over me for extra warmth, but despite the additional layer, I still shivered. It would be a long night, and though I was fatigued, my mind was reluctant to calm. Voices in my head insisted on being heard, and I could do nothing but let them speak.

I would sooner steal the song from the meadowlark than dampen your light with talk of darkness.

What the blazes was that to mean? A soft flutter rose deep in my belly at the memory of Quinn's words.

Did you know he's a one-man army?

Quinn D'Arturio was a deeper mystery than I could have

ever imagined. Why *hadn't* he joined the army anyhow? And, where had he learned to fight? It hadn't been in Barnham. Of that much I was certain.

He had always been somewhat of a loner. Until today, I hadn't given much thought to it, but now…well, now I was perplexed.

So, Quinn was a warrior.

And a poet.

And?

What else was he hiding beneath his quiet, solid exterior? Here I'd thought he just enjoyed chopping fallen sycamore trees.

CHAPTER ELEVEN

Gillesmere

Madam Laurelle Bonverno was not as old as I imagined she would be. Nor was she anything less than stately, though how she remained so after the trials she had been through in the last few years was beyond my understanding. Her flight from the castle was well known, even in villages as small as Barnham.

As mother to the former queen, and without a kingdom of her own, she had often served as the queen's advisor in the years before Queen Isobelle's death. When the queen died in childbirth, Madam Bonverno had taken on caring for the new prince. She had resolved to look after him regardless of what rumors might fly, ignoring all insistence by the wet nurses and nannies waiting to take on the role.

As she had just lost a daughter and the king a wife, the king allowed the unconventional arrangement. I could only imagine what she must have gone through when the prince baby was taken only a few months later.

After the king's death two years ago, Madam Bonverno ran for her life. I had heard that the first several months without a ruler brought Castilles one challenger after the next for the crown, and that any contender with royal blood left in his veins was often first to die, be it from the sword or from poisoned wine. Madam Bonverno was no fool and she fled to safety.

Despite all she had seen, her face showed few wrinkles. Her gown, though worn, still exuded royalty. Her silver hair remained swept off her neck in the latest fashion. She sat tall and straight in what looked to be an uncomfortable wooden chair, her shoulders back, neck long and elegant, hands folded in her lap.

To say I was intimidated would have been putting things mildly.

We'd made it to Gillesmere with enough time to obtain a room at the inn, but I had not had the chance to do more than wash my face and hands and run a comb through my snarled locks. Now, gazing upon the council, I sorely wished I'd had time to bathe and dress properly. I was sure I was quite the amusement, dressed as I was, to the nobility who sat before me. I pretended not to notice the raised eyebrow Madam Bonverno had given me upon entrance to Governor Kelford's receiving hall.

Aside from Madam Bonverno and Governor Kelford, the council consisted of Duke Schellingworth of Keswick, Governor McElson of Gathlin, and Governor Ollingswood of Langley. Of the once dozens of council members, they were the only ones now present. The council was seated at a heavy oak table at the far end of the hall. Niles, Quinn, and I stood at the end of the long table. We had not yet been invited to sit.

At one time, the large hall had probably been used for hosting grand parties, but it now served as an impromptu war room for a council with so little hope of ever defeating General Bruenner that they put their faith into finding a woman who would somehow absolve them of everything by taking responsibility into her own hands.

That woman was not me, and while my head told me it was time to let that be known, my knees turned to jelly. I swallowed hard.

"So," Governor Kelford began, "Captain Ingram, is it? My Guard tells me you have important news from Governor D'Arturio in Barnham. I must assume this news to be particularly significant, or my Guard never would have allowed you past Gillesmere's gates, let alone into my home."

Kelford didn't exaggerate. The Gillesmere Guard had given us a bit of difficulty, but it seemed showing the talisman made quick work of opening doors.

Niles stepped forth. "Governor Kelford, I assure you, there's nothing more important than what we have to tell you."

"And what news do you bring?" Madam Bonverno asked, her sharp eyes falling on me though her words were directed at Niles.

Niles did not hesitate. "The Faranzine Talisman."

Everyone in the room sat straighter with the words, their eyes a little brighter, breath held in hope. Niles turned to me. "Show them," he said.

My mouth was suddenly dry, as though I'd tried to swallow a mouthful of sawdust. Quinn stepped forward, placing a hand on my elbow. I glanced at him, taking unexpected comfort in his familiar face. He gave an almost imperceptible nod.

I took a breath and pulled the talisman from beneath my travel-stained tunic, its weight heavy in my palm as it sent curious vibrations pulsing up my wrist and to my elbow. I let it drop to my chest.

Governor Kelford let out an audible gasp. Every pair of eyes in the room seemed rooted to the pendant around my neck.

"Is it true?"

"It, um...yes and no," I answered.

Niles stared at me, willing me to continue speaking, but after all of our travels, after all we'd been through to get here, I suddenly wasn't sure what I wanted to say.

"Well, girl, it can't be both," Madam Bonverno said. "Make up your mind."

I cleared my throat. "What I mean to say is that it's true we've found the Faranzine Talisman."

Madam Bonverno's gaze roamed from my head to my feet and back again as she assessed me. "So you're the White Sorceress," she said.

"That's the *no* part," I replied. "It's true I was in the party Governor D'Arturio sent to search for the talisman. I helped locate it, but I was only to serve as a guide. The talisman no more chose me than it *chose* to remain hidden for so long."

"Please elaborate."

"Madam," Niles intervened, "Miss di Bianco believes she holds the talisman by sheer accident."

Madam Bonverno actually laughed. "That's not possible, my dear."

"It was thrown at me!" I said. "All I did was raise a hand to keep from being hit in the face."

"And do you think it flew in your direction by chance?' she asked. "Do you think someone else should have been there to catch it?"

"No," I answered. "No, it was thrown at my face because of a fight amongst the real candidates."

"Candidates, pah. If they argued over who would wear the talisman, they were never ready to be its owner at all, which means it chose exactly who it was supposed to choose."

"But, I—"

"You *are* the White Sorceress," Madam Bonverno finished.

I clamped my jaw shut. I had been prepared for many things in my life, but nothing—*nothing* in the world could have prepared me for the mantle of responsibility that came with such a title. As if to spite me, the talisman began zapping my skin again in short, annoying bursts. I was getting really tired of being shocked.

"I am but a village Healer," I pleaded. "I cannot stop a war."

Madam Bonverno's eyebrows rose slightly. "Is that the truth?" she asked.

"I'm afraid so."

She leaned forward then and smiled at me, her eyes almost kind, "And how would you know, child?"

It had been a long time since anyone had called me child. I blinked, confused. For once, I suddenly felt as though I were a child.

"How could you possibly know if you haven't yet tried?"

I had no answer.

"Please sit," Governor Kelford said, a hand extended toward the empty seats around the table. "I think we need to hear everything that's happened. Forgive me for not offering food or drink earlier. I'll have a member of my staff bring something immediately. It sounds as though you've had a difficult journey."

"You don't know the half of it," Quinn muttered beside me.

It took over an hour to recount everything from the beginning, during which time Governor Kelford's staff brought out trays heaped high with food more delectable than anything I had ever tasted. Or perhaps I had tired of eating stale bread and hard cheese over the last several weeks.

When I'd finished giving my account of the events that led us to Gillesmere, I waited to hear Madame Bonverno voice an opinion other than the one she'd already expressed.

It was no great surprise that I waited in vain.

Much to my dismay, the council members agreed in unison that I was, indeed, the White Sorceress.

"But, if that's true," I said, "then how am I to end this war? How do I save this kingdom from being torn apart? This blasted talisman hasn't shown me a thing, and it's been around my neck for nearly two weeks now!"

Tilting her head back just enough to look down at me with a slightly furrowed brow, Madam Bonverno addressed me, "And have you thoroughly examined it, my dear? Have you tried to wield its magic?"

"Well," I paused, "no."

Other than trying to figure out what made it alternately shock or hum at me, I hadn't tried to do much with it. But then I had also been hopeful that once we arrived in Gillesmere it would no longer be in my possession. I assumed that once the council heard my version of how it came to be in my hands, they would agree there had been a mishap and I was not fit to lead, let alone to lead a kingdom out of warfare and seat its new rightful king on the throne.

"Then perhaps it's time you start looking," Madam Bonverno said.

"We will make sure that Miss di Bianco uncovers its secrets," Niles said. "I have every confidence in her ability."

Madam Bonverno nodded. "And, as it is agreed she is the White Sorceress, she shall henceforth be addressed as Sibyl Moreina," she said. "If there's one thing I'm a stickler for, it's title, Captain. She shall be addressed with the respect such a title deserves."

I glanced at my travel-worn tunic and the layer of dirt upon my breeches, and I couldn't help but think I was not remotely fit to be addressed with such respect, now or perhaps ever. I refrained from expressing such opinions to Madam Bonverno, but mentally I squirmed at the thought of being addressed as Sibyl.

"Now, as it has been a long journey and you are likely in need of a warm room with a good bed, I will have Governor Kelford's staff prepare a room for you. Governor, I assume it will not be a problem if she is housed in my wing?"

Kelford nodded his head. "She is welcome here, Madam Bonverno. I would never say no."

"Oh, that's not necessary," I began. "We have a room at the inn already."

"My dear, you'll have better protection, a better bed, and most certainly better meals here. Therefore, you shall stay."

Since I wasn't exactly sure how to argue with Madam Bonverno, I nodded in agreement. "My thanks," I said.

"Madam Bonverno, Governor Kelford, as I am head of the

White Sorceress's Personal Guard, may I respectfully request to remain in residence with Sibyl Moreina?" Niles asked as he stood.

Governor Kelford opened his mouth to respond, but Madam Bonverno intervened. "That will not be necessary, Captain Ingram. The Gillesmere Guard has a long history of superior service. Rest assured she will be well guarded here."

Shifting his weight from one foot to the other, Niles was silent for a moment. It seemed he didn't know how to argue with Madam Bonverno either. He swallowed and nodded, his hands clasped tightly behind his back.

"Very well," he said tightly. "I shall return to the inn with the rest of the guard. Please call upon us as needed. We will be ready at a moment's notice." He stepped away from the table with a glance at Quinn, their cue to exit.

Preparing to leave, Quinn stood and met my eyes. "Send word if you should need me," he said quietly. I nodded in response, saddened to see the only familiarity in my world quickly disappearing.

With that, he turned to join Niles, but Madam Bonverno had more to say.

"One moment," she said. "You, sir."

Quinn stopped. "Yes, Madam?"

"You're not a soldier, are you?"

"I am not," he confirmed.

"You may stay."

My gaze slid to Niles. Anger flashed in the blue of his eyes, but it was quickly masked, and I wasn't sure anyone else noticed.

"I'll have the staff prepare another room," Kelford said.

"That won't be necessary," Quinn told him. "I can sleep in the servants' quarters."

Kelford deferred to Madam Bonverno, who nodded her approval with only mild surprise at his request.

"Very well," Kelford said.

Madam Bonverno addressed Niles once more. "Thank you, Captain Ingram. We will send for you and your men shortly, I am sure. For now, please rest from your journey and know that Sibyl Moreina is safe and will be working hard to figure out how to end this war and rid the kingdom of the insufferable blight that is Marcus Bruenner."

Niles gave a bow and exited through the large doors leading from the hall. The resulting slam echoed on the vaulted ceiling as they closed behind him.

I looked to Quinn who shrugged, then to Madam Bonverno. "Now, let's get you settled, shall we?"

Madam Bonverno led me to rooms furnished as I had never seen. I had read about such wealth, but never imagined I would ever see the inside of a sleeping room so grand. The whole of my own cottage could fit in the receiving chamber. The bed alone was nearly three times the size of my cot and covered in multiple layers of soft, thick quilts. There were half a dozen pillows against the headboard, fluffed and inviting. What would it feel like to rest my head on one of them after so many nights on the ground? My legs nearly weakened with the thought.

Governor Kelford was far wealthier than our own Governor

D'Arturio, though Gillesmere was a larger town than tiny Barnham, and I could only imagine what the tax on such commerce could bring. The inside of the town bustled with people of many castes, but there seemed a definite predisposition toward the wealthy.

"Please consider anything in this room to be yours," Madam Bonverno said as she bent to stoke the fire the servants had already started within the hearth.

She stole a glance at my tunic and men's trousers. Though she had not meant for me to see, my cheeks flushed.

"I don't normally dress this way," I reassured her.

Madam Bonverno let out a surprisingly girlish laugh. "I guess the delicacy I once possessed escapes me in my old age. There was a time when I was far more subtle, I assure you."

I smiled sheepishly. "I can hardly fault you for looking. I'm quite a sight."

"Oh, child." *Child, again?* "I assure you my laughter is not at your expense." She took my hand in hers, her skin soft and worn with age. "The truth is"—she leaned close, faintly smelling of roses, and gave my hand a squeeze— "you remind me of me."

The surprise on my face must have been evident. I never expected to hear such words.

"Oh don't look so stunned! I wasn't always an old ninny with a high collar."

I couldn't help myself. I outright laughed.

"Madam Bonverno, you do not appear an old ninny to me!"

"Laurelle, please," she said. "Call me Laurelle. Or Elle, I do prefer that. None of this *Madam* nonsense."

Confused, I said, "But, what about—"

"Pah," she said with a wave of her hand. "What I say in the presence of men and what I tell a woman of my equal are two entirely different things. One is meant to portray the strength others must believe I possess. The other is meant to convey the camaraderie and guidance I willingly offer to a woman I rather admire."

"*You* admire *me*? What on Liron could I have done to earn such distinction? You've known me but two hours."

"I know you just fine, child. I know you were chosen by the Faranzine Talisman, and if I knew nothing else, that would be enough. But, you also traveled far and wide to consult with the council simply because you believed there to be an error. That means you care enough about Castilles to ensure what happens is the right course of action, you want to see the war end, and you want to see our citizens live in peace. Lastly, you cared so much about consulting with the council that you came to us straight from the road, dust still on your trousers. Whereas most women would refuse to entertain the thought of appearing before the high council in such a state, you did not hesitate to come to us. That tells me vanity is low on your list of priorities. And between you and me, dear, we could use a few more like you."

I was stunned into silence.

"Now, I'll have Madeline bring the tub and draw you a hot bath. You should be able to find something to fit you in there." She pointed at a large, intricately carved armoire of a dark wood. "Take your time and enjoy the warmth. When you're ready, you can join me in my receiving room and perhaps we can figure out what to do with this talisman of yours."

At the mention of the talisman, the stone hummed excitedly on my chest. Unexpected tears welled behind my eyes. "Thank you," I said.

"I know what it's like to run for your life, child." She squeezed my hand once more and left, leaving me pining for the hot bath I gratefully anticipated.

CHAPTER TWELVE

To Search the Stone

I emerged from the water only when it had gone completely tepid. Breathing in deeply, I inhaled the divine scent of rosewater. My hair was shiny, the grime of many weeks had been removed from my face, and I had scrubbed every inch of my body three times. I was clean and even the edges of my fingernails showed little stain as it had been weeks since I'd pulled herbs from the ground or compounded medicines on my workbench.

Padding softly on the plush maroon carpet as I toweled my hair dry, I opened the doors of the armoire and admired the gowns that hung within. Almost reluctantly, I pulled a deep green silk gown from its hanger. Sage-colored trim lined the bodice and the sleeves. Like everything else in the room and in Kelford's home, it was far more extravagant than anything I had ever seen in my life. I searched the armoire for something less grand, but everything seemed of similar quality.

I couldn't guess who the owner of such grandeur would be, but if this was one of Madam Bonverno's—er, Elle's—rooms, then it stood to reason the dresses belonged to her. We were of similar body type, and yet I couldn't picture myself wearing the dress I had pulled out.

Reluctant though I was, I had little choice but to wear the splendid garment. I couldn't exactly parade around the castle naked, though that would make for interesting conversation. I vowed to pay Madame Bonverno back someday. The dress fit nearly perfectly, though it was perhaps two finger widths shorter than it should have been and the bodice was a hair tighter than I would have liked. I turned to face the mirror and met my own surprised eyes.

Perhaps there was something positive to be said for wearing one's bodice a hair tighter than it should be. I had never considered my breasts to be an asset, but in this dress, I looked almost, well, like a lady.

A soft knock at my door made me jump and I cursed myself for foolishly admiring my own body.

Through the door, there was a muffled, "M'lady?"

I let out my breath. 'Twas Madeline, undoubtedly come to see if I'd drowned in the tub.

"Come in," I called.

"Would you like me to braid your hair?" she asked as she entered, her eyes alight with the suggestion.

I pulled my fingers through the damp locks. "It's not yet dry, but if you wouldn't mind giving it a try, I'd enjoy that, thank you."

She nodded, and I sat on a plump velvet stool so that Madeline could comb the knots before working with my hair.

"You have rather amazing hair, Sibyl. So thick. It's beautiful," she said.

"Reina, please," I told her. "Call me Reina. I'm not royalty."

"Oh, Sibyl, I've been told otherwise, if I may say so."

I sighed. I supposed Madeline *had* been told otherwise. I'd likely never be called by my name again.

"I doubt there's anything I could do to stop you."

Madeline paused, seeming not to know what to say.

"I'm sorry." I turned to face her as I spoke. "You're only doing what you've been told."

She looked down at me, uncertainty clouding her face again. Oh, dear. I was making the poor girl even more uncomfortable. I doubted Kelford ever apologized to his staff. Not knowing what else to do, I turned back so that she could continue combing through my hair.

Before long Madeline's fingers were deftly working their way through my mane, pulling back piece by piece, gradually exposing my ears and neck.

"Mmm," I said. "It's been years since anyone has done my hair like this." The muscles in my body had begun to relax as she braided. If I weren't careful, I'd end up falling asleep in my seat.

"That's a crime, Sibyl. With hair such as this, you should be wearing it coiled every day. Do you never wear it up?"

"Well, it's not so easy to manage by myself," I told her. "Though I'd love to cut it, my mother always loved it long."

"Is she no longer with you?" Madeline asked, picking up on my past tense reference of my mother.

"No."

"I'm sorry."

"Don't be," I said. "She died years ago."

"Well, I can see why she preferred your hair long. Although, may I ask about this peculiar streak? I've never known anyone with one like it!"

It was perhaps bold for a servant to ask, though I was far from offended. It made me wonder what Madeline's life was like.

"I've always had it," I told her. "I would say I was born with it, but my mother used to love to tell me again and again how I was as bald on my head as I was on my bottom as a babe."

Madeline laughed outright, and I found myself laughing along.

"There you are, milady," she said, as she performed one final tug.

I turned to look in the mirror and nearly lost my breath. "Madeline, it's beautiful," I said. Madeline had taken my white streak and intricately woven it, ribbon-like, through the many braids she had intertwined into one main twist that hung halfway down my back. The effect was amazing, accentuating a slender neck I hadn't realized I possessed. Even when my mother braided my hair, I had never seen it look so regal. Then again, I'd never been dressed so elegantly either.

"Would you like me to show you to Madam Bonverno's room now?" Madeline asked.

"Yes, please," I said. I pulled the talisman from the night table and admired it. It had cleaned up nicely with only a cloth and some persistence on my part. I placed it around my neck and felt its weight settle heavily between my breasts with a contented buzz.

Madeline led me down the hall, around a corner and opened a door to a room larger and grander than the one in which I stayed.

Elle sat in a high-backed, blue velvet armchair next to

a crackling fire, a book open in her lap. She looked up as we entered.

"Ah, I knew those old dresses were worth saving," she said, a smile on her face.

"Elle," I said, toying with the hem of a sleeve, "I'll only wear this until Antony brings my belongings from the inn."

"Nonsense. It's yours. Although"—she gazed the length of me— "it looks as though we'll need to ask Madeline to let the hem out."

"But, I can't keep this. It's too much!"

"Child, I suggest you get used to owning fine things. Your position will demand it."

I sighed and let my shoulders drop.

"Come sit," she said, patting the arm of the chair beside her. I did as she asked. Madam Bonverno lowered the spectacles that sat on her nose, and looking over them, her gaze fell on the talisman.

I brought my hand to the stone and pulled the chain over my head to hand it to Elle. Though she was obviously fascinated by it, she seemed reluctant to take it.

"Go ahead," I said. "Have a good look and maybe you can tell me what I'm supposed to do with the blasted thing."

She glanced at me, eyebrows raised, and guilt crept through my veins in response. Perhaps I needed to learn to watch my tongue before snapping at a member of the royal family as though she were a patient who had refused medicine. Elle accepted the talisman with an *oh!* of surprise. I should have warned her about the jolt.

"I'm sorry," I said. "I should have warned you. If you hold it by the chain, it won't shock you. Or it won't shock you as much anyway."

Deep-set eyes took on concern as they viewed me. "Does it do this all the time, child?"

I shrugged. I had *almost* become immune to it at this point. "Mostly, but it tends to settle after a while."

"Oh!" she said, dropping the chain, the talisman falling to the thick-carpeted floor. "I think it bit me."

"Sorry. I guess the chain isn't very safe either."

She was sucking on the finger where she must have received a pretty strong shock. "Can I see?" I asked. Nodding, she held her hand out to me. Her thumb and forefinger were reddened and beginning to blister where the chain had come in contact with her skin. My lips parted in surprise at the severity of the burn. "I can treat that," I said, my mind already thinking of the right salve to ease the burn.

"Pah, it won't kill me. And now I've learned my lesson not to toy with the treasures of others!"

I smiled in response as I bent to pick up what I was slowly beginning to think of as my evil bauble. It buzzed at me as if in response to my thoughts.

"I swear this thing seems to be good for nothing, which makes me feel as though I'm not the White Sorceress everyone wants me to be."

"I doubt that," Elle said. "I think it's more likely you haven't really searched the stone."

I frowned. "Search the stone?"

She placed a hand over mine, her skin cool and soft against the warmth of my own hands. "When I was a young child, my grandmother once taught me how to read kai leaves. Oh, don't laugh. I see already you're amused, but there's truth in it."

Thinking of my sight, I assured her, "I wouldn't think of laughing. I believe you."

"Do you?"

I nodded.

"Hmm, I wonder." She set the talisman on the table beside her and, lifting a small pot of kai, she poured a generous measure of it into an empty cup. Handing the steaming cup to me, she instructed, "Drink."

The warm liquid slid down my throat with ease as I sipped from the cup, the slightly bitter taste of kai leaves combined with a hint of lemon and honey. Swallowing the last of the kai, I handed the cup back to Elle, but not before taking a curious glance at the bottom myself.

I couldn't discern what might make it interesting, but Elle hummed her approval upon examining it.

"Well?" I asked. "What can you tell?"

Elle gave me a sly smile. "Can't say."

"But, I thought you said you could—"

"I can."

I waited expectantly.

"Well, it doesn't mean I should tell! Some things are meant to be kept secret."

I laughed. "My own destiny is a secret from me?"

"Absolutely."

"But your knowing is fair game?"

In response, she only winked.

"Well, is it at least what you hoped you'd see?" I asked,

resigned to the fact that I wasn't going to get details.

"Oh, yes. That it is." Elle placed the cup back on the table. "Now, back to searching the stone. I think it would be better if you wore it while we perform a little test, so keep it round your neck. I want you to hold the stone in your palm. Yes, that's it, but don't cover the face of it. Make sure you can see it."

I loosened my grip and adjusted my fingers so I held only the silvered setting. The shock I first received settled into tiny sparks.

"Now, close your eyes."

I took a deep breath, shifted in my seat to get comfortable, and obeyed.

"Concentrate on your breath. Slow and even. In, out, in, out. Yes, just like that. Imagine what it is you want to see. See it in your mind's eye."

I was jolted internally—a sensation that had nothing to do with the talisman—when I realized Elle was walking me through the very process I used to evoke a vision.

"Relax," she said. "You've tensed up."

I forced myself to drop my shoulders. "Sorry," I mumbled.

"Think about what it is you hope to see."

I reined in my errant thoughts and focused on discovering the secrets within the stone. With all of my resolve, I pressed my will into the stone. Minutes passed. Perhaps hours. Slowly, I felt a pleasant low humming as the stone warmed in my hand.

"Ah!" Elle gasped softly, and I opened my eyes.

The aqua tourmaline glowed from within, a turquoise opalescence pulsing with light, the blues and greens shifting and swirling as though they had been stirred. Startled, I nearly dropped the pendant and the glow diminished.

My gaze shot to Elle's.

"What happened?" I asked.

"You found the stone," she said knowingly.

"How long was it glowing?"

"Only a moment. Surely you felt it."

I nodded slowly. "It felt warm, but I thought it was the heat of my palm."

"Try again," she said, leaning in with excitement.

With a deep breath, I closed my eyes and focused as I had before. Again, it felt as though hours passed, and yet nothing changed in my palm—no hint of warmth, not even a shock or a hum.

I gave a frustrated sigh.

"I think that's enough for now," Elle said. "We'll be called for the evening meal soon and you look as though you could use a rest."

Disappointed, I agreed. I wanted to know how the stone produced its glow, how I'd actually *found* it, and how on Liron I could find it again. Its glow was far more impressive than crushed glow beetle, and I was intrigued. Though I still didn't exactly believe in magic, this was the closest I'd ever come to witnessing something like it.

I sat back in the plush chair, feeling as though I might sink into the cushion, and stretched my feet to warm them by the fire. The jeweled slippers I'd been given were delicate and feminine but didn't do much to keep my toes warm. I wiggled my toes as the delicious heat began to finally touch them.

"May I ask a question, Elle?"

"You may."

"Why did you send Niles to the inn?"

I suspected she tried to hide it, but Elle's face clouded over. "Soldier," she answered. "Never trusted them."

"Never?"

She gave a bitter laugh. "Oh, long ago, in my foolish years, I may have trusted them once, but I've seen too much, my dear. Trained career soldiers will do whatever they can to be on the winning side of the war. They murder, pillage, and rape, taking what isn't theirs to take. And when the tides turn and signs show their opponents might conquer them, they won't bat an eyelash at switching sides. No loyalty. No respect."

The venom in her voice shook me. There had always been corruption, but I had to believe the majority of soldiers on any side of a war were faithful servants, loyal to their cause. I couldn't imagine why any man would volunteer to fight otherwise.

"But surely you can't feel that way about our own soldiers! The ones who have sworn to protect us, the ones who fight Bruenner at every turn."

"Oh, child. You are young."

I furrowed my brow. "I'm not as young as you think," I said half-defiantly.

Elle laughed—a husky sound. "You're younger than you know. And when you're my age, you'll see what I mean."

I didn't argue.

"I am grateful there are men who will fight against Bruenner's army, men who would protect us from complete domination, but I know for every one loyal man fighting for his family, there are no less than a handful of opportunistic parasites who couldn't be more delighted to have the chance to use their sword against another man. And that frightens me."

"Then why was Quinn allowed to stay?" I asked. "He may not be a soldier, but he's an able fighter."

"I suspect he is," she answered. "But, he didn't ask to stay, and that appealed to me immensely."

I guessed that Elle had reasons beyond that, but I couldn't fathom what they were.

"Besides," she said, "he's a handsome devil."

My eyes widened, surprise evident on my face. This was not a statement I expected to hear from a woman old enough to be my grandmother. Most of the women who encountered both Quinn and Niles seemed predisposed to swoon over Niles. Elle, however, had expressed no such statement about Niles.

"I suppose," I agreed slowly.

"He's also smart."

I could only stare at Elle questioningly.

"He requested the servants' quarters." When I clearly did not understand why this alone made Quinn smart, Elle paused and held up a finger. She rose from the chair and made her way to the window, pulling back the heavy blue drapes to reveal another wing of the building, one that appeared to attach to the wing in which we stood. Behind thinner drapes, the windows glowed with light.

"There," Elle explained. "The servant's quarters are in that wing. I have no doubt your Quinn has already positioned himself in the corner closest to where your room resides. Why, if he has, you could probably speak to each other right through the stone. Oh, but I'm willing to bet there's a passage back there.

Old castle, you know."

I drew a surprised breath. Quinn could not have known where I would be housed and where the servants' quarters were, and yet he *had* specifically requested the servants' quarters. I mulled over the new information in my head.

"How could he possibly have known?" I asked.

Madam Bonverno shrugged. "Men will be men," she answered. "And he's a smart one."

Elle and I bumped into Quinn in the corridor as we journeyed to the dining hall for the evening meal. A subtle smile crossed Elle's face. As I had, Quinn had washed and changed. Though his jaw was freshly shaven and his boots shined, he was no less imposing than he had been when we'd spent days in the wilderness.

"Sibyl Moreina," Quinn said with a bow of his head. I thought I caught the faintest hint of a smirk.

"Don't you dare," I warned him. "Not you."

His eyes met mine as he brought his head back up and a faint look of surprise overtook his features. His gaze rose to my hair, then lowered as he absorbed my entire change in appearance down to the very slippers I had donned.

I bit my lip nervously. As I had typically spent most of my time in indigo and mud-stained aprons with only my books as company, I wasn't accustomed to being physically assessed.

Quinn opened his mouth as if to say something, then under Elle's scrutiny, quickly closed it again.

We proceeded to the dining hall where Quinn held a chair for me. No doubt the governor's son was better trained in etiquette than I. I took my seat and nodded my thanks as he claimed the seat next to me.

Governor Kelford, his wife who was introduced to us as Falene, and Elle seated themselves around the table as servants brought platters of food before us.

In an attempt to be cheerful, Falene asked about Barnham and inquired about my daily routine. Though Falene had intended to keep talk merry, my heart grew heavier as the meal wore on, aching for the home of which I spoke.

By the time our dessert, a rich chocolate custard with briarmint undertones, was presented, Elle had steered the conversation into a new direction about what wares the latest vendors were selling in Gillesmere's commercial district. Relieved, I let my thoughts turn inward.

Quinn touched my elbow lightly, leaning in to speak privately to me.

"You're fatigued," he said.

I nearly laughed. "It's been a longer day than most," I agreed.

"Retire, and I'll walk you to your rooms," he offered.

I gave him a sidelong glance. Regardless of politics dictating that I should stay for the remainder of the evening, I was nearly asleep in my seat. Standing, I prepared myself for as much diplomacy as I could muster.

"Governor Kelford, Falene, Madame Bonverno, please allow me to thank you from the bottom of my heart for offering me guidance, shelter, a hot meal, and most importantly right now, a bed in which to rest my head. If you'll excuse my lack of proper protocol, I am exceptionally fatigued after many days on the road, and I have need of a long and decent night's sleep."

I was met with hearty agreement and found myself relieved as Quinn and I traveled the hall back to my rooms.

Typical of Quinn, he said nothing as he escorted me through the long corridors. Could what Elle had said about him be true? Had he known where I would be housed? How could he have fathomed they would ask me to stay?

As we drew closer to the wing that housed my rooms, there was an almost tangible tension in the air. I couldn't determine if its origin was Quinn or myself. Perhaps both, I decided.

"How did you—" I began at the same time he said, "That look becomes you."

It was enough to halt me in my tracks.

He paused. "Forgive me," he said, looking away.

I regarded him with what could only be confusion. "For what?"

"I speak out of turn."

"How so?"

"I shouldn't say such things to you," he said. "Especially now."

"Quinn, for goodness sake. I'm the same as I've always been."

"Quite the contrary, Reina."

Frustrated, I pressed on. "We grew up together. You retrieved my mother's favorite nanny goat the night we had that terrible storm when I was ten, remember? You were, what, eleven? You should never have been out that night yourself!" He continued to stare at the wall as though there were something of importance there. I continued, "My mother tended your broken arm, and I stood by her side as she splinted it and changed bandages every day. And I've treated your father through several bouts with his knee ever since it stiffened up on him two years ago. Don't act as though I'm a stranger to you. Say what you would say."

He turned his head toward me, his eyes growing dark with something I couldn't discern. I understood then that though it seemed I had known him forever, essentially, he *was* a stranger to me. *He's a one-man army.* The thought came unbidden.

His jaw clenched.

"Say it," I encouraged him.

He shot me a look, eyes glittering. "'Tis not my place to say!" he growled.

I took half a step back. In all the years I had known him, I had never heard Quinn raise his voice.

Closing his eyes, he drew an even breath, then looked away once more. "I'm sorry," he said.

I shook my head. "No need. I suppose I've never known when to let things be. It is I who should be sorry."

"Blazes, Reina. Will you not even let me apologize?"

I clamped my mouth shut to keep myself from apologizing again as we slowly resumed our walk to my rooms in silence once more.

"May I ask you a question?" I said. He looked hesitant, but I proceeded anyway. "Why did you request the servants' quarters?"

He thought for a moment as though contemplating how to answer.

"Did you know that I would be offered a room?"

Slowly he nodded. "I couldn't be sure, but I had my suspicions."

"How? How could you know where I would be? And how could you know where to place yourself?"

Our footsteps echoed in the hall as we neared my rooms. "When we first arrived, there was steam coming from that wing of the castle. The laundry, I correctly assumed. And in a building of this age, the laundry is typically between the servants' quarters and the kitchens. Easy access to hot water and the servants, both of which are essential to clean linens and clothing."

I narrowed my eyes. I should have figured, but why anyone would take such notice of castle design, I couldn't begin to guess. "Does nothing escape your notice ever?"

He shrugged.

"That still doesn't answer how you knew where I would be?"

"Again, I couldn't know for sure, but when we entered, the servant girls were coming and going to one particular wing more than any other. The kitchens are the opposite direction, which led me to believe the place they'd be most likely to go would be the guest wing where Madam Bonverno is staying. Given the layout of the building, I figured the servants' quarters probably offered the best chance of my being able to protect you should the need arise."

I gave an unladylike snort of disbelief and narrowed my eyes, scrutinizing him as I added, "Madam Bonverno said something about there being secret passages, as well."

"That could very well be so in a castle of this age," he said in a tone that gave away nothing as he met my eyes evenly.

I suspected he'd already discovered the passages Elle had mentioned. If anyone could, it would be Quinn.

At last, we stood before the door to my room. Quinn's hand reached for the knob.

"I'll check your room first," he said.

I raised an eyebrow. "To make sure it's safe?" I was fairly certain the Gillesmere Guard was capable of handling any threats, especially within the governor's own home.

"Of course," he said, his back to me as he entered the room. After a brief but thorough search, he determined it was safe for me to spend the night. I hadn't expected any differently.

Leaving, Quinn hesitated at the door for a brief moment. He turned to me, the expression on his face unreadable.

"Good night, Reina."

"Good night," I said softly as he closed the door. "Stranger."

I didn't wait for Madeline to help me from my gown. Giving the bed a single look of longing, I fell upon the feathered mattress and slipped into a dreamless sleep.

CHAPTER THIRTEEN

Decisions

For the next three days, I saw very little of Quinn. I suspected he was avoiding me, though I wasn't entirely sure why. I couldn't think of any reason for his odder-than-normal behavior. Though I hated to admit it, after his constant companionship over the last several weeks, I missed his quirky silence and solid company.

Over the following weeks, Elle and I spent almost every day searching the stone again, but with little success. It became routine for me to grow frustrated and anxious and get shocked often as a result. After the first immediate success, I had thought *finding* the stone again would be easy, but I couldn't have been more wrong.

A month and a half after we arrived, I awoke in the middle of the night to a vision I had not summoned. Not since my very early experiences with my peculiar gift had I experienced a vision I had not intentionally worked to *see* and the scream that caught in my throat as I viewed this one wasn't nearly adequate to express my feelings.

Blinded to everything around me, I threw the covers from my body and fled from the room, stumbling over my own feet as I ran. I didn't know where I intended to go, only that I was possessed by an overwhelming urge to run from the images I had seen. When I rounded a dark corner and crashed into Quinn's solid chest, I would have fallen straight onto my rear had his strong arms not caught me in their grasp. I clung to him like a child.

"Reina, what's happened? Are you all right?" he asked, his words muffled by my hair. "You screamed."

I tried to speak, but my voice evaded me. Raspy breath came in shallow, uncontrollable spurts. The talisman sent angry waves of electricity through my chest in response. Why had I left it on while sleeping?

"You're trembling. What's wrong?"

I swallowed, attempting to compose myself, trying to make sense of what I'd seen. Light from the oil lamp on the wall flickered with a breeze, causing our shadows to dance eerily on the stones.

"I...I had a vision," I told him.

His eyes searched my face, concern etched onto his features, and I hated that I must look like a raving lunatic.

"You're all right, though?" he asked, as he smoothed down my wild hair, tucking it behind my ear.

I sniffed as I nodded.

"Come," he said, giving me a squeeze. "Let's get you back to your room."

We walked in silence, my mind beginning to numb. I took a seat on the edge of the bed as Quinn stoked the embers in the hearth and added a log, coaxing the fire back to life.

When the flames had begun to lick at the new log, and he was sure it would burn, he turned and faced me.

"Do you want to talk about it?" he asked.

Truth be told, I wasn't sure that I did, but I needed to, whether I cared to admit it or not. "It was Bruenner," I said.

Quinn stiffened, immediately on guard and he shifted. "What's he going to do?"

I nearly choked on a sick laugh as I shook my head. "It's what he's already done." Quinn waited for me to continue. Though there were any number of evil deeds from which to choose, I was sure even Quinn could never have anticipated my next words. "It's…it's my mother."

"Your mother?"

"He killed her." Quinn's shadowed face showed his confusion. How would he ever believe me? It sounded crazy even to my own ears. "I know it's insane. I know…I know you must think I've lost it, but, Quinn, I swear to you, I saw it."

"Easy," Quinn said. "Take a deep breath."

I did as he instructed, shakily inhaling, tapping my foot rhythmically on the carpet in a failed attempt to soothe myself.

"Another," he instructed. I breathed. "Now, tell me."

"Remember when she died? She'd been called to Irzan. I never knew why, and I never did find out." Memories I had shoved away long ago came flooding back, trickling into every corner and crevice of my mind.

"Yes," he said. "I remember. She was"—he paused, searching for some acceptable way to say it— "attacked on the road home, not far from Irzan."

"Attacked by Bruenner himself," I said, trying to keep my throat from closing as I spoke.

"Reina, how can you know that? You were asleep. Perhaps it

was a nightmare."

"I know the difference between the truth and my dreams," I said, my voice breaking as it rose in anger. "I *know*."

He held up a defensive hand. "All right, I believe you. Tell me what happened."

I swallowed. "I offered to go with her, you know. I knew she shouldn't have made that long trip by herself. I wish she'd let me come."

"Then you wouldn't be here now, either."

"I don't know…"

"Reina, you're emotional. You're not thinking straight."

I continued anyway. "She completed whatever business she had at the capital, and she was a day's journey from Irzan on her way home. That's when she encountered three men on the road. At first, she thought they were thieves." The vision flashed again in my mind, my mother sitting straight-backed in the saddle. I hadn't seen her face in three long years and yet she looked exactly how I remembered, right down to the coarse, gray wool of her traveling cloak and the intelligence illuminating her bright, hazel eyes. She'd had no fear and held her head high, though she recognized the look on their faces and realized what fate awaited her. "She knew when she saw *him* that they wanted more than her horse or coin."

"Bruenner?"

I nodded.

"But why? What reason would he have to kill your mother, Reina?"

"I don't know," I said, my voice raw with emotion I couldn't hide. "But he did. I saw him. He…he pulled her from her horse, and he…he *enjoyed* it. I mean, he *really* enjoyed it. God, the look in his eyes…" I choked back a sob.

"You're sure it was him?"

"It was."

"But you've never seen him."

"It *was.*"

He nodded slowly. I was certain he didn't believe me, but I didn't care. General Bruenner, for whatever reason, was directly responsible for my mother's death three years ago. The fresh reminder of my loss was no less painful now than it had been when I'd first learned of it. Whatever it took, I vowed I would personally hold Bruenner accountable.

"Listen, Reina—"

"I know what I saw!"

"I believe you."

I squinted at his blurry form through my tears. "You do?"

He sat beside me. "Why wouldn't I?"

I placed a hand over my eyes, rubbing them, suddenly unsure of my own visions, unsure of anything. "I don't know."

"I'll look into it," he said. "I promise you. Beginning tomorrow morning, I will find out what happened."

I raised my eyes to him, wishing I could at least try to appear stable, but unable to bring myself to do more than give him a hug.

He stiffened in response, but I only hugged him tighter, registering the warmth and security he brought with his presence alone.

"Thank you. Even if you discover nothing, thank you."

He pulled back and I allowed him. "For what?"

"For believing me," I said, wiping another unshed tear from my eye.

He gave one slow nod as he stood to leave. "Reina," he said. "Does anyone else know of your…"

"Ability? No."

"Good. We should probably keep it that way."

I nearly laughed. "What, and single myself out further? No, there's no danger of that, Quinn. I won't tell a soul. Of that much, I can assure you."

If Quinn had discovered anything regarding my mother's death, he had not yet shared it with me. The next week passed as the previous several had. Niles visited frequently, as frequently as Elle would allow in any case. He never stayed long, but he would brief the governor and Quinn on news that had been heard at the inn and anything his men had learned in and around town. It seemed it was becoming common knowledge that the Faranzine Talisman had been found, and rumors had begun to swirl surrounding the unknown guest in Governor Kelford's home.

It wasn't difficult to see I endangered everyone in my presence simply by staying. Despite Kelford's and Niles's and Quinn's precautions, it wouldn't be long before anyone and everyone would put two and two together and figure out who the unknown guest in Kelford's home really was. Once that happened, whoever it was who tried to attack us on the mountain pass would have plenty of time to plot a more successful attempt.

I could hardly sit around waiting for that to happen while I fiddled with the blasted talisman day in and day out. As if recognizing my thoughts, the talisman crackled angrily.

"I have to leave," I said aloud to the empty room, wondering as I said it how and where I would go.

Winter had set in. Of that, there was no doubt. A perpetual light layer of snow coated every surface for miles. Though it melted each afternoon, a fresh blanket replaced it nearly every morning.

I contemplated where I would go in such weather. I didn't have extensive knowledge of the area and didn't know how the war had changed the borders in the months since I'd last seen Barnham. The last thing I needed to do was unknowingly wander straight to Bruenner, though that'd certainly be convenient for him. The image of my mother being pulled from her horse replayed itself in my mind, fueling my anger towards the monster and eliciting a series of small zaps from the pendant at my chest. I had almost stopped noticing the shocks.

Tomorrow, I thought. I'd make sure I was more than idly present when Niles came for the briefing. I needed to know exactly where our troops were, where Bruenner's troops were, and all the towns between Gillesmere and there. Had it been any other season, I could have lived happily off the land, sheltering in the trees and nearby caves. Winter was an entirely different creature, and, though I might be self-sufficient, I wasn't stupid. I'd likely need to stop frequently for food and supplies.

The next day dawned, bringing the seemingly requisite inch of snow with it. As long as I didn't interact with Quinn for too long during the day—which didn't seem to be a problem these days since he was scarce—I figured I could easily keep my plans secret.

Niles came to the castle early that morning, which could only mean one thing. Bad news. Elle and I were taking our morning meal when he stepped through the doors, chunks of snow still falling from the tips of his boots, a scowl on his face.

"Kelford?" he asked.

"Not certain," I answered. "He usually dines with us, but Falene wasn't well this morning. I believe he's fussing over her."

Niles looked mildly annoyed.

"She's newly with child," I explained, as if it would somehow make a difference.

Surprisingly, it did, and the irritation melted from his features.

"Would you care to join us?" I asked, though Elle's dislike of him emanated in waves from her.

He shook his head. "Thank you, but no. I need to speak with Kelford. And Quinn," he added as an afterthought.

There was an urgency in his voice I did not like.

"Perhaps you'd be more comfortable waiting in the parlor," Elle said.

Though Niles didn't care for her either, he nodded his head and retreated.

"Well, that was interesting," I commented.

"If by interesting you mean typical, then, yes, it was," Elle said.

I gave a dubious smile. "You might relax a little. He's been with me for months now and has yet to show this devious side you seem to think he has just because he's a soldier. If anything, he's been nothing but loyal to me."

"They all are, my dear," she replied. "That is, until they day they're not."

Elle had become almost a surrogate grandmother to me over the course of the weeks I'd spent in Gillesmere. She was the closest thing to a friend I had ever known. I regretted I couldn't tell her about my plans, but there was no doubt in my mind the older woman would probably attempt to come with me if I did.

We finished our meal as the governor entered. Wearily, he plopped into the nearest chair and rubbed his hands over his face, then through his hair, leaving it sticking up wildly in all directions.

"How's Falene?" I asked.

"Tired," he said, looking rather fatigued himself. The morning sickness was more severe than Falene had previously let on.

"Is she sick constantly?"

He nodded. "It appears so. I thought this was only supposed to happen in the mornings! It seems she is sick morning, noon, and night. She grows thin."

"I'll see her this morning," I said. "I have a tincture that might help."

Governor Kelford looked doubtful.

"She's a Healer," Elle added. "Let her heal."

I was grateful for her words. The longer I wore the title of White Sorceress, the more I seemed to lose the only part of myself I knew to be true. I hadn't had much to heal in the weeks since we'd arrived. While I was not happy for Falene's difficulties, I was thrilled to have something useful to do.

"Captain Ingram is waiting for you in the parlor," Elle told him. "Some urgent matter or another."

"He'd like to meet with Quinn, too," I added.

"Where is that man?" Kelford asked, looking around. "I swear, he's like a ghost; appears out of nowhere when you least expect him, and never in one place."

I shrugged my shoulders and fought a smile.

"I'm sure he's been doing a bit of reconnaissance work, himself," Elle said in Quinn's defense, raising her chin defiantly.

If I wasn't mistaken, Elle was taken with Quinn. It was entirely harmless, but sweet in a way I couldn't explain. Elle had a habit of drawing him into conversation, and I heard him talk more in her company than I'd heard him speak—possibly ever. It was positively adorable.

As if on cue, Quinn appeared. His cheeks were slightly reddened, as though he'd been in the cold.

"Ingram here?" he asked of Kelford, giving me only a cursory glance.

"Yes," the governor replied.

"We need to talk," Quinn said.

Kelford nodded. They seemed mildly surprised when I followed them to the parlor.

"Look," I said. "I'm not going to be the supposed saving grace of anything if I don't know what's happening, so expect to keep me informed from this point forward." I surprised even myself with my demands, justified though they might be.

Quinn's eyebrows raised in surprise, but he didn't argue.

Niles had been poring over maps laid out upon the large oak table, one hand flat on either side of the largest map, and he looked up as we entered. A lock of thick, blond hair fell into his eyes. He shook it back with a flip of his head.

"News?" Kelford asked.

"Not good," Niles replied, his mouth forming a grim line. He glanced at me as though unsure whether to continue. "They know her."

Quinn nodded in agreement. Apparently, that was the news he'd gathered that morning as well.

"What do you mean?" I asked, glancing from one to the other.

Niles turned to me, bright eyes turned dark. "They know who you are. Bruenner has a full description, name, and likely location, which, by the way, is wrong. They seem to think we're hiding you in New Tratham."

"Which could be a cover," Quinn commented, "as he sends either an assassin or a troop here."

"Or it could be the misinformation someone from Barnham fed them, right?" Kelford asked hopefully.

Involuntarily, I swallowed.

"We can hardly rule it out, but for the moment we have to assume they know her correct location," Niles said.

"Which means we need to find a new place for you," Quinn said, addressing me. If only I'd slipped away yesterday. It would be twice as hard to escape his notice now.

"Milord," one of the servants stood in the doorway, her dark brows knitted together in worry. "Madam Falene is requesting you. She's very sick again."

Governor Kelford wasted no time. Before another word could be said, he fled from the room.

I glanced at Niles and Quinn. Quinn nodded before I could say a word.

I hurried to my room for my bag before hailing another servant to take me to Falene's rooms.

I reached Falene's side as she finished retching into the pot next to her bed once more. Falene was pale and drawn, but she was far from the worst I had seen in her condition. I was grateful.

She looked up at me, an apology on her lips. "Don't be silly," I told her. "There's nothing to be sorry for. We'll have you fixed up shortly. I promise. It won't be a complete recovery, but you'll feel a whole lot better than you do right now."

"I'm miserable," she said, wiping her nose with a rag. "Had I known a babe would cause so much trouble, I might have tried to talk Milt out of it." She glanced upward at her husband, who anxiously shifted from foot to foot.

I smiled knowingly at her as I pulled the right vials from my bag. "You'll change your mind when you hold your newborn for the first time."

"How can you be so sure?" she asked, pulling matted hair away from her forehead.

"Falene," I said as I sat in the chair beside her. "I've delivered more babes than I can remember, and I stopped counting years ago. There hasn't been a woman yet who didn't forget every single misery she's been through at the very first sight of her little one."

She gave a weak smile.

"Now," I told her. "I'd like you to mix a pinch of this powder into a glass of warm water first thing in the morning, and I mean first thing." I turned to Kelford. "Have a member of the kitchen staff make it up before she's awake so that she can drink it right away."

He assured me that he would.

I addressed Falene again. "You can actually drink this up to three times a day if needed, but the first one is the most important. If you can't tolerate it on an empty stomach, see that you eat toasted bread with it. It must be plain, though. No butter or jams."

Falene nodded earnestly, color beginning to return to her cheeks as we talked.

"These," I said, pulling a jar of crystallized sugar pieces from my bag and handing it to her, "are nothing more than candy, but I've infused them with briarmint. When you feel the first hint of nausea, place one of these on your tongue, and let it dissolve slowly. Breathe deeply."

Falene accepted the jar and placed it on the nightstand beside her, thanking me.

"Lastly, I want you to make sure you eat."

"It's so difficult!" she said. "I find myself starving, but then my innards seem to want to expel my food before I can even swallow!"

I thought for a moment. "When do you eat?" I asked.

Falene looked bewildered by my question. "At the usual times."

I shook my head. "I want you to eat eight or nine times a day."

"But—"

I held up a hand. "Small morsels all throughout the day. Every hour, if necessary. Your stomach won't protest so much if you keep it busy with a little to digest all of the time. Do you get up at night to use the privy?"

She blushed. "Yes, of course."

I looked at Kelford again. "Ask the evening staff to prepare a covered dish of something small—fruit, bread, or something of the like. Have them place it at her bedside before she retires for the night so she can eat when she's up at night."

"I'll make sure it's done."

I reached for Falene's hand and gave it a squeeze. "I know it seems as though this will last forever, but I assure you it won't."

"Thank you so much," she said to me. "I could never thank you enough."

"Have a beautiful, healthy baby and it will be all the thanks I need." I rose to leave. "Oh, one more thing." I reached into my bag for another jar of the gingerene powder. "Just in case."

Falene looked confused. "There's a possibility my location has been revealed," I told her. "If that's the case, Quinn and Niles will likely move me away from here soon." I kept my tone light as though I had not already made up my mind to leave on my own. "I want to make sure you have enough to make it through the pregnancy without me."

"You have to stay," Falene said, "Or at least come back! I want you to deliver the baby."

"I would like nothing more," I said. It was true even if it could never happen. I bent to kiss the top of her head and left the room, pretending to myself the tears in my eyes were from the fireplace smoke.

I was in the midst of packing the necessities when there was a soft knock at my door. Quickly, I tossed the bag and its contents beneath the bed and took a seat in one of the plush armchairs, opening a book on my lap.

"Come in," I called, expecting to see Laurelle.

My heart gave an unexpected flutter when Quinn stepped through the doorway. I wished it would stop doing that each and every time I saw the man. I wasn't sure when exactly that sensation had started, but it was unnerving. Even the talisman hummed happily at his appearance.

"Is something wrong?" I asked. I hadn't been alone with Quinn since the night I'd had my vision.

He shook his head.

"I hope I haven't interrupted," he said.

"You're never an interruption," I replied. "I was just trying to keep up on my herbal knowledge." I held up the book for him to see.

Dark eyebrows rose in obvious disbelief as he glanced from the book to my face.

"Not the most interesting topic, I know—" I began.

"And especially difficult to understand when read upside down, I would imagine," he commented. His gaze shifted around the room.

"Oh…" I said, my voice falling away as I regarded the book, feeling exposed.

"So, what were you really doing?"

"I was searching the stone," I said without hesitation. The lie was smooth to my own ears, and Quinn seemed to believe it as easily as I had told it. I wasn't sure where it had come from or when I'd gotten good at lying.

"Any luck?"

"No," I said, picking up the stone around my neck. Startled, I dropped it again.

"What's wrong?"

"It's…" I pulled the pendant from my neck, staring hard into the deep blue center. "It's warm."

"It's been lying against your skin."

"No, not warm like that," I said, quickly becoming entranced with it. I could swear the cobalt abyss shifted. It seemed as though its green edge had swirled ever so briefly. "Remember Stonehaven? It's almost…my hand tingles."

"May I?"

"Of course," I said. I looked up at him, hearing a tiny snap in my ears as I did. When I glanced back at the talisman again, it seemed as though the stone was as it had always been. "Did you hear that?"

Quinn shook his head. "What did it sound like?"

"A pop."

"The fire?" he asked with a shrug, holding the talisman close as he examined it.

I felt silly. "Could be, I suppose." In awe, I watched him as he seemed not to be bothered by the shocks he was surely receiving. Finally, burning with curiosity, I asked, "Doesn't it hurt?"

He shrugged as he finished examining the pendant and handed it back to me. "You can get used to anything if you train yourself," he answered.

I raised an eyebrow. "And you've been training against

electric shocks?"

He gave a small smile that failed to touch his eyes. "You never can tell, can you?"

I could only shake my head. Either Quinn was weirder than I thought, or he was messing with my head. Accepting the pendant, I draped it around my neck and tucked it into the neckline of my amber-hued gown once more where it continued to hum happily to itself.

"Well?" I asked.

"There was a heat to it, yes."

"You felt it, too."

"But it faded quickly. It could be nothing more than warmth from your body."

"It wasn't." I'd been wearing it for months, and it was the first time I'd felt such a thing.

Quinn didn't argue. Instead, he ran a hand over his stubble. It was only midday, and he was already shadowed.

"Reina," he began, "I don't want to waste any time. We want to move tomorrow morning."

I nodded. I expected he would want to move right away.

"We can't risk keeping you here at this point. If Bruenner knows who you are, there's no reason to think he doesn't know *where* you are."

"Where will we go?" I asked.

"We're still discussing what's safest. Niles wants to head north, but I think that's foolish with the weather being what it is. It's farther from Bruenner's camps, but it's also running away. At some point, we won't have anywhere left to run. I'd rather make a stand on our terms, not because we've run out of places to go and we're forced to."

An anxiety rose deep in my belly. Quinn had used the term *we*, but I knew better. There was no *we*. Ultimately, I stood alone in this. The reality of the situation closed in quickly.

All too tangible, the enormity of it swelled before me. Somehow, I was to find a way to save the entire kingdom, and yet I didn't know where I would wake up tomorrow morning. I had accomplished absolutely nothing with this ridiculous talisman that supposedly contained untold phenomenal power when, in fact, I had seen little evidence of anything at all.

But then, I still didn't *really* believe in magic, which made it all that much more difficult to believe in the entire prophecy, regardless of what everyone else thought.

Quinn stepped closer. "We'll take care of you, Reina. *I'll* take care of you."

I nearly cried at the words. I wanted nothing more than to agree to let someone take care of me, but I'd already made up my mind. Images of Quinn covered in blood the day we'd traveled the pass flashed before my eyes. It could very well have been his blood. I could not let harm come to anyone else because of me.

And if I was ever going to discover what the talisman could reveal, I would need to be alone to find out. I hadn't tried to use my vision since coming to Gillesmere. I hadn't wanted to alarm anyone with knowledge I shouldn't have. To be honest with myself, maybe I was just frightened of what I might learn. But the time had come.

"Thank you," I finally choked.

Quinn studied my face, his dark eyes focused intently upon me, and a heated flush crept up my neck. Unconsciously, I reached to touch the scar to the right of his eye, where the arrow had grazed it. My fingertips had barely traced it when Quinn clamped a hand tightly around my wrist, slowly lowering it from his face.

"It healed well," I said absently. What the Saints was wrong with my voice?

Quinn's hand was still locked around my wrist, his jaw clenched, that same unreadable expression in his eyes again, and my breath quickened.

Slowly, deliberately, Quinn released my arm. With a step back, he took a deep breath, turned, and left the room and me standing bewildered in it.

I'd overstepped my bounds. Quinn did not like to be touched. I knew it. I'd seen it before in him, and yet I was so used to touching to heal that I never thought twice about reaching out to him.

Determined to focus on anything but my confusion, I made for the bed and the sack I'd thrown beneath it. I smoothed my skirts and took a deep calming breath. Now more than ever it was important that I leave as soon as possible. Quinn would be furious when he discovered me missing in the morning, and the sooner I set out, the more ground I could cover. If I was lucky, the morning snow would cover my tracks, and I would be untraceable.

Suddenly, the door burst open behind me. I swirled around, nerves frayed. But Quinn stood in the doorway. In three quick strides, he covered the length of the room and stood before me once more, his dark eyes searching mine for something unknown.

Puzzled, alarmed, I frowned as I looked up at him. "Was

there something else?" I asked, my heart hammering in my chest.

He hesitated only a moment and before I realized what was happening, his hands cupped my head and his lips were upon mine. His grip was firm, fingers wound tightly in my hair, calloused thumbs upon my cheek. I could not have pulled away had I wanted to.

And I did not want to.

My breath left me as he kissed me long and full. All thoughts fled my head, and I pressed into him, kissing him every bit as solidly in return. I breathed in his scent, clean and masculine, familiar and yet foreign just the same. The talisman roared to life between our bodies, burning with a heat like I'd never known.

I had been kissed twice in my life, but not by Quinn and *never* like this. My blood boiled. There was a humming in my ears, a music as I had never heard before, like birds before the sunrise.

Then, with no warning at all, he pulled away, quickly stepping back. His breath came as heavily as my own. I stared at him, speechless.

"Forgive me," he said, and before I could answer, before I could tell him there was nothing to forgive, he was gone, leaving my pounding heart and swollen lips as the only proof he'd been there at all.

CHAPTER FOURTEEN

Alone With Company

I stood in the stable, pondering whether or not to saddle Aeros. By horseback, I could make ground faster, but by foot, I was more easily hidden should the need arise.

And I didn't need to worry about starving poor Aeros half to death if I left the mare in Kelford's stables. I had every confidence she would be well cared for.

She whickered softly as I stroked her velvety nose.

The sudden feel of Quinn's lips.

I squeezed my eyes shut against the memory.

His thumb stroking my cheek, his scent lingering on my skin long after he'd gone.

I could still smell him. Worse? I wanted to. I could no longer tell if the spectral scent was real or imagined, but it made my head swim.

Swallowing, I forced the thoughts away. Such thoughts were dangerous.

And yet, no matter how hard I tried, I didn't seem to be able to rid myself of the memory entirely. It continued to hover annoyingly at the edges of my conscience. What had happened? What had changed?

With a huff, I made a decision. As much as I hated the thought, I would leave Aeros behind.

I planted a kiss on the horse's warm nose, registering the pleasant smell of alfalfa on her breath. The mare nuzzled into me, looking for a treat, no doubt.

"Be good," I told her. "I'll come back for you."

With that, I pulled my cloak around me, fixed the bag upon my back, and set out. I slipped from the castle grounds easily enough. I tucked the length of my hair beneath the hood of my cloak, and was once again dressed in a tunic, trousers, and boots. No one paid any attention to a stable boy.

I wasn't far from the castle when Aeros yelled for me.

I'll care for you and you'll care for me.

I hadn't said it to her. I'd left her behind.

Sorry, girl, not this time.

I quickened my pace as I traveled the road. I trusted Quinn's instincts. If he didn't want to go north, then neither did I. Plus, the southern terrain provided a line of caves and protective mountainside that might offer some shelter from the weather.

The thought of Quinn produced an odd sensation in the pit of my stomach. Curiously, my eyes felt hot.

I gritted my teeth and continued to place one foot in front of the other. I needed to make distance—as much distance as possible. I had left the table early after the evening meal, feigning a severe eye-headache. I now had only an hour or so before dark. I aimed to make it into the surrounding countryside before then.

I tugged the hood farther down on my head and kept my eyes downcast as a cart rolled by on the road beside me. The driver's gaze fixed on me, and I fervently hoped he wouldn't stop. I only passed as a boy from afar. Up close, I stood no chance. My heart thumped even as my luck held.

Darkness fell just after I left Gillesmere's gates. Slipping out hadn't proven difficult, though I wouldn't have wanted to be seeking entrance. The guards were questioning everyone on the legitimacy of their business. Undoubtedly, Kelford had given them explicit instructions to follow in order to ensure my safety. Guilt tugged at my heart. Quinn, Niles, Kelford, Laurelle, all of them—would stop at nothing to keep me safe. And yet that was exactly why I couldn't continue to hide. I couldn't keep endangering everyone around me. To do so would be selfish. Cowardly.

I followed the road after dark, my breath condensing in the still night air. Andra was near full and partially risen. It provided enough light for me to place my feet without fear of stumbling in the occasional wagon wheel or hoof divot.

When the mountains rose to my right, I allowed myself to stray from the road. Thus far, I'd remained warm enough despite the cold. My cloak and boots were lined with the warmest fleece from Langley sheep, courtesy of Elle, who'd gone out of her way to have clothing made for me during my stay. Regrettably, I'd had to leave the many beautiful gowns behind. As lovely as they were, my journey demanded practicality and there was a high probability that I'd never get the chance to wear such nonsensical, but beautiful, clothing again.

Andra was high in the sky and Stellon had risen above the treetops when I found a cave suitable to spend the night. I gathered enough wood to last through the night, then started a fire with the help of a small sprinkle of the *sulfuria* I'd pulled from a jar in my bag. Far from the road and tucked into the cave as I was, I had no fear of being discovered should anyone be about at this time of night.

Within minutes, the space was cozy, a slight draft from deeper within the caves serving to push the smoke from the mouth of the cave. I laid out my bedroll and sat upon it, pulling my cloak over me.

My stomach growled. I ignored it.

There would be time to eat in the morning, and I had to be sparing with the food. I had pilfered a decent amount from the kitchen, hoping Kelford and Falene would forgive me, but I was reluctant to break into it too early.

Pulling out the talisman, I held it in my hand and gazed deeply into its depths. It appeared more green than blue tonight, though perhaps that was a trick of the firelight. I couldn't really tell. It seemed to change appearance every time I looked at it.

Closing my eyes, I inhaled deeply. If I was honest with myself, the reason I had not attempted to use my vision was plain and simple. I was fearful of what I might learn. I didn't *want* to be the kingdom's only chance. I didn't *want* that responsibility.

I cleared my mind, opened my eyes, and let them focus on the smooth stone wall opposite me. I sat like that for many breaths, slowly letting go of all thought, pushing it all away, no matter how difficult.

Finally, a familiar tingling began in my toes. As the warmth made its way upward through my body, I trembled ever so slightly, unsure that I really wanted to *see* at all.

And then it was too late.

Bruenner's troops were widespread. There were numerous

camps, mostly to the south. Bruenner held control over everything east of the Black Mountains and was slowly extending his reach south and westward. A light, but ominous presence pulsed to the south—Bruenner.

Slowly, I turned my attention to the stone.

What's your secret? Tell me what to do.

Frustratingly, there was no response. Why had I thought there would be? Adamant, I focused harder.

How? How do I make it happen? How do I do what you need me to do?

Nothing.

I let out a howl of frustration, ripped the talisman from my neck, and tossed it into the dirt beside me.

Throwing my head into my hands, I dug my palms into my eyes. Why was this so difficult?

"What do you want me to do?" I yelled at it, throwing my hands in the air. "I don't understand!"

Giving a frustrated sigh, I gave up. I had somehow assumed things would be different once I was alone, that the talisman would respond to me when I used my vision. Now—another failed attempt and I was at a loss for what to do.

Against my will, my mind slowly wandered to Quinn. Normally, I wouldn't put it past him to discover I was already gone, but given our earlier interlude, I didn't think he would be quick to see me alone again. Like the rest of my company at Gillesmere, he would discover my absence in the morning.

My thoughts began to steal toward memories of earlier that afternoon, and a warmth grew in my belly. In my wildest dreams, I hadn't imagined Quinn had such feelings for me. He'd said things to imply as much here and there, but I'd always thought he was simply being nice.

Stupid girl!

When had Quinn ever simply been nice to anyone? That wasn't to say Quinn was terribly mean, but indifference seemed to be his normal state. Quiet, aloof. At least with others.

He'd never been that way with me. The explanation now was plain to see. How had I ever missed it?

I didn't know what to think. Of all the people I'd known in my life, Quinn was probably the closest friend I'd had growing up. I'd known him since I could remember. Since the beginning of this journey, he had become something more, but I couldn't define exactly how or why.

I needed to think. I needed to sort out emotion from logic.

When I remembered his kiss…*Saints, that kiss.*

I was lightheaded all over again. If I let myself imagine for even a moment, I swore I could feel it again. The pressure of his hands on my face, his mouth against mine, his scent.

I gasped. The pendant had begun to glow a pulsing cobalt. I snatched it from the ground and held it close, brushing the dirt from its surface.

"What?" I whispered. "What do you need from me?"

There was no response, though it wasn't as if I'd expected the stone to speak to me.

Clenching the pendant in my fist, I closed my eyes and cleared my mind, attempting to access my vision again.

I was rewarded with an instant scene of Bruenner's camp as I'd previously viewed it, but I couldn't detect anything different about my vision with the talisman in hand. Maybe I could make something happen from afar? And if so, what?

I viewed men—soldiers—gathered around a campfire, laughing at a vulgar joke one had told. There on the ground, next to one of the soldiers, was a tin cup with liquid inside. I focused in on it and attempted to knock it over using every ounce of concentration I possessed.

Nothing happened.

I tried again and was met with the same frustrating response.

Finally, I pulled away from the scene, drawing back until I had completely returned awareness to the cave.

I looked down at the talisman and realized it was no longer glowing. I frowned. Why had it stopped? Then again, why had it started? At least it confirmed that I had done the right thing, even if I had no idea what that actually was.

When I awoke, dawn was breaking and the fire was but embers. I fought the urge to stir it back to life, knowing I wouldn't long be staying.

I ate and drank quickly, all too acutely aware of the miles I need to put between me and Gillesmere, lest the others decide to follow when they realized I was no longer in my room. Tying my hair back into a fresh braid, I packed my belongings, and tucked the talisman into the neck of my tunic. I scattered the remnants of the fire with my boot, adjusted my pack, and was on my way.

The next two days were very much the same. I kept a good pace, fast enough to keep warm, but slow enough to keep from perspiring. Though I had veered off the main road several nights before, I soon found myself running alongside a smaller, less used path and, for ease of travel, decided to follow it. The morning snow had begun to melt. In another day or two, I'd be completely out of the snow's reach.

I had followed the smaller road most of the day, stopping only to drink and eat a light meal, when the sound of hooves came from around the bend ahead. My heart thudded as I glanced to thick evergreen shrubs over my shoulder. I hesitated only a moment too long.

Two horses and riders came into view, and as I had spotted them, so they also spotted me. I made the best of it, pulling my hood down low and arranging the neck of the tunic so it fell across the bottom half of my face. I adjusted my stride and tromped onward as any man would.

As they approached, they spoke in low tones to each other, though they ceased talking as they grew closer. I risked a quick glimpse of them and then wished I hadn't.

Two more unsavory characters I could not have hoped to avoid. Neither looked as though he had bathed or shaved in a week or more. Unkempt beards, missing teeth, a long scar across a cheek, and a filthily bandaged hand on one were all I caught, and I didn't risk looking longer.

"Ho, there," one called to me as I trod past.

"Aye," I said as gruffly as possible as I continued walking.

What happened next was everything I desperately hoped wouldn't. The sound of hooves ceased and the uncomfortable weight of their eyes upon me was nearly crippling as I made my way onward.

"Eh, boy, where're you headed? Nothin' tha way for miles," the one closer to me called as I kept walking.

I shrugged my shoulders, keeping my back to them.

"Hey, I'm talkin' to you!"

I continued to walk.

"Girl," the other one said in a voice hardly more than a hoarse whisper.

I stole a glance from the corner of my eye. A lock of my hair had escaped from my hood, trailing defiantly behind me in the breeze. There was a moment of silence before the first man mumbled in return to his companion.

I sensed rather than saw him dismount and had only seconds to act. Hoping to gain distance, I broke into a run. Though I had a pack, I was lighter and faster than he was, and I prayed it was enough.

I glanced over my shoulder in time to see his shocked face as he turned to his companion who motioned with annoyance for him to pursue.

I wasted no time. Dashing into the first opening within the dense brush, I kept running, twigs tearing at my face, scratching my skin in a dozen places. The cold numbed the welts and I didn't slow down even when a low-hanging branch nearly took out my left eye.

He entered the wood behind me and I ran blindly, praying to the Saints above that I didn't misstep. At this point, I had only two choices—outrun him or drop beneath the thick brush and hope he couldn't find me.

It was doubtful I could outrun him over any distance. He was easily twice my size, and it wouldn't take him long to close the gap between us.

That left me with only one option, and I wasn't sure I could make it happen. A new wave of fear surged through my body. I dodged to the left and ran. My pursuer was following slower now as the evergreen brush and winter-dried featherfern became thicker. He cursed as bare branches from larger shrubs lashed at his face.

I dodged back to the right. Before he realized I had changed direction, I dropped to the ground and pressed myself into the frozen carpet of leaves, beneath the fern and evergreen, my heart pounding loudly within my ears, the talisman pulsing wildly at my chest. I ignored the pain.

Reaching into my boot, I unsheathed the only weapon I had brought, a dagger no longer than the length of my hand. I held it in front of me and stilled.

Waiting.

Praying.

He slowed, then stopped, clumsy footsteps falling as he circled, trying to determine where I had gone.

My breath came in shallow spurts, condensing in the cold air. It took every ounce of willpower to slow my breathing. I waited for him to lose interest, go away, but he was more persistent than I had given him credit for.

The other rider called from afar.

The ogre called back, "Nah. Lost 'er. She's here som'ere." Then, lower, he spoke words meant for me, "Come on, pretty. I'll help keep you safe." He laughed, an edgy rumble in his chest.

Footsteps fell closer.

There was a call from the road again, a summons for the ogre to return to the road.

"Hold yer horses!" he yelled back. "I'm jes lookin'."

A boot appeared inches from my face, only a thick spray of featherfern between us. I tightened my grip on the knife. I would go for his heel if I needed to. A slice to the tendon wouldn't be fatal, but he'd likely never walk again without the help of a crutch. *Could* I cut through the boot leather with my meager blade?

Another shout from afar.

"Yah, all right! Fine," he answered. As he tromped away, he muttered, "Jes wanted to have a bit a excitement is all. Been too long since the last piece. Dressin' like a boy. You'da been a fun one, girlie."

I couldn't guess how long I remained flattened to the ground. My fingers and toes had grown numb with cold and my very core had been chilled by the time I finally moved. At first, I didn't dare do more than breathe until I was certain the ogre and his friend had moved on. Even then, a residual wave of fear kept me paralyzed, unable to bring myself to move onwards.

Steeling my resolve, I gritted my teeth and rose. I dusted the dirt and pine needles from my front and hesitantly began moving southward once more.

This time, I stayed off the road.

It would soon be dark, but I was reluctant to stay anywhere close to the vicinity I had seen the riders, so I pushed forward through the woods, hoping to find a place to spend the night well away from anyone or anything.

An hour later, I still hadn't found any suitable caves for spending the night. In fact, I had found no caves at all. The terrain here was slightly less mountainous than that closer to Gillesmere.

Finally, I located a rock outcropping with enough of an overhang to provide at least some shelter from the elements. I had made it far enough south that I hadn't seen snow that morning, but I didn't know if I would be so lucky again. I assessed the large rock. As I had no other choice, it would have to do.

I trekked back into the brush and began pulling dried featherfern from the ground. In the summer, featherfern grew lush and pink, its willowy fronds as soft as their name implied. Now, though, they were dried and brown, and would make for a scratchy bed, but without a fire, I needed anything that would help me conserve body heat tonight.

Returning to the rock outcropping, I laid the fern thickly on the ground. I took off my cloak and draped it over the rock, allowing it to hang so it provided at least some shelter from the wind, then secured it with several smaller rocks.

Without my cloak, the frigid air bit through my tunic quickly. I climbed into my tiny shelter, pulled my pack towards me, and concocted an *Andral essence* lantern. I'd been contemplating the idea all afternoon. It was my hair that had identified me as a girl earlier in the day and another incident like that might well end with me raped, injured, or dead. I had no desire to be any of those things. Holding the shears I pulled from my pack, I inhaled slowly through tight lips.

"I'm so sorry," I breathed to the spirit of my mother. "I promise I will grow it again."

With that, I began snipping. I was surprised at how cutting the thick mass affected me. I'd never attributed much importance to my physical appearance, but I was saddened to see the growing pile of hair on the floor of my makeshift shelter.

When finished, I pushed the cuttings into the slant of the overhang, where the rock submerged into the ground. I ran my fingers through my hair, surprised at how quickly they met empty air, though I had only cut to shoulder length. Many men wore their hair long and if anyone were close enough to see my hair now, then my gender would already be known as nothing about my face or body could pass for a man.

Reaching for my bag once more and using my vision to assist, I pulled out a tiny jar of black oak gall dye. I didn't relish the thought of dying my hair, but the white streak that ran the length of it might as well have been a trumpeting fanfare no matter where I traveled, especially since they knew who I was. I would be better able to go unnoticed without it. Reluctantly, I worked the dye into the strands, further erasing the most noticeable traits about Moreina di Bianco. When finished, I wiped my hands on a rag from my sack and replaced the jar of dye.

I shivered involuntarily, surprised at how exposed my back suddenly seemed without the extra protection of the thick hair that once covered it. Without removing my boots, I slipped into my bedroll. It would be a long night without a fire.

Since I was reluctant to go to bed without at least attempting to search the stone again and, given the events of the day, wasn't feeling remotely sleepy anyway, I held the stone in my hands and slowed my breathing.

I had made slight progress with the stone over the last couple of days, managing to entice it to glow each time I worked with it, but I'd noticed something strange the night before. I hadn't yet determined whether it was the result of working with the talisman or whether I simply hadn't noticed it before.

When I'd first started using my vision with the talisman, I had focused on accessing Bruenner's camp and attempting to manipulate the environment. I had not succeeded either time.

The last time, I had tried to breathe life into a dying campfire, something that wouldn't necessarily be noticed by anyone, but something I might be able to visually observe. I focused intently on the flickering flames, willing them to grow in size.

Grow. Grow! I had commanded silently to no avail.

Finally giving up, I pulled away, ending my meditation, escaping my vision. And when I slowly became aware of my surroundings, I leaned back...and placed my hand directly into a patch of grass. I was sure I had previously seen only dirt and rock, but there was instead a small tuft of newly emerged and vibrantly green grass.

I examined it closely, brushing it lightly with my fingertips, feeling the blades spring back beneath the pressure of my hand. I hadn't noticed it before I'd searched the stone, but its presence was undeniable. I couldn't imagine how it had grown in the midst of winter.

Perhaps I'd *done* something with the talisman after all.

Tonight, I focused on that result. Instead of using my vision to access Bruenner's camp, I'd remain wholly in my own location and attempt to make a change here. If I were lucky, maybe I'd discover something more.

Taking a deep breath, I focused on making the talisman glow again. Clearing my mind, I took the talisman in my hands and concentrated.

But nothing happened. I frowned at it. Why was it that I had been able to get it to glow three nights in a row, but not now? As if answering my question, it zapped my fingers.

I tried everything I could imagine but was met with disappointment time and again. Weary, frustrated, I tucked it back into my tunic, ignored its obnoxious buzz, and attempted to close my eyes. An hour passed, maybe more. Sleep was difficult as I was cold and unable to stop my teeth from chattering.

So I was already awake when I became aware of a rustling outside of my provisional tent. I threw my sack over the *Andral* lantern to douse what remained of the dim light and grabbed my dagger, gripping it fiercely.

Through my cloak curtain, I saw a torch slowly approaching. Whoever it was had spotted my shelter as they headed straight for it—and for me.

It was the second time today I questioned the wisdom of my decision to journey on my own.

CHAPTER FIFTEEN

Old Friends and New Enemies

The shadow stopped directly outside and thrust the torch into the frozen ground with force. My trembling was not from the cold now. Silently I waited, ready to surprise the invader with more than he had bargained for, praying that I would be able to.

I held my breath. The man reached to pull the cloak aside.

I lunged.

I pulled back only a split second before it was too late and rolled myself sideways to keep from stabbing Niles. He gave a surprised yell and lurched backwards as I changed direction and fell into a pile of leaves.

"Blast it, Moreina!" he said at the same time I began apologizing profusely.

"What are you doing here?" I exclaimed.

"Trying to find *you*," he said, dragging himself from the dirt and offering me a hand.

I took it gratefully and allowed him to help me to my feet.

"You're freezing!"

"Well I didn't exactly want to be found, so I thought it best not to light a fire."

"In these temperatures? Are you out of your mind? You'll

freeze to death and then we'll all have no hope."

Firelight from the torch flickered on his face, illuminating a scowl and eyes dark with anger. Gently, he took both of my hands in his and rubbed them. He put them to his mouth and blew, his hot breath both painful and a relief on my skin at once.

"How did you find me?" I asked.

"As soon as we realized you were gone, I knew I had to find you. I started tracking you right away." He blew into my hands again. "Come," he said, "we need to get a fire started. Sit here while I get some wood. Won't take long."

He quickly gathered enough wood and lit it with a touch of his torch, the flames radiating their warmth. Though I was still uneasy with a fire in the open, Niles was a far more skilled fighter than I could ever hope to be, and I needn't worry any longer about facing the type of character I'd met on the road earlier that day.

I sat as near as I could without scorching my clothes, drinking in the warmth. It was good to have fire.

"*Fiermi*! What have you done to your hair, Moreina?" Niles exclaimed as he took in my appearance.

Instinctively, my hands flew to my shoulder-length locks. "I wanted to disguise myself," I told him. "My hair makes me recognizable to anyone who would know me, so I changed that." I almost dared him to contest my reasoning.

Instead, still wide-eyed and incredulous, he replied, "I suppose it will grow back."

"Thanks for the compliment. Where are the rest of your men?" I asked, eager to change the subject.

Niles pulled biscuits and a sack of dried fruit from his pack and offered them to me. I accepted gratefully. My own supplies had begun to run low and I had eaten little, trying to conserve as much as possible.

"I ordered them to stay behind. They would have slowed me down and I needed to be able to track quickly and well. I do best when I'm alone."

"I know the feeling," I said, giving a weak smile.

Niles pursed his lips. "What *were* you thinking?" he asked.

I shrugged. "My very presence endangered everyone, Niles. Kelford, Falene, Madam Bonverno, you, Quinn…" There was a funny catch in my throat. Nonchalantly, I added, "Frankly, I'm surprised Quinn let you come without him." I ignored the butterflies in my stomach, the ones that stretched their wings at the mention of Quinn's name.

"Yes, well, D'Arturio had other errands to tend to, I suppose," he replied, capturing my full attention.

I hid my confusion poorly.

"I guess he thought your absence was as good a time as ever to run back home. I'm sure his father will be relieved."

"He went home?" I asked, the words like a knife to my gut.

"Said something about having to let his father know of the situation. I'm sure he had his reasons. I don't claim to understand him." Niles waved a dismissive hand.

If I had been pressed to reveal who I believed would attempt to track me down, Quinn would have been my first guess. And yet, here I sat with Niles while Quinn made his way back to Barnham.

A wave of jealousy—or maybe it was anger—surged in my breast. How nice it would be to go back to Barnham and pretend all of this had never happened, that my little protected world could continue while the rest of the kingdom waged war around us.

Quinn might have told Niles he needed to inform his father of the *situation*, but I knew better. I was a fool. What must he have thought after I'd left? Had he believed *he* was the reason? Was he now so ashamed he could no longer bear the thought of facing me? And, if he truly felt something for me, why let me slip away?

Anger, guilt, and bitterness swept through me in a whirlwind so violent I didn't have time to discern whether I was furious with Quinn or finally coming to terms with the fact that I had fallen in love with him. I almost laughed at the absurdity. I had known him all my life and had never known my own feelings, and now he was gone, well, it seemed to be so clear.

"Where were you going?" Niles asked, interrupting my personal revelation.

"Nowhere, exactly," I answered softly. "I just knew I needed to be far away from where I was a danger to everyone."

"Are you aware you're traveling directly into Bruenner's path?"

"I'm not as brainless as you think," I replied. "Of course I know I'm headed that direction. I checked all the maps, and you and Kelford had the boundaries clearly marked."

"I didn't say you were brainless, but what exactly did you plan to do when you reached him?"

"I didn't intend to reach him," I told him, rubbing my temples. "Look, I didn't have everything planned out the way you think. I just needed to learn how to make this talisman do what it's supposed to do, and I thought it would probably be useful if I was close enough to Bruenner to strike once I figured it all out." Saying Bruenner's name sent chills down my spine. He would pay. For my mother, for Selena, for Ramus, and for every soul he'd wronged. I swore it.

"Have you discovered how to make it work?"

I chewed my bottom lip as I contemplated whether or not to tell Niles what I had discovered. He still didn't know about my vision and I didn't intend to tell him.

"I've managed to wake it," I said. "But, I'm not sure how to make it actually *do* anything."

"Intriguing." He rubbed the back of his neck with a hand as he thought. "Do you have any idea how it should work?"

"I think I might know, but I haven't been able to verify it yet," I told him. "It requires complete concentration, and I suppose I haven't had much of that since this afternoon."

Niles looked puzzled.

Somewhat reluctantly, I relayed to him my earlier encounter with the men I'd met on the road.

He looked visibly shaken when I was done. "Blast it, Moreina. You could have been killed. You could have been... you could have been..."

I nodded and drew a shaky breath. "I know."

He kneeled before me and clasped my hands in his again. "Please tell me—reassure me—that you will not leave on your own again. Allow me to escort you. If you need to be alone to do whatever you do with the talisman, I'll disappear. I'll gather wood. I'll get water. I'll stand guard a hundred paces away, but please do not leave again. I beg you. Let me be the guard I was meant to be for you."

His pleading eyes drew me in, threatened to drown me in emotion, as he made his argument.

"Why do you care so much?" I asked him.

"I...I just feel it. Haven't you ever known that there was something you were *meant* to do? That's how I feel when I think of you. I need to protect you, Moreina. For me. If we lose you..." His voice fell away.

I swallowed. Slowly, I nodded. "All right," I said. "You may be my guard."

I hated myself. Even as I said it, a little voice inside my head chimed in, wishing it had been Quinn who offered to escort me, Quinn who found me, Quinn who wanted to protect me. I blinked back tears of frustration. Quinn was gone. *I* had left, it was true. But he hadn't cared enough to follow. Why should I want someone who hadn't cared enough to follow?

I looked up at Niles. His sincerity was not lost on me. Here was someone who was truly concerned about my existence, while Quinn...

"Then as your guard, I have one request," Niles said.

I raised an eyebrow. "I'm not sure you're allowed requests in your position."

"Sleep," he continued, ignoring me. "There are circles beneath your eyes that even the generosity of the firelight cannot mask."

I almost cried at the thought of sleep, but it was difficult to leave the fire for the cold ground beneath the overhang. I glanced at it. My cloak still lay in a heap on the ground where Niles had pulled it after I had surprised him with a near-knifing.

Niles followed my glance.

"I will sleep aside you," he said.

Alarmed, my eyes met his.

"You need heat," he said, his gaze serious. "So do I. My body may not be as warm as the heat from the fire, but we'll both get through the night if we stay together. Tomorrow, we'll find a better shelter, or build one if necessary. We need to stay out of the weather and still be able to have a fire nearby."

I had never spent the night close to *anyone*, save perhaps my own mother, and certainly not a man. I didn't know if I would be able to sleep. And yet, the very thought of crawling back into my bedroll on the cold ground made me shiver. Reluctantly, I agreed.

He picked up my cloak and shook it, then fastened it around my shoulders. I looked at him questioningly.

"But we'll need something to block the wind."

He removed his own cloak and draped it over the top of the ledge, arranging and wedging it between stones to keep it in place. He held back the corner and gestured to the opening he'd created.

I didn't hesitate. I climbed in, Niles following close behind me. I tried to push myself as near to the rock as I could, but once there, the penetrating cold forced me to retreat into Niles, my back against his chest.

He *was* warm.

He jumped suddenly, hissing through clenched teeth, as if burned and I realized the talisman had shifted and dropped to his arm.

"Sorry!" I said, shifting to remove the talisman from around my neck and wedging it against the rock where he would be safe from its wrath.

Readjusting again, I pushed my back into Niles for warmth, forgetting any inhibition I'd ever been taught to have. I practically burrowed into him. Niles wrapped his arms around me beneath the blanket, holding me tight, rubbing the sides of my arms to generate additional warmth.

"Relax," he said. "You're safe."

My eyelids fluttered open, a dull, pre-dawn light illuminating the gray rock wall in front of me. I was pressed tightly into Niles, his arm resting lightly on my hip. The intimacy of such contact should have had me blushing, but I was too appreciative of the warmth to care.

I lay unmoving for a while, unwilling to wake Niles despite the fact that a small rock had become wedged beneath my hip at some point during the night.

He had been right last night. I needed the sleep. I marveled at how much better I felt—rock in hip aside—after having gotten a decent night's sleep.

Niles sighed deeply and nuzzled his face into my neck. Almost against my will, I registered the comfort of his presence. He smelled good. After days on the road and nights spent on the ground, the only sign he'd not had the comforts of home recently was a slightly masculine musk that was not unpleasant.

Eventually, a numb leg forced me to move. It was then that I noticed the talisman glowing from its place in the dirt. I frowned at it. I hadn't even been trying to work the stone. What had encouraged it to glow? What had changed?

I contemplated the obvious. Niles? Had his presence impacted the talisman's activity? It would explain why I hadn't gotten the talisman to respond to me while in Gillesmere. I had hardly seen Niles at all with Elle having had such an instantaneous dislike of him. But as quickly as it started the glow faded away, leaving me thoroughly puzzled.

Shortly after, Niles awoke. Seemingly embarrassed about the placement of his hand, he pulled it from my hip, mumbling his apologies. I waited until he'd gotten up and left the makeshift shelter before rolling over and stretching.

We set out soon after eating and walked most of the day before we found a large cavern—much bigger than the ones I'd previously stayed in. It would keep us out of the weather and allow for a bonfire had we wanted one. The only disadvantage was that it had a narrow entrance and descended below ground level, but staying out of the cold and being able to have a fire was well worth the discomfort of a little claustrophobia. Within a few moments, Niles had a blazing fire started and I stood close, allowing the heat to warm my frigid hands.

"I'm going to see what I can catch us for dinner," he said, slinging his bow over his back.

"But, I—"

Before I could argue, he was gone. *Let him.* With any luck, he wouldn't catch anything. I would survive fine on bread, nuts, and cheese. At least until we could stop at the next village.

I took the opportunity to pull out the talisman.

Several deep breaths later, the stone was glowing, I had

accessed my vision and was concentrating on the life that surely stirred somewhere within the cave. I willed it to grow, to bloom, to sprout however it might. I lost track of all time, and it began to feel as if I'd closed my eyes eons ago. My vision felt off. I could see, even with my eyes closed, but everything around me was a shade of cobalt and a hair out of focus, as though I'd had one pine ale too many.

Grow! Spring forth! I commanded, feeling ridiculous as I spoke the words in my mind.

I could feel a change even if I could not fully see it. When I opened my eyes, I was rewarded with an overwhelming sense of accomplishment. I stood, eyes wide, turning circles as I gazed at the wonder that had grown around me, in the dark cavern which should not have provided such bounty.

Mushrooms—hearty black morels, horned trumpets, bright yellow chanterelles, and delicate truffles—had sprouted throughout the length of the cave floor. I grew breathless with excitement, a smile wide on my face. I had never seen so many mushrooms.

Life.

That was what the talisman brought forth. Life.

I was so thrilled with my discovery that the fact that I couldn't begin to imagine how such a power could help me bring down an entire army was only a mildly annoying afterthought. I shook my head, pushing it aside. I'd worry about that later.

For now, I collected the mushrooms as swiftly as possible. It wouldn't do to have Niles come back to the cave in this state. I had no way to explain the change and was not ready to share in my discovery—not until I could figure out a way to turn this skill to my advantage anyway.

I plucked the last mushroom from the dirt and added it to the pile, still in awe of the life I had managed to create. I set a small pot of water to boil on the fire and had just begun adding the mushrooms to it when Niles returned empty-handed. I breathed a small sigh of relief that there were no dead animals to add to my mushroom stew.

His eyes widened in surprise at the pot and its contents. "Where did all of this come from?"

"This feast, good sir," I said with a smile, "is courtesy of yours truly."

"I thought you'd work with the talisman while I was away."

"I tried, but I was hungry," I lied, surprised at how easy it had become to do. "So, I decided to see what I could find in case the hunt didn't fare so well."

"Where did you find all of this?" he asked, gesturing to the large pile. I could only imagine how strange it looked. "It's so cold out! I wouldn't think anything could grow. Even fungus."

"There were whole piles of mushrooms deeper back in the cave. In the dark," I said before adding, "And some by fallen logs outside, round the other side of the rocks. There were mushrooms there, too." I was glad when he didn't attempt to check my story.

His eyes grew anxious. "I wish you wouldn't go exploring alone. It worries me, Moreina. What if something had happened?"

"I'm all right," I reassured him. "There's no one around, perhaps for miles." I gestured to the space around us. He didn't look convinced, so I continued with a fluff of my shortened hair, "Besides, no one would recognize me now for certain! I'm just a peasant boy, remember?"

Niles gave a hearty laugh. It was a warm sound, a sound reminiscent of normalcy. "You could never pass for a peasant boy, Moreina."

I furrowed my brow and frowned at him, feigning insult. "Are you insinuating I've done a lousy job with my guise?"

He grasped my hand in his and stepped close. My heart skipped a beat as the smile dropped from his face. The heat from his body radiated against my own, and my breath quickened involuntarily. "Trousers or not, there's nothing about you that could ever be confused with a man." His voice had grown husky as he slowly delivered his words. Looking into his eyes, alarm bells began to ring in my head, warning voices telling me that I was approaching a dangerous emotional abyss. And yet, I wasn't sure I wanted to back away.

Niles cleared his throat, released my hands, and added, "Besides, your feet are terribly small for a man."

I laughed despite myself. The tension dissipated as though it had never existed, and I questioned whether it really had.

We feasted on mushrooms that night, toasting the remainder of the stale bread and eating that as well. We would soon be out of food, but I now remained hopeful that I could grow more of anything we needed with a little more practice.

I slept well that night, warm by the fire, protected from the wind, a belly full of food, and safe in my own secret knowledge that I had finally discovered the true power the talisman held.

The next several days and nights were much the same. I practiced with the pendant and Niles removed himself from the cave, so I could concentrate. He found numerous reasons to leave—collecting firewood, checking the traps he had set for small game despite the fact that he never caught much, scouting for the unknown enemy, whatever reason he could think up. But we both knew he left for my sake.

There was something about Niles. Something I couldn't put my finger on. He had become more genuine, more real when no one else was around. Perhaps it was that he had dropped all pretenses. Our conversations were lengthy and interesting, and we talked a lot about his life before the army. It was almost as though I'd grown up knowing him.

We sat by the fire one evening, perhaps closer than was proper, definitely closer than we should have been sitting and I was mid-sentence when Niles's hands gripped my arms and pulled me to him. He kissed me, his lips eager upon mine, and I responded, confused with myself as I kissed him back.

It felt good to be close to someone, to be warm, safe, and wanted. His kiss was softer than Quinn's had been, seeking—as if presenting me with a question and unwilling to go further until he was sure of my answer. He was apprehensive, ready to pull back at any second.

Until he finally did.

He rested his forehead against mine. "Saints, I'm sorry, Moreina," he breathed, his eyes searching mine. "No, I take that back. I'm not. I'm not sorry. I've wanted to do that since I first laid eyes on you."

I swallowed. "I don't know what to think," I said. It was the truth.

"You feel something for me, though. I know you do. I felt it," Niles said, drawing back, but still holding me in his arms.

They were strong arms, long and formed. "And that must mean, I mean, that would imply—"

"You're one of the two suitors," I whispered. There was no point in denying it.

The truth was I didn't know how I felt. Niles offered a protection no one else had ever given me. He'd plunged into the ocean after me when I tried to rescue Emylia at the Plymann Cliffs. He'd acted as my protector when we'd been attacked on the mountainside on the way to Gillesmere. He'd tracked me now, following me for days into the remote wilderness despite the cold and discomforts. He was willing to put his life at risk to ensure my own life was safe. How could one not feel something for such a person? How could I *not* have fallen for him?

Yet, how could I?

I recognized my feelings for Quinn but a week ago. How could I possibly fall for someone else? The bitterness of Quinn's betrayal had apparently stung far worse than I'd originally realized. Had my anger with him pushed me to Niles? I tried to clear my head, to make sense of the confusion that clouded my befuddled brain.

"Ah, don't worry, Moreina," Niles said soothingly. "We'll figure this out." Then, in true Niles fashion, he flashed a dashing smile and added, "Well, we know I'm the good suitor then, right? So, whoever you may meet next, tell him no and everything shall be fine."

I smiled at him but swallowed hard. He didn't know of my feelings for Quinn. I resolved to say nothing.

I took a deep breath, shakier than I would have liked. I needed to be alone, to sort through my feelings and figure out what was real. Only days ago, I felt one step closer to defeating Bruenner and fulfilling the prophecy. I had tapped the talisman's power.

Now, I'd never felt more lost. Yes, I'd accessed the talisman's power, but I was far from controlling it. Now the two suitors had shown up after all, making the entire prophecy a little more solid. I was stupid not to have seen it before. Governor Arden had seen it clearly and that was months ago. I was a fool.

Niles's studied me closely. "Are you all right?"

I nodded. "Fine," I lied. "A lot to absorb. I think I'd like to get a little fresh air. I need to think, Niles." I looked into his eyes, hoping he'd see the truth within my words.

"But, I—"

"I won't go far," I promised. "I'll be fine, really. Please. I need space to breathe."

My pleading seemed to do the trick. He nodded slowly and took a step back as if releasing me.

Once outside, I drank in deep gulps of cold, cold air, stumbling over the leaves and roots on the forest floor. How had I let this happen? How had I fallen for two separate men, knowing full well that I was told I would?

I swore. I swore if I ever saw Quinn D'Arturio again, he would face my full wrath. Who did he think he was, making me feel such things and then running away like a coward, tail between his legs, racing for home? Running home, of all places, when I could not. Going back to the place I loved while I was forced to march farther and farther from it with each passing day. It was like rubbing sea salt into an open wound. I would never forgive him. As long as I lived, I would never forgive him.

Let Quinn run home. 'Twas better he should be there than here where I might do or say any number of undesirable things.

Out of steam, spent, I collapsed into a pile of leaves, drawing my knees to my chin and rocking softly back and forth. I bit back an insane laugh that threatened to escape from my throat. What had I thought fresh air would do for me?

There was a single snap of a twig behind me a split-second before a strong, calloused hand clamped over my mouth. Panic welled within as I fought to reach the dagger in my boot.

I struggled, even as a familiar voiced hissed in my ear, "Shhh! Quiet yerself, Reina!" Spinning me around to face him, he removed his hand from my mouth, but kept a hold on my arm.

Speechless, I could do nothing but stare. Quinn looked all the worse for wear. An enormous gash over the top of his eye into the side of his scalp had mostly closed, but was only a few days old, dried blood holding the skin in place.

"Don't think of it," he whispered, seeing my stare. "I'm fine. I know what you're thinking, and I'm fine."

All the things I thought I would say to Quinn if I'd had the chance flew from my head. "You're hurt," was all I could manage.

"Shhh, keep your voice down." His eyes shifted nervously.

"What happened?" I whispered.

Quinn gritted his teeth. "We have limited time before Niles comes looking for you," he said quietly.

I frowned. "How did you know I was with Niles?"

He didn't answer, just shook his head.

"Have you been following us?" I asked, anger growing in my blood again.

"Listen to me," he said. "I need you to listen closely. Niles is not who he seems."

I narrowed my eyes. "Right. That's what I would expect *you* to say. Why aren't you home by now anyhow?"

Quinn's confusion was evident. "What are you talking about?"

"Did you change your mind after all?"

"I never went home, Reina."

Now it was my turn to be confused. "But, Niles said—"

"Blazes," Quinn cursed through gritted teeth. "Listen. We don't have long. Go along with his game, whatever it is. Follow his lead. I'll be watching, and I will *not* let anything happen to you."

"Quinn, what are you talking about?"

"Just promise me."

"I don't—"

"Promise!" he hissed.

"Yes, yes, I promise."

Quinn paused, letting his eyes roam over my face, raising a hand to my cheek. He touched my shortened, dyed hair and for a second, a smile hinted at his eyes. "I'm just so glad you're safe."

With that, he was gone, vanished behind the trees and boulders. I stood open-mouthed, staring into the space where Quinn had stood, suddenly unsure of everything I thought I knew.

CHAPTER SIXTEEN

Two Suitors

"Are you all right?" Niles asked me for what seemed like the seventeenth time.

"I'm fine," I reassured him. In reality, I was anything but. I hadn't been able to think straight for days since Quinn's appearance. I was on edge. I didn't know what to believe or whom to trust. My brain had run through every possible scenario at least a dozen times, and I was beyond fatigued.

Niles is not who he seems.

The statement disturbed me. Quinn didn't like or trust Niles and that had always been the case, but this, well this implied something far more sinister.

To make things worse, Niles had been nothing but a gentleman since our shared kiss. He seemed to realize I needed space and that it was in his favor to give it to me as much as he could.

Now that I had a basic understanding of the talisman, we decided to move forward again. I was reluctant to leave the large cavern which served to shelter us so well, but the longer we stayed in one place, the better the chances were that one of Bruenner's scouts would eventually locate us.

We followed the foothills to the southwest, finding another suitable cave miles away from our last. I set about gathering wood while Niles went hunting. He was hungry, and yet I still hoped he wouldn't catch anything.

Niles had not been gone long when Quinn appeared. I had seen no sign of him since his first visit. I wondered where he'd been staying and how he'd been keeping warm and fed.

The wound on his head looked only slightly better, but, *Saints*, why did he still look so good to me?

"Will you let me treat you?" I asked him.

"There's no time for that," he said. "Has Niles suspected anything?"

I shook my head.

"Can you tell me what's going on?" I asked. "Where did you come from? When you appeared that day, where were you before that?"

He pressed his lips—*those* lips—together as if debating what he should tell me.

"Quinn, please," I added softly.

"Yes," he said. "But, first, I need to know. You're safe? You've not been hurt?"

"Niles wouldn't hurt me!"

He swallowed. "Not Niles," he said. "The riders. About a week and a half ago."

My eyebrows rose on their own. "You were there?"

"Aye," he said, gesturing to his head.

I gasped. "They did that?"

His eyes grew dark as he flexed his jaw. "No, someone lower managed this."

"I don't understand."

"Reina, I'd been following you for days."

"What? Why didn't you make yourself known?" I asked.

"I worried maybe perhaps you were running away from me, and if that were the case, well then, I'd be the last person you'd want as company. I figured I'd protect you from afar if need be."

"No, that wasn't it at all," I told him.

He looked hopeful as he searched my eyes. "It wasn't?"

"No, Saints, Quinn. I just...I knew I was endangering everyone. And I thought if I could be alone, I might unlock whatever secrets the talisman held."

"So you weren't running away from me?"

"No," I almost whispered. "Never."

He looked shaken, as I'd never seen him before, as he rested a hand on the trunk of a nearby tree. He gave a half laugh as he said, "You have no idea how relieved I am to hear that."

"So if you were there the day I ran into the riders on the road, what happened?" I could hardly believe Quinn would have left me to fend for myself no matter the circumstance.

"Niles happened," he said through gritted teeth, touching his head.

"What!"

"Just as I was about to reach the road, I heard someone behind me. It was stupid. After all the years of training I've had, I should have been more aware, but all I could think was that I needed to get to you. All I could see was you. I turned to defend myself and just as I did, I was hit."

"With what?" I asked, taking in the size of the wound.

"A tree branch that might as well have been a club."

"*Fiermi!* How can you be sure it was Niles?"

"I can't be a hundred percent certain, but when my gut tells me something, it's never wrong. I panicked when I woke. I thought for sure you were gone, that you'd been taken, hurt, killed... When I began tracking you again, I wanted to weep with relief."

The mental image of Quinn weeping over me gave me a jolt.

"And that's when I realized you were no longer alone. That's when I saw someone else was also following you. By the time I found you, the two of you had already set up camp and I thought three would be a bit of a crowd. He obviously didn't intend to hurt you, or he would have done it already, so I decided to watch and wait."

"You've been following us ever since?"

"Aye. I need to know what he's up to. He's not on our side, Reina. I can't explain it. I think I've sensed it from the beginning, but I chalked that up to my general dislike of the man. Being clubbed in the head by him rather solidified my opinion."

"And obviously I *should* have hit you harder." The harsh sound of Niles's voice made us both jump as we turned to face him. He made his way through the trees, bow pulled taut, an arrow aimed at Quinn's chest.

"Niles!" I exclaimed as I leaped in front of Quinn.

"Clearly, it wasn't enough of a deterrent," Niles said, growing closer.

Quinn pulled me aside by the arm. "What do you want, Niles?"

"Well for starters, I'd like you gone."

"That's not going to happen."

Niles chuckled, sauntering towards us. "Frankly, I'm in a very good position to make it happen right now."

Quinn's jaw clenched again as he stared hard at Niles.

"Niles," I intervened. "What's going on?"

"I could ask the same question of you."

"What?"

"Is this—can this be—fair suitor number two?"

I hesitated and decided to play daft. "Quinn? Saints, no! Niles, put down the bow."

For an instant, he looked as though he might have believed me. "Here's what's going to happen, Moreina. I'm going to shoot Quinn with this arrow," he said with some degree of glee. "But, don't worry yourself over it. I'll make sure not to kill him. I will, however, make certain he will no longer be able to follow us. Can't have you falling for the wrong man, now, can we?" As if threatening to shoot Quinn would somehow heighten my opinion of Niles. "Then, without the extra company, you and I will continue on our trek, just as we were."

"Niles, I'll come with you. There's no need to harm Quinn."

He gave an exaggerated sigh. "Women are fickle creatures, Moreina, and I need insurance."

"Niles," I said, doing everything I could to coax tears to my eyes, which didn't take much. "Quinn is a childhood friend, no more a love of mine than any brother."

I was getting somewhere. He *wanted* to shoot Quinn—he did—but he didn't want to upset me. Quinn wisely let me continue without interruption.

"Why the need for violence?"

Niles ignored my question and kept the arrow pointed at

Quinn. "I have a very good inkling that you were onto something with the talisman," he said. "In fact, I'm almost certain of it. So, you and I are going straight to Bruenner."

"Niles, I can't defeat Bruenner now. I haven't *that* much control!"

He smirked at me as though I were missing some key piece of information. "Well that's lucky for us, then, because we're not going to defeat him. We're going to join him."

"I knew it!" Quinn breathed.

"Yes, so clever as always, Quinn," Niles said with a snicker.

"*What?* Niles, have you lost your mind?" I cried.

Icy eyes turned on me. "No, in fact, I may be the only one thinking clearly. And maybe he'll acknowledge me for it."

"Do you really think he would reward you?" Quinn asked.

Anger flashed in Niles's eyes. "When I bring Bruenner the only person on the planet who can defeat him, why, yes, I do believe he'll reward me. The sooner Bruenner is seated unchallenged on the throne in Irzan, the sooner he'll name me his top general. Top generals aren't sent to the front lines, you know. And perhaps I'll treat Bruenner kinder than he treated our own late King Edgar." He turned his eyes toward me, softening. "Do you know what a general gets paid? You'd make a lovely general's wife. I could offer that to you, Moreina. He won't kill you if you're on his side, if you're with me."

Niles was possibly insane. I tried not to think it since I'd always been a terrible liar, and Quinn's life depended on my ability to deliver a convincing performance.

"You told me you wanted to stop this. You said you wanted the killing to end, but what about the destruction mentioned in the prophecy? Aren't you concerned about that?" I asked quietly.

"Desolation, death, and despair? Well, I imagine if you choose *him*," he gestured at Quinn with the arrow, "there will be plenty of that. This war will never end."

"He's not the other suitor," I said gently.

"Well, choose me and you will help to end this war. Bruenner will be king, armies will stop fighting, and a new ruling family will establish order in the land. Think about it. It makes sense."

I wasn't sure in what world this could possibly make sense, but I could hardly say that to Niles.

"Don't you see?" he continued. "The desolation, death, and despair are what we've currently got with this war anyway. The way to end it is to put someone on the throne. Once the Resistance stops challenging Bruenner's seat, all of this ends."

I had nothing to say. Nothing he would accept anyway.

"Enough talk now. Moreina, step away from Quinn and take your place beside me."

I glanced uncertainly at Quinn, hesitating. Almost imperceptibly, he nodded.

Slowly, I covered the ten feet between Quinn and Niles. Looking at Niles, I couldn't believe I'd once been affected by his charm. For a moment, Niles's gaze turned to meet mine, a sick adoration in his eyes. He was well and truly broken. That my lips had once touched his, that I had even contemplated... bile rose in my throat.

Niles loosed his arrow as Quinn plowed into his stomach, knocking him to the ground, and everything became a blur of motion.

I heard a scream and realized only afterwards it had come from my own throat.

The bow went flying from Niles's grasp as the two men wrestled on the ground. Fists flew as dirt and leaves splayed everywhere. For a moment, Niles was on top, and a dagger flashed in his hand, but then they were tumbling once again, and I couldn't make out who was winning as arms and legs flew in all directions.

Finally, Quinn pinned Niles to the ground, dagger to his throat.

"Stop!" My voice was foreign to my own ears. "Quinn, don't!"

No matter how crazy Niles might be, I didn't wish to see his blood spilled.

"What would you have me do, Reina?" Quinn yelled.

"Don't. Don't kill him. Please," I begged.

"Let him live? Why? So he can kill us in our sleep?" His fury wasn't directed at me and yet I cringed all the same.

"I don't want his blood on my hands," I pleaded.

"Not *your* hands, Reina. Mine."

"Quinn, please."

With a growl of frustration, Quinn shoved Niles into the ground with his free hand, grabbed the neck of his tunic and pulled him close. "Saints help me, Niles. If I ever so much as *see* your face again, I will kill you, no questions asked."

He stood, releasing him.

"Get out of here."

Niles, wide-eyed and disheveled, gave me one glance before retreating. There was no adoration in his eyes now.

"You'd better run, Niles. Before I change my mind."

It was one command of Quinn's that Niles obeyed.

CHAPTER SEVENTEEN

The Forgotten Threat

When Niles had gone, and we could no longer hear the crunch of dry leaves with his footsteps—when I was sure he had really gone—I turned to Quinn.

"Who are you?" I demanded, wide-eyed, with as much steel as I could muster.

He stared. For a moment there was so much emotion in his eyes I thought he was about to confess some dark, long-held secret. I braced myself.

"I deserve to know. After all we've been through, the least you can do is be honest with me. There was an arrow pointed at your chest, and you had him on the ground in half a second."

"It wasn't hard," he said. With his response, I could almost hear the door closing on the fleeting emotion I had seen in his eyes. And on any hope I had of getting a real answer. "He looked at you. It was an opportunity, and I took it."

It was the biggest crock of horse manure I'd ever heard.

"Quinn D'Arturio, I mean it! *Who* are you? I swear I don't know you at all." My voice faltered. That I didn't know him as I'd always thought shook me to my core. That he was a stranger...

Apparently, it scared him, too.

"I was trained by the Order of the Southern Cross," he said, dragging his eyes to meet mine almost painfully.

I couldn't have been more shocked if Quinn told me he was the crowned prince of the Southern Plains and had taken three wives.

"What?"

"I'm a spy, Reina."

The trees around me spun. Abruptly, I plopped into a pile of leaves, twigs poking at me through the fabric of my pants.

"Remember the years I left Barnham?"

"Yes," I said slowly.

"When I was sixteen, I was chosen to become an agent for the Order."

"That's absurd." But even as I said it, I realized there was nothing absurd about it. Quinn had disappeared from Barnham shortly after completing school, and we'd all assumed he'd gone on to see what the world had to offer before settling down to study with his father for his future role as governor. When he returned last year, I'd thought nothing of it.

In reality, he had been learning some of the deadliest skills any human could possess. Any agent of the Order was essentially a one-man army, at least as far as legend was concerned. Suddenly, Antony's description of Quinn made perfect sense.

I had heard stories about the Order of the Southern Cross. Everyone had. It was said that upon the telling of the White Sorceress Prophecy, Magnus Tarrowburn had handpicked elite soldiers to carry out the duty of training protectors for the White Sorceress. For a thousand years, very specific men had been chosen to carry on the tradition. No one really knew much about them or if they actually existed at all.

I couldn't imagine a tradition continuing for a thousand years with no indication that what was mentioned in the prophecy would ever truly come to pass. The very conviction involved... the faith these men must have had throughout the years even though they would never live to see the day the prophecy was fulfilled. It was nearly beyond comprehension.

"My father is an assessor," Quinn explained and suddenly Governor Arden's obsession with the White Sorceress Prophecy fell into place.

Assessors were responsible for recruiting new agents. In order to recruit successfully, being thoroughly familiar with every aspect of the prophecy was a job requirement. Governor Arden had taken that requirement seriously.

"But, I thought you...I mean..." I couldn't seem to find the question I wanted to ask. Finally, I settled on, "How?"

Quinn shrugged. "I suppose my father thought it was a family duty."

"But couldn't you have said no?"

"He didn't force me into it, if that's what you're implying. I chose to do it."

"So you never escaped the *Choosing* after all. You were simply *chosen* for other things," I said. "You've believed in the White Sorceress all along, even though you led me to believe that you didn't."

"That's not entirely true. Trust me, I had my doubts, Reina. There's something very surreal about being part of a long line of agents who've been waiting for the appearance of one single, very special person. For hundreds of years, decade upon decade, one generation to the next, these people, *my* people, have done nothing but wait for that one woman. To know I was in the line who might finally get to know her identity was daunting. There were times I preferred not to think on it."

Quinn found something daunting?

"Come," Quinn said, offering me his hand. "Let's get a fire started in the cavern, and I'll tell you what you want to know."

Grasping his hand, I stood and we returned to the cave that only a short time before I had thought to occupy with Niles. In no time at all, Quinn had a roaring fire and I knelt close, warming my hands. I watched him, marveling at how little I truly knew of him and his life, as he stacked more wood against the wall of the cave. Childhood friends we might have been, but what more was there beneath his calm, levelheaded exterior that could apparently stop arrows and fight wars single-handedly?

"You said you're a spy," I said, unable to wait for him to return to the conversation in his own good time.

"Yes," he said. "By trade, agents are spies."

"Who did you spy on?"

"Everyone. We're ghosts. We blend in, disappear, and wait to hear whatever there is to hear. I have heard and seen about every and any conversation that was thought to be private."

I shifted, uncomfortable with such knowledge. "You didn't feel ashamed listening in on conversations that weren't yours to hear?"

"When I heard lovers coupling or a dying man's last wishes desperately bestowed upon a stubborn son, yes, believe me, I was ashamed." Against my will, I blushed at the mention of coupling. Had he really heard such things? He continued. "But the things I learned that I wouldn't have otherwise known? No, I've no shame. It's part of the trade. It's my duty."

"Were you afraid when you were chosen for the Order?"

Surprised, he paused a moment before giving me a half smile. "I suppose there was an...anxiety in being chosen," he said. "A secret organization with secret practices? The unknown variables were intimidating. But afraid? No, I don't think I was ever actually afraid."

I was not surprised.

"Does nothing scare you?"

He sat beside me and the firelight played off his dark features. I fought the urge to touch the wound above his eye. The skin around it had turned a deep purple and yellow. His eyes met mine directly, and though I wanted to look away, I returned his gaze evenly.

"The thought of losing you terrifies me."

Butterflies flitted deep in my belly. Did he know how he affected me?

I gave a tight-lipped smile. "As an agent of the Order, I suppose I should expect no less."

Quinn looked as though he wanted to say more, but he turned away.

"Is the training what they say?" I asked, remembering the scars I had seen on his back. They made sense now. Saints, what had they done to him?

He took a far-off look as he gazed into the fire. Absently, he snapped a twig repeatedly and threw the small pieces into the fire. "And what do they say?"

I swallowed nervously and chewed my bottom lip, debating

how to delicately phrase the mutterings I'd once heard. "That agents are…tortured just to learn to withstand it. That they're taught to kill in every way possible with any and every instrument. And when no instruments are available, they learn to use their bare hands. Oh, and, um, that they…*practice* on vile criminals."

He waited an eternity before answering, the snapping of his twig and the popping of the fire the only sounds echoing in the cavern. Finally, he replied, "Much of it is true." He didn't elaborate further, and I didn't ask him to.

I inched closer to the fire, plagued by a chill I was unable to shake, hoping it was from the cold and not from newfound knowledge.

"Who do you report to?" I asked. "If you're a spy, surely there's someone you report all of your findings to?"

He nodded. "I send weekly transcripts to Director Grant, detailing anything of interest."

"So that's why you've never joined the war efforts," I said, more to myself than to Quinn.

He nodded.

"Do you have secret meetings, too?" I half joked. The look on his face prompted me to continue. "Oh, Saints, you do!" I breathed.

"Well, we have to have a way to stay informed, right? If not, there's hardly a point to the Order's existence."

"And where do you meet?"

"I can't say."

"Ah, right, *secret* meetings."

He rolled his eyes. "South Trellington."

South Trellington was as far south as one could go before

leaving the borders of Castilles for the Southern Plains. It was several days' journey from Barnham.

"How many agents are there? Do you all meet there?" My mind teemed with questions. How had I not known before that Quinn was an Agent? How had I never noticed?

"I don't know how many agents there are. Only Director Grant is privy to that information. It might make it difficult to keep secret if every agent knows where other agents are and what they're doing, aye?"

"I guess."

"Anyway, those of us not directly on an assignment report to the meetings. The ones on assignment can't leave without endangering their mission, so they usually resort to other means of communication."

"Other means?"

He gave a cryptic smile. "We can be creative."

Suddenly feeling the urge to change the topic to something that made my head spin slightly less, I said, "I believe I've discovered what the talisman does."

Quinn's interest was piqued. "Have you?"

I nodded. "At least partially," I said as I pulled it from my tunic. "I'd like to show you," I added, surprising myself. I had never accessed my vision in someone's company—not even my mother—having always preferred to be alone. I wasn't sure what prompted me to say such a thing.

"I'd love to see it," Quinn answered before I could retract my words.

Slowly, I nodded. "I have to access my vision, and that may…strike you as odd. So if you think it will be too strange, we could always try this another time."

His eyebrows drew together. "Why on Liron would I think it's strange?"

I shrugged. "I know it's strange, Quinn. I know *I'm* strange."

"Well, then you're in good company. I'm not exactly the kingdom's most normal specimen, aye?"

I smiled despite myself. There was no backing out now.

"So the state needed for my vision," I said. "It's a trance of sorts, so don't be alarmed."

I waited for him to tease, but instead he nodded seriously.

"Oh, and I should also tell you I've never done this in front of anyone. I'm not sure if it will work. It might take a while."

"Reina," Quinn said. "'Tis only me. The boy who broke his arm rescuing your mother's favorite nanny goat. Remember?"

"I'm sorry," I replied. "You're right."

Slowly, almost reluctantly, I closed my eyes.

What will Quinn think of me?

I pushed the thought from my head and concentrated hard on lengthening each breath until they were all deep and even.

Is he watching?

Of course he is.

Shut up and concentrate, Reina.

I pressed the talisman tightly into my palm and rubbed a thumb repeatedly, almost rhythmically, over the silver scroll-worked edges as it hummed happily at me.

It didn't take nearly as long as I thought it would. My fingers and toes began to tingle. Accessing my vision was surprisingly easy, even in Quinn's presence.

Within minutes, I could *see* the cavern—and Quinn—

without opening my eyes. Once again, an aqua haze signaled to me that the stone was glowing.

Focusing on the talisman, remembering my previous successes, I began an internal dialogue with it.

Grow. Please. Bring forth new life, I silently requested. *Emerge from the ground. Emerge from the ground and stretch your petals to the light. Yes, the cave is dark, but there is a light here that can sustain you. I am here.*

My vision blurred. I couldn't see the change happening, but judging by Quinn's gasp, I had succeeded.

I pulled back slowly and opened my eyes to reveal the lush jungle I had created. Mushrooms, yes, but also orchids, passionflowers, trumpet vines, lilies and dozens of other varieties of flowers and fruits the likes of which I had never before seen. My lips parted in shock as I let my gaze roam from one species to the next.

"This is amazing," Quinn said, unable to pull his eyes from the clusters of delicate purple flowers that hung from the cave ceiling. "You've done this before?"

"Yes. No. I mean, not like this. Nothing like this."

"What did you do differently this time?" he asked.

I shook my head. "I don't know. I...I said please."

Quinn stood and ran his hand along the perimeter of the cave as if needing to feel the reality of my work. He plucked a ripe, purple fuisberry from a vine that had spread along an entire wall and popped it into his mouth. There were dozens more on the vine.

He shook his head in disbelief. "This is incredible."

I nodded.

"If I hadn't seen it with my own eyes, I would not believe it."

"What did it look like?" I asked. "And how long did it take?"

He gave me a look of confusion. "Are you…not aware when you're like that?"

"It's an odd thing," I said. "I can *see*, but where things grow, my vision blurs. And I have no sense of time. This could have taken seconds or hours."

"Somewhere in between," he said. "Not long, though. Not long at all. A few minutes at most."

He plucked another berry from the vine. "It's real," he said to me, placing it in his mouth. "This is no illusion."

I joined him with the pot from my pack and helped him pull the berries from the vine. I placed a few in my mouth. The berries made a pleasant pop as I bit into them, releasing a sweet juice as I had not tasted in many months. The taste brought to mind the fuisberry patch I kept every summer in Barnham.

Abruptly, I sat.

"Are you all right?" Quinn asked, kneeling next to me.

"Aye," I answered. "Just missing home is all. I can't help but wonder if we'll ever know summer again. If we'll ever see Barnham again."

He took my hand in his. "We will, Reina. I swear it."

I met his eyes. He believed what he said.

"I don't know how," I told him. "I just don't know how."

"But you're halfway there already. You've discovered how to wake the talisman. You've done something no one else has dared imagine to be possible for hundreds upon hundreds of years."

I gave a choked laugh. "And what shall I do with it, this

awesome power of life? Do I grow vines to strangle Bruenner while he sleeps?"

Quinn stroked his chin as if truly contemplating the idea.

"Quinn!"

He raised his eyebrows. "It's a legitimately good option," he said. "But it would have to be something strong and it would have to be fast, faster than what grew here."

"I wasn't serious!" I nearly shouted at him, throwing my hands in the air.

He shrugged and fell quiet.

"You were right about your mother," he said, breaking the silence as he stared hard into the fire.

"*What?*"

"It was Bruenner."

"I *know* that. What happened? How did you find out? When?" I didn't know what I'd expected to feel when I heard the news, or if I'd actually expected Quinn to discover anything. But then, I hadn't exactly realized the scope of his influence at the time that he'd made his promise to me, either.

"I don't know the details," he said. "And I doubt anyone does."

I clenched my jaw. "Bruenner does."

"Tomorrow will be a long day. We'll need to find new shelter," he said, attempting to draw my mind elsewhere.

"We only just found this one."

"Yes, but Niles knows where we are."

"You really think he'd come back after your warning?"

"Not without reinforcements."

"Bruenner."

He nodded. "If I know anything about Niles, and I believe I do, he's on his way to Bruenner now. At best we've got two to three days before he'll be back, searching for us, *if* Bruenner actually believes him, that is."

"Good. I'd like to lay my hands around Bruenner's neck right now," I said through gritted teeth.

Quinn wisely had no answer.

I let out my breath in a huff. "About Niles," I said. "Would you tell me what it was you didn't like about him? Please? I mean, aside from the most recent and obvious reasons."

Quinn appeared to mull over the question as if debating how he would answer.

"I want to know what you know," I told him. "After all, had I known it from the start, I might not have been so quick to allow him to travel with me."

Quinn snorted. "You wouldn't have had much choice. I'm fairly certain he would have taken you hostage at that point."

"Fine," I conceded. "But, what did he do before?"

"Niles is a soldier," Quinn said.

"Elle—Madam Bonverno—said the same thing. What the blazes is that supposed to mean? Aren't soldiers supposed to protect? I don't understand why being one should make anyone a suspect."

"It's not that," he answered. "I know of things he's done in battle that were neither fair nor just."

"Is there anything just about a war?"

"There are the right reasons to fight a war and the wrong reasons to fight a war, as there are the right reasons to kill and the wrong reasons to kill. Killing is never justified, but there are times when it is necessary and times when it is not."

"And how is his killing someone any different from yours?" I asked, regretting the words as they left my mouth.

Quinn's gaze hardened, but I refused to back away.

"It is *very* different," he said. "He didn't care who he killed. He *doesn't* care who he kills. There were…there were so many children."

I inhaled sharply.

"It was towards the beginning of the war," Quinn explained. "Niles was young, daft, hungry to see action, and wrongly placed in charge. Actually, I take that back. Niles has never been daft. That's part of his problem. He's always been one step ahead of almost everyone, and that's how he was able to get away with what he did."

I could barely find my voice. "What did he do?"

"Early in the war, maybe a month in, the Resistance forces had gathered children and wives of many of the King's soldiers. It was a foolish attempt by untrained leaders to force Bruenner's army into laying down their weapons. Attack close to the heart. No one had ever done anything like it."

I swallowed as Quinn continued speaking. He stared into the fire again, as though he saw something more within the dancing flames.

"There was never any intention to harm any of them. Saints, they were children!"

"But, it happened anyway," I whispered.

"Niles led the slaughter. His soldiers didn't know what to do. They were young, inexperienced, untrained militia. Most of them followed him because they were too afraid not to."

"You were there?"

He nodded. "And I could do nothing to stop it. Not one cursed thing."

My heart twisted in my chest. I could almost hear the screams of women and children, could almost taste the fear in their throats.

"Why?" I asked.

"Because I was a ghost," he said.

My lips parted involuntarily. "You mean you—"

"Risked blowing everything had I made myself known, yes," he said, his voice catching in his throat.

I licked my lips, unsure of what to say.

"And that," he said, "is why I have never *liked* Niles Ingram."

"Why wasn't he caught?" I asked. "Was he not tried for war crimes?"

Quinn shook his head. "You've heard him speak. He's smooth, calculated. He was called out and reprimanded by the general, but nothing more ever came of it. A slap on the wrist in turn for dozens of innocent lives. It sickens me."

There seemed nothing more to say.

"We'll move tomorrow," I said. "Far from here."

We laid out bedrolls, and I tried hard to sleep, but some time later, the imagined screams of women and children still echoed in my head, and I found it difficult to close my eyes. How did Quinn ever live with such a thing?

"Quinn," I nearly whispered, turning to face him.

"Mmph?" His back was to me, broad shoulders outlined beneath the blanket.

"It wasn't your fault."

He said nothing.

"The children. It wasn't your fault."

There was a long silence and I thought he might be asleep before he said softly, almost inaudibly, "Thank you."

We moved early the next day. There was a stillness to the air, a crispness that could almost be smelled, and I was nearly certain we'd see snow—a lot of it—before the day was through. An urgency in Quinn's pace assured me he felt the same.

By the time we located another suitable cavern, we'd walked most of the day, and I had begun to feel the fatigue from many days and nights on the road with little food to sustain me. Three finger-widths of snow had fallen. Despite the stillness of the air, the bitter cold seeped into my boots and into my bones. I was relieved when we found a place to settle, and I helped Quinn gather as much wood as possible.

"*Fiermi!*" he cursed as he tried unsuccessfully to coax flames from the damp wood.

"Here," I said, crouching next to him. "Let me help." Pulling *sulfuria* from my bag, I poured several pinches into a small pile beneath the tinder. "Now try the flint."

It lit in a small whoosh, and Quinn narrowed his eyes suspiciously at me. "Are you certain ye've no witch's blood in those veins?" he asked.

I glared at him in response.

Surprisingly, he met my glare with his own. Slowly, he leaned in, and I thought he might kiss me again. My heart quickened in response, my breath catching in my throat.

"Don't be so serious," he said, his gaze dropping to my lips.

"You're one to talk," I replied, my voice weak.

Abruptly, Quinn stood, and I let out a breath I hadn't realized I'd been holding. He added more tinder to the fire until the flames were hot enough to burn through the damp wood, trapped water sizzling as it steamed within the logs.

"Think you can grow us something to eat?" he asked some time later.

I nodded. Within minutes, I had grown a trove of berries, leaves, legumes, and mushrooms despite the snow that continued to accumulate outside.

It had been easier to access my vision this time than it had been the first time I'd done it to show Quinn. Quinn's presence seemed to make the entire process faster. As I admired his profile, I mused why this should be the case. It was almost as if he were a conductor for my ability, magnifying it so it was easier to access.

"You'll make me nervous if you keep staring at me so, Reina," he said.

"Sorry," I muttered, feeling a heat creep to my ears. Suddenly lightheaded, I placed a hand on the cave wall to steady myself.

"Are you all right?"

"Yes," I answered slowly. "A bit dizzy is all."

He examined my face, eyes darting back and forth between my own. Without warning, he pulled me to him and placed his lips on my forehead. I had no time to resist.

"What are you—?"

"Blazes, Reina. You've a fever," he said, pulling away.

I brushed his hands from my arms. "I'm fine," I said stubbornly.

"Were you not going to tell me?" he asked, his voice rising in anger. He pulled the blanket from his bedroll and draped it over my shoulders. I pulled the woolen material close to ward off a sudden chill, trying to ignore that it smelled divinely of Quinn and only contributed to my vertigo.

"I'm fine!"

"You are *not* fine." He began rummaging through my sack, pulling out a small pot. He disappeared outside and when he returned, he had filled the pot with snow. He set it to boil on the fire. "Of all things, of all things," he muttered to himself.

"Quinn—" I started.

"Don't," he said. "For one blasted minute, stop trying to be so bloody strong all of the time."

I clamped my mouth shut.

"For once in your life, let someone help. Let *me* help. I didn't travel hundreds of miles through rain, through snow, through getting my brains nearly bashed in, only to have you die from an illness that you, yourself, would have easily prevented in any child in Barnham."

He grabbed my sack and dumped it, sorting through the contents as though they somehow offended him. Finally, he found the vial he'd been looking for, and, grabbing my tin cup, he dumped several spoonfuls into it.

Wordlessly, I pulled the blanket closer. When the water boiled, he poured it into the cup, stirred it, then handed it to me.

"Drink," he commanded.

I sniffed at the rising steam. "Yarrow," I said, impressed.

"My mother used to make it for me whenever I had a fever as a child."

I suppressed a mild laugh at the irony of the Healer being treated. I hadn't had a fever since childhood.

"Yes," he said, "she likely learned it from your mother."

I sipped, wrinkling my nose at the bitter brew, but swallowing anyway.

"I have a hard time imagining you ever being sick," I croaked. "Come to think of it, I have a hard time thinking of you as a child at all."

He frowned at me.

"You knew me then," he said.

"But it seems so long ago. I feel as though it was someone else I knew, some other child long gone."

He shrugged.

A chill ran through me, and I shivered involuntarily.

Quinn gave a frustrated sigh. "Oh, Reina," he said. "I wish you'd told me earlier you weren't well." He sat next to me, rubbed my arms, then pulled me onto his lap. My bones ached, but I was too cold to protest. He wouldn't have listened anyway.

It felt good, sitting curled on his lap, his muscular arms wrapped tightly about me, his chin resting on the top of my head. It was the first time I'd felt warm all day.

He alternated between stroking my back and smoothing my hair, and I pondered how hands that killed so efficiently could also touch so softly. I pushed the thought away. My mother used to stroke my hair, too, when I was sick. All at once, I realized just how much I missed her.

"Tell me about the favorite parts of your childhood," I said to Quinn.

He stared down at me quizzically. "You were there," he answered.

"I know, but you're rather a mystery, you know."

"Oh, I am?" he said, now sounding amused.

"Mm hmm," I said into my cup as I sipped. "All the girls wanted you and all the boys wanted to be you."

Quinn couldn't hide his surprise. "That so?"

I narrowed my eyes as I looked intently into my cup. "What else did you put in here? I speak far too freely."

He chuckled. "I suspect your fever has the best of you."

"Mmm."

"There's not much to tell, I'm afraid."

"When did you find out you were adopted?"

"When I was drafted for the Order. I suppose I'd always known to some extent, but that was when my father actually told me."

"Do you know anything of your birth parents?"

He shook his head. "I've been told that I look like my birth mother."

"They knew her?" I asked, surprised. It was uncommon for adoptive parents to know anything about the birth parents, the child often having been placed on their doorstep or having come from an orphanage with little information.

"Somewhat. My mother's sister worked for them for several years from what I was told."

"Were they well off?"

He shrugged. "My father implied something along those

lines, but I don't really know." There weren't many people in the kingdom who had a hired labor force, and I wasn't sure in what capacity Quinn's aunt had worked for them.

"You said your birth mother died from the sweat plague. What about your birth father?" I asked.

"I don't know much about him or even if he's still alive. I can't imagine how a single man would raise a baby on his own, or that he would want to."

"You'd be surprised," I said. "There are plenty of fathers who have raised strong and healthy babes on their own."

"Then he's probably dead, too," Quinn concluded.

"I'm sorry," I said.

"Don't be."

"Where did you go when you left Barnham?" My, my. Fever made me talkative.

"Many places," he answered.

"Such as?"

"South, mostly."

I didn't know much about the southern part of the continent, only that it was supposedly warm and lovely year round.

"Is it what they say, the south?"

He smiled as he gazed down at me, and I was suddenly struck by the intimacy of it all—me on his lap, tucked into his arms, our faces inches apart—only I was unable to muster the concern I should have had in such a situation.

"The sun shines warm almost every day and the fruit grows through the entire year. Exotic fruits, too, the flesh like none you've ever tasted."

I closed my eyes, trying to imagine warm breezes and lush

fruit. "Are the people different?" I asked.

"Oh, I don't know. They have different customs, but they're a warm people."

"Warm, hmm, like their weather?"

"Yes, like their weather." A cryptic smile played on his face. "You really don't get sick like this often, do you?"

"Not since I was eight." My voice sounded small. "What do they look like?"

"Who?"

"The southern people."

"Oh. They're mostly dark-haired with golden skin kissed by the sun, not at all like most of the fair-haired folk in the north. Actually," he turned me slightly in his arms and squinted at me, "*you* could pass for a Southerner."

"Really?"

"How odd. I hadn't noticed it before."

"Perhaps my father was Southern. I never knew him."

"Something we have in common, I suppose."

"A couple of misfits with no lineage on the run," I said, yawning.

Quinn laughed, a deep rumble in his barrel of a chest. "Sleep," he said as he stood, lifting me in his arms as though I weighed no more than a frond of featherfern.

"You're so bossy, Quinn D'Arturio."

"Aye, I am. And a good thing, too. Someone must look after you."

"I'm fine," I attempted to argue again, though I could hardly keep my eyes open. He laid me gently on my bedroll near the fire and covered me tightly.

"Of course you are. Now, sleep."

I wanted to protest, I did. Instead, I slept.

CHAPTER EIGHTEEN

The Ticking Clock

When I came to, I was surprised at the ache in my joints and the hunger in my belly. I placed a hand to my head, trying to recall anything that had happened over the last few hours.

Days?

Saints, how long had we been here? Sporadic, jumbled memories of Quinn holding a steaming cup of yarrow tea to my lips, of being force fed some sort of horrible tasting broth, of him wiping hot tears from my cheeks as he rocked me like an infant suddenly came spilling forth in my mind.

I inhaled sharply and sat up, looking for Quinn. I found him beside me, sleeping in the dirt floor of the cave, breathing softly as though the lightest sound might wake him. I realized then I had both my bedroll and his.

Shifting so as not to wake him, I pulled myself from the covers and slipped outside to relieve myself.

I was greeted by hills of sparkling snow, drifts piled several feet high against the outside walls of the cave. I could hardly believe I'd been asleep for so long. Footprints trekking to and from the cave had been mostly filled in again.

I reentered the cavern as quietly as possible and added a log to the dying fire. The logs shifted as if to spite me, and Quinn shot to his feet, instantly on guard.

I stared at him, wide-eyed. He looked dangerous—dark hair wildly splayed, a thick beard covering the lower half of his hollowed face, smudges of dirt and ash on his face and clothes.

"I'm sorry," I whispered.

He grabbed me in a bear hug, holding me so tightly I could hardly breathe. One hand stroked my hair repeatedly.

"God, Reina. God." His voice was husky in my ear.

Tears blurred in my eyes as I repeated myself. "I'm sorry. I'm so sorry."

"Don't," he said. "Please. Just don't. Not ever again."

I swallowed.

Finally, he pulled himself back, holding me at arm's length. "I thought I'd lost you. I thought…I thought you were gone." His eyes darted over my face as though he didn't truly believe what he saw.

"I'm sorry," I repeated. I could think of nothing else to say.

"I was so afraid. I didn't know what to do. All I kept thinking was that if *you* were here, you'd know the right tincture to mix up, or you'd have a poultice to keep the fever away, or some tiny pill to take to make it all stop. I couldn't find it. I just couldn't find the right jars. I didn't know what to do. You don't have instructions."

Quinn was babbling.

Quinn.

Babbling.

"I'm all right," I said. "I'm fine. Quinn, I'm fine."

"Sure, and that's what you said three days ago."

"Three days!"

"Aye."

Dread filled my gut. "But we wanted to keep on the move," I said. "Niles, Bruenner…"

"The storm was a blessing," he said, finally regaining his composure and sounding more like himself. "They're no closer than they ever were."

I touched a hand to a gaunt cheek. "Quinn, you're wasting away. Have you eaten nothing since I fell sick?"

"'Tis nothing," he said. "I've extra to spare."

I glanced around the cavern. Most of what I had grown had wilted and the berries were picked clean.

"You need meat," I told him, surprising myself. "Are you able to set traps?"

Quinn's eyes suddenly shifted from me, and he nodded slowly. "I was able to catch one hare," he said.

"Good." It was then that I followed his gaze to the pot near the fire.

I looked at him. "You didn't."

He was silent.

"Oh, God! You fed it to me?"

"You needed something more than water and a few fuisberries! You needed something to replenish your strength."

"You fed me a rabbit!"

"Not the whole thing."

As if that would somehow make it better.

"Not the whole thing!?"

"You weren't awake enough to eat. I boiled it and made a broth you could drink."

I wanted to retch just thinking on it. I wanted to gag. I wanted nothing more than to purge myself of it.

"It was two days ago," Quinn said as though he'd detected my thoughts.

"How could you?" I asked, horrified that he'd thought such an action could ever be warranted.

"Reina, trust me, had I believed there was any other way to make you well, I would not have thought twice. If making you well involved removing my own fingers from my hand, I assure you, I would have done it."

As quickly as it had flared, my anger faded.

I still wanted to vomit.

What choice had he had? He did the only thing he'd been able to do. Without me, he could grow nothing to eat and the bread and cheese had long been gone. Really, honestly, what choice *had* he had?

"I'm sorry," he said. "Truly, Reina, I am. I knew you'd be furious. I only hoped you'd live long enough to lash out at me."

I turned to him, thoughts swirling through my head faster than I could sort them. "You look pathetic," I said. He narrowed his eyes and pressed his lips together as he tried to determine whether or not I was still angry.

"I'm glad you're well, too," he replied.

Softly, I added, "Thank you."

He nodded, a dark lock of unruly hair falling onto his forehead. Unconsciously, I reached to push it back. He stiffened.

I should have remembered his distaste for touch. Was it *my* touch or was it all touch? One day, I would ask.

"Now you're on the road to recovery, we'll have to discuss a plan of action," Quinn said.

I nodded in response. "I suppose we'll need to move soon."

"If we want to keep ahead of Bruenner's scouts, yes, it's probably wise, but I don't intend to travel until you're completely well. The last thing we need is for you to relapse."

"I'm certain I'll be all right," I told him, though I was anything but sure. The thought of hiking through snow made me cringe.

"Stop."

"Stop what?"

"Lying," he said. "Any fool can see you're not ready to travel, so don't tell me you're fine."

"What, then, shall I say to you, Quinn?"

"The truth," he answered. "Or nothing at all."

Reluctantly, I kept my mouth shut.

"We'll see how you feel tomorrow morning. Do you think you can access the power of the stone? To grow something to eat?"

"I don't see why not."

"Well then, let's start there. The sooner you can get some nourishment, the sooner we'll be ready to start moving again."

"It's not like *you're* the reason we've stalled," I muttered.

"Yes, well, *we* are a team, like it or not, and *we* are in this together. So when I say *we* are ready to move again, *we* will."

"You're testy when you haven't eaten," I said as I pulled the talisman from the neck of my tunic and closed my eyes.

Ignoring the look he was surely giving me, I stilled my mind. Within moments, I had unleashed the power of the stone. If I'd had any prior doubts that the stone's power would be impeded by my own frail state, I had none now. I had once again grown a lush jungle that provided us with enough food to feed at least five.

We ate raw berries, made a stew with newly grown trumbor roots, potatoes, half a dozen fresh greens, and mushrooms, and had fresh melted snow water to wash it all down. It was a feast like I hadn't eaten in weeks.

"It gets easier to use the talisman each time," I observed.

"That's a good thing," Quinn said. "We'll need that advantage. Now, get some rest and I'll figure out a plan for tomorrow."

"I'm not tired," I said, stifling a yawn. "I've been sleeping for days."

"No," he said. "You've been fevered and hallucinating for days. There's a difference."

Finally, I agreed. "You need sleep, too," I said, climbing into my bedroll. "You've circles beneath your eyes."

"Soon," he replied, raising his gaze from the lines he'd begun drawing in the dirt.

I sighed and tried to get comfortable in the blankets, but it was difficult. "I smell," I said.

"You've been very ill and perspired a lot. I was worried you might dehydrate."

"I'm sorry you have to be near me."

Quinn sighed and rose, stopping over me. "Take off your clothes," he said.

"What?"

"You're in your bedroll. Take off your clothes. I'll wash them for you while you sleep."

"Quinn D'Arturio, that is in no way proper!"

"Aye, but cozying up to Niles Ingram was plenty proper, I suppose." There was an angry glint in his eye.

My mouth dropped open. "That's not fair! We had no fire."

"Mmph."

"You were there?"

"I caught up to you that morning."

"I wasn't...I mean, we didn't...do anything."

His dark, impenetrable eyes stared into mine.

"I know," he said.

How much did he know?

"Clothes," he said, a hand extended.

I opened my mouth to argue again and realized the futility in it. Begrudgingly, I undressed beneath the covers, muttering to myself.

"Until I wash my body, I'm still going to smell," I said.

"Well, I'll bring you water to wash, then."

"Shall I wash beneath the covers, too?" I asked sweetly, blinking innocently at him.

"I'll take the opportunity to check my traps," he said with a tight smile, "and you can wash near the fire."

Once again, I had no reply. I handed my clothes to him, careful to keep the blanket pulled up to my neck.

He accepted the bundle and within minutes had put a fresh pot of snow on the fire for bathing. I waited until he was gone for several minutes before I ventured to climb out from beneath my cover. The cool air washed over my skin, eliciting a rippling gooseflesh that prickled my arms and legs.

I set the talisman atop a rock and removed a rag from my pack. I soaked it in water and scrubbed circles on my skin.

Without soap, I would never feel fully clean, but a bath with water alone was preferable to the sour sheen of perspiration that had dried upon my body.

Gazing at the flowers dangling from the cave walls, inspiration hit. I grabbed a handful of the purple blooms and pressed the petals solidly between my fingers. The oils from the crushed petals released a pleasant aroma—a light floral perfume that reminded me of the scent my mother had always worn.

It didn't take long to make the rest of my body smell as pleasant. I was careful to wash my hair last, pouring the flowery water over my scalp and hoping it was enough to make a difference.

Finished, naked and with dripping hair, I was chilled even near the fire. I slipped the talisman back over my head without a shock, climbed into my bedroll, and waited for Quinn to return.

I made an effort to work the talisman while he was gone. Was it possible to grow things from afar? I had joked about strangling Bruenner with a vine grown from the talisman, and while I didn't believe that was possible, it didn't stop me from considering what I *could* do from afar.

But I was in for a surprise. I could not coerce the talisman do much more than pulse dully with a weak blue light. I told Quinn only hours before that it was getting easier to use the talisman. Now this.

I attempted several more times, but never succeeded in fully accessing it the way I had in the last several days. Angry and frustrated, I gave up and fell asleep despite my earlier insistence that I wasn't tired.

When I awoke, Quinn was sitting by the fire, roasting the

carcasses of two rabbits. My stomach turned looking at them, but I held my tongue. It was clear to see he needed nutrition. Nothing I could grow would replenish his strength as fresh meat would.

My clothes had been laid out to dry, tunic and pants draped over sticks that Quinn had wedged into the ground. When I returned my eyes to Quinn again, his intense gaze was fixed on me. I couldn't decipher the expression on his face, though I'd seen it before. Why was he always so hard to discern?

"Blazes, Reina. Cover yourself."

I was suddenly very conscious of my exposed bare shoulder and half a breast, as I had draped one arm over the covers while I slept. Slowly, I tucked back beneath the covers, pulling the blankets to my chin.

"Um, my clothes?" I asked.

"Aye, they should be dry," he said as he grabbed them and handed them to me. "I'll be outside. Be quick. I'd not like to eat burnt rabbit."

I dressed quickly. The clothes were still slightly damp, but not uncomfortable if I sat close enough to the fire. I kept my gaze averted from the rabbits on the spit.

We ate in relative silence, Quinn his rabbit and I my berries, roots, and mushrooms. Finally, I decided to ask. "So, what do you propose we do?"

He took a stick and began drawing a map in the dirt again. "We're still on this side of the mountains," he said, pointing the stick to the little hills he had drawn. "That's good and bad. We're in the right place to strike at Bruenner if and when we finally figure out how, but that also means we're in the right place for him to strike at us." As an afterthought, he added, "Should he find us, that is."

"And with Niles intent on that…"

"I've been thinking on that. He was behind the attack on the mountain pass that day. I'm sure of it."

I frowned. "Back then? How can you be certain? He rode ahead with me, protected me." I swallowed. "If you'd asked me that day, I would have sworn he'd lay down his life for me."

"And perhaps he would have. He is clearly insane, after all."

"Then why would he have had someone attack us—attack me? I could have been killed."

"Debatable. He may very well have given explicit instructions that you were not to be harmed."

"There was an arrow inches from my head," I reminded him.

"Or he may not have been concerned with whether or not you remained alive. Either way, he had something to gain. Bringing you to Bruenner—dead or alive—would, in his mind at least, ensure a favorable position with him."

I fought the chills that shot down my spine.

To think I had kissed Niles.

Yes, but it hadn't exactly been like kissing Quinn, had it?

Quinn's kiss raced to the forefront of my mind, and my insides grew warm with the memory as he sat before me ever so logically reviewing tactical information.

"I knew something seemed odd about that attack. It was too soon for word to have gotten out about the finding of the talisman and the identity of the White Sorceress. It didn't fall into place, but I couldn't put my finger on it. This," he said, "This makes sense."

"So what next?"

He rubbed the stubble along his chin. He had shaved when he'd washed my clothes, but it wasn't a close shave and a deep shadow adorned his cheeks and chin. "We run," he answered.

"That's not much of a plan."

"Until we can find out exactly what you need to do with the talisman, and I do suggest figuring that out sooner as opposed to later, we'll run."

I scrunched my nose. "About that…I had trouble with the talisman earlier."

He frowned. "That's not good."

"No, it's not. I haven't had trouble like that since before I first was able to access it."

"What kind of trouble?"

I relayed how it hadn't wanted to glow and how I didn't seem to be able to tap its power. "I'm worried that I may have somehow depleted whatever energy source fuels it."

"Is that possible?"

"I—I don't know."

"I doubt it. I mean, it's been in existence for a thousand years, unused."

I shrugged my shoulders. "I don't know what to think. There are no instructions."

"Can you try again now?"

I took a deep breath and nodded. A tendril of fear snuck into my gut despite my efforts to dispel it. Before I could be consumed by the thought, the talisman flared brightly, and my vision blurred as vines sprouted and twisted up the walls once again.

"Odd," I said, perplexed. "Very odd."

"Again, good, but not good. You still have the power and that's a good sign, but if it's no longer dependable, we don't know how much we can trust it. We need to find out why it didn't work before. Without knowing that, we can't be certain it will work when you need it."

I was immensely relieved I hadn't lost the ability to power the talisman, but now I was terrified it might come and go at will, and I would have no indication of when I might be left without it. The thought was daunting.

The next morning, we both agreed I was ready to travel. I didn't relish the thought of hiking in the snow, but there was no other option. I was shocked when Quinn suggested we try venturing through the cave system instead.

"Do you really think that's wise?" I asked. I hated to think about getting lost in the dark with no way out.

"Most of the caves we've been staying in are connected somewhere farther back. I can't guarantee we'll get where we'd like to go, but given we have no destination in mind, it's worth a shot. If the air can get through, so can we. It'll keep you out of the snow, anyhow."

I cringed. "Spelunking is not my idea of fun," I said. "And just because air can get through doesn't mean we will."

"So you'd rather walk in the snow?"

I sighed. "Fine, caves," I agreed.

"I promise I won't make you squeeze through cracks and

crevices. If we find ourselves in a tight spot, we'll turn around," he reassured me.

This didn't make me feel any better.

"Besides," he added. "People lived here long ago."

"In the cave?"

"Well, not this particular cave, perhaps, but all along this cave system."

"I didn't know that. How'd you learn about it?" I asked as I tied my bedroll to my pack.

"I learned a lot while training for the Order."

"Did you miss Barnham while you were gone?"

He gave me that odd look again—the one I couldn't discern. "Yes," he said.

When he didn't elaborate, I pressed further. "You must have seen and done so much. I can't imagine what it must be like to have that kind of adventure in your life."

He lifted a dark eyebrow at me as he slung his pack over his shoulders and cinched the belt tightly around his waist. "I've got news for you, Reina. You're already in the midst of *that kind* of adventure."

I rolled my eyes and followed him as he led into the passageway at the rear of the cavern, his torch lighting the way.

"That's not what I mean. This is an *adventure*, for lack of anything better to call it, but it must have been different when you were away for the Order. There must have been more to it."

"Actually, this is pretty much it."

"Oh," I said, disappointed. "Seems like there should be more excitement, more planning somehow."

"There was a lot of travel," he said. "I saw a lot and did a lot, but never truly had time to appreciate any of it. I was busy working."

"Being a ghost." The phrase bothered me. I couldn't say why. Perhaps it was because it implied he never really existed anywhere at all.

"Yes."

"What is it you do as a ghost?" I asked.

"I told you before. I listen." But there was more to his profession. I was sure he had given me the rosy-hued version.

"Have you ever killed anyone?"

He didn't answer.

"Well?"

"Reina, do not ask questions to which you do not wish to hear the answer."

I scowled. "I don't care what I *want* to hear. I want to know what it is you do, Quinn. I'm at a significant disadvantage here, and I find it more than a little unfair."

"Disadvantage? How?" He turned to face me.

"You know me," I said. "You know who I am. *What* I am."

He narrowed his eyes. "*What* you are?"

"Yes."

"And *what* exactly are you?"

"I…my…abilities," I stammered.

"You're a person. A woman. A stubborn one for sure. And, right now one who's trying to somehow define herself as though she should be ashamed of who she is. There is no *what*. You are Moreina di Bianco. Be proud."

I glared at him. "Don't change the subject."

He scoffed. "All right, you want to know?" His eyes glinted

dangerously and for half a second, I wanted to take back my question. I wanted to pretend I'd never asked it at all. "Yes. Yes, I have killed. I've killed far more than I care to admit. Are you happier knowing it?"

"Am I happy that you've taken lives? Of course not! But for God's sake, Quinn, the least you can do is share with me some small snippet of who you are. I've known you almost all my life, and yet I'm finding out only now I've really never known you at all. I might as well be traveling with a complete stranger."

There was that look again. What *was* it?

Finally, he said, "Ask your questions. I'll spare no detail."

"Quinn," I said, lightly touching his sleeve. He pulled away. "I'd never think less of you."

"You don't have to," he said. "I already do."

"Quinn, look at me."

He clenched his jaw, his mouth set in an unhappy line, but he met my gaze nonetheless.

"You have nothing to be ashamed of."

"You don't know the things I've done," he said, his voice soft as though if he spoke quietly enough he might be able to hide the truth even from himself.

"Ah, but a good friend once told me you should be proud of who you are. You're Quinn D'Arturio. Be proud."

To my surprise, he gave what could have been a laugh through his nose and shook his head. "You're incorrigible."

"Thank you kindly. Now, march onward Agent D'Arturio."

He shot me raised eyebrows but said no more. I had won a small battle and in doing so learned something I had not truly wanted to know. And yet, I wanted to learn who Quinn really was. If I expected him to be comfortable telling me, I needed to be sure I was able to respect his answers, even if they weren't what I wanted to hear.

We walked onward in silence for the better part of an hour before I dared to attempt conversation again. This time, I deliberately kept the focus off specific work with the Order and stuck to happier subjects.

"So you've been to the south," I commented lightly.

"Mmhmm."

"Where else?"

"Why the sudden interest in all my travels?"

"Well, we've miles to walk together and nowhere in particular to go. And," I added, "Since I've learned you're suddenly an agent of a secret society formed a thousand years ago with the sole purpose of protecting me."

"My being an agent of the Order is hardly sudden."

"Right, well, it's sudden that I learned of it, then. So, where else did you travel?" I said, refusing to be deterred.

I stepped lightly around a large boulder in the path through the cavern. The damp air was chilly, but far warmer than the weather we would have faced had we been traveling outdoors.

"After training, I spent the first few months trying to track down my birth family in Brynwenn."

"Even though you suspected they were dead?"

"Yes."

"Why?"

"I needed to know more. I wanted to know where I came from and who I was, I guess."

"And what did you find out?"

"That I didn't need to know where I came from to figure out who I am."

"Cryptic. So, where else did you go?"

"I spent four months at sea."

"Really?" I didn't bother to hide my surprise. I'd never known a sailor. I'd seen ships from afar at times off Barnham Bay, but Barnham had no port and there was nowhere to dock a seafaring ship. "What's it like?"

He thought for a moment. "Freeing."

I could easily picture Quinn on a ship. I didn't have to try hard to imagine him at the bow of an enormous vessel as it crested a giant wave, then plowed downward into the trough below. He'd probably be smiling.

"There's no place you need to go and no one you need to see. There's only the ship and your duty to it. There's sun and spray and when you catch the wind just right, you feel as though you've wings."

"You almost make it sound appealing."

"What's not to like?"

"It's hard work," I commented.

He glanced over a shoulder at me. "You've never shied from hard work."

"You're right. I guess the sea just seems lonely to me."

He stopped and turned to look at me, his features flickering with torchlight. "For a ghost like me, what more is there?"

My heart quickened with a yearning I was now beginning to understand all too well. *Me,* I wanted to answer.

I reached out to touch the bruise on his head, the one he had refused to let me treat. His reluctance to be touched confused and wounded me. I wanted so badly to be able to do the one thing I was capable of doing. *Let me help.*

As expected, he flinched, drawing away from my fingertips. Why had I fallen for the one man who seemed not to want me to touch him at all? I blamed him. I never would have known I'd fallen for him if he hadn't kissed me in the first place.

That kiss.

It was time, I decided. Time for confrontation. It was he who had kissed me after all. Besides, I'd already angered him several times today anyhow. At least this way, answers would be had.

CHAPTER NINETEEN

Confrontation and Expectations

"Why do you shy from my touch, Quinn?" I asked softly. "Is it truly so repulsive to you?" I tried unsuccessfully to hide the hurt from my voice.

He shot me an incredulous look as he pulled away, his dark eyes impossible to read.

I waited for an answer as he continued to examine me. "You're serious," he said.

Confused, I shook my head. "Shouldn't I be?"

"You're truly serious."

"You kissed me once," I said, searching his eyes for some sign of what burned in my own soul. "I thought...why? Why then? And yet, you pull away when I touch you."

"Reina, every time I have ever pulled away from you, it has been with your best interests in mind," he said. Bending over, he placed his hands on his knees and laughed, a desperate sound that echoed off the cavern walls. "God, I can't do this any longer."

I clenched my teeth, fighting against the rising temperature of my blood and for the first time in a long time, the talisman sparked angrily. "I fail to see what's so amusing."

He fell to his knees. "You do not know what it is you do to me."

"What?" I asked. "What is it I do?"

"Saints' blood, Reina, I know I cannot possibly be one of the suitors. You've said so yourself—"

"When have I ever said such a thing?"

"A week ago, with Niles. You told him I was no more than a childhood friend. I know I can't hope to be anything more than that to you, but Reina, I need you to understand. There's a fire in my soul that burns at the mere mention of your name. And when you're in the room, God, when you're in the room, I can hardly think straight for wanting you."

I stared.

"When I shrink from your touch, it is only because if I give in—even for a moment—if I allow myself that contact, I will lose all control. I have spent my life trying to harden myself against those feelings, walling them up, keeping them from ever seeing the light of day, and yet with one touch, a single finger, you send those walls tumbling as though I'd built them of sand."

I swallowed. What was that lump in my throat?

"You want to know why I really begged my father to forego on the *Choosing*? It had nothing to do with a career in politics. It was because if I couldn't have you as my *chosen*, I didn't want anyone. I figured I had nothing to lose by waiting a year, when you would be up for *choosing*. But everything went to hell. Your mother was killed, everyone had an agenda for you, and you fought tooth and nail against being paired with anyone."

He slammed a fist against the surrounding rock, staring somewhere far off to my right. "*Fiermi*, I was so, so proud of you. You wouldn't let anyone call the shots. You were so strong, even then. So stubborn. I made my father withdraw his proposal before it was presented it to assembly. By then I was already accepted as an agent, assigned in the south.

"And I very nearly stayed south, too. The thought of going back to Barnham, returning to see you again, waiting for you to be *chosen*, paired with someone else eventually, watching you day after day, knowing I could never have you, it was worse torture than anything my training for the Order could have inflicted upon me."

"But you came back."

He nodded. "No matter how hard I tried, I couldn't stay away. I finally decided I didn't care. If you'd accepted another, if you'd married and had children of your own, I would somehow find a way to live with it, but I couldn't stand to not be near you. I can't tell you how overjoyed I was every time one of your prospective suitors was turned away."

"You've felt this way for some time." There was an odd buzzing in my ears and my own voice sounded far away.

"Almost as long as I've known you." His eyes burned. I wished he would get off his knees.

"As long…as long as you've known me? Why have you never made such things known?" I nearly cried.

"Would you have noticed?"

Yes! I wanted to yell, but he was right. Blazes, why was Quinn always right? Boys had never been on my list of interesting topics to learn, not even in my school years. I had always wanted to heal, to keep death away. And yet, would that have been different had I known Quinn's feelings?

Almost certainly.

"And that," he said, "that is why I withdraw from your touch.

Your hands fuel that fire until I no longer have any control at all, and I assure you that's a very dangerous thing." His eyes flashed at his words, and my heart nearly leaped from my chest in response.

"Quinn," I said, sinking to my knees beside him, fighting the frustrating moisture that suddenly blurred my vision, "for someone who's so blasted observant, you're awfully daft." I hadn't meant to say it so, but I couldn't think straight, couldn't find the words I wanted.

He waited expectantly, confusion on his face.

"I've been in love with you for months!" Pain swept across his features, as though I had punched him in the gut.

He opened his mouth, closed it, then opened it again. "Do not toy with me, Reina," he warned, his voice like steel.

"I don't know when it happened—or how—but you're my home," I rushed onward. "Quinn, somewhere along the way you've opened my eyes to what it means to love someone, and not because I want to or because I have to, but because I have no choice *but* to love you."

Now it was his turn to stare.

"I've been so many people in my life. I've worn so many different faces, made myself whoever I needed to be in order to do whatever it was that needed to be done. My whole life has been about taking care of others. Collecting plants that only grow in mid-spring a hundred miles from home. Putting hours of time into mixing *just* the right remedies in *just* the right dosages so as to heal and not kill. Helping birth babes in the midst of snowstorms and hailstorms. Taking care of sniffles and sneezes, coughs and hiccups all night long without complaint—even when it sometimes meant missing a holiday meal—and let's not forget chopping fallen sycamores," I said, smiling at the memory. "All of it, I've done without complaint. I don't expect everyone to want my life. The Saints know it's not a glamorous one. But, I've never wanted anything else! That is…until you."

"Can this be…true?"

"With you, all of that seems to fall away. Everything or everyone I've ever tried to be ceases to exist and, in the end, with you, I'm just Reina," I paused, searching for the right words and feeling that I was failing miserably in finding them. Finally, I concluded, "I've never been *just* me with anyone."

When the echo of my voice faded from the cave walls, I feared the silence would go on forever. Then all at once Quinn had me in his arms, his mouth searching mine, fingers woven into my hair.

I responded, meeting his need with an urgency of my own, and as before, I began to hear a song the likes of which I'd never before heard. I wanted to question it, to figure out why such a thing should occur, but rational thought was impossible, and my entire body pressed forward as though my life depended on Quinn's understanding of the depth of my emotion.

When at last he pulled back, his breath came in enormous gulps as a drowning man might gasp for life-giving air. My own was not much different. Hands on either side of my head, he looked hard into my eyes. There was so much emotion there, uncertainty, hope, love.

And fear.

It was the fear that scared me.

"Why are you afraid?" I nearly whispered.

He exhaled. "Because now that I finally have you, I might lose you."

"You will never lose me," I said, as certain as I'd ever been of anything in my whole life.

He closed his eyes as if in pain. "Can it really be?" he asked.

I laughed, tears rolling from my cheeks. "Yes!"

He wiped the droplets from my face and kissed each cheek lightly, a move so uncharacteristically unlike him I hardly knew what to make of it. Then his eyes were drawn downward.

"You're glowing."

"What? I—" I followed his gaze. From within my tunic, the talisman was glowing brighter than I had ever seen. I pulled it out and examined it. The blues and greens within were swirling with vibrant light.

Suddenly it all made sense.

"It's you," I said.

Quinn looked puzzled.

"It's you! Kiss me."

Surprised, he nonetheless obeyed. The humming resumed and the glow intensified.

I pulled away. "It's you," I repeated.

"What does that mean?" Quinn asked.

"Did you hear it?"

"Hear what?"

"There was…I don't know how to describe it. Music. Like songbirds, like the wind. It was a harmony of sound. I can't explain it." I sounded like a babbling fool. "You didn't hear it?"

He shook his head. "No, but the talisman is brighter than I've ever seen it, even when you were working it to grow a small jungle."

There was more to the talisman than we'd originally thought, and I sorely wished I had access to the scrolls and books in Governor Arden's study. I cursed myself for not having studied them earlier, as if I should have somehow known then I was the White Sorceress and I'd be forced to single-handedly find a way to save the kingdom.

But I didn't have to do it single-handedly. I gazed at Quinn and blinked against the sudden moisture in my eyes. I would never have to do anything alone again.

"What's going through that head of yours?" he asked.

"I'm not sure yet, but I've some ideas I need to mull over," I answered. What I needed was hard evidence to support the idea that had taken shape in my mind, but I wasn't sure how I would obtain proof of anything living like a cave-dwelling bat.

"You'll tell me when you've finished mulling appropriately?" he asked, humor dancing in his eyes.

"You have my word," I answered with a smile.

With that we moved forward again, Quinn grasping my hand securely as we went. My eyes remained fixed on the physical connection between the two of us, proof I had not imagined our entire exchange. How was it possible for everything to have changed so significantly in the space of a few minutes—in the breadth of a single conversation?

We emerged shortly into another large cavern that led to the outside world, though how Quinn navigated the maze of passages was beyond my comprehension.

It didn't take long to set up yet another makeshift camp and when we were done, I followed Quinn outside and squinted. The late afternoon sun had melted much of the snow. The white stuff was still more than ankle-deep, but no longer mid-calf the way it had fallen only days before. While I enjoyed the thought of no longer traveling through the caves, how long would it be before we saw signs of Bruenner's men? They were closer. The burn in my knees and the ache in my wrists told me as much. How many had they killed today?

Quinn, apparently, shared my concerns. "After we've built a fire, I'll do some scouting and see what I can find."

"I'll go with you," I said, reluctant to let him ever leave my sight again.

He gave me a quirky, rarely seen smile. "You'll stay here. Where you're warm and safe and out of sight." When I protested, he added, "Besides, I can move faster without you. Ghost, remember?"

Only slightly irritated at being left behind, I clamped my mouth shut against further argument. Instead, I concentrated on pulling together something that would pass as a meal. With a roaring fire, I made a stew of the roots and potatoes I had grown. I had accessed the powers of the talisman right after Quinn left and I was proud I had managed to produce not a single mushroom, given Quinn's general dislike of them. He had not said as much, but I was certain I'd seen him cringe with each mouthful. There were *some* things even I was able to observe without much effort.

Now, with the stew simmering on the fire and Quinn still nowhere in sight, I focused on working with the stone again. As I'd suspected, it lit dimly—barely pulsing—and I was able to grow nothing, proof that my theory had been correct.

Quinn was the key.

He likely always had been. I'd just never known it. I thought back to all of the times I had tried to work with the talisman, the times it had reacted to my touch and the times when it had remained cold, refusing to glow.

It had to be.

It was nearly an hour before he returned for me to confirm it. Sure enough, in Quinn's presence, the talisman glowed, and I grew greenery all about the cavern walls.

I wanted to share with Quinn what I had learned. I wanted to reassure him I had discovered the talisman's power and that my ability depended upon him, but I still didn't know why. I needed more time to think.

I dreamed that night, frequent and disturbing dreams. The same Bruenner I had previously seen in the vision of my mother's death held Quinn captive, threatening to end it all. There was bloodshed and screaming. I awoke in a silent wail and was relieved to see I had not disturbed Quinn, who lay breathing long and evenly beside me.

The fire dwindled throughout the night and I added more wood, relishing the instant warmth added to the cavern.

When I returned to my bedroll, Quinn lay on his side, dark eyes observing my every move.

"What is it?" I asked, taking in the handsome angles of his face, a face I'd seen nearly all of my life.

"Was it a dream?"

"Was what a dream?"

"Yesterday."

I smiled. "No," I said. "'Twas real."

"Good, because if I'd been dreaming, I'd go back to sleep and wish never to wake."

He clasped my hand in his and we lay side by side in silence.

Finally, I spoke, reluctant to break the peace, but unable to settle completely while the previous day's thoughts played through my mind.

"I know what makes the talisman work."

Quinn propped himself up on his elbow, alert.

"It's you."

"You mentioned that yesterday."

"Right, but I mean what *really* makes it work. It won't work at all when you're not near."

He looked dubious. "You're sure?"

"I tried it yesterday. After you left, I was able to access it. I tried again later and couldn't make it work at all. When you returned, I attempted and had no problem."

"But why should that be? Why should I make a difference?"

"I've been thinking about that."

"And?"

"I'm not sure."

He snorted.

"Well, I've a couple ideas, but I'm not sure that either of them fits. Maybe you can provide some insight. I assume you know a bit more about the prophecy than I do, your father being an assessor and all."

"I'd say that's a fairly good bet."

"First, and obviously, you're the *right* suitor."

"Which means you've chosen correctly, so everything should be fine, right?"

His words reminded me of Niles's, and I told him so.

He looked as though he might be sick. "Please don't ever compare me to him."

"My point is that surely you must be the right one."

He let out a long breath. "But that's not necessarily true."

"How could it not be?"

"The prophecy doesn't specify that either suitor is good or evil, right or wrong. It simply states that in choosing one, the result will be death and despair while in choosing the other, all will be right in the kingdom."

"That's ridiculous. How on Liron could choosing you ever result in death and despair?" I asked.

"Any number of ways. Choosing me could mean that I fail to protect you, you're killed, and Bruenner reigns. Or, Bruenner strikes and kills me and you are either killed as well or worse— forced into service beneath Bruenner. Perhaps he'd attempt to use you as his instrument of death. Or, I could—"

I held up a hand to stop him. "All right, no more. I see your point. I don't agree with it, but I see it."

"All I'm saying is that prophecies are twisted words of wisdom. Sometimes it might be better never to have heard them at all. Correct interpretation is nearly impossible, which is why men like my father dedicate their entire lives to studying them."

"For argument's sake, let's suppose you're the right suitor, the path which leads to *all things good*. Then it makes sense the talisman only works in your presence. That would be the exact reason *why* I would be able to succeed."

"Unless it only works because you've chosen me. Say you'd chosen Niles. Perhaps then, the talisman would work only in his presence."

"Don't be difficult."

"I swear to you, I'm not trying to be difficult. I'm trying to show you how tricky cause and effect becomes when you're dealing with a prophecy. Am I the right suitor because the talisman works for you when I'm near, meaning you chose correctly? Or does the talisman work for you when I'm near because your choice *made* me the right suitor?"

"Either way," I said, beginning to become frustrated, "it works in your presence. To me, that means you are a key piece in this puzzle."

"We can agree on that."

"The first time I got the talisman to glow, even a little, we were in the castle in Gillesmere. You were there, weren't you?"

He didn't answer.

"You were in the passageway, the one that Laurelle knew about."

He nodded slowly, guiltily.

"And the times I got it to glow when I set out on my own. You were nearby, weren't you?"

"I never left you alone," he confirmed. And there it was—that fear in his eyes again.

"The morning I was beneath the overhang with Niles. That was when you caught up to us. I hadn't tried to tap into its power then when it began glowing on its own. I hadn't made any choice at that point. I didn't know what I wanted."

"You actually considered Niles, didn't you?"

"Well, of course! I didn't know what you knew about him. Because," I added, "you refused to tell me."

"Mmph."

"And I was angry with you."

"With me? What had I done?"

"For starters, you made me fall in love with you."

"And that was bad?"

"When I thought you were willing to let me go, yes. When I thought you'd gone back to Barnham and left me to face this on my own, yes."

"Never."

"I know that *now*."

We agreed to remain in our current shelter for another day, provided Quinn's scouting detected no sign of Bruenner's men nearby. When he left to check, I put my theory to the test once more. Sure enough, I could not make the talisman work without Quinn.

"Plans changed," Quinn said upon his return, his face once again wearing the serious expression I had grown accustomed to seeing.

My heart began to race. "No, not already."

"They aren't close—not yet—but they will be. We need to get going before they get close enough to discover we've been here at all."

Fighting a growing sense of panic, I agreed. I'd known it was coming. Bruenner had the means and the reason to hunt for me, and even though I'd anticipated it, I shuddered at the reality.

"Where are they?" I asked Quinn later as we traveled southwest in the slushy remnants of the snow.

"They're on the far side of the ridge. When they cross, they'll be north of us, and likely headed farther north in search of us.

That's why I've been pushing so hard."

I hadn't noticed that he'd been pushing any harder than usual.

"The other side of the ridge," I said, stopping in my tracks. "You trekked over the mountain this morning?" I couldn't believe he'd traveled that far in the amount of time he'd been gone.

"I told you I move fast," he said with a half-smile as he turned to look at me.

What had he done? Climbed the face of the mountain? I shook my head as I stared at his back.

We traveled another mile or two when I was hit with the uncanny sensation of being watched. The talisman hummed and the hair on my arms stood. Picking up my pace, I fell into step beside Quinn.

"Quinn," I said quietly. "I think we're being followed."

He took my hand in his and swung it a few times as though we were two betrothed out for a stroll.

"I know."

I blinked in confusion. "Then why on Liron are we still walking happily along?"

"I'm waiting for the right moment," he replied. "And here it is."

CHAPTER TWENTY

The Measure of a Life

As if on cue, a young man wearing the uniform of the King's Army stepped from the trees and onto the road, sword drawn. He couldn't have been but fifteen or sixteen at most. Had he even been allowed to finish school before being pulled into the army?

"Halt," the boy said with an attempt at conviction, his voice still an octave too high to portray confidence. "I need names and destination."

Quinn and I stopped on his command, but now Quinn eased forward toward the soldier as he spoke. "Anton Grubben, sir. This is my betrothed, Violetta. We're heading south to—"

I jumped as Quinn relieved the soldier of his sword and snapped his neck in one swift move that left me unable to comprehend what I had just witnessed. It happened so quickly the familiar pain in my bones that simultaneously arrived with any death seemed to come long after the soldier's final breath, robbing me of strength, pulling me to the ground in a searing agony.

On my hands and knees, I fought rapid, panicked breaths as I tried feebly to push the pain from my body. I had trouble tearing my eyes from the soldier on the ground as Quinn pulled the body off the road and into the brush.

"Reina. Reina!" Quinn's voice finally reached my ears, though it seemed it came from far away. He was in front of me again. My eyes met his and he took my hand, pulling me upward and encouraging me forward. "Come on."

"You killed him."

Quinn pulled me into a hug, holding me, sheltering me with his barrel of a chest, as he kissed the top of my head. His heart thudded beneath his ribcage, a rhythm that might have soothed me any other time. "Saints, Reina. There was no other way. I'm sorry you had to see it."

I looked up at him curiously, feeling in a fog. "But…not sorry you did it."

He pursed his lips. "I'm sorry I *had* to do it. I'm not sorry I did it. How long do you think it would have taken for him to figure out who you were?"

I didn't answer.

"We would have ended up in sword fight, and he would have had a much more difficult and painful death. I made it painless and instant."

"Couldn't you have let him live?" I squeaked.

"That scout would have been back to his troop by this evening and the entire army would be searching the area hours after that. I did what I had to do, Reina."

Dully, I nodded. Walking forward again, I placed one foot in front of the other, leaving yet another death in my wake.

Quinn was right. He was always right.

We didn't find a suitable cave for shelter until almost dark, which left us collecting whatever damp firewood we could find nearby. A little *sulfuria* helped to start a fire and in no time at all, we had food to eat as well. I was at least getting faster with the talisman.

"We're running out of time," I said, stating the obvious.

"Nonsense. There's plenty of time."

I raised an eyebrow.

"I will buy you as much time as you need," Quinn said. He believed it. I wasn't so certain, even with his actions this afternoon.

In my bedroll that night, I recited the pieces of the prophecy I remembered, trying to extract the important bits. Truth. Truth will guide to save the day.

What did that mean? It was the truth I was the White Sorceress. Even I could no longer deny that. It was truth Quinn was one of the suitors, and very likely the *right* one, or so I continued to hope.

What bigger part could truth play? It was true there was a good and a bad side to this war. In the past, there had been wars where both sides appeared to have a legitimate cause for fighting, or where each side at least claimed to have been wronged by the other. All of the history lessons I had ever been taught about Castilles showed that. In this instance, though, it seemed rather clear to me that one side was forcefully trying to take while the other side was obligated to defend a position they had never wanted in the first place.

I tried to imagine back to the days when the war first started. When King Edgar died, there were many folks who insisted there had been a conspiracy at the heart of it all, a mutinous rebellion by those who planned the king's death. The cause of his death had never been fully determined and it was widely believed he had been poisoned, but there were few poisons on Liron that would leave no trace for a physician to find. Most toxins left at least some evidence they had been the cause of such demise. Since I assumed the King's Physician to be the best in his field, I could not imagine him missing such a thing.

Unless he was part of the conspiracy. That would change things entirely, and it would make much more sense as to why no cause of death was ever released.

Without a direct heir, the next in line would have fallen to the king's younger brother, but no one had seen him for a dozen years at least, and it was assumed he was dead. Members of the royal family had a tendency to disappear under unusual circumstances.

After that, the royal line became a bit hairy. There was an aging uncle somewhere in the midst, two distant cousins to the royal family, and if I recalled correctly, a young woman who claimed to be the king's illegitimate daughter in the months following his death.

Once General Bruenner declared his intent, each of those contenders met a rather untimely death—including the young woman who had never really been a threat even if royal blood had indeed run through her veins.

Bruenner soon declared himself king of the so-called *new* kingdom. He then publicly insisted that King Edgar's death had been caused by poison and that he would personally apprehend the seditious forces responsible.

As he gained control, rumors flew that he was forcing men of a certain age to join his army or systematically eliminating them if they refused. There had never before been a requirement in the kingdom for men of any age to join the army. Many men chose to enlist simply to gain the skills necessary to carve out a successful life in any profession.

The odd part was that Bruenner only eradicated men between certain ages. In a matter of months, falsifying birth records became common practice. It was as though he feared the prince baby somehow lived and would eventually challenge him to reclaim the throne. Did any man Quinn's age actually remember when he was really born?

One thought led to another and I mused if Quinn himself knew his own birthday. He'd talked about trying to discover his own history, but since I'd been more intent on learning about where he'd gone for Order, I hadn't really pressed him on what he'd discovered.

Sleep clouded my brain and, giving in, I resolved to talk more with Quinn tomorrow. I prayed fatigue would keep me from additional disturbing dreams tonight. My mind didn't need to face imagined threats overnight. Surely, I faced enough of the real kind during the day.

We were on the move again, traveling through a mess of wet leaves, snow, and sticky mud. I wondered if traveling through the caves wouldn't have been preferable after all.

"I bet there's no mud in the south," I muttered.

Quinn smiled. "No, no mud. Lots of sand."

"Must be glorious."

"It can be, but sand presents its own discomforts."

"How so?"

"It's horrid in wind. Grit everywhere, in everything. Your eyes, your ears, your mouth, and, well, everywhere else."

"I hadn't thought of it like that." I stepped in a particularly mushy spot, and the mud made a sucking sound as I pulled my foot from it. "Quinn, you said you went to Brynwenn."

"I did."

"What did you discover?"

"I told you already, not very much. It's a large town, and they've an orphanage there. Knowing almost nothing of my history, I checked there first."

"I thought you said your aunt worked for your birth parents."

"As far as I know, but I would imagine she didn't make the decision on her own to snatch me up and carry me off. There would have to be official paperwork of some sort, yes?"

"Oh. I guess I hadn't thought of that. Did you find any?"

He shook his head. "No. There was a fire in the records house years ago. They'd lost everything three years prior."

"That's terrible."

He shrugged. "Not much could be done at that point."

"Did they direct you somewhere else? Was there anywhere else to go?"

"Not really. They recommended I check with the church since they frequently worked closely with them, but they didn't have any information for me either."

At Quinn's mention of the church, I was reminded of a story

Laurelle told me when I'd been in Gillesmere. Elle's family hailed from Brynwenn and she spent her childhood there. Early in my stay, she described to me her first visit to the enormous cathedral with its beautiful stone archways and intricate stained-glass windows. She'd confided in me that had she not been of noble blood, she would have joined the nunnery right at that moment.

"Madam Bonverno was from Brynwenn," I mentioned, studying Quinn's face.

He seemed surprised. "Is that so? She hadn't mentioned it to me."

"She wouldn't have had particular reason to, believing you to be from Barnham."

"True."

"You know," I began, "she took a liking to you. I don't think I've ever seen you speak so much to anyone."

Quinn chuckled. "I suppose that's so. To be honest, I rather took a liking to her, too. She's…unique."

"No nonsense with her."

"You're right about that."

"So how long did you stay in Brynwenn?" I asked.

"A week, maybe a little more. There was nothing to discover there."

I chewed my lip thoughtfully, wishing I could rid myself of the nagging sensation that I was missing an important connection.

"Have you ever asked your aunt?"

"Well, yeah, but I was six the only time I ever saw her."

"And?"

"Have you met my Aunt Beatreece?"

I frowned. "No."

"She's a little...off."

"Off?"

"She's kind enough and smart enough, but she's got at least a thousand...let's say *questionable* beliefs."

"Oh?"

He glanced at me, as if trying to gauge my reaction.

"Some might say the same about me," I reminded him.

"I suppose that's true."

"So what did she say on the matter?"

"She told me to be thankful that I'd been given the parents who'd raised me and that Cadnum had wished it to be so."

"Cadnum? The planet?"

"I told you she was a bit off."

"Hmm."

"She would never say more, and believe me, I tried."

"That seems odd, but there are entire leagues who study the night sky for signs of what will happen on Liron below."

Quinn coughed.

"You don't believe?"

He rubbed a hand in his hair, as if trying to buy time as we walked. "I don't know, Reina. I guess that kind of thing never really struck me as being legitimate."

"You're serious? This, from the man who's been assigned to protect a sorceress he could only assume would come along based on a thousand-year-old prophecy."

"It sounds ridiculous when you say it that way."

"No more ridiculous than studying planets."

"I see your point."

"Does your aunt belong to any such league?"

He shot me a look. "I really wouldn't know."

I shrugged. "Fair enough."

We spent the next week shuffling from cave to cave making our way south, then north, then east and back again in an attempt to stay well away from Bruenner's scouts. In that time, I pieced together a reasonably crazy theory I was nearly convinced was truth.

It explained everything.

The only problem was presenting it to Quinn. He would discount my hypothesis, and I had no evidence to prove the truth behind it. And yet, the more I thought about it, the more it fueled my conviction. It fit.

"Quinn," I said one morning. "We need to get to a messenger."

He stood alert. "What for? What have you discovered?"

I took a deep breath. "Nothing I can tell you yet."

"What do you mean nothing you can tell me?" he asked. I hated the insult upon his face.

"If I could tell you now, I would. And the time will come for me to share my thoughts, but it's not now." I reached for his hand and squeezed it.

"There's nothing you cannot say to me, you know," he said gently, studying my face.

"Not this," I said. "Not yet."

He nodded as he withdrew his hand from mine and looked away, but not before I saw the pain. He truly thought I didn't trust him. I didn't know how to convince him otherwise.

"Gathlin," he said, looking into the distance. "We're near Gathlin by now. We should be able to find a reliable messenger there."

"Gathlin," I said. "Governor McElson?"

"Aye, he should have a man or two. To where are we dispatching them? Or is that to remain a secret as well?"

I touched his elbow. "Please don't be like that." At least he no longer flinched at my touch.

"How shall I be, Reina? I'm to protect you, to help you, to escort you all over this great kingdom, and yet you won't share with me what it is you're onto. What exactly am I to think?"

"That's not fair! There was plenty you never shared with me," I reminded him.

"Aye, and maybe it was wrong of me."

There was little that could have prepared me for his admission, and I had no way to combat it.

"Quinn, please," I said softly. "Please?"

He shifted the pack on his back. "Let's go, then."

CHAPTER TWENTY-ONE

The Inevitable

Governor McElson seemed more than surprised to see Quinn and me on his doorstep, but was happy to receive us, even in our disheveled state.

"You've taken great risk in coming here," he said. "Bruenner's forces are not far. We've been trying hard to figure out how to keep them from taking the city. We've held the line so far, but I fear Gathlin is lost."

I shuddered to think of the bloodshed. "Aren't there troops protecting the city?"

He snorted and pushed his spectacles farther up his nose, a nervous habit I remembered from the last time I'd seen him. "Resistance troops are half their number at best and spread thin as it is. We're doing all we can, but it's not enough."

"That's part of the reason we're here," I said.

McElson's eyes lit with hope. "Sibyl Moreina, please tell me you've discovered the key to the talisman and whatever will save us from this horror."

"Not exactly."

His shoulders fell.

"We need a messenger," Quinn said.

"Several, in fact," I said to Quinn's surprise. I ignored him as he watched me.

"For you, Sibyl, anything. How many will you need?"

"How many legions are on the ground?"

"Not enough."

"Yes, I've gathered that," I said, fighting my own fatigue to remain patient with him. "How many precisely?"

"Total?"

"Yes."

"Two dozen legions totaling sixty-five hundred men."

"How many of those two dozen are within three days of here?" I asked, mentally calculating.

"Most of them," he answered. "I'm afraid Gathlin is not in a good position at all."

"Believe it or not, Governor, that's actually good to hear."

He looked at me as though I'd grown a second head.

"Can you spare twenty messengers?" I asked.

"Twenty!" He clasped his hands together. "I haven't nearly that many," he said.

"Twelve, then. Have you a dozen men?"

He nodded. "Surely, I do."

"I'll need a writing desk," I told him. "Paper and ink, too."

"Whatever you desire," he answered.

What I desired was a hot bath and to be absolved of my duties, but that option didn't seem to be in my stars. And if nothing else, it was the starry sky that had brought forth the truth in my own mind. Should I ever meet Quinn's Aunt Beatreece, I promised myself I would hug her tightly and thank her for her wisdom.

"I need someplace quiet to write two dozen copies of a letter I want delivered to the commanding officer of each legion."

"I have a scribe in my employ," McElson offered.

I shook my head, "No," I answered. "It's crucial I write them myself."

"As you wish. I'll be happy to provide my seal to verify your authority."

I nodded my thanks.

As promised, everything I asked for was delivered to me in McElson's parlor. Behind closed doors, I wasted no time in drafting a letter. I wasn't sure exactly what I needed to say, but I scribbled furiously nonetheless. It was nearly two hours later by the time I had twenty-four copies written and sealed for messengers to carry.

Standing from the oak chair, I stretched my back, stiff muscles protesting. I sorely wished we could stay and take McElson up on the hospitality he offered, but I'd be less conspicuous had I painted a glaring red target on my back. No, it was far better to keep on the move until the messengers had ample time to deliver my letters.

The only problem with sending the messengers now was that I still didn't have a very good design of how I was going to pull together the spark of an idea I'd started to form. Calling the troops too early might be a foolish move, but I couldn't risk them arriving late. That would ensure my own death, and I didn't particularly wish to meet the Saints now or anytime soon.

I opened the parlor door and nearly collided with Quinn, freshly washed and shaven. The gash on the side of his head had healed, though the skin around his temple was still bruised a sallow yellow.

"You're clean," I said, stating the obvious.

He handed me a bundle of clothes. "And you're next."

"We really cannot stay, Quinn. You know that."

"No, but there's plenty of time for a hot bath in the springs. McElson has a bath house behind the main building."

"A bath house?" I asked. Not concerning myself with anything but finding messengers, it hadn't occurred to me that we were traveling to the infamous Gathlin, known throughout the kingdom for its bubbling hot springs.

"Aye, a real bath. Go. I'll stand guard so no one disturbs you."

It was impossible to refuse, and my feet were heading for the rear of the house before my mind could process the wisdom of such a decision. The bathhouse was essentially a very basic wooden shack built around a bubbling spring. I wrinkled my nose at the sulfurous odor that reached my nostrils almost as soon as I opened the door.

I poked my head out from the door to meet Quinn's eye. "It's horrid!"

He squinted in amusement, hawk-like eyes dancing at my surprise. "Did you expect it to smell like Keswick roses? It's hot for a reason, ye know."

"I suppose I hadn't thought about it."

"Don't worry, you won't notice once you're immersed."

"Ah…all right," I said doubtfully.

With that, I closed the door again and undressed. I hadn't even entered the water yet and my face was dewy from rising steam and perspiration. I examined the faintly cloudy surface of the water, unsure if I really wished to bathe in it. Surely it was harmless enough, given the fame it had brought Gathlin over the centuries.

Slowly, I stuck a toe into the water. It was almost too hot for comfort, but I slid in regardless, enjoying the deliciousness of no longer being covered in filth and plagued by cold as I had been for weeks.

Either Quinn or McElson had left a scrub stone for me and there was an assortment of soaps laid out upon a small shelf above the spring. I selected a lavender-hued one and scrubbed the weeks of grime from my body. It was glorious. Quinn had been right about the smell. While I still detected a slight sulfurous odor, it was no longer overwhelming and the floral scented soap had overcome almost all traces of it.

When I'd finished scrubbing every inch of my body and washing my hair twice, I immersed myself deep within the spring and attempted to allow my body to relax enough to produce a vision, but despite Quinn's presence outside the door, I was unable to coax myself into the right state.

Reluctantly giving up, I settled for examining the rocks that surrounded the spring. They were smooth, worn by the touch of many hands. I rubbed them with my own fingers, surprised at the slick coating on them.

Rubbing my fingers together lightly, I brought them to my nose and gave a delicate sniff. I could detect nothing unusual, and the sticky substance quickly washed off in the water.

Perhaps a natural flora of the spring. Definitely odd. Wondering what sort of medicinal properties outside of my traditional repertoire it might offer, I wished I had more time to study it. I hadn't made any new additions to my medical stores in a long time.

Finally, I pulled myself from the water, dried and dressed in the deep blue tunic and pants that had been provided for me, savoring the feel of the soft, clean fabric on my freshly washed skin. I toweled my hair dry the best I could and joined Quinn. Together, we walked back to the main house for the hot meal McElson insisted we stay to enjoy.

By nightfall, we were back on the road despite Governor McElson's protests that we at least spend one night in the comfort of his guest rooms. Neither Quinn nor I felt it wise to stay any longer than necessary.

As McElson insisted on providing us with the basics to continue living outdoors, we now had a tent to use. It served us well over the next several days. While we couldn't make our fire as large as those we'd had in the caves, it at least negated the need to hunt for a place to stay every night. I was grateful for any small way to make our lives a little easier.

"Why did you have the troops head straight for the center of Bruenner's camps?" Quinn asked.

My mouth dropped open. Why I was surprised, I couldn't say. I should have known better.

"You weren't meant to read that," I told him, narrowing my eyes.

He shrugged. "It's my duty to know."

"I think I liked it better when I wasn't in love with you," I muttered. "Easier to be angry that way."

"And why do you have them meeting us there?"

I pressed my mouth into a tight line and stared at him.

"Maybe you don't feel as though it's important to tell me, but I've got a right to know," Quinn said, anger fused into his words. "Especially," he said, "if I'm to protect you as I lead you straight into the enemy's hands."

I couldn't yet tell him. I couldn't tell him what I had figured out. He wouldn't believe me. I needed something that could prove my theory beyond any shadow of a doubt.

"I have my reasons," I answered, trying my best to sound as though I knew exactly what I was doing and praying I was right.

Quinn didn't respond as he added a log to the fire. Finally, he said, "I hope you know what you're doing."

Nearly palpable waves of cold frustration rolled from him. My heart cried in response. Did he not understand how much it hurt me to keep something from him? I wanted so badly to tell him.

With a sigh, and already angry with myself for knowing what I was about to reveal to him, I opened my mouth to share my thoughts, but just as I did, three soldiers wearing kingdom uniforms burst through the flap of the tent.

Quinn reacted almost instantly, reaching for his sword, but the first soldier's sword was inches from his throat before his hand could touch its hilt. The second soldier grabbed my wrist and pulled me to him, holding his own sword above my collarbone, the metal like ice upon my skin. I swallowed and breathed deeply as I tried to convince myself to remain calm and think rationally.

"Well," said the first soldier, "It looks as though we've finally caught up with the fugitive sorceress." Glaring at Quinn, he barked, "Throw down your sword."

The fight sparked in Quinn's eyes.

"Quinn," I said quietly. "Do as he says."

Confusion crossed Quinn's face. There was little doubt that on his own Quinn—even on his knees as he was—would have taken down all three men without hesitation. What had Antony called him? *A one-man army.*

"I suggest you do as the lady requests. If ye mean to be thinkin' you're going to kill us all, *Agent,* then you're in for a surprise. There are sixteen more just outside."

"Quinn," I nearly whispered.

He threw down his sword.

"Now the boot," the soldier said.

Slowly, Quinn reached down to his boot, plucked the dagger from it and threw it to the ground.

The flap to the tent opened again, and Niles strolled in, looking as smug as ever, bright blue eyes glinting with a hint of insanity. How had I ever thought him attractive?

His gaze met mine, the cold within it sending shivers down my spine. He looked away, focusing on Quinn.

"D'Arturio, we meet again."

"How lucky for me."

With no warning, Niles kicked him hard in the gut, causing Quinn to double over. I jumped instinctively to go to his side, but an arm clamped over my chest, holding me tightly.

"You arrogant bastard," Niles spat.

Too busy trying to breathe, Quinn could say nothing.

"Kill me the next time you see me? I don't think so. Fancy new tent you've got. I suppose the seductive sorceress didn't want to cozy up to you the way she did with me."

"Niles," I said. "This isn't going to work. Taking us to Bruenner won't solve anything." I didn't know what I hoped to achieve. Perhaps I just wanted to remove his attention from Quinn.

It worked.

Turning on me, he came close, voice filled with malice, breath reeking of pine ale. "Ah the sorceress, the infamous White Sorceress. How blessed the kingdom must be to have you as a savior." Using the tip of his dagger, he ripped the talisman from my tunic and snatched it from my neck, but not before the chain bit hard into my skin. I winced at the sting of the fresh laceration.

The talisman sparked angrily, furiously trying to jolt its holder. I wished Niles would take a hold of it with a hand, but he had been burned by it before and was none too keen on touching it again. Instead, he placed it into a thick leather pouch, then cinched it shut tightly before placing it in a second bag.

I struggled hard against a rising swell of panic in my chest. The talisman. *My* talisman. I hadn't realized until now how much it had become a part of me since I first tapped its power. And now its power had been muted, silenced.

"Ah, Reina," Niles said, putting a hand to my cheek. I fought the urge to pull away. "I could have offered it all to you, you know."

I met his gaze evenly. "It's not yours to give."

He narrowed his eyes. "You think you're the only one they can write a prophecy about? Well, I've got news for you. I've got a little prophecy of my own. You're not the only important person in these times."

Reaching down deftly, Niles plucked the dagger from its fleeced sheath inside my boot. I had hoped it might go unnoticed, but he hadn't forgotten about the weapon.

"No need for this," he said, flinging it on the ground next to Quinn's while smiling at me. Still caught on his prophecy statement, I could not pretend to hide my shock. "Oh yes, there are prophecies written about me as well. Looks like I'm an important man after all."

I opened my mouth, but before I could reply, Niles turned to the soldier holding Quinn at sword tip. "Bind him. And make it tight. That's one you don't want escaping."

The soldier did as he was told, binding Quinn's wrists tightly behind him.

"Her?" he asked Niles.

Niles appeared to think a moment. "Not that she should be much trouble to us as I've already stripped her of her talisman, but yes, her, too," he said. As an afterthought, he added, "Bind hers in the front though." He turned to me. "No need to make you more uncomfortable than you have to be."

He seemed mildly annoyed when I didn't thank him.

The soldier bound my hands tightly, coarse rope biting into my wrist bones. I held my tongue against the curse on my lips as he gave one final yank to test the strength of his knots.

"Let's go," Niles demanded as he swept open the tent flap.

"What shall we do with their possessions?" the third soldier asked.

Niles waved a hand. "Take what you want, burn the rest."

Quinn and I were marched from the relative warmth of the tent into the cold night, the remainder of the soldiers surrounding us as we walked.

"Are you all right, Reina?" Quinn asked leaning close.

"Fine," I said, though I was anything but. It was too soon. It was too soon for this to be happening. I hadn't worked out the details, and the Resistance troops would not be in place.

"No talking," barked one of the soldiers.

I was pushed to the front of the group, where I could no longer see Quinn and my stomach knotted in anxiety.

We marched through the dark for hours before we came upon a camp, several large tents set up within a field. There were dozens of soldiers milling about, tending fires, and dozens more snoring from unseen cots.

Niles issued commands immediately. "Place her in my tent. I want to keep an eye on her. Him," he pointed at Quinn, lip curled in disgust, "have him guarded. Do not leave him alone for a moment. I'll make sure you regret it for the rest of your miserable, short life if you do."

"Yes, sir."

I glanced back at Quinn as we were separated. His eyes did not relay the confidence he always possessed. That alone was perhaps more frightening than anything.

We'll find a way, I wanted to tell him, though I fought the rising panic in my breast at the thought of being separated from him.

Then I was escorted into Niles's tent, giving up my last view of Quinn stumbling as he was prodded forward by one of the soldiers behind him.

"Now," Niles said, lighting the lamp that hung above the cot. "About these prophecies."

I stood inside the doorway as he sat upon his cot, kicked his boots up on the mattress, and placed his hands behind his head as though he were relaxing lakeside on a summer's day. I said nothing.

"Oh, but where are my manners? Please sit." He gestured to the second cot.

I remained standing.

"Maybe I didn't make myself clear. *Sit*," he said, his voice hard.

Reluctantly, I sat as straight-backed as possible, my tied hands clasped in my lap. I regarded him coolly, relaying no hint of emotion.

"You haven't even asked. Have you no interest in the other prophecy?" Niles seemed perplexed.

"I don't believe there is one," I answered.

He stood hastily and pulled papers from the collapsible writing desk that had been placed in the corner of the tent.

"Then what's this?"

He placed the papers inches from my face, far too close for me to read, and I backed away in response.

"Not interested? Well, let me read it to you.

He comes from afar,
Lineage unknown.
During a time of trouble,
He comes alone.

Another in power,
One that he will pursue.

> *A power that's his,*
> *The new king true.*
>
> *Surname different,*
> *But disposition the same,*
> *A fighter to king,*
> *Soon he will reign."*

"It's not true," I said, but I hated that a cold twinge of fear crept through my spine.

"Don't be a fool. Of course it is. It's one of Tarrowburn's and he was never wrong. In sixty-three years of telling prophecy, not a single one was known to be false."

"How can you be sure it pertains to you?" I challenged.

"Did you not hear what I just read?"

I didn't answer.

"A fighter to king. It's me. I *know* it. Just as you knew the White Sorceress prophecy was about you."

I wanted to remind him that I'd never thought such a thing, but the point seemed moot.

"That means *I'm* meant to be the new king. Oh, Bruenner might reign for a time, but *I'm* the true king. To think I would have been satisfied with the title of General Ingram!"

"That's not how a prophecy works. You know that. Besides which, were you not the very person to explain to me about the misinterpretations that occur throughout the years?"

"Not this one," he said, tapping the paper. "This one is right."

"So what do you plan to do?" I asked. "Kill me? Take your rightful place at the throne?"

His eyes softened. "I don't think I have to kill you, Moreina. I think…I think I need to tame you."

Trying not to vomit, I bit back on my retort.

"To…tame me?"

He bent forward and stroked my cheek. I couldn't help but flinch. Before I could stop him, he put his hand to the back of my neck and pulled me to him. The laceration on my neck screamed as his hand pressed into the flesh, not allowing me to pull away as he forced his mouth upon mine.

Though I might have been better off complying, I could only fight with every fiber of my being. There was no part of me that wanted a touch from Niles Ingram and—crazy or not—I didn't care if he knew it. I could not even pretend to hold an interest in him now. I bit down on his lip—hard.

Angrily, he pulled back, pressing fingers to his bleeding lip. "Wench," he said as I spat the stale taste of him from my mouth. "Perhaps I'll let Bruenner decide what to do with you after all." He yanked my wrists by the rope and tied me to the cot, not making the slightest effort to be gentle.

"I'll return later," he said. "I don't suggest trying anything, as I've guards stationed outside the tent." He gave a sick grin. "Although, I imagine Captain Brigantino would probably enjoy an escape effort."

I narrowed my eyes at Niles. "Don't tempt me."

He threw his head back and laughed as he strolled from the tent, leaving me alone with my thoughts.

CHAPTER TWENTY-TWO

Playing on Sympathy

If we were to be taken to Bruenner tomorrow—and I assumed we most likely were—the Resistance forces would never arrive in time to save us. And if they appeared after Quinn and I were killed, they didn't stand a chance of saving themselves, let alone anyone else. I'd be responsible for the deaths of sixty-five hundred men.

Sixty-five hundred.

This journey had forced me to leave too many dead in my wake already. Tears stung my eyes and I fought against the bile that rose in my throat as I shook with fear and anger.

My entire existence had been about bringing life into the world, healing it, and—yes, sometimes helping a person to move forward to join the Saints. But not like this. Never like this.

I twisted the best I could to get my arms into a semi-comfortable spot and pulled my knees to my chest.

Life had always been my purpose.

It was *still* my purpose.

I stilled.

Life.

The talisman brought forth life. I had figured that out at least to some extent early in my journey from Gillesmere. What I hadn't realized, and couldn't be entirely sure of even now, was that it must allow me to access *all* life, not just fungal and plant life. I had only experimented with plant matter because plants were all that had been available to me, but, oh! If I could bring forth life, if I could encourage it, what else could I do with it? I bit my lip in excitement before my hopes came tumbling back down to reality again. How could I defeat an army of twelve thousand with the gift of *life*?

Closing my eyes, I tried to remember of all of the books I had ever read, all of the medical knowledge I had retained. How could I take life by encouraging it at the same time? Then my eyes flew open and I gasped with sudden realization.

"Yes!"

It made perfect sense. It was the last piece of the puzzle, and I needed only to figure out when to execute it. It would work. It had to.

And then it hit me. It didn't matter that I finally had an answer. The talisman was no longer in my possession.

I had already failed.

I couldn't evoke any power without it, and there was no way Niles would allow me to hold it even for a minute. Not even a *pretty please* would earn me that. Perhaps I should have led the bastard on.

But supposing I had the talisman, I still needed Quinn's presence in order to tap into its power effectively. If there was one thing Niles was intent on doing, it was keeping Quinn and me far apart. Did he have any idea just how dangerous Quinn and I could be together? I hadn't known it myself until now.

Blast it, why was I always half a step behind? Had I figured this out six hours ago, Niles and Bruenner's band of cronies would all lay dead on the forest floor.

The flap to the tent opened and a daunting solid wall of a soldier stepped through. He looked as though he'd seen and conquered more than his fair share of battle—his angled face cruel and weathered, jaw lined with stubble the same steely shade as the hair on his head. Fear knotted in my stomach. Surely, this was Captain Brigantino.

"I don't know what you think you're mumbling about in here," he said, his voice like gravel, "but you'd better keep it to yourself."

Too terrified to say a word, I swallowed and nodded, trying to pull myself into as tight of a ball as I possibly could.

"Aren't you all high and mighty?" he growled. "Aye, I know your type. You're in for a rude awakening. The truth shall be known."

Saints, I hope so.

I had fallen asleep at some point during the night despite my unwillingness to close my eyes. Apparently, my body's need for sleep had eventually overcome my anxiety. I awoke in the early morning hours to the sounds of camp stirring and my numb fingers tingling.

I opened my eyes at the nickering of horses and my gaze shot to the cot where Niles should have been. Seeing it remained empty, I breathed a sigh of relief.

I flexed my tingling hands, trying to bring them back to life, while I attempted to ignore the growing discomfort in my bladder.

It wasn't long before Niles rocketed through the tent flap with bloodshot eyes, reeking strongly of pine ale.

His gaze fell on me and he looked mildly surprised as though he'd forgotten I was here.

"I have to, um, relieve myself," I said as he turned his back to me and began to root through some possessions he had laid out upon his cot.

He turned, eyes focusing on me for an instant, and left. A moment later, Captain Brigantino appeared, untied me from the cot, and escorted me wordlessly outside to a copse of trees not far from the main camp. He held my arm as though he expected me to bolt. Where did he think I would go?

Given the man's general disposition, I wasn't surprised when he offered me no privacy while I tended to business. I did my best to ignore his stare, focusing my gaze instead on the hand that held me. It was extensively scarred, as though the skin had healed improperly in jagged layers upon itself. I wondered how many times it had been burned.

When we returned to the camp, tents lay askew and fires were slowly being burned down and kicked out. It confirmed my fears that we would soon be leaving.

Less than an hour later, and after I'd been offered what I could only assume was porridge to eat, we traveled east on the main road. I'd been placed on one of the wagons and had not seen any sign of Quinn at all this morning. Saints, I hoped he hadn't tried to do anything stupid.

"Do we have far to travel?" I asked the soldier assigned to guard me, trying to gauge how long the Resistance troops had to reach Bruenner.

"Half day, maybe. More likely a day, though," the young soldier answered.

Not enough time. I needed to buy at least a couple more days for the entirety of our forces to reach us. But how?

I searched for Niles and spotted him riding near the front of the platoon. My eyes returned to the soldier next to me. He looked hardly old enough to consume ale, and I guessed he could not have been part of the King's Army for long, which meant he might not yet be thoroughly conditioned. I also caught him looking perhaps more than a little smitten in my direction.

"So," I began hesitantly. "What does Bruenner intend to do with me?" There was no way he would know such a thing, but I needed to make friends and fast.

"Couldn't say," he answered.

I looked down at my hands in my lap, letting my hair fall forward, and gave a small sniffle.

He leaned forward to glance at me, alarm on his face.

"Oh, please don't do that," he said. "Don't cry."

I sniffed again. "I can't help it," I said, letting a stray droplet fall to my knees. It wasn't difficult to conjure the tears. "Do you know what it's like to not have done anything wrong at all and still be hunted as though you were a common criminal?"

Actually, an army would never bother hunting a common criminal, but I didn't think he'd put too much effort into thinking on it.

I was right.

"No, no, I'm sure it's not like that."

"What do you mean it's not like that? I'm bound!" I said, wide-eyed, holding my wrists for him to see as though he didn't already know. "I haven't done a thing to anyone and yet, simply because of who they *think* I am, I'm going to be killed."

"Well, now, there's no saying that he'll have you killed."

I made no reply.

"I mean, if the General wanted you dead, surely he would have issued that command from the start, right? I'm sure it will work out. He just wants all this sorceress nonsense put to rest. Now that he has the talisman, there's no reason to fear you, so he'll probably let you go, right?"

God, he must have been even younger than he looked. I couldn't imagine anyone having less of a concept of war and what was done to the enemy when caught. Once again, I answered with silence.

"It will be all right. I'm certain of it."

"How can it be all right? I have nowhere to go even if he does let me go."

"Well…" he said, hesitating.

Come on, say it.

"I'll make certain it's so. And if you need a place to go, I promise I'll help you figure something out."

Yes.

"You would…but no, how could I trust your word?" I threw my head into my hands. "You're driving the very cart that's taking me to him in the first place!"

"It's a job," he said so softly I wasn't sure I'd heard him correctly.

"What?"

He gave an exaggerated roll of his eyes. "This. It's just a job."

I feigned confusion. "I don't understand."

"These are harsh times, and I wasn't given much choice. My father is a captain in the thirty-first brigade. He's always been one of General Bruenner's top men. So what was I to do? Refuse service? Dishonor him?"

"You mean you don't want to be here?"

"Nah, but it will be over soon enough, and I'll have enough gold in hand to buy my own vineyard."

Could my new *friend* somehow provide me with more of an advantage than I'd dared to hope?

"Everyone has dreams, it seems," I answered.

"Ayuh. And what's yours?"

"To be free," I said, staring into the distance ahead of me. "To have no title to wear. To…be me. What's a vineyard like?"

Saints, my acting skills weren't the strongest. I was laying it on thick. Maybe he wouldn't notice.

To my relief, he brightened at the mention of vineyard. "Oh, lots of work, but a sweet, sweet reward. My uncle has one." He turned to face me as he spoke animatedly about different types of wine and how the grapes must be grown a certain way and in certain conditions, and how if they were blended just slightly differently, they'd produce an entirely different flavor. "I've got ideas for a full new blend, but I need to invest in land before I can think about actually giving it a try. It'd be years before I'd see any payoff."

"It sounds amazing. I sincerely hope you get the chance to

follow your dream, um…I'm sorry, what's your name?"

"Henley. Private James Henley."

"James," I said. "I hope you get to follow your dream someday, James."

He blushed straight to his hairline.

Thank you, Private Henley, I thought. *Thank you.*

CHAPTER TWENTY-THREE

Where Past and Future Collide

With the exception of more gray in his hair and slightly more weathered skin, General Bruenner looked exactly as he had when he'd murdered my mother three years ago. It ignited instant unease in my gut. Before I'd seen his face in my vision, I imagined him to be larger, more intimidating somehow. That wasn't to say he was a small man. In fact, he was actually bigger than most, but I had previously pictured him to be physically daunting, more like Captain Brigantino.

To see him match the image in my vision only solidified my hatred of him. I wanted to rip his heart out with my bare hands. Instead, I forced myself to remain calm and show no sign of anger.

He was a solid, dark-haired man with prominently graying temples. His long hair was slicked back from his face and a thick, dark mustache adorned his top lip, matching his bushy, black brows.

"I see I finally have the privilege of meeting the infamous White Sorceress," he said. "Welcome to my kingdom, or at least what will very shortly be my kingdom now that you're here."

We were alone in a tent and I was seated, once again tied to another piece of furniture—this time a chair. I raised an eyebrow at his pretense of a welcome.

"I've waited a long time for this, almost my whole life, in fact," he said, grooming his mustache with his fingertips as he spoke, smoothing it downwards with half a palm.

Against my better judgement, I replied, "You've waited your whole life to tie me to a chair?"

To my surprise, he threw his head back and laughed heartily. Saints, he was just like Niles. No wonder they got along. Leaning in, his face inches from mine, he stared uncomfortably into my eyes, as if searching for a clue to solve some riddle. I fought the instinct to look away and met his gaze evenly, refusing to flinch from the pale gray eyes that betrayed no emotion.

"Odd," he said, straightening again. "You don't look like you should be someone so spectacular."

I bristled. "How peculiar. My thoughts about you, as well."

With no warning, the back of his hand met my cheek, and I fought the gray haze that threatened to overcome me. I should have anticipated a volatile temper.

"Insolence will not be tolerated," he said through the buzzing in my ears.

I could not reply, which was probably for my own good.

"Do you know how long I deliberated before I executed the plans to remove Edgar from the throne?"

He was silent for a moment as if waiting for a response.

"No smart comments now, I see. Perhaps you have some brains after all." He lit a pipe he pulled from the drawer of a nearby table, puffed a few times, and slowly paced as he enjoyed it. "Sixteen years. Sixteen long years of actively planning, plotting, and putting together the right team to make it happen. It's not as if you can interview for this type of job, you know. No 'Ho there, you ready to kill the king? All right then, the job is yours.' No, none of that."

He paced back and forth as he spoke.

"Would you like to know the best part? I probably wouldn't have thought about it if it weren't for Prince Eron's disappearance."

That caught my attention. Until a few days ago I, like everyone else, had assumed General Bruenner was responsible for the missing prince. His admission otherwise seemed a confirmation that my most recent suspicions were correct. Had I not been tied to a chair with Marcus Bruenner for company, I might have been elated at the discovery.

As it was, it didn't matter, given the circumstances.

"That was the first sign the Tarrowburn War Prophecies were about to unfold."

I could no longer hold my tongue. "You mean the White Sorceress Prophecy. The one seen by Magnus Tarrowburn."

"No, that's not what I mean at all, and I'm fairly certain I wasn't unclear." He shot me an annoyed glare and I half expected another blow, but none came. "The Tarrowburn *Prophecies*."

"But there was only one about the war, about the White Sorceress."

"Only one was ever made public knowledge. No sense in panicking the masses. If you'd had access to the Royal Libraries as I had, you would know there are dozens of additional prophecies."

First, Niles introduced the idea of one additional prophecy

and now there were dozens. Part of me resisted believing and yet Bruenner had access to much more information than I could ever have dreamed.

"And what do they say?" I asked.

"I'm sure you'd love to know," he answered with a sly smile, pipe clamped between his teeth. He puffed a few more times before continuing. The sweet scent of tobacco and something else—cherry maybe—had begun to fill the tent with each pull on the pipe. "The general consensus is that they tell of the beginning of a new age—a new kingdom if you will—starting when Cadnum lines up with the path of the rising sun in the east and an infant prince disappears."

"But you said you had nothing to do with that, so why would you think you had any role in the prophecy?"

"There were signs," he answered. "And I was the only one clever enough to read them. Edgar and some of the other council members knew of the scrolls. They knew, but they chose to remain daft—to hide, to ignore. Edgar wanted to pretend such a thing could never happen. Stupid man. Amazing he was ever king at all. No ambition. That's how I knew."

His eyes glinted in a way that reminded me of Niles when he began to spout insanities. Maybe they were related.

"In all of the prophecies, though, there was only one person who would ever stop me from ruling the kingdom."

"Me," I said dryly.

"Yes, you, although I have to say again how unexpectedly unremarkable you are. I suppose I'd anticipated a fair-haired goddess aglow with power."

Sorry to disappoint. I bit my tongue, afraid of what he would do.

"But you, I mean, you're not at all what was called for. You're hardly more than a child."

"I'll gladly relinquish the title," I lied. True as that sentiment might have been months ago, I could feel the power of the talisman now. It coursed through my veins with every pump of my heart even though its weight no longer fell on my chest.

His eyes opened in surprise. "Is that so? Well, yes, I imagine you would *now*, given the circumstances and all."

I didn't know what he wanted from me. Did he want me to beg? Was I to barter? My cheek still stung, and I didn't risk asking questions.

"Now the question is what to do with you," he resumed his rounds in the tent and was silent for a moment. "I should kill you straight out, get it done with. Then you'll no longer be a thorn in my side," he paused. "But if I do that I'll be forced to deal with the disbelievers. Better to have you publicly executed. We'll put on a show. Let it be *seen* that General Bruenner—no—King Marcus, has eliminated the White Sorceress. What is it—Sibyl Moreina, they tell me?"

I nodded slowly.

"Yes, let it be known publicly that King Marcus is responsible for the execution of Sibyl Moreina, and I'll have no disbelievers then."

"What of my escort?" I couldn't help but think of Quinn.

"Agent D'Arturio?" He snorted. "I'll execute him first. Get the crowd warmed up."

"No!"

Fiermi. Too hasty. Too emotional.

"Ahh, I think I understand." Bruenner's mouth twisted into that slow, sick grin again. I looked away, cursing myself.

"A double execution for the lovers, then? We'll make it a story to remember, a tragic romance to be told for centuries in every schoolbook in the kingdom."

He was trying to rile me. I breathed deep and even, attempting to find the calm center of my universe. I needed to buy time. There were at least two full days before the Resistance forces would arrive. I had to be alive at that time.

"Tomorrow," Bruenner said, slicing through my thoughts. "Tomorrow, at sunset. That should be relatively dramatic enough, don't you think?"

Was he actually asking me what I thought about the timing of my own death?

"Yes, I think that will be fine," he continued. "And it will give me enough time to spread the word so the local townsfolk can be here to take it all in."

As if my execution were a circus or an orchestral performance, some entertainment for simple amusement purposes. He'd force the townspeople to come, at sword tip if necessary.

"How unusual! I thought that when I finally caught you, I'd have hundreds of questions for you. I thought I'd want to know all about where you came from, what powers the talisman has bestowed upon you, and how you possibly thought you'd be able to defeat me. But now that I have you here, I find…I really don't actually care."

I remained silent, unwilling to take the bait.

"Don't you want to know why?"

Saints, but he truly loved the sound of his own voice.

"Because it doesn't matter! It no longer concerns me. I've no need to know how or why any of it occurred. You're no threat to me now—none at all. You're nothing but a has-been hope for all those resisting a new age. But the new age *will* come, and I will be here to usher it in."

He reached forward and stroked my face. I flinched and pulled away, unable to suppress a shiver of disgust.

"There is…" His voice faded as he squinted, examining my face. "Yes, you know, there is something exceptionally familiar about you, though I can't place my finger on it."

My breath quickened.

"You killed my mother," I said, my voice thick with anger I failed to keep from showing.

He smiled slowly. "I've killed a lot of people," he said. "That's true. I doubt I would recall your mother."

I shook with rage.

"Although, you really do look familiar."

"You attacked her on the road from Irzan," I accused. "She'd done nothing to you."

Recognition flickered on his face and he cocked his head, giving two quick puffs on his pipe. "On the contrary, if she's who I recall, she set me up for a fall I couldn't afford to take."

I swallowed. "What could my mother have possibly done to you?"

"This was what—three, four years ago?" I responded only with a hard stare. "Yes, I know who she was," he continued. "Edgar summoned her."

I squinted. "I don't believe you."

"Why should you?"

"Why would the king summon a small village Healer?"

He smiled. "She was better at her craft than you knew. Good enough to replace the King's Physician, in fact. I'd spent years positioning Dr. Jorgenson into the right place in order to be promoted to his station. And in a single visit, your mother threatened all of that."

My confusion must have been evident. My mother hadn't known King Edgar and had never been to Irzan before then. How could she have threatened anyone?

"Edgar had issues with his heart and he wanted a second opinion, preferably from someone outside traditional medicine. He requested the names of the best Healers in the kingdom. Your mother's name topped more than one list. Esmé di Bianco, was it not?"

I swallowed and gave a dull nod.

"She had Edgar charmed in a matter of minutes. When he offered her the job of Physician's Assistant something had to be done."

"My mother was no threat to you!"

"Ah, but she was. I'm sure she would not have been bought nearly so easily as Dr. Jorgenson. I couldn't risk it."

"You poisoned King Edgar."

"Saints, no! Most poison takes too long. Although," he paused to scratch his temple. "Had I used poison, your mother might have actually been an asset in verifying it. Then I could have had definitive proof of the Resistance's plan to overthrow King Edgar and obtain control of Castilles, but that's neither here nor there. As it was, a simple knife thrust to the heart was enough."

I stared at the monster before me. "You killed him yourself?"

"Well, no, not personally. I hired someone for that. Killing the king is treason, you know. Couldn't have my hands involved with that. Although I did kill the man who killed the king. Didn't want him ruining my plans with the potential to blather on down the line, now, right?" He took one last puff on his pipe before placing it on the table.

"And killing a harmless woman alone on the road wasn't a problem for you, either, was it?"

He gave a slow leer and leaned close to my ear, so close the sweet tobacco on his breath made me gag. In a low voice, he confessed, "She was fun, your mother. You should know I had a good time with her before I sliced her neck. She was a fighter. I like that."

I closed my eyes and fought back the bile that rose in my throat. A hand cupped my breast and my eyes flew open again. His thumb roughly scraped against my nipple through the fabric of my tunic. Tied or not, I attempted to pull away.

"I've had the mother. Shall we see how the daughter compares?"

"You monster," I breathed, unable to think of anything but getting away. "Don't. Don't you dare."

"Or what? You'll wield your magic? I've already taken care of that problem. We both know that without the Faranzine Talisman, you *have* no power." He smiled, revealing teeth yellowed by tobacco. I wanted to vomit. "I want to feel your fight. I want to feel it *here*." He shoved his hand between my legs and I stiffened.

Pulling back, he began to undo his breeches. Involuntarily,

I whimpered. He smiled as he placed my hands upon him and held them there, forcing my hands to massage him. I tried to pull away, but he held my hands firmly in his, keeping my fingers wrapped around him. I squeezed my eyes shut and turned my head away, a tear sliding from the corner of one eye.

This is not happening. This is not happening.

Bruenner removed his hands from mine and I yanked them back, cradling them to my chest. I had little time to consider his actions as he turned the chair to dump me to the floor. He untied the rope that confined me to the seat and kicked the chair aside. He'd left both my arms and my legs bound and I fought to slither away on my hands and knees, not caring it was exactly what he wanted me to do, exactly how he wanted me to fight.

He gave a sickening laugh as he grabbed the back of my tunic to keep me from moving further and, with little effort, he flipped me onto my back. I tried to lodge a knee into his groin, but he'd anticipated it and pressed into my leg with the full weight of his body, pinning me to the ground. I cried out as my muscles screamed in pain.

He'd done this before. He'd done this many times before. Despite the struggle, he had hardly broken a sweat. I fought to keep my wits.

With one knee on the rope between my legs to keep me pinned, and one hand holding my tied arms to my own chest, he had little resistance as he pulled my breeches down to my knees. A rough hand assaulted me, and I cried out against my will.

Then I prayed. With every fiber of my being, I prayed to each and every one of the eight Saints for a miracle.

And then I was blessed with one. A shockwave rumbled

through me and a brilliant blue light flashed from behind closed eyelids. Bruenner jumped from me as though he'd been struck by lightning.

My heart pounded in my chest as I opened my eyes, every bit as shaken as Bruenner himself. He lay stunned in the dirt of the floor, and as I focused on him, he scrambled backwards.

"Witch," he hissed, pulling at his breeches and fumbling with the belt. His eyes were wide, and my own must have been nearly as large.

Too afraid to move, I lay motionless, waiting. I could do nothing but stare. His hair had gone white, and his fingers trembled as he tightened his belt in place. He took one last look at me, and the breath left my lungs as I realized he had easily aged ten years. The wrinkles around his eyes had grown in number and the lines upon his forehead had deepened, but perhaps the biggest shock lay in his eyes. Once a clear grey, they were now occluded—milky with cataracts—and my mind reeled, trying to make sense of what had just happened.

"You'll meet your fate tomorrow," he said, then he spat on my boots and marched from the tent.

It was only when he'd gone that I let out a breath I hadn't realized I'd been holding. I pulled up my breeches hastily, ignoring the dirt and scrapes on my thighs. Then I righted the chair and collapsed onto the ground beside it into a mess of sobs. I pressed a cheek into cold, hard wood of the seat and gripped a leg of the chair as though it could somehow save me.

The stench of Bruenner's pipe lingered in the air—a reminder that even though he'd left, he'd never truly be gone. Not while I was still here.

Hours later, in a reminder that I was still alive, my stomach growled. Weeks of surviving on nearly nothing had caught up to me. Bruenner hadn't returned and after the *incident*, I didn't really expect him to, though he sent Brigantino in to tie me to the chair once more.

Bruenner's pipe sat on the small table, a memento of the hateful man, as though I needed one. My eyes kept returning to it as I tried to comprehend what exactly had happened to him. Had I been responsible? Without the talisman, I was powerless. Or was I?

Perhaps the talisman wasn't the source of the White Sorceress's power after all. Maybe…maybe *I* had the power? And the talisman helped to channel it. The thought was terrifying and alluring at once.

As time ticked on, I hoped Private Henley would make good on his earlier promise to me. Would he seek me out when he learned of my public execution? He was low in rank and high in personal ambition. Regardless of whether or not he had been besotted with me on the trip here, he'd not likely go against high command. He was, well…too young to be a rebel. I stared at the tent flap as if willing it to open, regardless.

When it finally opened, my stomach sank. Captain Brigantino stood inside the tent's walls looking fierce as ever, as if he somehow hoped I'd resist him so he would have an excuse to break my neck himself rather than wait for the promise of tomorrow night's entertainment.

He cracked his knuckles and slowly worked his jaw.

"If you wish to intimidate me, try something else," I said, surprised by my own show of anger. "I've had about all I can take today."

His eyes narrowed as he slowly approached. "And what makes you think I can't intimidate you further?" he said, his voice laced with more than a hint of malice and gravel. "I can do whatever I want. Whatever. I. Want."

Almost beyond the point of caring, I gritted my teeth. "Well, get on with it, then!" I nearly yelled.

He looked half-surprised by my outburst, if someone of his demeanor could, in fact, look surprised. He grabbed another chair and lifted it with a single hand, placing it directly opposite me, then sat.

"How does the talisman work?" he asked, leaning back and folding his arms across his chest.

I blinked in surprise. An interrogation? What was the point?

"What do you care?" I spat. "Bruenner already made it clear I'm no threat to him and that he couldn't care less about it. So why should *you* care?" It was true that Bruenner had expressed such thoughts, but he had done so before I had aged him a decade. At least, I think *I* had aged him a decade.

I expected some violence in response. I expected to elicit a reaction similar to the blow I'd received from Bruenner earlier.

Instead, Captain Brigantino kept his expression neutral. "Answer the question," he said.

"Or what?" I asked. "You'll cut off my fingers? I'm pretty certain General Bruenner would like me in one piece for tomorrow's execution."

He leaned forward, speaking slowly and clearly, surprisingly white teeth carefully enunciating each word. "I've spent many years learning how to torture without leaving a mark. I assure you, if I wanted to torture the information from you, you would have already told me everything I wanted to know—and more—within ten seconds of my sitting down."

I swallowed, half tempted to tell him to go to the farthest reaches of hell.

"Now, I'll ask again. How does the talisman work?"

"I don't know," I answered.

"You've done nothing with it?"

I contemplated lying, but I was sure a man like Captain Brigantino would smell a falsehood from a mile away.

"I didn't say that. I said I didn't know how it worked."

"Let me phrase this differently. Tell me everything you *do* know about the talisman."

"It works, if that's what you're asking."

"Yes, that would be what I'm asking, and you are sorely testing my patience."

"It gives life," I said. "It grows and nurtures. It is the exact opposite of everything *your* would-be king has ever done."

"That's all?"

"That's all? As if the breath of life weren't responsible for the existence of every person on this entire planet! You say it as though you don't believe it's anything special. If that's the case, why don't you go take your own life, if it doesn't mean all that much to you? Oh, but you won't do that, will you? So I guess it must matter a little bit after all. The power of life is the *only* thing that will ever matter." I was rambling now, and I didn't even care. A rage boiled in my veins.

"And how could you have defeated General Bruenner with command over such a power? Would you grow a new army? An army of babes grown into men overnight? What purpose could such a power have?"

He'd finally gotten under my skin. "Rest assured. Should that talisman ever come into my possession again, I will obliterate Bruenner's army, and it will happen so quickly no one will realize what I've done until it's entirely too late," I told him, my voice seething with anger.

He smiled slowly. "That's all I needed to know."

With that, he stood and strode from the tent.

How daft!

Wonderful. Just wonderful. I had all but told Brigantino exactly what I planned to do. Now he'd make sure I had no help and that the talisman was destroyed. Oh, but how I made a horrible savior. I couldn't even manage to save my own breath.

CHAPTER TWENTY-FOUR

Hope and Chance

A private brought my food to me that evening, and I was disappointed when it was not Private Henley. I hoped I might speak with him again. Long shot though he might be, he was perhaps the only person I might be able to depend on for help. I had a feeling that perhaps Niles had been onto the boy's captivation with me, and I would likely never see Henley again.

I didn't expect to see Niles again, either, so I was taken aback when he appeared in the tent's opening. The last time we'd spoken, I had very clearly turned him down. I couldn't imagine why he would be here now.

"What's happened to you?" he asked, touching my face. "Your cheek is bruised. Who did this?"

Bewildered, I stared at him. For once since joining the King's Army, he didn't reek of alcohol.

"Was it Brigantino? I'll have his rank pulled. I swear it."

Had Niles truly lost his mind? I wanted to remind him that yesterday he'd threatened to send Brigantino after me if I attempted escape and he, himself, had seemed relatively thrilled with the idea of me being caught.

"No," I answered. "It was Bruenner."

He pursed his lips together. "He's not who I hoped he would be." Looking thoughtful for a moment, he sat hurriedly in the chair Captain Brigantino had pulled over. "That's why I'm here."

He grabbed my tied hands and clasped them in his, looking down at them.

"Moreina, listen, I know I've done and said some things that might seem...well...crazy to you." I bit my tongue. *Might seem crazy?* "And the truth is I've been out of sorts lately. I defected, yes. I came to Bruenner. This is true. But all I wanted to do was end this bloody war. Since finding out there's an entire prophecy written about me, I've not known exactly how to handle it. It's a lot to take in, you know." I still didn't know where he'd gotten the idea the prophecy he'd shown me was about him, or how he'd gotten his hands on the prophecy at all.

"Yes, actually, I *do* know."

"I suppose you do. I don't know how else to say this, so I guess I'll just come out and say it. General Bruenner says you're to be executed tomorrow night." He looked up as he said it, his eyes filled with unshed tears.

"Yes," I told him. "That's my understanding."

"Come with me," he said. "We'll leave now and be gone before they realize it. No one will question me. I'm the one who brought you to Bruenner to begin with. If I move you, they'll all assume it's under his orders, and we can walk right out of here."

This? This was my salvation? A lunatic who changed moods faster than the winds changed direction in Barnham Bay? If I'd been told I would be rescued by my three-legged goat, I could not have been more surprised.

"Niles, I—I don't know what to say."

"Reina, if it's true I'm meant to be king, it will be so one way or another. But Bruenner wants a public spectacle, and that just stirs things up. It makes people angry. Do you know what happens when people are angry? They fight. And when people fight, people *die*. They no longer care whether or not they live. The anger takes over the fear. Well, I'm not willing to die for someone else! Let Bruenner have his time on the throne. He doesn't have long anyway."

"Where did you get the prophecy?" I asked.

Niles glanced to the tent flap, as if debating whether prying ears might be listening. His hands were still around mine, rubbing them with a thumb. Finally, he answered, "I found it on the cot in my tent when I returned from a meeting with Bruenner."

"So you don't even know who left it? *Saints*, how do you know it's real? Niles, anyone could have written it! It could be complete rubbish, meant to confuse you. It could have been placed there by a soldier in hopes you would challenge Bruenner and muddy the waters further!"

He shook his head vehemently. "No. It's real. Bruenner thinks it's about him. He has the original in his possession, which I only learned later. What was left on my bunk was a copy."

If my hands had been untied, I would have rubbed my temples against the confusion fogging my brain. As it was, I pulled them from Niles's grasp and set them in my own lap.

"Don't you see?" he asked. "Someone believes I'm the real heir. Someone who knows both Bruenner and the prophecy thinks *I* am the real center of the prophecy."

"So what do you plan on doing?" I asked. "How can you think you're the true heir and still want to run away?"

He glared at me, his pale eyes glinting in lantern light. "It's not running away. It's strategic planning. I want the kingdom, Moreina, and I think I could be good for Castilles, but it's a safer bet to let Bruenner have it and let the Resistance die down. They're nearly crushed as is. They've got nothing left. It won't be long even if Bruenner doesn't get to execute you. He *will* sit unchallenged on that throne."

I eyed him. Did he have any understanding of the man he once called a commander? Bruenner wouldn't stop if the Resistance died. He'd look to extend the borders of Castilles. He'd turn to other lands. This was not a man with an easily satiated appetite for power. How could Niles *not* see this? Furthermore, what kind of king could Niles be if he was willing to let others die while saving his own hide? I bit my tongue to keep from voicing my thoughts.

Finally, I asked, "So, what? We come back when he dies? Wait until he's eighty and run him through like he did Edgar?"

Niles gave an exasperated sigh as he threw his hands in the air. "I don't know, Moreina! I don't. I only know there's time to formulate a better plan later. But I have to be *alive* to do so."

"So you want the kingdom...just not badly enough to actually die for it."

"Well, if I die, it does defeat the purpose, doesn't it? Reina, I can come back for the kingdom. I can. Right now, there's something I want more than the kingdom. I can save you."

I grew quiet, contemplating my options as though I actually had any.

"Say yes. Come with me."

If I said yes, I might live to fight another day. The Resistance might live to fight another day. "What about Quinn?" I asked.

"I can't."

I couldn't use the talisman without him, and so living to fight another day didn't really make much sense unless Niles could also rescue Quinn. And now I'd really finally *found* Quinn, I'd never be able to live without him, and that had nothing to do with the talisman whatsoever.

I looked down at my lap. "Then I'm afraid I cannot come."

"If I could free him, I would! Don't look at me like that! I would. I still dislike the man, but if it would mean you coming with me, I would free him. But I can't, and it has nothing to do with my will. He's heavily guarded. It will be hard enough to leave with you. How would I also get him out of the camp?"

"If you want to free me, you'll find a way. Otherwise, I'm sorry, but I can't go with you."

"You would choose instead to die?" he hissed. "You would *die*. Over Quinn. When hundreds of thousands of lives depend on yours, you choose death?"

I met his eyes, took one slow and even breath, wondering if perhaps I was the one who'd gone insane. "Yes," I said. "I choose death."

He narrowed his eyes as he stood. "So," he said. "I guess I know for certain where I stand now, don't I? Thanks for that."

"That's not it—" I started to say as he stormed from the tent.

Well.

I'd blown that one.

Had I thought Niles would agree? Had I believed he'd cheerily opt to free Quinn and bring him with us on a runaway journey from the kingdom to only Saints knew where?

"Just as well," I said. I'd been honest with myself if nothing else. I didn't want to live a life without Quinn.

After Niles left, I gave in to exhaustion and dozed where I sat. I dreamed of horses and men, charging over hillsides and through valleys. I dreamed of the Resistance forces making their way to free us, to return my talisman and declare the war over for good. I could almost hear the hooves pounding into the hardened ground.

I awoke with a start as a hand gently shook my shoulder. Jerking my head upwards, I looked straight into Quinn's penetrating dark eyes.

"Quinn," I said, trying to stand even though I was still tied to the chair. Had Niles found a way?

Slow to wake from sleep, it took me a few seconds to realize it was not Quinn who had touched my sleeve to awaken me.

Captain Brigantino had thrown Quinn to his knees in the dirt floor before me. I glanced back and forth between Brigantino and Quinn in the light of the lantern, panic setting fire to my veins, my heart thudding in my chest.

"What do you want?" I asked.

"Reina," Quinn croaked, his voice hoarse. "God, you're like the sun."

"That's enough!"

Our attention focused on Brigantino as he grabbed Quinn by the scruff and backed him into the other chair. There were few men who could make Quinn appear small. Brigantino was perhaps only one of a handful in all of Castilles. With his hands tied behind him, Quinn sat uncomfortably at the edge of the seat.

"What do you want?" I asked again. "I told you what I knew

of the talisman."

Captain Brigantino ignored me as he leaned close to Quinn, fierce warrior eyes gleaming. God, were they all insane?

"You," he said to Quinn. "You will tell me everything you know about the talisman because so help me, by the Saints, the truth shall be known."

Quinn's expression changed as his eyes sparked with a recognition I did not understand. Jerking his head upright, he met Brigantino's eyes.

"Yes," he began slowly. "The truth…the truth *shall* be known."

I blinked in confusion. Brigantino had said something similar to me earlier.

"Brother," the captain said, hugging Quinn with a slap on the back. I could only stare in confusion.

"Agent Brigantino," Quinn said with a nod. *And a smile?*

"I'm only sorry I didn't get to you earlier. Please believe me, I tried."

"Apologies are unnecessary. You're here."

"But I have one more confession to make. I told them you were an Agent. I couldn't be sure, but they needed something to go on and I needed a way to keep you alive."

"Think nothing of it. It was the job."

Brigantino nodded. "Whatever the job requires," he replied.

"Excuse me! *What* is going on?" I finally interrupted.

Quinn grinned. "Only the best thing that could possibly happen to us. Agent Brigantino is a brother—an Agent of the Order of the Southern Cross." He turned back to Brigantino, eyes alight. "Are there more?" he asked.

The captain shook his head. "We're spread too thin. There was another in this legion, but he's fallen. Six weeks ago."

"I'm sorry," Quinn said.

"Honor in duty."

"And duty with honor."

Captain—*Agent*—Brigantino nodded. As if suddenly remembering I was in the tent, he turned to me. "I'm sorry I was forced to address you so roughly earlier. I hope you'll understand it was what was required of me."

I was too stunned to speak.

He continued in a voice as gravely as it had ever been, "I needed to be sure you could defeat Bruenner. If not, I couldn't risk blowing my cover wide open, not yet. I've spent too many years working very hard to make sure my identity has never been known. I couldn't throw it all away without knowing for certain that you will defeat him."

"You've figured it out?" Quinn asked.

"I—yes. Yes, I believe so."

Agent Brigantino's eyes grew wary. "You believe so? You told me you would *obliterate* the forces."

I pressed my lips together. "Yes," I said. "I know what needs to be done."

"Then we act at sundown, when there will be no doubt. What do you need?" he asked.

"For starters, the talisman."

"I don't know how we'll get to it," Brigantino said. "Ingram passed it along, so it's with Bruenner."

"We're going to need more help," Quinn said. "Is there anyone else you can recruit?"

Brigantino shook his head. "No one I'd trust."

"Private Henley," I said.

Both men turned to look at me.

"James Henley. He'll help."

"Who's Henley?" Quinn asked suspiciously.

"He'll help. I know it," I insisted.

"Young kid. Why would you think he could handle it?" Brigantino asked.

"He doesn't really want to be here to begin with."

Brigantino's eyebrows rose in surprise. "Is that so? I've never noticed anything to indicate that, and there's not much I don't notice. His father is loyal to Bruenner—one of his closest men, in fact."

"I know. That's the only reason he's here."

"He's never given any sign of being anything but supportive of Bruenner."

"Would he indicate anything otherwise to you?" I said.

"Not if he wants to keep his fingers intact."

I couldn't repress a shudder. "Exactly."

"All right, so how do we gain his help?" Quinn asked.

"I'm his commanding officer," Brigantino said at the same time I said, "Bring him to me."

Agent Brigantino thought for a moment, then nodded. "I'll have him bring your meal tomorrow morning. In the meantime, I need to get you"—he pointed to Quinn— "back. I may have rank, but even I'll rack up suspicions if I question you too long."

"There's one more thing," I said as Quinn stood to go with Brigantino. "The closer I am to Quinn, the better."

"What do you mean?"

"Tomorrow. When all of this happens, I need to be sure that Quinn is close. I need every advantage I can get. He's critical to me accessing the power of the talisman. You must ensure we're as close as possible."

"It will be done."

A wretched pressure squeezed my heart as Brigantino pulled Quinn's arm, ready to escort him from the tent. I hated the thought of having him out of my sight again.

Before they left, Quinn bent and kissed me. Those five seconds were a screaming confirmation we would find a way out of this horrible predicament somehow, that Quinn would help me conquer the world if need be.

"Come on," Brigantino goaded. "There'll be plenty of time for that later if we do this right."

Quinn gave a sideways smile. "Aye. We'll have to make sure of it."

"Ready?"

Quinn nodded.

"Act as though I've roughed you up a bit, eh?" Brigantino said. "We don't want to risk being exposed too soon."

"Hit me," Quinn responded.

"I'd rather not."

"It's not going to be convincing unless I show up with a few new bruises, so hit me."

"I understand that, and I know you'll understand when I tell you this, Agent D'Arturio. I've had to do many terrible things in these last months and years. I've no desire to do anything more than I must." His eyes took on a distinct haunted look that made me wonder what kinds of things he had done, and I fought the images that came to mind.

Quinn nodded. "I understand."

"I suspected you might."

Before I could open my mouth to protest or Agent Brigantino could reach to stop him, Quinn flung his head violently downward onto the desk where Bruenner's pipe lay. I let out an involuntary gasp while Agent Brigantino closed his eyes and shook his head.

Quinn stood again, a large knot already forming on his forehead. "You can thank me later," he told Brigantino.

The next morning, exactly as Agent Brigantino had assured me would happen, Private Henley arrived with my breakfast. He looked disheartened to see me still tied.

"Does General Bruenner really still believe you to be so much of a threat he can't untie you?" he asked.

"That he does, and would you like to know a secret?" I asked, bending close.

His eyes darted nervously toward the flap of the tent, but he leaned in.

"He's right, but I need your help."

Henley looked apprehensive. *Please don't let me be wrong about you.*

"I don't know what I could do," he began.

"Shh, just listen," I said, and he quieted. "There are others who will help," I told him, feeling only somewhat guilty that I exaggerated slightly, "others who are in a very good position to help, but there's one thing they can't do."

"What's that?"

"I need to recover the talisman, James."

He inhaled sharply and cursed. "What would you have *me* do? I cannot help."

"You can! You're maybe the *only* one who can."

He looked away. "Sibyl Moreina, I swore to you that I would help you after all of this is over, but there is nothing I can do for you right now."

"James, you must. I know you want to do the right thing. I can see it in your eyes!"

"My father is Colonel Alfred Henley in the thirty-first. What do you think will happen to me if you fail? I'll lose everything. Everything! And that's if they don't try me for treason and have me beheaded. My father would probably be first in line to watch!"

I switched tactics. "Have you seen Bruenner recently?" I asked. "Have you noticed anything different?"

"Well, yeah. It's all anyone's talked about since yesterday."

"And?"

His eyes grew. "You're telling me you did that?"

I nodded.

"Then you don't need the talisman at all!" he said, looking thoroughly relieved as he ran a hand through chestnut locks.

"It doesn't work that way. I need the talisman to focus my efforts. I can't control it without the talisman."

His shoulders dropped and he shook his head. "I can't," he said. "I can't help you."

I let my gaze fall. "Then I was wrong about you."

"I'm sorry," he said, rising to leave.

I wanted to scream at him, watching him walk away. I'd put all of my hope in him, and I had been wrong. My mind reeled as I tried desperately to think of an alternative plan. He stopped at the opening of the tent, though his back was still to me, and his shoulders slumped forward. I held my breath in hope. *Turn around. Turn around!* But he shook his head and moved forward again.

And then he disappeared from the tent, and my hopes crashed down upon me like the swiftly tumbling future of the Resistance. I had been so sure he would help. I had seen the good in him. He wasn't loyal to Bruenner any more than the draft horse was loyal to the plow it was tied to. He was tied, that was all.

Frustrated, I rested my chin on my knees, my eyes fixed on that disgusting pipe, and wondered what to do next. I doubted I could get word to Brigantino that my plan had failed. Was there enough time for him to formulate something else?

What else could we do?

Think, Reina. Think!

But I couldn't. I could think of no way to gain access to the talisman. I could still feel its magic coursing through my veins, but I would never be able to touch its full power without having it in hand, especially enshrined as it was in two thick leather pouches. Niles must have warned Bruenner of its electrifying capacity. I had not strongly sensed its presence since it had been taken from me.

Still, I had difficulty believing that Bruenner's ego hadn't urged him to take a peek. The temptation seemed too great. I suppose he figured he'd have plenty of time to examine it once I was dead.

But even with the talisman sheathed, I *had* accessed its power. At the moment when I'd needed it most, I had been able to grasp and bend the power to my will. That should offer some consolation. I could do it again if needed, but the knowledge alone was hardly encouraging.

No, I'd need to form another plan.

Quickly.

CHAPTER TWENTY-FIVE

Those Things Sacrificed

My pulse raced despite having reassured myself I could access the talisman, that there was no other choice. If something went wrong, if I somehow couldn't tap its power, it wouldn't matter how close Brigantino could get me to Quinn. We would fall as swiftly as the kingdom had upon King Edgar's death.

Knowing what I did of Bruenner, I now relied on his love of showmanship to do what I felt down to my very bones he wouldn't be able to resist. He would pull the infamous talisman from the double-lined pouches Niles had used to obscure it from me, feeling the need to show it off to the hundreds of townsfolk and thousands of soldiers under his command.

The temptation would be too overwhelming. He'd need to prove his undisputed greatness and what better way to do it than to show off the Faranzine Talisman? My presence wasn't enough. I could be any common girl pretending to be a sorceress, but the talisman? It could never be faked, and neither could the power within.

The challenge for me would be to tap the talisman and control its power without holding it. I had never before attempted it, but the lives of thousands would depend on my ability to control its effects. Without that control, I could just as easily kill them all. My nerves were raw at the thought, but my bones weren't aching with death. Not yet anyway.

I was nearly confident in the part Brigantino would play. As an agent, he could be trusted to get Quinn close enough to ensure I would be able to touch the talisman's power as soon as it was in the open.

And yet, being *almost* confident wasn't the same as actual confidence. There was the nagging question as to whether or not he was truly loyal to the Order. A wave of relief at knowing we had someone so powerful on our side had washed over me when I learned Brigantino was an agent, but the interaction with Henley lingered in my mind which resulted in me fighting my inner voices—the ones that asked if Brigantino was any more our ally than Henley.

Above it all, though, was my fear the Resistance forces wouldn't arrive in time, and I wouldn't be able to maintain control for as long as it would take for them to reach us. I'd count myself lucky if they got here by tomorrow morning, and my execution was scheduled for sunset, leaving me now with a mere two hours to figure out what I would do without their presence. Technically, I didn't need them to carry out the plan. I needed only for them to help enforce my position, and to assist in tying everything up once I'd acted with the talisman's power.

Pushing all worries aside, I settled for meditation. I'd always resorted to it before any call of duty, focusing my energy inward and reciting the Healer's Oath. A quick and efficient way to inwardly calm and prepare at the same time. Just as I had once prepared for birthing babes and stitching wounds, I now prepared for battle. Either way, lives were on the line.

Breathing deeply, I allowed myself to fall into the meditative state, a pseudo-consciousness that allowed an awareness of both internal and external surroundings at once. The beating of my own heart reminded me of the hoof beats from my dream the night before, the rhythm soothing and even. I focused on my own part of the plan, ignoring the whispered *what ifs* that could negate the need for me to do anything at all.

Feet will guide,
And fingers heal.
Soothe my soul,
Let me feel.

Calm my breath,
Steady my hands.
As I lay out,
Most important plans.

Swiftly I move,
Deftly prepare.
For all that comes,
May I be aware.

Feet will guide,
And fingers heal.
Saints watch over,
Here, as I kneel.

"Let's go," a rough voice said, startling me from my meditation.

"Where? Now?"

"Well it ain't sunrise, sweetheart," the soldier said, grabbing me roughly.

My pulse leaped. How long had I been meditating?

I could hope to be the kingdom's savior as much as I wanted, but the sheer terror at having to put a real plan into motion overwhelmed me.

I hardly had time to think as I was escorted outside. We made our way amidst the tents, rounded a corner, and my breath left my body as though someone had squeezed it from me. Though I had heard the sound of sawing and hammering all day, nothing could have prepared me for the enormous stage that had been erected and the thousands of soldiers and nearby townsfolk who had gathered. Regardless of the fact that I should have anticipated such a spectacle, I hadn't expected *this*.

For me. This was all for me. A show of Bruenner's control, a pretense of his power.

My hatred for Bruenner and all the ways he had twisted the kingdom came boiling to the surface. I let my gaze roam the crowd as I was led to the stage, meeting the stares of innocent bystanders who would watch this ordeal only because Bruenner had sent his troops into the towns with threats of maiming and death had they not agreed to come. They didn't wish to be here any more than I did. The fear in their eyes made that clear. I caught the gaze of a little girl who could be no more than six, her disheveled strawberry blond hair wrapped into twists at the nape of her neck, tearstained face turned into her mother's skirts.

Who would insist children witness such an event?

Someone intent on striking fear into their hearts forever. That's who. A man who insisted on making an impression never to be forgotten, someone who would warp them for life. They were future tithes to him, future soldiers, expendables. He would never be content. Taking the kingdom completely might tide him over for a few years, but he would soon move to the rest of land, making a tyranny of his rule over Castilles and continuing the slaughter and bloodshed. Why hadn't Niles been able to see that?

My eyes fell on Bruenner himself, smartly uniformed, his newly whitened hair well-groomed as he stood on the stage, eyes wild and glittering. A fire ignited in my veins. There was no sign of Niles, and I wondered how far he'd gotten since those midnight hours. To Gathlin? New Tratham? Was he halfway to South Trellington by now? Should I have gone with him?

I searched for Agent Brigantino and spotted him to the far side of the stage, his bulk and demeanor making him difficult to miss. Quinn kneeled before him, facing the audience of soldiers and townsfolk. The soldiers toward the front of the crowd snickered and leered as Quinn stared nobly past them, his hands tied behind his back. One of the soldiers spat at Quinn, the viscous wad landing a foot short onto the stage in front of his knees. The fire that had sparked in my veins slowly roared to life.

Brigantino met my eye, then looked away, giving no indication of whether or not the plot we'd worked out was already in motion on his end. Maybe I'd misjudged him. Private Henley—looking paler than I had seen him last—appeared at the edge of the stage as I arrived with my escort. Perhaps the thought of a beheading bothered him more than he cared to admit. Maybe he wished he'd agreed to help me after all.

Then again, maybe not. Sneering, he grabbed hold of my other arm forcefully, pulling me toward the stage.

"We'll see how much your powers are worth now, won't we? Without your talisman, you aren't fit to lead anyone. You should thank General Bruenner for putting you out of your misery," he said derisively, scowling at me. I was overcome at the malice in his voice until the smooth stone and familiar, radiating heat of the talisman was pressed forcefully into the palm of my hand.

Sudden understanding washed over me. His warning look curbed any response, and I was ushered to the stairs roughly, but not before I noticed his thoroughly burned hands. Blistered, swollen, and shaking, he had held the talisman even when it had burned his skin and the tissue beneath beyond repair. I couldn't imagine the excruciating pain, and yet other than his pallor, he showed no outward sign, acted as though nothing were amiss.

A soldier hauled me unceremoniously to the stage, and I nearly tripped over the final step. Having someone on either side of me was the only thing that prevented me from smacking my face against the hard wood.

Cold hands yanked me upward until my eyes met those of General Bruenner inches away. I clasped my hands together as though praying, feeling the talisman's growing heat within. Being caught now would be very bad indeed.

"And here she is," he shouted to the crowd in a voice made for oration. Spittle flew from his mouth, leaving me with a keen desire to wipe my face. "The very witch who has declared war on the kingdom's forces, the one who would attempt to split the kingdom in two, the one responsible for *this*." He gestured to his whitened hair. "*White* Sorceress is exactly what she is, and don't be fooled by her diminutive stature. Believe me, she'll do the same to you as soon as she has the chance. She's a menace to Castilles.

"We will not tolerate it. *I* will not tolerate it. After all the work we have so diligently put forth into keeping the kingdom united. After the cities we've claimed back from the Rebel Resistance, after the families we've helped reunite when the rebels forced them to scatter, now, we've finally apprehended the villain. She is here. And she will pay.

"I know what you're thinking. Yes, I can see it on some of your faces. No, it's all right, don't hide it. It's plain to see. You're thinking, 'She didn't lead the Rebel Resistance. Why should she pay? What good will this do?' Well, let me explain.

"You see, the Resistance has been based around a false notion that *I* am the evil on which the White Sorceress Prophecy was based. How such a ridiculous idea could come to be after I've spent so *many* years serving King Edgar so loyally, I do not know. But, I suppose it's easy enough to guess. Even as I set out to protect the kingdom against pretenders who would attempt to take the throne, the Resistance forces were mounting their attack, building their armies, and waiting for the right moment to declare me the traitor. The prophecy gave them every reason to point the finger my way to declare death and destruction.

"And what ensued? Why, death and destruction, of course! When you start a war, that's what will occur every single time, I assure you. And as top commander for the good King Edgar,

Saints protect his soul, I can verify the truth in such a statement."

The soldiers nodded in agreement, but the townsfolk didn't seem nearly as convinced. Frankly, they seemed too frightened to do more than huddle together in hopes they would soon be allowed to go home. *Soon*, I vowed.

I turned the talisman in my hands as Bruenner continued to deliver his speech. Quinn was still on his knees at the opposite end of the stage. Glaring at Agent Brigantino, I willed him to bring Quinn closer. I needed as much power as I could summon. Brigantino would not meet my eye. Blazes, was he not who I thought? I held the talisman firm in my hands, hoping the distance between us was close enough.

The executioner sharpened his blade as Bruenner continued on, spinning his tales about his defense of Castilles. The scraping sound of the ax upon the grinding stone set my nerves on edge— just as it was meant to do. I swallowed, my mouth having gone dry. Gaze drifting back to Brigantino, I caught Quinn's stare. I had never before viewed Quinn as helpless. Seeing him on his knees now served to remind me of the gravity of our situation. Our very lives teetered precariously on a single hope, one shot in maybe a hundred million. And that was being generous.

The faces in the crowd blurred together as my eyes roamed across them. They might as well be dead, too. But the ache in my bones, the one that announced death's arrival, was hardly present. It was there, but not in quantity. I wanted to be hopeful, wanted to believe it meant there would be no death at all today, but maybe I just hoped the death wouldn't be mine.

I lowered my head as if in prayer. And maybe I was.

Bruenner was making his closing statements now. "And so

justice will be served today. This war *will* end. The Resistance forces will lay down their arms." He paused for effect. "The witch is defeated."

Now.

Whether Quinn was close enough or not was no longer a concern. Now was the time.

"NO!" I shouted, surprising myself with my ferocity. "It is you, General Bruenner, who is defeated."

I had the attention of the crowd. Even Bruenner looked surprised. Had he expected me to die quietly?

"Oh, is that so? And yet, it is you who are tied before us. It is you for whom the executioner sharpens his blade."

"There will be no need for his blade today or any other day," I said, not recognizing my own voice.

"And what will you do when I have *this*?" he asked, reaching for the pocket where surely the pouch containing the talisman had been before James Henley had swiped it. There was confusion in his eyes, followed by a panic I relished in the moment before I accessed the talisman's full power and fell into a vision.

Grow now! I commanded. *Grow swiftly. Multiply quickly, quickly!*

As I worked, soldiers doubled over in the crowd, grabbing their sides, holding themselves. Their moans rose through the air in a chorus as they clutched at their abdomens, their insides suddenly in far too much pain for their minds to contemplate the curse I had bestowed upon them. It took all of my concentration to differentiate between soldier and citizen, leaving townsfolk unscathed. This was far beyond growing fuisberries and callogh root.

I turned my head to find Quinn beside me. Brigantino had held true to his word. I reached further into the stone, grasping its power, pulling it forth, and unleashing it with as much force as I could muster. The troops continued to fall to the ground in waves, those closest falling first as the magic of both the Faranzine Talisman and the White Sorceress swept through them.

Villagers looked around at the empty spaces that had opened beside them and at the men who had fallen to the grass. They were wide-eyed, terrified at the sudden turn of events, and if I could have spared an ounce of energy to soothe their fears, I would have. But I didn't dare turn my attention from the task at hand.

"You," I said, addressing General Bruenner, who had gone still and pale. "You are the most false *king* any kingdom could ever hope to have. You have done nothing but bring death to this land, crushing villages and towns that would otherwise prosper, beating down their people, and slaughtering all who would oppose. You," I said, "are a monster. And your time is over."

He didn't appear to know how to respond. His eyes shifted as he searched for help—for someone to come to his rescue— but even the executioner was in my grip, doubled over in pain, unable to stand, let alone come to Bruenner's assistance.

"There is no one to help you now, Bruenner. It's just you and me. So, tell me again how you saved this great kingdom. Tell me now how you believe yourself to be king."

"I am the closest thing to a king this kingdom has got," he attempted, though his voice wavered as he said it. I almost enjoyed the fear in his eyes. Finally, I would repay the man who was responsible for taking my mother from me.

"You lie!" I spat. "You lie, and you *know* it. It's why you live in fear. It's why there is fear in your eyes now. But the true king *is* here, and he stands before you." I turned to address the crowd, though most of the soldiers couldn't hear my words above their own pain. The villagers would witness. "This," I said, pointing to Quinn. "This is the true king. This is Eron Alexandre Morel of Brynwenn."

"Reina," Quinn's warm voice breathed into my ear. "What are you doing?"

I ignored him. Bruenner's gaze darted nervously between me and Quinn.

"You've been searching the kingdom for him all this time, Bruenner. You knew. You knew the baby lived. Why else would you be so eager to recruit young men of such a specific age? If he was on *your* side, there would be no way for him to ever discover his birthright. There would be no means for the White Sorceress to find his true heritage and claim him as the rightful king."

"The prince died long ago. Everyone knows that. I don't know what you're talking about!"

"You couldn't recruit every last one of them, though, could you? And soon they began to lie about their age because when they couldn't all be recruited, they would end up dead. What a noble king you must be to kill your young men. All because you feared one day the wrong one would show up and reveal your sham to the kingdom."

"Reina! What are you doing?" Quinn gripped my arm.

"Trust me," I whispered.

Through the blue haze of my vision, his eyes questioned mine, but he did not persist.

"At the first hint of Cadnum's positioning, the baby was taken into protective custody by those who would see he grew strong and healthy and safe. Yes, it may have been the baby's disappearance that placed the idea of high treason in your head, but the wheels were already in motion. The prophecy had already been put into play. Recognize him, Bruenner? He looks remarkably like Edgar, doesn't he? Isobelle, too."

"You lie."

"I do *not*!"

There was a thundering in my ears, a pounding like horse's hooves again. I had never before accessed my vision—or the talisman—for such an extended period of time. The blue haze wavered ever so slightly.

"Give up," I said. "Surrender."

Bruenner snorted. "Never. I applaud you for your abilities in crippling my men, but regardless of what you've done to those here, you'll never be able to take them all. I've got thousands, placed all over the countryside. Kill these if you want. More will come."

I gave a mental tug on the talisman and elicited screams of pain and sharp moaning from the soldiers who had already fallen to the ground. Those who had somehow remained standing dropped to their knees.

A wave of fear passed over Bruenner's features, but he stood his ground, determined not to give in. Did he think I couldn't harm him while I held his troops? I could.

I didn't want to. I wanted the council to have him. I *wanted* him to pay for his crimes. I wanted him to be punished in a way that would last far longer than the pain I could give him.

"Agent Brigantino," I said. "Perhaps you would be so kind as to extend the same courtesies to General Bruenner as he has extended to me. Tie him up." With his troops unable to come to his aid, I had confidence that he would no longer resist.

I was wrong.

As Brigantino reached for Bruenner, the general launched himself at Brigantino, pulling the agent's sword from its sheath and lunging directly at me. I was thrown from my feet as Quinn rammed me with his shoulder to take the sword that had been meant for me. The blade sliced cleanly through his middle.

Time slowed, and my scream pealed through the air.

In a heartbeat, the rage that had been simmering in my blood boiled over. Through the deep blue haze, I glared at Bruenner and dropped him to the ground. He curled into a ball, motionless. I sensed his life hanging in the balance, but I no longer cared about taking him alive. He had caused harm to Quinn. I didn't care if his lungs never took another breath.

Reaching Quinn's side, I raised his tunic to look at the wound. His breath came in gasps, a nasty gurgle accompanying each inhalation. Men did not survive such wounds.

"Quinn, you stupid, stupid man. What were you thinking?"

"You," he said. "Always you."

Tears rolled from my cheeks, plopping soundlessly onto his stomach. The wound was a clean puncture, straight through his middle, but it bled profusely with each breath.

I pressed my hands to his middle to staunch the flow. There were shouts around me now, but there was nothing and no one that mattered but Quinn. I no longer cared what else happened around us.

"Thank you," Quinn said as he closed his eyes. "For loving me."

No.

I would not lose him.

"No, you don't," I said through gritted teeth. He opened his eyes—dark, glassy pools regarding me. "You will *not*."

He gave a half smile. "If I saved you, that's all that matters."

"To you, maybe."

With that, I reached further into the talisman, grasping at every ounce of power I could find. I surged, liquid fire coursing through my body. For an instant, I thought I might be consumed by the heat that poured forth. We'd both die. Heady blue flames within my veins flowed through my fingertips and into Quinn—into the gaping hole in his body. Rivulets of power streamed forth, a wild and raging river under my command.

Grow, I commanded to the tissue. *Mend.*

I couldn't tell through the haze that was my vision if my commands had any impact at all. I tried to close my eyes and *feel* the result. I tried to *see* without the use of any vision at all.

The talisman's blue fire consumed my sight.

And then all went black.

CHAPTER TWENTY-SIX

Of Magic and Miracles

There was sound. Muted at first, but gradually growing in volume. Before I opened my eyes, the familiar sounds of men conversing reached my ears. Someone was being debriefed, though I couldn't make out the words. It was the tone. Perhaps I recognized the voice? But no, it wasn't anyone I knew. I slipped in and out of consciousness, not caring to know more, not interested in who it was or what they were saying.

But my body wouldn't let me sleep any longer and whether I wanted to or not, reality insisted I wake. Metal clinked and the stringent odor of medicinal alcohol became overpowering as someone passed nearby.

I tried to open my eyes, panicked at the realization I could not. My hand flew to my head and grabbing the oppressive weight from my eyes, I flung the compress aside with violence that was surely unwarranted.

"You're awake," someone said. I turned my head to find the source of the voice. It belonged to an older uniformed man with faded, once-red hair and kind eyes. "No need to take out vengeance on the compress," he said with a smile, stooping to pick it up from where I had thrown it on the floor.

"Where's Quinn?"

"Relax, there'll be plenty of time for questions."

Quinn was dead. Saints, he was dead. God, it was my fault.

"Where am I?" I asked, ignoring the growing nausea in my stomach.

"Medical tent. Resistance, Legion Eight. I'm Dr. Ludwick."

I tried to sit up and my head spun wildly. Placing one hand on the side of the cot and one to my forehead, I laid back again.

"Resistance? What day is it?"

How long had I been out? Dr. Ludwick looked alarmed at my question and came close to look into my eyes. He took a firm hold of my chin—a doctor's touch—and tilted my head to the light. Looking for signs of a concussion, of course. How hard had I hit the ground when I passed out?

"When did you get here?" I asked as he held one of my eyelids open to examine, then the other.

"Sibyl, did you not see us arrive? I, myself, saw you on the stage last night. What a performance!"

"That's impossible." I tried to calculate the days that had passed from the time when I had sent the messengers, but my head was foggy—too foggy even for simple math.

He mixed a liquid concoction as he spoke. "Very possible, I assure you. Here we are. Now drink this," he said, handing me a mug full of a viscous green liquid. "It will help you recover your strength."

Mildly annoyed, I took the cup from him and placed my nose to its rim. Fluted pear nectar with a hint of harkspun nettle. I almost wished it were something else so I could argue with him. Instead, I obeyed and drank.

"I'll tell the Captain you're alert," Dr. Ludwick said, accepting the mug as I handed it back to him.

There were partitions in the tent, and nurses tended to other patients behind the canvas veils.

God, Quinn, I'm so sorry. I'm sorry I couldn't heal you.

Could he hear me? Did he know? I wiped away a tear before it could crest the rim of my eye. They wouldn't see me cry. Not here. Not now. I'd cry my tears for Quinn later.

"Sibyl Moreina," said a man in a captain's uniform as he came through the partition. He was younger than a captain ought to be, but the Resistance forces hadn't exactly had a large selection of experienced men when they'd formed. He kneeled before me, grasping my hand. "To you, my allegiance. Captain Collins, at your service."

Not having a response, I swallowed and watched him rise. "How is it you're here?" I asked.

He looked confused. "Your note. We're here because you asked us to be."

"But, you shouldn't be here until right now—today, at earliest."

"Your help made all of the difference. We can't thank you enough. I don't know how you did it, but it was…truly amazing."

It was my turn to be confused. "What do you mean?"

"The horses. The men. It was amazing. They marched on as though never plagued by fatigue or hunger. I've never seen any unit move so fast in all my life. As though the wind helped to carry each step. Surely it was your doing."

My lips parted involuntarily. "No, I—" I thought back to the times I'd heard hoofbeats, wondering. Could I have done such a thing? Captain Collins stared at me intensely, awaiting my response. "I suppose it was."

"Well, it was truly a feat unlike anything I've ever known."

"Are...are all of the troops here?"

He nodded. "All sixty-five hundred."

So even those from the farthest reaches had made it here in time. If only I'd figured it all out sooner, Quinn might still be with me.

At that moment, a commotion arose from a bed on the other side of the partition. A metal pan full of instruments clattered to the floor and a scalpel slid across the floor into my bedpost. An already heated conversation grew angry, and a man's voice began to yell.

"*Fiermi*, no, I will *not* calm down. She's here. Where is she? *Reina!*"

My heart leaped into my throat as Quinn burst through the partition. His dark hair was spread in every direction, eyes nearly as wild until they rested on mine. My jaw went slack as he covered the distance between us, gathered me in his arms, and showered my face and hair with kisses, murmuring tender words I couldn't make out.

"I don't understand. I don't—"

He kissed me on the lips, silencing me.

"You're alive," I breathed, tears springing to my eyes.

Hands still upon my face, Quinn wiped the droplets from beneath my eyes with his thumbs. "Because of you," he said, dark eyes smiling. God, those eyes. "You."

I remembered then. An image of blue fire pulsing through my fingers into his body, willing the flesh to heal.

Captain Collins cleared his throat loudly. A nurse stood in the open partition, hands on her hips, glaring at Quinn angrily.

"Listen here, Stellon," she began, "You may have your Andra later *when* I've finished checking you and making sure that you're fit to go chasing after her."

He waved at her and lifted his tunic. "I'm fine. Dr. Ludwick already determined that. See? No holes." The newly healed skin on his upper abdomen was pink and tender. Aside from that, there was no other sign of injury.

The nurse continued to glare at him for a moment longer, then turned on her heel and left without another word, undoubtedly to speak with Dr. Ludwick.

"I'll come back later," Captain Collins said with a twinkle in his eye before taking his leave as well.

I turned back to Quinn, drinking him in. "You're real," I whispered, fighting back tears again. So much for not letting them see me cry. I'd never cried so much in my life.

"Never more so. Hey, now, no tears."

"They're happy tears," I laughed, my eyes roaming the length of him. I never wanted to let him go. "I thought you were dead. Saints, and I thought it was my fault."

He frowned and tilted my chin upwards. "No, never. Reina, I did what I was meant to do. I'd die to protect you."

"Yes, well you almost did, you dolt!"

He smiled at me again. "I'd do it again."

"Please don't."

"Besides, you returned the favor pretty well, don't you think?" He lifted his shirt again and I brushed my fingertips over the newly healed skin on his otherwise perfect abdomen. He winced slightly.

"Tender?"

He nodded. "A little. Sensitive more than anything."

"What about the back?"

He turned, revealing a smaller pink scar just to the left of center in the middle of his back. It would eventually be indistinguishable from the others.

"Amazing," I breathed.

Quinn sat on the bed with me, holding my hands. "How did you do it?" he asked. "All of it. Start with the soldiers. What did you do to Bruenner's troops? Half of them are still recovering!"

"Oh, that."

"How did you decimate them? It was incredible. I thought you said the power of the talisman lies in life."

"It does."

"So how did you take down thousands of men at the same time? They were curled on the floor like babes—and nearly crying like babes, too."

"I didn't focus on the men," I explained. "I focused on the natural flora within."

"The what?"

I laughed at the look Quinn gave me as I searched for a way to explain it without sounding crazy. "It's like the hot springs at Gathlin. Do you remember how there was a film on the rocks? It felt slippery."

He frowned. "Sure, I remember."

"That's just an example of a natural flora that lives in that environment. That slime was alive in a way." I put a hand to my head, searching for another way to explain it. "Yeast!" I said. Men understood beer. "When a brewer makes ale, the brew needs to go through a fermentation process, right?"

He nodded.

"That entire process depends upon a type of organism that thrives on sugar. Without that organism, nothing can happen. What most people don't realize is we have plenty of that kind of organism living within us. It's a natural part of our bodies— our natural flora, if you will. So, all I did was grow that natural flora."

"I don't understand why that would be harmful."

"What happens during the fermentation process?" I asked. "As the yeast digests the sugars, what happens?"

"I'm not a brewer, Reina."

"It produces gas," I said. "Lots of gas."

His eyes lit with amusement. "Gas."

"Very *painful* gas," I added.

He laughed heartily in response.

I nodded. "That's all. Nothing more, nothing less."

"They thought they were *dying*...and it was gas! God, I wouldn't want to be in *that* medical tent right now," he said between laughs. "You gave them nothing more than intestinal upset."

I couldn't help but laugh with him. I laughed until my cheeks hurt, until my sides ached, until I no longer remembered why I was laughing.

When we finally recovered, Quinn asked, "And what on Liron made you say I was the king? In front of all those people, nonetheless."

I sobered. "Quinn, you *are*."

He snorted as though I were joking.

"No, truly. You *are* the king."

"You're serious."

"I didn't realize it right away, but it fits. The talisman glows only in your presence. Long ago, a sorceress was the king's trusted companion, responsible for keeping the kingdom balanced. A bad king could do very bad things without someone to keep him in check. Just having a sorceress meant a king was less likely to be tempted by greed.

"At the same time, the sorceress also reported to the king. What if the sorceress grew greedy? Having her power work only within the king's presence helped to ensure that it was used only for the good of the kingdom. That's why it glows when I'm with you. I am at your disposal, Your Majesty."

"That's only your theory, though. You can't believe people will accept it if you can't prove it. Blazes, *I* can't accept it."

"She's right." I hadn't heard Agent Brigantino enter the tent.

Quinn turned to face him. "Where did you disappear to?" he asked him.

"Sent word to the Order. They'll be here in time for the coronation."

"Don't be absurd. I'm not the king," Quinn said.

I placed a hand on his. "It's not easy being someone you never wanted to be."

"Reina, you can't assume I'm the king because a talisman glows when I'm around. That's just not solid reasoning."

"That's not the only reason, Quinn. You told me half of the story yourself, but you didn't know the rest of it. Your aunt brought you to your parents. Your aunt. I'd bet my life she worked for the royal family. And she knew exactly when you needed to disappear because she's a Starwatcher."

"She's right," Brigantino said.

"And how are *you* so certain?" Quinn asked him.

"Because I issued the command."

"What?" Quinn and I spoke at once.

"My assignment at the time was to watch for the signs and make sure the prince was protected. You were in Beatreece's care when I issued the order to have you removed from the castle."

Quinn studied Agent Brigantino's face, as though trying to sense a lie. Judging by his expression, he was unable to find one.

"When she suggested her sister's house, I was skeptical. We couldn't have the prince under just any old roof. And then she told me. I couldn't think of a more fitting home, given that the man who would be raising you is one of the Order's best assessors."

"My father knew?"

Agent Brigantino shrugged his shoulders with uncertainty. "I'm sure he suspected, but rather wisely, he never asked. The fewer people who knew, the better."

"Then why didn't anyone come forward after Edgar was murdered? Why didn't you just say something then? My aunt *knew*." Quinn threw a hand in the air.

Brigantino shook his head. "That's not how the prophecy was to unfold."

"You're Prince Eron," I said. "Niles read me the prophecy. He just assumed it referred to him."

Brigantino snorted. "I knew he'd think so. That's why I left it there."

"It was you," I said. "But why?"

"Because he was a nuisance. As long as he held Bruenner's favor, he would have continued pushing his own agenda. And his agenda would have undone all the progress I've made in the last six months."

I nodded absently. "Quinn, Niles was wrong. The prophecy was never about him. It was about you." I turned to face Brigantino. "What happened to Bruenner?"

His eyes turned downward. "You took care of that problem."

I breathed. "I didn't mean to kill him. He should have been tried for treason, for war crimes. He should have been made to pay."

I wanted to feel remorse at taking a life. I wanted to feel some sense of repentance, but relief was all that came. I swallowed, unsure what to make of my emotions. Nothing could ever take away my mother's death, but at least her killer no longer roamed free.

"He did pay. Sibyl, you've nothing to apologize for. This is war and you did as any agent would," Brigantino said. Somehow, this knowledge was not reassuring.

"How did you kill Bruenner?" Quinn asked.

I thought for a moment before responding. "I aged him."

"You—"

"Aged him. I increased the speed his body aged at until he had no life left within him. I did it once earlier, when he...well, when he tried to attack me."

Anguish crossed Quinn's features as he berated himself for

not being able to come to my rescue. "I wondered," he said. "When I saw him, I wondered. With the hair and the eyes and all."

"I didn't realize at the time that I had such power. And without the talisman I had no control, but I don't...I don't think the talisman is the source of the power," I confessed reluctantly. "I think it's me. I think it's always been me, but the talisman awakened some part of me, allowed me to access it with ease—control it somehow."

"What happened to not believing in magic?" Quinn asked with a small smile.

I returned his smile with one of my own. "I suppose I can't deny its existence any more than I can deny the air I breathe." I turned to face Brigantino. "What about Niles?"

A shadow crossed Brigantino's eyes. "Don't know. The little weasel slipped away sometime yesterday morning. Bruenner had me too occupied to keep tabs on him."

Quinn squeezed my hand. "I'll hunt him down myself if I have to."

I gave a tight-lipped smile in reply.

"You," Brigantino said, "will do no such thing. You have the entire Order at your disposal."

"Fine, then one of my first commands will be to have the Order hunt him down, Agent Brigantino. And by the way, congratulate yourself. After the coronation, my first act as King will be to promote you. I want you head of the guard."

"My allegiance is yours," he replied with a nod.

"Precisely." Quinn glanced at me, then back to Brigantino, hesitating only a moment. "If you wouldn't mind, would you wait for me outside? I'd like to go over some thoughts with you, but I need to talk with Reina first, privately."

Brigantino nodded, gave a small bow, and took his leave.

Quinn faced me again. "I suppose this changes things," he said.

I blinked. "How so?"

He gave a long exhale, his hawk-like eyes examining my face. "All you've wanted all this time was to go home. And now…"

I waited for him to continue.

"What?" I asked.

"It's all over. And you," he said, putting a hand to my cheek. "You can go back to Barnham, and back to being the best blasted Healer in the entire kingdom. Surely there are still infants to be born and twisted ankles to mend." He gave a smile that didn't touch his eyes.

"And you?"

"I suppose I must head to Irzan. I'll admit I don't feel remotely fit to lead. I'm sure there's a learning curve I can't possibly anticipate."

I pressed my lips together. "Mmhmm. And how far do you think you'll get without the White Sorceress by your side? Have you thought about that *Prince* Eron?"

Taken aback, he winced at my words.

"Do you suppose I'll go quietly back to Barnham while you continue on with your adventures? After all the upset this kingdom has experienced in the last two years, do you think everyone in the kingdom will be assured that you're actually the royal heir? You think there will be no challengers?"

"I...I suppose I hadn't thought that far ahead."

"Of course you hadn't. You were too busy trying to get rid of me."

"I—no! That's not true."

"I've got news for you Quinn D'Arturio Eron Alexandre Morel of Brynwenn. You can't get rid of me so easily." I climbed onto his lap as I spoke, etiquette be damned. "You've supposedly spent years pining for me—"

Surprise and a hint of amusement touched the corners of his eyes. "Pining?"

"Yes, pining. And now that you've finally got my attention, you're ready to hightail it out of here as fast as possible. Well let me tell you something. You can't just awaken a desire—"

"Desire?"

"Yes, desire. You cannot awaken a desire in the White Sorceress and then think you'll pat it gently back to sleep as you would a child. You can't get rid of me, and I will never let you."

Quinn bit back a smile. "Is that so?"

I kissed him in response, nearly tasting his surprise. His dark stubble pressed into the palms of my hands, but I only held him harder. He wove his hands into my hair in response and a sound that could have been laughter escaped from his throat.

Finally, I pulled back. "I've told you once before, Quinn D'Arturio. Home will be wherever you are and if that's in Irzan, so be it. We'll make that our home together."

Quinn's dark eyes shone with a happiness I'd never before seen on his serious features. He squinted knowingly and tapped a finger on his lip in thought.

"Maybe I should save Brigantino's promotion for my second act as king," he said.

I smiled questioningly. "And your first?"

"Marrying you."

THE END

ACKNOWLEDGMENTS

When I began writing this story during NaNoWriMo of 2012, I never actually believed that I'd one day publish it (let alone finish it). I was working full time, raising a young family, and writing late into the night most days. Time got away from me, I stopped writing for a while, and then jumped into it again during NaNoWriMo of 2013 when I was finally able to type what every writer dreams of typing—"The End." It took me many years of revisions, numerous beta readers, five title changes, and more drafts than I can count (seriously, I stopped counting a long time ago), but I'm so happy to release *A Thousand Years to Wait* into the world. It never would have been possible without all of the amazing people who helped me along the way.

To my critique partners and beta readers who read the manuscript at various stages (some of which were very, very bad—I'm sorry), I thank you from the bottom of my heart. To my parents who encouraged me to follow my dreams and my husband who put the kids to bed so many nights while I played with my imaginary friends on the page, thank you. Thank you to everyone who has helped me along the way—Jess Bieber, Donna Gerhart, Jean Grant, Margaret Herrick, Nancy Kershner, Barbara Longo, Frank Longo, Jennifer Longo, Shanah McCready, Jessica Metzgar, Leann Quire, Alex Roscher, Brig Seitzinger, Vanita Shastry, Nathan Storms, and Sarah Valentine. A giant thank you to my amazing and talented editor, Sorchia DuBois! And another thanks and special mention to Mrs. Maria Stout's 2018-2019 8th grade class at Park Forest Middle School for their invaluable input.

To the readers who enjoyed this book, thank you for letting me take you on this journey. I sincerely hope we can travel together again soon. Writing for me is fun, but writing for *you* is even better.

ABOUT THE AUTHOR

L. Ryan Storms is a writer, photographer, traveler, and dreamer. She's a member of the Eastern Pennsylvania chapter of SCBWI who enjoys working PR & Marketing for her local library. She has written articles featured on the front page of local newspapers, but mostly she writes novels near and dear to her heart. She holds a B.S. in Marine Science from Kutztown University of Pennsylvania and a Master's in Business Administration from Marist College, but writing young adult fantasy has always been her true passion.

Storms lives in Pennsylvania with her cancer-survivor husband, two children, and a "rescue zoo" featuring two dogs, two cats, and an ex-racehorse. When she's not writing, reading, or keeping her kids in line, she enjoys hiking, photography, and planning the next big adventure.

L. RYAN STORMS
(Photo credit: Laslo Varadi)

Find out what L. Ryan Storms is working on & visit her blog at www.lryanstorms.com. You can also find her frequently tweeting about writing (and parenting) on Twitter (@LRyan_Storms).

Lightning Source UK Ltd.
Milton Keynes UK
UKHW040800260619
345071UK00001B/60/P